THE ANGEL'S WING

Pamela Gordon Hoad

Mauve
Square
Publishing

For Francis Gordon and Donatella Tronca, residents of Verona, to whom I owe acquaintance with and devotion to the cities of the Venetian *Terrafirma*

Acknowledgements

I should like to record thanks to the friends who have supported me during the process of writing and preparing *The Angel's Wing* for publication. Their kind reception of the first book in this series, *The Devil's Stain*, has given me great encouragement to continue the story of Harry Somers. I owe a particular debt of gratitude to Iona McGregor and Oliver Eade, who both read the draft and advised on innumerable matters. They introduced me to Mauve Square Publishing and I am pleased to have joined the authors whose writing has been supported through this facility. In particular Annaliese Matheron has given enormous help in preparing for publication. Oliver Eade has surpassed his usual helpfulness on this occasion by resolving a difficult problem and it is to his daughter, Fiona Ruiz, that I owe my cover. I am also most grateful to my sons: James, who cast his eagle eye over the draft as proof-reader extraordinaire, and Francis, who checked the 'local colour' in my story with pedagogic thoroughness.

Any errors are of course my own.

CONTENTS

Principal Characters in *The Angel's Wing*

Fugitives from England

Harry Somers, physician
Rendell Tonks, his servant
Geoffrey du Bois, his friend, an apothecary

Residents of Padua and the surrounding area

Giorgio Clemente, an apothecary
Antonia Clemente, his wife
Pierpaolo Clemente, his son by his first wife
Professor Andrea Bonalini of Padua University
Berthold Zimmermann, a student from Bavaria
René Pellino, a student from Savoy
Gasparo da Friuli, an apothecary
Gregorio, senior apprentice to Gasparo da Friuli
Gabriele, apprentice to Gasparo da Friuli
Leone, apprentice to Gasparo da Friuli
Samaritana, a prostitute
Giovanna Lendro and her family

Visitors to Padua

Carlotta Schioppa, wife to Enrico Capello, from Venice
Signorina Carlotta Capello, her daughter, from Venice
Matteo Maffei, a condottiere
Orsola Guarienti-Schioppa, from Verona, mother to Carlotta

Residents of Verona

Sandrino, steward to Signora Orsola Guarienti-Schioppa
Iacopo, fool to Signora Orsola
Constanza, attendant on Signora Orsola
Diamante, attendant on Signora Orsola, Constanza's sister
Bernardino Biagio, notary to Signora Orsola
Alessandro Biagio, his nephew and assistant notary

Alberto, Sandrino's nephew, captain in the Venetian garrison, cousin to Leone
Marghetrita Fratta, Alberto's sister
Father Mario, a priest at San Zeno Orador

Visitors to Verona

Beatrice Gonzaga from Mantua
Signor Giustiniari from Venice
Carlo, Matteo Maffei's henchman

Residents of Mantua

Ludovico Gonzaga, son and heir to Gianfrancesco, Marquis of Mantua
Madonna Gabbia
Paolo, her brother
Father Mario's mother

Residents of Venice

Guglielmo Guarienti, brother to Singora Orsola
Francesco Foscari, Doge of Venice
Enrico Capello

Visitors to Venice

Ambassador from King Henry VI of England
Bartholomew, member of the Ambassador's entourage

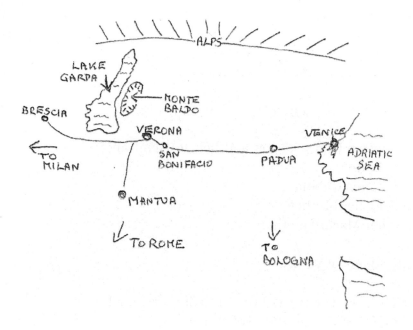

Sketch map of cities in Northern Italy

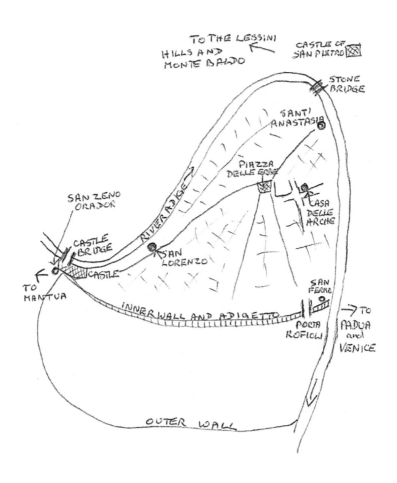

Sketch map of Fifteenth Century Verona

Part I – Padua: 1442 -1443

Chapter 1

In the late afternoon the shadow of the squat tower fell across the window of my room and frescoed the wall with the pattern of its battlements. In the sweltering heat I had discarded my gown and sat in tunic and hose, trying to concentrate on the astrological chart of signs and humours which influence men's nature. Sometimes my eyelids grew heavy and I shook my head to banish the risk of dozing but the greatest threat to my studies came from the competing thoughts which distracted me.

So often the image of Bess came to me, as last I saw her, standing on the wharf when I boarded the ship which would carry me from England into exile. She had smiled as she promised to wait for my return but her trembling lip reflected my own misgivings about the duration of my absence. Nearly nine months had passed since then and I had journeyed far through Flanders and Burgundy to my resting place in northern Italy, at the University of Padua. For a young physician, the opportunity to add a doctorate from the foremost place of medical learning to my other qualifications was irresistible but Bess had no such compensation for uncertainty about my return. She served a capricious mistress in a household full of latent tensions and malice. If a well-intentioned yeoman offered her a secure and cherished home, I could not hold acceptance of his hand against her. So I reasoned, a dozen times a day, and so I grieved.

On that sultry afternoon, however, it was not my familiar longing for Bess which troubled my mind but unexpected anxiety about a situation nearer at hand. I had travelled to Italy in the company of my friend, Geoffrey, a skilled apothecary who had left England, not under threat of execution, as I was, but nevertheless in peril from influential foes. He had been fortunate in finding employment quickly, in an established pharmacy sited beneath the loggia of the imposing Palazzo della Ragione, a stone's throw from our lodgings, and his earnings enabled us to eke out the money we had been given by well-wishers to ease our passage. He had spoken at first of his ambition, in time, to have his own pharmacy in Padua, as he had in the household of Duke Humphrey of Gloucester, where we both served in our earlier existence. Yet within a few weeks he seemed reconciled to acting indefinitely as assistant to the elderly apothecary, Messer Clemente, and the previous evening he had announced his intention of quitting the garret which we shared in order to stay in the house of his employer. He offered to continue paying his share of our rent but seemed mightily anxious to remove himself and his possessions to his new quarters without delay.

I was puzzled but accepted his decision and helped him carry his belongings across the piazza to the narrow fronted house where the apothecary lived. On my return I needed to explain the new arrangements to young Rendell, the pert and not wholly dependable lad who had accompanied us from London and described himself as my factotum. Only then did I learn the alarming implications of Geoffrey's removal.

'God save us, Doctor Somers, have you lost your wits? Don't you know what he's up to? Ain't you seen the apothecary's wife? Bit of all right, Madonna Antonia is! About eighteen, I'd say, with enormous eyes and a heaving bosom that strains her tight bodice.' He gave me a pitying look and with his hands depicted in the air the outline of a shapely woman.

'That's enough, Rendell. I doubt Master du Bois has ever met Madonna Antonia.'

The lad guffawed. 'You should be lodged in a monastery cell, you're that unworldly. The lady often goes to the shop. She simpers at her drooling husband and, when

2

his back's turned, she flashes those dark eyes at all and sundry. Dare say it's been good for business: bringing the men in to buy spices and candles, as well as their wives and servants after potions and remedies.'

'Maybe, but Geoffrey's not wet behind the ears. He's not such a fool as to flirt with his employer's wife.'

The wretched boy sighed heavily and sank onto a stool. 'Doctor, you should put down your books and take a peek at the outside world sometimes. D'you remember when you sent me over with a message for Master du Bois last week? Messer Clemente was fast asleep in his chair at the back of the pharmacy and your good mate had his hands up Madonna Antonia's skirt and his tongue halfway down her throat.'

'In full view of all the passers-by?' I did not hide my annoyance and disbelief.

'They had the shutters drawn,' he said patiently. 'I just squinted through a crack and left them to it. I went back later with your message.'

I'd sent Rendell away after that exchange and returned to my work but I could not dismiss what he had told me from my mind. I'd never known Geoffrey besotted with a woman, or behaving so indiscreetly, but I had seen him rattled when under pressure and liable to act unpredictably. If at least some of what Rendell suggested was true, there was certainly cause for concern on my friend's account, so I was worried for him and a little irked for my own sake. There were few Englishmen in Padua and the reputation of the small English 'Nation' at the university could do without scandal by association.

The afternoon dragged on as I tried to concentrate, first on one thing then another, but to little effect. I put aside the astronomical chart and stood up, stretching my arms, and out of the corner of my eye I seemed to detect movement among the shadows on the wall. I turned in surprise to look more closely and realised there was an unfamiliar shape just below the silhouette of the battlements. I stared and saw the shape move slightly to the right. Then I span round and leaned out of the open window.

Just below the battlements of the tower across the piazza there was a narrow band of stone moulding which relieved the starkness of the sheer brick walls, although serving no practical purpose. It was an arm's length beneath the parapet and, I estimated, no more than six inches wide but on this precarious ledge a small creature had ventured and, even above the cries of the gathering crowd in the street, I could hear a thin mewing and still shriller screams. The kitten was clearly unable to jump back to the ramparts and, when it wearied, would undoubtedly fall to its doom. I pondered whether a bystander below might manage to stop its fall but quickly realised others were not prepared to take that risk. A head crowned by a halo of blonde curls appeared between the machicolations on top of the tower and little hands scrabbled for a grip on the coping. Fortunately there was no possibility of the child hauling herself up but her shrieks were becoming frantic.

I was about to turn aside from the sad scene when I glimpsed a second person by her side, who lifted the infant down and then proceeded to clamber adroitly over the wall and onto the frail foothold a yard or so from the terrified animal. A susurration of excitement rippled through the watching throng but I caught my breath and gripped the window sill to steady myself. 'Rendell,' I said out loud. 'Dear God in Heaven!'

The lad was agile and sure-footed, I knew, but he was not yet twelve years old and inclined to be reckless. I thought of his sister, Grizel, now married to my old friend Thomas, and wondered how I would ever have the courage to tell her if Rendell fell to his death. What was he doing inside the tower anyway? I'd heard it belonged to some grand family from Venice who visited occasionally but I had no dealings with members of the household. Rendell must

4

have met their servants in the marketplace – he was an inveterate chatterbox – but he had no right to visit them without my permission. My useless indignation passed in a flash as the boy began to edge sideways, inch by inch, towards the kitten and I fancied his lips were moving as if he was speaking words of reassurance to it. His ploy was successful and the frightened creature did not move.

He balanced himself with both hands on the wall behind him as he side-stepped but, when he had reached the cat, he needed to bend down to pick it up and that manoeuvre would be extremely hazardous. I could scarcely breathe as I watched, expecting him to topple forward when he shifted his weight to stoop, and I was aware of absolute silence in the square, despite the growing audience of normally garrulous citizens. There was a moment of stillness while he stood frozen and I feared that his bravado had collapsed as the reality of his situation became obvious, even to him. 'Don't look down, don't panic,' I begged silently, willing him to control the terror he must feel. Then, after that heart-rending pause, he flattened his back against the wall and in a fluid movement slid into a crouching position, scooping the kitten into one arm, and straightened again to stand upright. Only then did one of his knees begin to quiver.

I cursed myself for a fool as I realised that his predicament was now worse than before. The animal lay quietly in the crook of his elbow, but might begin to squirm at any time, and he had only one free hand to ease his way back along the ledge towards the gap between the battlements, where the parapet was lower. If he succeeded in sidling that far without being thrown off balance, it was impossible that he could climb up and over the wall and the small girl who had watched him continuously throughout his escapade could give no help. Were there no adults at hand to help the boy? Why was he risking his life for an ungrateful household? Did they think him a vagrant beggar-boy of no account to anyone, whose life, like the kitten's, was wholly dispensable? I turned from the window and left the room, hurrying down three flights of stairs as fast as I could manage with the halting gait I acquired in a childhood accident. At least, I thought sourly, I could be there to gather Rendell's broken body in my arms and give him Christian burial.

When I emerged from the house to cross the piazza I saw he had miraculously maintained his toehold on the slight projection and even moved nearer the place from which he had climbed down. The little girl had disappeared and he was quite alone on his eyrie but, below him in the crowd, men were stretching out a sheet which some sensible woman had fetched. This gave some hope of arresting his fall but I noticed how thin and worn it was and feared that the material would split when his weight crashed onto it. I hurried to join the would-be rescuers but the sound of movement on the tower caused us all to look up, dreading that the instant of disaster had come. Instead, a row of heads had appeared and a man was scrambling onto the coping with a rope in his hand. I heard his calmly resolute voice. 'Stay absolutely still, lad, and I'll get the rope round you. Then we'll haul you up.'

For once in his life Rendell was obedient to a command and was soon anchored by a noose pulled tight under his armpits. As their companions tugged, two men straddling the wall seized his shoulders and assisted his ungainly ascent onto the ramparts while his feet dangled in the air. Only at this point did the kitten start to squeal and I heard Rendell swear in English when his face was scratched. Rather unkindly but with delirious relief, I laughed at the creature's ingratitude as the boy grasped the scruff of the its neck and held it up to outstretched hands. Those in the watching throng started to cheer and slap each other on the back but I made for the gate in the wall beside the tower which gave entry to the house.

I hammered on the door, demanding admittance, and when I had explained who I was an attendant led me upstairs to a grand chamber with a polished tiles on the floor and fine tapestries on the walls. I took in no details of these opulent surroundings because at the other end of the long room a short figure emerged from the bustling horde of people surrounding him and strode towards me. His face was pale but his expression one of arrogant self-satisfaction. 'Did you see me, doctor? Good, weren't I?'

'I did and you put the fear of God into me. Whatever made you do something so rash?'

It was a stupid question and it never received a reply for as I spoke the cherubic little girl who had been on the tower skipped forward and tugged Rendell's sleeve. She was richly dressed, in pale blue silk slightly scuffed from rubbing on the stonework. 'He's my valiant hero,' she lisped.

She was clearly not the child of any inferior servant and I gave her a respectful bow as Rendell puffed out his cheeks in what I took to be approval of my gallantry. Others had moved to join us and foremost among them was a stern-faced young woman in her twenties, exquisitely robed and bejewelled. I gave a deeper bow and only then, looking down at my shabby hose, did I remember I had rushed from my lodgings without my gown and was most inadequately clad for such company.

'You are the boy's employer, sir?' The noblewoman gave no sign of noticing the vivid birthmark which disfigured one side of my face and I gave her credit for her civility.

My Italian by this stage was serviceable but slow. 'Madonna, yes. Harry Somers, physician, at your service.'

'I am Carlotta Schioppa, wife to Enrico Capello, of the Venetian magistracy. This is our daughter, also Carlotta.' Again I bowed, acutely aware of my unseemly garb but the lady was far too well-bred to show any surprise or disdain for my shortcomings. 'Your servant, Rendell, has risked his

7

life to save my child's kitten and bring her comfort. She will be whipped for her part in such dangerous sport but the boy merits the highest commendation.'

Small Carlotta pulled at her mother's skirts. 'Mamma, Mamma. Please do not have me beaten.'

Rendell had dropped to his knees, endorsing her appeal, but her mother was unswayed by their pleas. 'Carlotta, you know you are forbidden to go on the roof. You disobeyed me. Not only that but you bolted the door so you could not be followed. Because of this no one could come speedily to help and your brave champion might well have perished.'

'They should have shouted louder. I'd have unlocked the door if they said they'd come to help.'

Childish petulance was met with grown-up fury. 'How dare you argue with me, you senseless minx! A louder noise could have startled Rendell and caused him to lose his footing. Nurse, take this wicked girl to her room to await her thrashing.' Carlotta Schioppa ignored her daughter's wailing, as she was led away, and turned to me. 'You are already a physician, Doctor Somers, yet you come to Padua to study?'

I was unused to such questions and did not welcome probing into my background. I took a deep breath. 'Madonna, I studied at the University of Oxford and have been admitted to the Guild of Physicians in England but the chance to claim a doctorate from Padua will add unparalleled lustre to my reputation.'

'Silver-tongued,' she said tartly but then she smiled. 'Our Italian maidens had best look to their defences with this persuasive Englishman in their midst.'

It has always been a matter of embarrassment that I blush so easily and I felt the blood colouring my one smooth cheek but the Venetian lady trilled with laughter and in her merriment she sounded like her daughter. I started to demur but she had turned to Rendell and I shut my mouth

8

as she asked the question to which I also was anxious to have an answer.

'How was it that you were in my house and in company with Carlotta?'

He looked at me out of the corner of his eye. 'Madonna,' he said, 'for a week or two I have come to help in your kitchen – when I had time and my master did not need me. In England I assisted the Duke of Gloucester's cook. It is my trade.'

It was true he had been a scullion at Duke Humphrey's palace, and turned the spit at the undercook's behest, but the grandeur with which he gave his credentials suggested a far more elevated position and I smiled. The Signora hid her amusement and raised her eyebrows to signify that the second part of her question had not been answered. Rendell understood.

'Signorina Carlotta visits the kitchen sometimes. She has a sweet tooth and the cook gives her treats – for her and her kitten. I showed her how to teach the little thing to jump up for a titbit and then to chase a string. Today she took me onto the rooftop so we had more space to play. We had a ball of twine to throw for it to chase.'

The explanation was credible and the lady nodded. 'My daughter and I will be leaving Padua in two days. I think it best that you do not offer your skilled services in my kitchen again.' Rendell looked crestfallen and she pursed her lips. 'My cook was paying you something for your assistance?' As my factotum confirmed that this was so, she beckoned one of her attendants and held out her hand. 'Here is a purse of coins, Rendell,' she said, 'to reward your bravery and recompense you for bringing your employment in my house to a conclusion.'

He felt the weight of the pouch and grinned but he uttered no word of thanks and I motioned to him to mind his manners. 'You think the payment insufficient?' the lady asked.

9

He looked her straight in the eye. 'It is generous, Madonna, but I would ask a different recompense.' She held up her hand to prevent me intervening and Rendell continued unabashed, dropping to one knee. 'My reward would be greater if I knew the little Signorina would not be beaten. I think she was badly frightened and will not repeat her disobedience.' A mesh of scarlet scratches showed on his cheek and a trickle of blood had dried beside his nose.

The lady turned to me. 'Doctor Somers, the boy justifies every word I spoke of English persuasiveness. I fancy you may wish to pursue with him how he came to play truant from his duties on your behalf and I leave any chastisement to you. As for my daughter, I am impressed she has won the pleading of so gracious and glib a champion. I will speak to her with displeasure, Rendell, but, at your request, I shall not have her thrashed.'

Rendell rose and kissed Carlotta Schioppa's extended hand then, as we both bowed, she swept from the chamber and we made our way out of the house. In the piazza many bystanders were still waiting, ready to cheer the hero of the hour in person, and it was illuminating to realise how many of them already knew him by name. He accepted their congratulations nonchalantly, nodding and smiling to acquaintances, moving into a knot of supporters to shake hands and receive embraces, and I saw him bend down to scoop something from the ground. He still had this object in his hand when we reached our lodgings.

'What's that you picked up?' I asked, attempting to keep any hint of criticism from my voice.

He opened his fingers to display a flattened ball of twine. 'The cat must have had it in its claws when it jumped over,' he said equably and smiled his most ingratiating smile.

I took hold of his shoulder. 'That seems improbable. More likely it leapt after a badly thrown ball which dropped on the ledge.' He was trying hard to stop his mouth twitching. 'Or was it intentionally thrown there?' I added as appalled understanding came to me.

He shrugged. 'How was I to know the daft thing wouldn't be able to get back again? Not that I admit anything, mind. It all happened fast and my head's a bit confused with all the danger and excitement. But I did save it!'

He did and, as always, he was entirely plausible. After the shock he had given me I hadn't the heart to interrogate him further and he knew this very well. 'Any way, doctor,' he said with a wink, 'you never know where an adventure like that might lead, do you?'

I gave him a gentle cuff and dismissed the platitude from my head; but he never spoke a truer word.

Chapter 2

Four weeks after Rendell's rash adventure I was summoned for interview by Professor Andrea Bonalini, the eminent scholar and physician who had oversight of my medical studies at the university. I had attended his lectures since the day I was admitted to the roll of students and I revered his intellect and knowledge but I had never met him face to face. His reputation was of one who did not suffer fools gladly and, although I did not believe myself a fool, I was aware of my shortcomings and the errors I had made in the past, not as a physician but as a misguided, susceptible young man. I was afraid the erudite doctor would find me wanting in the austere capacities he looked for in members of his profession and I dreaded the prospect of the meeting.

Time was reckoned with precision in Padua thanks to the great astronomical clock, high on its commanding tower, such as I had never seen in a public place. Nevertheless, in my nervousness, I arrived far too early at the gatehouse to the courtyard where the Professor had his lodging. I was surprised when the custodian beckoned me into his cubby-hole and the joyous thought came to me that Andrea Bonalini had been called away and was unable to see me. I was soon disabused of that base hope but rewarded with unexpected pleasure.

'You're the Englishman, Messer Somers? That's right, isn't it? I have a packet for you – brought by messenger from Venice this morning.'

Puzzled, I took a battered bundle from him, but then my heart gave a jolt as I recognised the seal fastening it – the arms of Duke Humphrey of Gloucester, uncle to King Henry, who had been my patron and lord, in whose service I had practised as a novice physician before my flight from England. I gave the gatekeeper a coin and hurried to a bench across the courtyard where, with fumbling fingers, I broke the seal and unfolded the papers inside the packet. A brief note, signed by the Duke himself, recorded his receipt of the book of philosophy I had sent shortly after my arrival in Padua, in accordance with the instructions he had given me, and enclosed with his words of gratitude was a generous letter of credit to be presented to Venetian bankers. He also asked me to purchase and dispatch two further volumes but he made no reference to my predicament as an unwilling exile or the fate of his wife.

I replaced Gloucester's letter in the pouch and smoothed open the longer communication, in hand writing I knew and rejoiced to see – that of the Duke's chamberlain, the incorruptible elderly man who had always been a friend to me. His inscription was, characteristically, formal but the sincerity of his words brought tightness to my throat.

Dear Doctor Somers

Dame Margery and I send you our greetings and trust you are finding value in your sojourn across the Narrow Sea, despite its circumstances. We, here at Greenwich, were all relieved to know of your safe arrival in Padua and your admission to the respected university there. All goes peaceably here, now we are freed from the pernicious influence of those who brought about the Duchess's downfall and your own unhappy flight. The Duke lives quietly among his books, in the company of learned men, and eschews attendance at court. Duchess Eleanor is imprisoned for life for witchcraft and treason – but that you know – and we have no hope that we will see her again.

My daughter, Lady Blanche, and her husband, Sir Hugh de Grey, send good wishes and the assurance that your mother, who remains in their service, is in good health although anxious for assurance of your continued well-being. Your old attendant, Thomas Chope, and his wife, Grizel, also ask weekly for news of you. They are now the parents of a fine infant, who from the noise he can already make bids fair to be as disruptive to our peace as was his uncle, Rendell, when he served here. Mistress Chope asks that you convey her affection to her rascally brother and the hope that he has not caused you too great embarrassment. Remember us also to Master du Bois, if he remains with you in Padua.

Alas I can give you no comfort as to your safety, if you were to return to England. Until the Duke is able to establish himself once more in his royal nephew's confidence, there is small chance that the grave charges against you will be dropped and your innocence proclaimed, so I can but counsel patience and devotion to your studies. I know you have one supporter at court, Lord Walter Fitzvaughan, whom the King trusts, but he can do little while the Duke's enemy, the Cardinal Beaufort, retains his pre-eminence.

Send us word of your fortunes when you can. Dame Margery is in indifferent health these days and would be cheered to know all is well with you.

The chamberlain signed himself with official correctness and I was deeply grateful for his thoughtfulness in giving me cheering news of those for whom I cared but two things gave me concern. His careful and unprecedented allusion to his wife's health was worrying, for I was fond of the formidable and intelligent Dame Margery, but his reference to Walter Fitzvaughan was more painful. The history of my dealings with Lord Walter and his wife, Maud, was conflicted and my dear Bess served in their household. The chamberlain would know nothing of my devotion and, in any case, Lady Maud and her tiring maid were likely to be far away from Greenwich, on the Fitzvaughan estate in Norfolk. Silence, in the letter, as to Bess's welfare was inevitable but the absence of what I most wanted to know made me sorrowful. Perhaps fortunately, I was given no time to indulge my sadness for I saw Professor Bonalini's servant approaching and realised the hour of my interview had come. I tucked the package into my gown, smoothed the folds of its skirt, straightened my cap and followed the attendant into the building.

*****

Andrea Bonalini was tall and lean with sharp eyes and emaciated cheeks. He reminded me of a heron, poised and watchful, ready to swoop onto his victim and savage them, not physically but with the force of his mental powers. He stared at me when I was ushered into his room, as if he had forgotten who I was or what I had come for, but this was momentary delusion on my part soon to be dispelled by his blunt introduction.

'They tell me you have already practised as a physician in England, Harry Somers. You are very young to be so qualified.'

I tried not to appear disconcerted. 'The Guild of Physicians gave me a dispensation to be admitted early, Professor.'

'Patronage of the Duke of Gloucester was valuable no doubt.' I had not expected that he would know my background and I was alarmed by his thin-lipped smirk of disapproval but he did not expect a response to his statement. 'You have attended a university previously?'

'At Oxford, sir.'

The curl of his lip showed that this information did not impress him. 'To have studied theology at that institution would be a commendation. Medicine is a different matter. The teaching would have been highly theoretical and arcane, I imagine. Were you admitted as a physician on the strength of that instruction alone?'

'No, indeed. After leaving Oxford I worked under the guidance of skilled and experienced doctors, in the household of Duke Humphrey. I have treated many ailments and conditions.'

He said nothing but his raised eyebrows indicated his scepticism and I froze in embarrassment, trying not to look away from his glare. 'You have seen the inside of a dead man's guts?'

'No, sir,' I murmured.

'Speak up, boy.'

This was a humiliation too far and I bridled. 'In England the prohibition of Holy Church against dissection is observed but since I came to Padua I've seen diagrams of how the internal organs are placed and I am anxious to learn more.'

Professor Bonalini's stern expression relaxed into the hint of a smile. 'Papal decrees on such matters do not carry weight in this university. You will attend my next dissection.'

'I should be honoured, sir. When will it be held?'

'When the justices next pass sentence of execution on some vagabond and the jailor releases the body. I expect to receive a cadaver in a week or two. Meanwhile we shall hold a disputation next Tuesday and I should be obliged, Doctor Somers, if you will take part.'

I gulped, unclear whether his use of my title was ironic. The Professor had a reputation for astringent appraisals of his students who spoke in these public debates, conducted all in Latin. 'What will the subject be, sir?'

'Can sleep be harmful? What are your first thoughts on the suggestion?'

I marshalled my ideas quickly. 'If an excess of sleep comes from an inclination to idleness and the shirking of exercise, it could be detrimental. Both wits and body should be kept active. But I would argue that unnatural drowsiness is an important symptom that something more serious may be amiss in a patient's constitution. It should not be ignored.'

To my amazement Professor Bonalini clapped me on the shoulder. 'Good – for an impromptu start, good. You will develop those concepts and speak in favour of the proposal.

The Bavarian, Berthold Zimmermann, will oppose you and then there will be open discussion.'

Berthold was in the third year of his doctorate studies and would be a formidable opponent but I suppressed my anxiety. 'I'll do my best, sir.'

'Bravo. I can see now why Giovanni di Signorelli thinks highly of you.'

'Giovanni! He was my good friend at the Duke's palace.'

'And he was one of my first medical students, many years ago. He wrote to me on your behalf. I respect his judgement.' I bowed my head in acknowledgement and relief. Then, as the Professor remained silent, I thought perhaps I was dismissed and moved towards the door until he held up his hand to detain me. 'He told me of your accomplishments in investigating crimes.'

I had much rather Giovanni had left that unsaid, given the misfortunes into which my last enquiries had led me. 'I achieved only mixed results, sir.'

'I'm well aware what you achieved and the deeper waters into which you fell latterly. The task I should like you to take on will not test you so severely.' My mouth opened but I could not form the words to query if I had heard him aright. He gave a surprisingly merry chuckle. 'I have a good friend, an apothecary, who believes there have been thefts of medicinal substances from his premises. I thought you might identify the culprit.'

My hand was trembling and I clutched my gown to still it. 'Is his pharmacy in the Piazza delle Erbe?'

'No, it's not one of those pretentious establishments under the loggia. You'll find it on the Molino Bridge – a spice shop, he calls it – and he does good business with the pilgrims coming to the hospice nearby. His name is Gasparo da Friuli. You will visit him?'

Thankful that the commission did not involve Messer Clemente or Gregory du Bois, I did not demur. 'I may not be successful in determining who is to blame.'

'Don't fear, that is understood.' Professor Bonalini accompanied me to the door. 'Just do your best, Doctor Somers. You have the makings of a sympathetic physician, young man. Study well.'

I reeled from the room, astonished to receive such encouragement, uneasy at the prospect of enquiring into missing medicines and tense with trepidation at the idea of confronting Berthold Zimmermann in formal disputation.

*****

Next morning, before the heat of the sun was intense I set out for Messer Gasparo da Friuli's establishment. My route took me past the old church of S. Niccolò and I stopped for moment to admire the stone mouldings above its windows until I was hailed by a figure crouched on the ground beneath the arched portico in front of the entrance. He was a scrofulous beggar with a withered leg and suppurating lesions on his neck who bleated at me for alms. I threw him a small coin and hurried on but what I longed to do was to provide him with a balsam to ease the throbbing of his sores. I wondered if I could obtain some from Geoffrey for a modest price but realised the impossibility of treating the ailments of all the mendicants in Padua. In my heart I knew that the insignificant incident had taught me how greatly I missed the practice of medicine – I relished the acquisition of new learning but longed to be active as a physician again.

I shrugged this inconvenient lesson aside as I approached the river with its floating water mills but, before I crossed onto the bridge, I hesitated in surprise when I recognised the man coming towards me, whom I had met a handful of times. His face was set in a scowl but there was no way for us to avoid each other and, when he saw me, Messer Clemente's expression mellowed, although he was evidently disconcerted to see me. I acknowledged him and would have been content to pass on without conversation but he stopped in front of me.

'Doctor Somers, this is a happy coincidence. I had not expected to meet you in this neighbourhood.'

'I'm on a commission for my Professor.' I thought I sounded defensive but he ignored my awkwardness.

'You should not run errands, doctor. Geoffrey du Bois has told me of your prowess. We were speaking of you last evening and I said you must join us at dinner. I was intending to send you a message. My wife and I would be pleased if you would come next Saturday. Would that be satisfactory for you?'

'Most certainly. It's kind.' The enthusiasm in my voice did not match the discomfort I felt at the prospect of dinner with that trio of hosts.

'Excellent. We shall await your visit with happy expectation. Good day.'

He bowed and hurried away, leaving me grateful not to prolong our discussion so near the shop I was to visit, which undoubtedly belonged to one of his rivals in the town. I stepped thankfully onto the bridge to pass between the close-packed buildings overhanging the river. Three or four apothecaries had their premises by the roadway but Gasparo's was the largest and most ostentatious. The sign of St. Michael Archangel, protector of spice merchants, creaked on its post outside the open door and coloured ceramic storage jars stood on a trestle inside the lean-to shop. An apprentice was using a small funnel to fill paper cones with an assortment of powders while a serving man waited patiently for his master's order to be prepared. I stood to the side until the transaction was completed and the customer had left. Then I enquired for the proprietor, saying Professor Bonalini had sent me, and while the youth went into the house behind the shop I looked around with care. I was then beckoned into the inner room where an imposing, although not portly, man rose to greet me and dismissed his assistant. I introduced myself with the briefest possible particulars of my background.

'I am glad to see you, Doctor Somers. I'm anxious to get to the bottom of the business. To harbour a thief in the household is not pleasant.'

'You believe one of your servants is to blame?'

'I suspect one of the apprentices.'

'Perhaps you should start at the beginning and explain what has happened.'

He motioned me to a stool and lowered himself back into his curved chair. 'There have been two occurrences. The first time a bunch of herbs seemed to be missing and I thought one of the lads had damaged it and been too cowardly to confess. The second time, three days ago, was far more serious. I have been leaving the shutter in the roof of the shop open for an hour or two after dark, due to the heat. When I went into the shop to fasten the catch, it was apparent there had been an intruder and a quantity of a valuable substance had been taken.'

'Just one substance?'

Gasparo da Friuli paused before replying. 'Yes. A special compound of my own, very efficacious for ladies' headaches and the fainting sickness.'

'So the thief knew what he was looking for?'

'Exactly. There will be scoundrels ready to pay him well for it.'

'For a sum less than you charge?'

'Precisely.' He folded his hands on his stomach and smiled complacently.

'There are other apothecaries nearby. Might they have coveted your special compound?'

He beamed. 'Oh, they do, they do. But I am confident they would not use underhand methods to obtain it. Besides, the shutter is not easy to manipulate unless you are familiar with it.'

'Hence your suspicion about members of your own household. I understand. But why should they go to the trouble of climbing in – it looks a small opening? Couldn't they just come back into the shop from the house?'

'I lock the door to the shop when darkness falls and keep the key on my belt. We all eat together when the shop has closed and then the lads go off into the town – to visit their families or for less desirable purposes. I'll brook no nonsense, mind you. They are required to be back in the house by nine o'clock. They enter by the side door.'

'Who are the members of your household?'

'My housekeeper and man-servant are both elderly and stiff in the joints. Besides they were in the house with me. Only my apprentices are used to the shutter and only they are agile enough to have climbed in. The theft must have occurred between the hour of darkness and when the town clock struck nine. Everyone had returned home and that is when I went into the shop to lock up.'

'So the theft took place within a period of less than two hours. Who are your apprentices?'

Again his smile seemed one of satisfaction. 'There are three. Gregorio, Gabriele and Leone – in descending order of seniority.'

'I'd better interview them all. Do you have reason to doubt the integrity of anyone?'

Gasparo drew himself up in his seat and brushed a fragment from his sleeve. 'I'd take my oath on the honour of Gregorio and Gabriele. They are both lads from worthy homes; their fathers are known to me.' He cast his eyes down as if waiting for me to prompt him but I kept silent and eventually he continued. 'Leone is a poor boy. I took him as an act of charity when his father was killed in an accident. I regret I do not receive the gratitude from him that I would look for in the circumstances.'

'May I proceed to question them all?' He nodded and I stood, fighting back the dislike I felt instinctively for his self-satisfied aplomb. He retired into an inner chamber leaving me his office for my interviews.

Gregorio and Gabriele were pleasantly polite and open in their answers. Neither seemed to be concealing any information and both claimed they would be vouched for by their families whom they had gone to visit after supping with their master on the evening concerned. Gregorio must have been about twenty and was clearly Gasparo's right-hand man. He seemed very knowledgeable about the spices and drugs in the shop and I asked him about the special compound.

'Do you know the ingredients?'

'Not all, nor how they're mixed. There's a multitude of herbs, half the contents of the physic garden: sage, parsley, betony, foxglove, wormwood, fennel, roots of Alexanders and dozens more, I don't doubt. He never lets us see him prepare the mixture and he won't tell you the truth of it, if you ask. It's too precious a secret for his business.'

'Could the compound be dangerous if taken without directions?'

Gregorio looked at me pityingly. 'All medicines can be dangerous if misused,' he said with disdain. 'The dosage is critical.'

I supressed a grin at his pedagogic tone of voice.

Gabriele was a year or two younger than his colleague and more diffident so I tried to put him at ease, speaking casually. 'You're not the most junior apprentice, are you? How long has Leone been here?'

My tactic did not work and he looked more uncomfortable. 'Eighteen months. He came after his father drowned.'

'How did that happen?'

'Leone was lucky to be given a position here. His father was a common porter. He worked at one of the mills on the river, humped the sacks of grain and flour on and off the boats for the miller. It seems he slipped and was hit by the sail, fell in the river, must have been stunned and carried away. They found his body somewhere downstream.' Gabriele's face turned pale and I did not press him further. He could add little otherwise to what Gregorio had said.

Leone was tall but slightly built, with delicate features, and I judged him to be about fourteen. He quickly made it obvious that he was not in the mood for pleasantries and I could sense his fizzing annoyance. 'I know what Messer Gasparo will have told you,' he said before I'd even asked a question. 'He'll be pointing the finger at me but I didn't do it, Doctor. That's all I can say.'

'If you didn't do it, you've got nothing to worry about.' I frowned at my use of such a trite expression and the sight of his contemptuous twitch of the lip. 'Where were you that evening?'

'I go to see my mother most evenings. She lives across the bridge.'

'She'll vouch you were with her that day?'

'You're not to ask her. She'd be upset and I won't have it. You'll get nothing more from me. If you think I'm a thief, denounce me. That's what he wants. That's why you're here. If you won't take my word for it, I've nothing more to say.'

I grabbed his arm as he moved to the door. 'Whoa, Leone. Not so belligerent. I'm not here to do anyone's bidding. I've got an open mind. But don't make it difficult for yourself. Your mother will understand if I ask whether you were with her.'

'No, she won't! She's had enough trouble and she's not well. I've told you I didn't steal the stuff and that's enough for you.'

I turned him so a beam of light fell on his truculent face and I was aware of his clenched fists. 'You weren't with your mother were you, Leone? Where were you?'

'I was!' He broke from me and thumped the table in anger but when he looked back to me his mouth was pinched with distress. 'I can't tell you.'

I sat him on the stool and crouched beside him. 'That's better. Now listen. For what it's worth, I'm prepared to take your word. I think it most unlikely you broke into the shop and stole that compound but I can't prove it. For some reason Messer Gasparo believes you're the culprit and he'll need proof that you weren't. So if someone can vouch for you, however disreputable they are, I need their evidence.'

To my surprise he hooted with laughter. 'Disreputable! That's a good one!'

'Were you with a woman, Leone?'

He fixed me with a mischievous stare. 'D'you think I'm not old enough for the stews?'

I decided to chance my arm. 'I don't think that's where you were. But I believe you wouldn't want Messer Gasparo to know what you were doing.'

'You're a sharp one, Doctor.' There was a hint of admiration in his voice. 'How could you tell?'

'You remind me of my servant, Rendell. He's a bit younger than you but I dread to think what the pair of you might get up to together.' He grinned and, once again, I let instinct direct me. 'You won't be earning anything as an apprentice.'

'My master provides board and keep.' The assertive tone had crept back.

'But you are trying to provide for your mother. If I had to hazard a guess what you were doing that evening, I'd say you were selling your labour to someone other than the apothecary. Am I right?'

'I'm bound to give all the labour of my body and mind to Messer Gasparo,' Leone said. 'My articles prohibit me from any other work.'

'Quite so. But I don't need to give your master details if I have confirmed your alibi. Tell me: where do you go for your illicit employment?'

'Anywhere less illicit, you can't imagine.' He chortled. 'Will you really not tell my master? I want you to believe me, Doctor. You're all right, I reckon.'

I was cheered by this endorsement but I kept any twinkle of merriment from my face. 'Where, Leone?'

He shrugged. 'The Convent of the Carmelites. Sister Maria Iacopina would vouch for me. The Infirmarer's fingers are stiff and she can't chop the herbs or mix the potions so well as she did. She welcomes help with the garden sometimes as well. I've done it since I was a little lad, before I came here. The Prioress says I'll have to give it up soon.'

'For fear you'd ravish one of the nuns?'

'More likely I'm starting to turn the nuns' thoughts from their prayers to my manly attributes.'

'You're a rogue, Leone, but I believe you. Why do you think Messer Gasparo suspects you might be a thief?'

'He regrets his generosity in providing for me after my father died. He took me as apprentice without the usual payment. Now I'm bigger, he's counting the cost. I've got a good appetite. He'd be glad to be rid of me.'

I was afraid this assessment was all too true but I repeated my promise to keep his secret and thanked him for his honesty. I opened the door for him to return to the shop.

'Would you do something else for me, Doctor?' He winked at me.

'What's that?'

'Introduce me to your servant, this Rendell; I'd like to meet him.'

*****

Later, when the apprentices had been sent off to eat their midday meal, I went back into the shop with Gasparo

25

da Friuli and looked more closely at its layout and contents. It was crowded with provisions and the utensils of an apothecary's craft. Every shelf was crammed with bottles and jars, overflowing boxes and untidy packets, bowls and dishes of varying designs; every solid wall held an assembly of tongs, ladles and pestles, hung on hooks and brackets. I picked up a stick of charcoal which was used to mark the prices of the different sized candles, and began to draw round the bases of the huge jars on the counter.

'What are you doing? Be careful with my albarelli! My father got them years ago from a merchant who traded with the east.' There was no mistaking Messer Gasparo's indignation.

'They're very fine. I'm taking great care. If anyone needs to move one of them during the afternoon, make sure they're set back just as they are, within the circles I've made. I'll come back when it gets dark to try a small experiment. Let the boys go off as usual after supper and then stay inside the house unless you hear anything amiss.'

'Are you going to try to climb in? You'll never manage it.' He cast a deprecating glance at my lame leg.

'No. My young servant will do it. He's not as tall as Leone but he's very sprightly.'

This seemed to satisfy the apothecary and, with fine condescension, he offered me a fee for the time I had spent at his premises. I declined to take money but asked for a pot of ointment to ease festering sores and he was happy to indulge my inexpensive whim.

I hurried back past the church of S. Niccolò but the beggar I had seen before was not there and a shrivelled old woman sat in his place. When I enquired where I might find him she shrugged. 'No business to be here, he hadn't. Sent him on his way.' She held out a grimy hand, extending an arm which was scraggy but free from sores, and I put a coin into her palm. Then I turned away from the direct route to my lodgings, towards the Convent of the Carmelite sisters.

26

*****

'If you don't stop giggling, Rendell, we'll have to abandon the whole idea. From the moment we set foot on the bridge, we have to be absolutely quiet. I'll wait outside the shop and if there are any passers-by, I'll explain what's happening. Let's hope there won't be any. You must try not to make a sound and let yourself down into the shop as lightly as you can.'

'Working for you, Doctor, is full of wonders! Mind you, it ain't the first time I've made an entrance through a roof-vent. You'd be surprised!'

'No, I wouldn't.'

The dryness of my wit was exceeded by the dryness in my throat as we approached the apothecary's shop and Rendell at last fell silent. I lifted the torch I was carrying so he could see where he needed to go and in an instant he had scrambled up the uneven wall onto the low roof of the lean-to. I watched nervously as he crawled across the tiles to the unlocked shutter and began, very gently, trying to raise it. He needed to insert his fingers into the gap beneath the boards in order to release the internal catch to the furthest extent and, as I had been advised, this was not easy. When he eventually succeeded I heard the hinge creak but I persuaded myself that this would not have been audible within the house. I held my breath as he wriggled into the opening and let himself down by his arms to dangle over the well-stocked pharmacy.

There was a moon that night but it would have thrown little light into the shop. To guard against mishaps, I had explained to Rendell where goods were stacked and how a slight shuffle to the right should ensure he landed directly on the floor, without crashing onto a shelf and spilling its contents, but I had not prepared him for anything else. I saw his fingers change their grip as he angled his body in the way

I had described and then they disappeared. Immediately there was pandemonium. The clatter of metal, rattle of pottery and a sickening splintering of glass were joined by a tersely basic English expletive, followed very promptly by the bang of a door thrown open and the sound of Messer Gasparo's irate voice.

'Mother of God, what have you done? My albarelli! Have you smashed my albarelli?'

Luckily Rendell had the presence of mind to ignore the distraught apothecary and unbolt the door to the street so that I could enter and light the candle-sconces from my torch. Mercifully all the large ceramic jars on the counter were intact but several smaller receptacles had bounced from an upper shelf and the vibration of the intruder's landing had dislodged heavy tongs from their hook on the wall. The damage was not serious.

'I'm sorry, Messer Gasparo, but I think this has shown how unlikely it is that anyone could break in through the shutter with drawing attention to their crime.'

'It's done no such thing, Doctor Somers. Your servant is a clumsy buffoon.'

I could see the boy's tight fists and stepped between him and the apothecary. 'I have entire confidence in his skill and had told him exactly where things were. The reason I marked the position of the great storage jars was because I could see that the slightest movement would cause them to judder against each other and make a noise. I thought it possible that some of the small bottles would fall from the top shelf – and I'm ready to pay for those – but I didn't know the tongs were so insecurely fixed to wall.'

Messer Gasparo continued running his hands over the albarelli until he was satisfied there were no cracks in their surfaces. Then he grunted acknowledgement of what I had said. 'I am not convinced by your experiment. Leone is taller and would not have had so far to drop.'

'But he's heavier than Rendell. I think he would have shaken the shelves just as much. I maintain no one could break into your shop in that manner without being overheard.' The apothecary snorted but I continued. 'Besides, Leone is vouched for by the Lady Prioress of the Carmelites. See.' I held out a paper.

Astonishment spread over Messer Gasparo's face as he read the note. 'Visiting a sick cousin, who is a nun, in the convent's infirmary? Why didn't the boy tell me?'

'I understand the Prioress made an exception to let him make the visit and she asked him to say nothing. I'm afraid, Messer Gasparo, I can think of nothing else to solve your mystery of the missing mixture. There is no useful evidence to follow.'

For a moment there was fury in his expression but he controlled himself and folded his hands across his stomach. 'You have been thorough and ingenious, Doctor. I am grateful. Perhaps, after all, I was mistaken.'

He insisted on giving me modest payment and this time I accepted, on Rendell's behalf, but I was glad to bid him farewell and to escape from the neighbourhood without encountering Leone. In time I would honour my promise to introduce the volatile apprentice to my servant but that was not a conjunction I could contemplate with ease.

As we walked back towards the Piazza delle Erbe, Rendell looked up at me with a quizzical glint in his eyes. 'Did that sodding apothecary set it all up in order to get rid of the poor apprentice and disgrace him?'

'Maybe. We can't prove it.' I did not wish to pursue that unpleasant possibility.

Rendell gave me a sidelong glance. 'Did you forge that note from the Prioress?'

'Certainly not. She wrote it herself after I'd explained the position.'

'Telling a bald, bloody lie?'

'She told me Leone had been carrying heavy pallets into the infirmary and, being a cheery lad, he exchanged words with the patients there. In God's eyes we are all brothers and sisters so allusion to him visiting a cousin was a minor inaccuracy.'

'You thought of that, didn't you?' When I simply grinned he let out a great whoop. 'Christ, you're a good 'un, Doctor!'

I wished I could share his uncomplicated merriment but the episode at the apothecary's shop had left me uncomfortable and now I needed to turn my attention to the forthcoming disputation with Berthold Zimmermann.

Chapter 3

I approached Messer Clemente's house without enthusiasm. I felt I had enjoyed adequate acquaintance with apothecaries in the last few days and knew I must steel myself for embarrassment, sitting at table with Geoffrey and the man he might have cuckolded. I told myself Rendell had a lively and scabrous imagination and was quite capable of embroidering what he thought he had seen, but I did not want to put it to the test. I must resist the temptation to watch for meaningful glances, exchanged in secret between dishonest lovers, and try not to read more into the conversation than was intended. I berated myself for being too ready to indulge my curiosity and pry into what was not my concern but I did not expect to find pleasure in my meal.

I was soon disarmed by Giorgio Clemente's hospitality and relieved that Geoffrey seemed genuinely pleased I had come. The three of us took wine together and chatted harmlessly about public affairs in Padua and the growth of its university. I knew it was some forty years since the town had fallen under the aegis of the Venetian Republic and become part of its *Terrafirma*, the large area on the mainland it controlled, and subject to its generally benign rule; but I was interested to hear Giorgio's reminiscences of the disorderly time before and after that transfer of control.

'I was only a little lad when the Carrera family was ousted from Padua but I picked up my father's nervousness about the change. He'd served them for many years, when they dominated the town, and he feared retribution from their enemies. He judged it wise to keep a low profile, especially when the Carrera tried to regain power, but he was always afraid. He died before his time with that dread preying on his mind. I learned from his misfortune and when there was unrest in the *Terrafirma* three years ago I declined to have anything to do with it.'

'Was Venetian rule seriously at risk so recently?'

'They soon re-established control. There was more excitement in Verona than here. There's always friction between Venice and the Visconti in Milan; they were behind the trouble then and they stir things up whenever they see an opportunity. Things can still be edgy in Padua, under the surface, and there's some in the town who hold it against me that I wouldn't declare for the Carrera – ironic when my father's problem was due to his association with them.'

Geoffrey swirled the wine in his goblet. 'That's how you incurred the hostility of some other apothecaries in the Guild?'

'Gasparo da Friuli had always seen himself as my rival. Different allegiances were grist to his mill. He never put himself at risk by coming out in opposition to Venice but it suits him to proclaim me unpatriotic, to anyone who'll listen.' I froze while Giorgio was speaking, uncertain whether to admit my contact with Gasparo or to keep silent and hope it would not be discovered. Happily for me, Giorgio decided to move on to other topics. 'You find your studies at the university invigorating, Doctor Somers?'

I explained how Professor Bonalini and his colleagues taught medicine in a very different manner from the academic approach I had learned at Oxford and I described the disputation in which I was to play a part. The apothecary clearly approved of me praising my tutors and he clapped his hand on my shoulder.

'My son studies law at the University of Bologna. You will know that our establishment in Padua welcomes foreigners, not citizens of the town. Otherwise I would have Pierpaolo closer to home. He is inclined to be wayward.'

'As is not uncommon among students,' I said lightly.

'He took the loss of his mother deeply, too deeply for a youth of his years, and he has behaved badly towards his step-mother.'

'You remarried recently, sir?

32

'Two years ago my angel came to me.' He spoke with reverence in his voice.

As if summoned by her husband's words, Antonia Clemente appeared at the door to the inner chamber and bade us come to the table. I bowed low as we were introduced and, raising my eyes, I saw she was fully deserving of Rendell's precocious praise. She was of medium height, with olive skin and slender hips but it was the luxuriance of her breasts which drew a man's gaze, despite his best intentions. They were decently covered by the soft material of her summer gown but the shape of her firm nipples was visible and her tightly clad bosom rose and fell with exaggerated elegance. She smiled and took my arm to lead me forward and I marvelled how Messer Clemente could consider it safe to allow any virile guest under his roof.

When we were seated and served, Giorgio reverted to the subject of my studies and told his wife that I was to speak against the desirability of too much sleep. She seemed completely at ease and told her husband, with a laugh, that he had best beware the dangers I might describe as Giorgio was inclined to nod in his chair after meals. She was so enchanting that it was only later I conjectured whether there had been suggestive mischief behind her words; at the time so vile a thought never crossed my mind. She leaned towards me and asked me to summarise what I planned to set out in argument and when I had concluded my summary she said simply, 'Doctor Somers, is it not possible that different people need varying amounts of sleep for health and energy?'

'Madonna, you should take my place in the disputation. You have put your finger on a significant fact.'

'I would wager Madonna Antonia could better a dozen Germans in debate; her wit is sharp and her skill undoubted.'

It was Geoffrey who had spoken and I trembled at his tone of undisguised admiration but Giorgio was not troubled. He raised his glass to his wife and we stood to drink her health, adding to the catalogue of her virtues as we did so. I noticed she had eaten little of the food on her plate and while we paid her extravagant compliments the faint colour left her cheeks and she turned pale. It struck me that she was feeling unwell and the heat was troubling her so I was not surprised when she summoned her woman and begged to be excused from our company. Giorgio beamed at her with besotted devotion.

Shortly after she had gone and the servants left the room, Giorgio leaned back in his chair and lifted his glass once more. 'Doctor Somers, I am happy to share our joy with you. As a physician, you will understand. My dear wife is with child and, after so many years, I am to be a father once more.'

Geoffrey was staring straight ahead and I could not tell whether or not he already knew of Madonna Antonia's condition. He gave no sign that the news was of any account to him but a horrid memory came to me of another young woman, my own sister, whose much older husband had longed for a child, but whose future had been blighted and curtailed with vicious finality. I forced myself to dismiss the thought and gave Giorgio hearty congratulations. Then to divert my companions and fasten my mind on a less painful topic I regaled my host and friend with the tale of Rendell's exploit on the Capello tower, with the cat.

'So you met Carlotta Schioppa-Capello? That might serve you well. They are a powerful family. Her husband is a notable Venetian.' Giorgio lowered his voice. 'But her mother is still more formidable! She is Veronese and still has influence in that city. Take care not to cross her path, Doctor, and counsel your servant not to play tricks when she's at hand.'

Giorgio began to laugh but was overcome with coughing and gave us a moment of concern when his face turned purple and the veins on his temple bulged. I moved to loosen his gown while Geoffrey thrust a glass in his hand, thumping him on the back, and the episode was over in a twinkling. He made a joke in poor taste, I thought, saying a crumb had lodged in his throat, like his seed in his wife's belly, and he filled his platter once more. It was some time before he finished eating and I could make my escape. I left him and Geoffrey drinking together amicably but I could not dismiss my unease about the seething emotions which might lie beneath the surface in the apothecary's house.

*****

I worked hard on my presentation, extolling the virtues of moderation in sleep, and I prepared some elegant Latin phrases to employ in debate. I developed Antonia Clemente's idea of appropriate measures of sleep for different ages and conditions, pondering that any old wife would swear the time spent by a baby in sleep fostered growth of body and mind. It occurred to me that the drowsiness of an elderly grandsire, slipping towards his second infancy, might also have some restorative function. Observation of such natural characteristics was as important for a physician as study of the zodiac and the four humours. Dared I assert that, even in Padua? As for the relationship between sleep and dreams, and the interpretation of dreams as indicators of health and fortune, I resolved to mention various theories but to put my trust in physical evidence.

It was not easy to concentrate for long on such abstruse notions. The thought of Antonia Clemente roused other sensations which were not conducive to scholarly detachment and I found myself remembering encounters I knew I would do better to forget. It was not gentle Bess who filled my thoughts but the noblewoman she now served, Lady Maud Warrenne as she had been before she married Lord Walter Fitzvaughan, with whom I had coupled in shameless sensuality. I had lived a life of monastic

35

temperance since I came to Padua, but the apothecary's wife challenged my determination to endure a celibate exile and the possibility that Geoffrey had enjoyed her favours tormented me. A feeling of desolate solitude afflicted me.

Berthold Zimmermann had many supporters, eager to undermine my confidence, and they became vocal in their derision and abuse, likening my person to a scabby toad and my intellect to the feeble logic of a green girl. I shrugged off their words but I did not care for the threat of intimidation in their beetled brows and twisted mouths. There was only one fellow student whom I considered to be my friend, the Savoyard, René Pellino, and he was appalled by what he saw as my docility in absorbing these insults. He berated me on our way to a lecture.

'You shouldn't be so supine. Their effrontery is outrageous. I'll rally everyone from outside the Bavarian "Nation" at the university. The French and the Flemings have no love for Zimmermann. They'll sharpen their daggers and give his minions something to think twice about before they bad-mouth you again.'

'No. I want no violence. I'd rather defeat him in the disputation than in the street.'

'But if you do defeat him in debate, it'll be in the street that the next episode will take place. You'll be a marked man, Harry.'

I was surprised by the anxiety in his voice. 'Little chance of that. I'll be satisfied if I can get through without disgracing myself. Berthold is far more experienced than me in set-piece debates. If by some miracle I do win, you can marshal your supporters and I'll take them all to celebrate. I can't believe the Bavarians will nurture a grievance after the event.'

René shook his head at my obtuseness but we had reached the door of the lecture hall. A dozen pairs of Bavarian eyes narrowed with contempt as we entered but Professor Bonalini was mounting the podium and silence fell across his audience. I was sure Berthold's followers guessed how I lacked assurance and their scorn reflected belief that I was a puny opponent, worthy only of disdain. When their champion had triumphed they would jeer at me but they would have no cause to harass me further.

That evening Geoffrey came to see me and we shared a flagon of wine. He seemed out of sorts and I sent Rendell away so that my friend could talk to me freely, if he was willing to share what was troubling him. I assumed he was finding it stressful to lodge with Giorgio Clemente and his wife so I tried to give him an opening to refer to his situation but he did not take up this opportunity, talking instead in vague terms about dangerous rivalries. His reluctance to be explicit led me to be more outspoken. 'You'd be welcome to move back here, Geoffrey, if that's what you'd like.'

He stared at me, uncomprehending, as if I'd spoken in a foreign tongue. 'You don't understand. My presence is a protection for them.'

'A protection? From what?'

'Those who describe Giorgio as a Venetian stooge. He hinted at it when you came to dine. It's a stick to beat him with as they play out the jealousies between rival herbalists in the town. They all strive for patronage from the leading families and it doesn't help him to be thought unreliable in his allegiance to Padua. You see he has the custom of the Schioppa-Capello household and it brings him good business, but Enrico Capello was unpopular when he held the position of Venetian Podestà in the town. Other apothecaries claim Giorgio is the lackey of Venice's chief representative and that damages his reputation. I have some credibility as an experienced foreign apothecary, who served a royal English duke, and that lends a measure of independence and esteem to Giorgio's affairs.'

Geoffrey had once staged his own apparent death and chosen voluntary exile in order to escape the complex enmities of great men at the English court. It seemed incomprehensible to me that he would now embroil himself in the petty squabbles of Paduan tradesmen – unless of course he saw himself as defender of Antonia Clemente's interests. 'So you are content to bind your fortunes to those of your employer?'

'I respect Giorgio.'

I drank deeply from my glass. 'And his wife?'

His brow puckered and then cleared. 'My admiration for Madonna Antonia is profound. It is my friend who causes me embarrassment.'

I thought at first that he was chiding me for implying impropriety in his relationship with Antonia but as he held my gaze and tightened his lips, I realised he was challenging me about something quite different. 'What do you mean?'

'You are become familiar with Giorgio's principal enemy and you've tried to keep it secret from me. You've spent hours in company with Gasparo da Friuli and purchased his ointments, rather than those I could have supplied. These are not the actions of a friend, who crossed half the continent in my company, nor those of a courteous guest who has been entertained at Giorgio's table.'

I shook my head with a sigh. 'I should have told you. It was quite innocent but I see how it could be misinterpreted. It was because I felt awkward I didn't say anything. I hoped you'd never know. My Professor asked me to investigate a theft at Gasparo's shop. That's all I did. I accepted a jar of ointment for the sake of a beggar with running sores. I didn't expect there'd be gossip about it.'

The anger had left Geoffrey's eyes. 'You won the appreciation of a talkative apprentice who has been singing your praises to his cronies across the town.'

'Leone?'

'I'm sorry I mistrusted you, Harry. I'm glad you explained. I should have known you wouldn't be involved in some underhand plot against Giorgio.'

'Does Giorgio think I was?'

'I don't believe he has heard Leone's chatter. Anton... Madonna Antonia picked up rumours in the market place and she told me, knowing you were my friend.'

I noticed his slip in starting to use the lady's Christian name without her formal title but I made no comment. After restoring my own credentials as a trustworthy colleague, I was in no position to probe the nature of Geoffrey's feelings for his employer's wife.

*****

When I followed Professor Bonalini and Berthold Zimmermann onto the podium I saw that the hall was crowded. Disputations were held in public and citizens of Padua were welcome to attend but I had not expected that they would do so in such numbers. Students at every level and from the disciplines of law and philosophy, as well as medicine, comprised the majority of the audience but the ranks of sober gowns and chains of office in the front rows startled me. I had no wish to be distracted by knowledge of who was present so I cast down my eyes and concentrated on the Professor's introductory words, trying to control my upsurge of nervousness. I rejoiced that Berthold, as the more senior student, was to speak first and I listened to him carefully, memorising points which I could contest or query in my presentation. He was a skilled orator, used to debating in Latin, as I was not, and he soon won murmurs of appreciation from his listeners.

When it was my turn to stand at the lectern, I was conscious of my trembling voice and when I stumbled over the pronunciation of a tricky phrase I heard a titter of amusement from the side of the hall. To my surprise Professor Bonalini banged his gavel on the stand in front of him, indicating his displeasure at the interruption, and that strengthened my confidence: I was to be accorded a fair hearing and I should not underrate my capacity. My delivery gained assurance and, shortly after, I departed from my prepared speech to dispute one of Berthold's assertions, before returning smoothly to my own argument. I heard an encouraging grunt from one of the distinguished gentlemen below the rostrum and noted that Professor Bonalini did not use his gavel to signal disapproval of this extraneous sound. I moved on to my peroration and returned to my bench satisfied that I had not made a fool of myself.

As Berthold's seconder moved to the lectern, I breathed deeply in relief and allowed my gaze to travel over the audience. The be-chained dignitaries were the officials of various guilds and there, on one side of the hall, stood Giorgio Clemente, corpulent, very red in the face and doubtless extremely uncomfortable in his thick robes. Just a few places along from Giorgio, and pointedly ignoring him, was Gasparo da Friuli, leaner and untroubled by the heat, it appeared, listening with chin in hand and accompanied by Gabriele. Gregorio would be in charge of the shop on the bridge, I assumed, as would Gregory in the premises beneath the loggia in the Piazza delle Erbe. I rallied my wandering thoughts to attend to the continuing disputation but not before I had observed an unknown man, seated on a carved chair in the midst of the standing guildsmen. He was dressed in black with a flash of crimson and silver at throat and wrists and his short silken gown suggested he was not a councillor or tradesman. Standing around him were half a dozen sturdy attendants in red and black livery with fixed expressions and probably little interest in the debate. Their master was swarthy in complexion, with handsome features and a demeanour that suggested he would tolerate no disobedience to his will.

When the principal speakers had finished Professor Bonalini called other students to make short contributions and then, before his summing up, he invited any of the illustrious guests to comment. The guildsmen shook their heads respectfully, perhaps a little overwhelmed by the academic rigour and unremitting Latin, but the unknown visitor leaned back his head against the back of his chair and stretched out long shapely legs.

'An excellent debate, Professor. Your students do you credit. In my opinion the misshapen little Englishman has the edge on the Bavarian protagonist in his arguments. I always take care to guard against too much somnolence for the sake of my safety as well as my health. A man of action needs to be alert to the dangers of a knife between the ribs. Will you award Doctor Somers the victor's palm?'

I kept a hold on my exhilaration and watched with interest how the Professor bowed his head courteously, showing no sign of the indignation I was sure he felt. It was for him alone to make an assessment of our qualities and to determine the outcome. He moved to the lectern and permitted himself one deprecating cough.

'I am most obliged, Commendatore, for your judgement and compliments. I shall give a few critical comments on what we have heard but my conclusion is that the disputation has been finely balanced in terms of logic and proficiency of presentation. I shall declare it a tie.'

He went on to dissect much that had been said and the manner of our speaking, but I lost many of the details. I was joyful to know I had been judged Berthold's equal and that this success would be reckoned in my favour as I continued with my doctorate studies. I was immensely grateful to the elegant stranger who had praised me and I was sorry to see him and his acolytes stride from the hall as soon as the Professor finished his oration. I would have been pleased to make his acquaintance. Berthold, inevitably, was frowning for he had clearly expected to be proclaimed the unquestioned winner but my tentative supporters were now willing to display their partisanship openly and they gave a cheer. Professor Bonalini made no effort to control the hubbub which erupted in the hall but he invited me to accompany him to his room and I was glad of the excuse to slip from the rostrum by his side, immune from catcalls and brickbats while in his company.

*****

The Professor handed me a goblet of exquisite wine, far superior to anything I customarily drank, and he congratulated me on holding my own so robustly against an experienced debater. I wondered if Berthold was also to join us and, when a tap on the door announced another arrival, I presumed I would see my erstwhile opponent and hoped to end our previous contention by sharing a draught in friendly fashion. The person who entered, however, was not my fellow student but the apothecary, Gasparo da Friuli. Gabriele was no longer in attendance.

'Well done, Doctor Somers, well done! I told Professor Bonalini I had confidence you would excel. I promised to come to drink your health if you did.'

His enthusiasm surprised me because I was convinced he must have been disappointed by the inconclusiveness of my enquiries into the theft at his shop but I acknowledged his congratulations. I was puzzled by his evident wish to see me until Professor Bonalini patted my shoulder and began to explain with customary dry humour.

'You are not unique, Doctor Somers, in studying at Padua for a doctorate after being admitted to the company of physicians in your own country. It is a measure of our prestige that we attract such qualified gentlemen – whatever the circumstances of their coming here.' He permitted himself a curl of the lip at this allusion to my flight from probable execution in London. 'However much you are stimulated by the superiority of our teaching, I suspect it is sometimes frustrating for you to be unable to treat patients as you have done in the past.' I had not expected such considerate understanding from the pedagogue but he did not require me to reply. 'It is open to me to grant permission, in appropriate cases, for gifted students to undertake the practice of medicine in limited circumstances. Some of our more enterprising apothecaries engage a physician to attend their premises for a few hours each week, to advise and prescribe treatment for their clients. My friend, Gasparo, has asked if I would give agreement to your employment one morning a week at his shop. I am confident this would not adversely affect your studies, indeed it may benefit them, and I am pleased to consent.'

I stared stupidly from the Professor to the apothecary while struggling to suppress the panic which seized me. It was a splendid chance to do what I longed for, to recognize myself as an active physician once more, to apply the knowledge and experience I had already gained. Yet I had no particular wish to work with Gasparo da Friuli and I dreaded Geoffrey du Bois's response if I accepted a commission with a rival establishment, reluctant to imperil our friendship. I stammered thanks for the unexpected honour but begged to be allowed to consider whether I was ready to assume this responsibility in addition to my studies. Professor Bonalini was displeased by my equivocation.

'By all the saints, Harry Somers, have you no gratitude? Your colleagues would give their right arms for such an opportunity.'

Gasparo raised his hands in protest at this harsh response. 'No, no, Andrea, don't be so hasty. Show some appreciation of our young friend's position. He has just achieved a notable success after what must have been a gruelling encounter for him. He deserves respite to consider my offer, coming to him without warning when he is both weary and exultant.' He turned to me with a sympathetic smile. 'The Professor neglected to say that I would make you a small regular payment to retain your services and you would of course be able to charge your patients fees as you deemed fit.'

I blinked in surprise at his kindly manner and the prospect of a modest income to supplement my fast diminishing resources. 'I'm confident you will accept,' he continued, 'but I respect your wish to reflect. Be assured I have no doubt as to your abilities. Let me know in two days' time what you decide and your place will be waiting for you next week. Which morning will fit most conveniently with your commitments at the university?'

'Tuesdays will be best,' Professor Bonalini replied. 'That will only mean the loss of a lecture by my junior associate, which a practised physician should be well able to dispense with. I hope you appreciate, Doctor Somers, how generous Gasparo is to indulge your ingratitude and grant you time to consider. You will notify us of your decision within twenty- four hours.'

'I am truly grateful, sir, but my head is spinning.' I must have sounded inane but Gasparo tapped my arm in avuncular style and showed me from the room with renewed compliments as to my skill in debate. I vowed to go at once to speak to Geoffrey.

*****

As I opened the outer door to leave the lecture hall I was greeted by a small but boisterous company of fellow students, led by René Pellino, who swept me up onto their shoulders and accompanied me to the tavern with much merriment. I was reminded with hearty geniality that I had promised to take them all to celebrate if I was successful in the disputation and being judged Berthold Zimmermann's equal was undoubtedly a triumph. I did not argue for what they said was true and the chance to lose myself in oblivion, postponing a difficult meeting with Geoffrey until the morning, suddenly became seductive. I drank far more than I was accustomed to and we were still carousing happily well after darkness fell. Ordinary students at the university were expected to observe a curfew and return to their quarters during the evening but the position of the older, doctoral students was always less clear. Provided we behaved ourselves with sober decorum we were unlikely to be challenged as we made our way through the streets but, on that particular occasion, our animated group might fail to meet the correct standards of rectitude. It was thought wise to divide up as we spilled out of the inn and to return home in twos and threes, rather than as a rowdy cluster of revellers attracting the unwelcome attention of the officious town guards. René lodged not far from me and we set off together towards the Piazza delle Erbe.

As we neared his lodgings he lounged back against a wall with a foolish grin on his face and he put his hand to his crotch. 'I've another call to make, Harry. You might like to come too. I'm horny as hell and there's this girl I visit. She's got a sister, a pretty little whore. She'd suit you well. I told them I might bring you one night.' He burped amiably.

I put out a hand to steady myself on the stonework. 'Bloody cheek!' I giggled. 'Wouldn't do myself justice tonight though.'

My words didn't sound quite right and he punched my chest with amusement. 'I'll tell Samaritana you'll come when your manhood is restored.'

'Sa . . . Samaritana?'

'Well chosen name. She'll do a good turn for anyone.' He roared with laughter. 'You all right to get home from here on your own?'

I took my hand from the wall and although I wobbled slightly I remained upright. 'I'll manage, you reprobate.'

'That's a big word in your condition! See you tomorrow, glorious victor of the disputation.'

He beat out a rhythm on the doorpost and I stumbled on my way, round the corner and across a small square to the alley which led directly to the piazza where my lodgings were situated. I wondered blearily what Samaritana was like and, although I had always shunned bawdy houses, it seemed at that instant that what she offered would ease my loneliness. I began to hum a ribald ditty to myself but could not remember all the words.

I was dimly aware of a shape moving towards me through the alley but my normal instinct for caution had deserted me and I thought nothing of it. I was wholly unaware of the second rogue padding along behind my back. It was the second fellow who pounced first, seizing my shoulders and forcing me to the ground. I could offer no useful resistance as he hauled me to my feet, gripping my arms, while the man in front pummelled my face and stomach with his fists. I heard myself groan when a punch smashed into my mouth and I saw the flash of metal as he drew a knife. I cursed fortune for devising so ignominious an ending for my futile life and I fell insensible onto the roadway.

Chapter 4

The bucketful of water brought me from my short-lived stupor and after a moment my mind cleared. I was propped by the wall, water streaming down my battered face and my gown was drenched. Torches illuminated a tall aristocratic-looking man, who seemed faintly familiar, standing over me. He cradled a knife in his hands until an attendant gave him a cloth on which he wiped the blade before returning the weapon to his belt. Turning my head with some difficulty I could see my two attackers in the grasp of liveried servants. One of the ruffians clutched his wrist and blood was seeping between his fingers.

'You are not seriously injured, Doctor Somers?' The authority in his voice made his words sound more like a command than a question. 'No don't try to stand yet. You've suffered rough treatment and I fancy you were not in a fit condition to sustain it. Your lodgings are nearby?'

'Round the corner in the piazza, sir. I owe you thanks.'

'It is fortunate we were passing the end of the alley, returning from dinner with the Venetian Podestà. We heard the scuffle and were in time to prevent worse villainy. Do you know these men?'

I peered at the prisoners and shook my head but the movement made me dizzy and I leaned back against the wall. My rescuer turned to the wounded captive. 'Who paid you?'

The man scowled. 'We were after his purse,' he said.

An expensively gloved hand slapped his truculent face. 'You were not! A drunkard's purse may be easily cut and is unlikely to contain much. You have been paid to maim or murder. By whom?'

The fellow clamped his mouth shut but his companion, who was clearly in pain, protested. 'We don't know, sir. Never seen them before.'

47

The tall man addressed his followers. 'Take these rogues to the town officers. Charge them with affray and attempted murder and order that they be put to the instruments to improve their memory. Your lives are forfeit, gentlemen, so you might as well enjoy the satisfaction of naming those who initiated your demise.' He clapped his hands and his servants led away my assailants while another attendant helped me to my feet and took my arm. 'You had been rightly celebrating your achievement, Doctor Somers, but you would be wise to remember that success breeds resentment. You placed yourself in danger by walking the streets alone and in an enfeebled condition.'

I summoned whatever dignity I could. 'I accept your rebuke, sir. I didn't think I had enemies in Padua. Perhaps that was my mistake. I saw you at the disputation. Professor Bonalini called you "Commendatore". May I know to whom I owe my life?'

'Few need to ask that question but you've not been long in the Venetian lands. My name is Matteo Maffei. My cousin's husband owns the Capello tower across the piazza. I am staying in Padua briefly but tomorrow I leave for Verona. I have, shall we say, a degree of notoriety throughout the *Terrafirma*.' I glimpsed his ironic smile as we turned the corner and came to the door of my lodgings.

'Signor Maffei, you have preserved me from my own foolishness and taught me a much needed lesson. I'm deeply grateful.'

'I admired your skill in debate and am gratified to have rendered this small service. However, you should know that I rarely act without purpose. We shall meet again, Doctor Somers, have no doubt, and there is always the possibility that I shall put a claim on you one day, in recognition of the assistance I've been able to give you tonight.'

He laughed as if his words were in jest but I solemnly acknowledged his right to claim some favour from me in return for my life, and we both smiled as if the idea was amusing. Then he reached out his hand to grasp mine. 'Good fellow. I bid you good evening and trust you will now experience the restorative powers of sleep about which you spoke so eloquently in the disputation.'

He strode off, leaving a servitor to escort me across the threshold of the house, into the care of a twittering landlady and an incandescent Rendell, furious to have missed an exciting brawl.

*****

Next morning my bruises ached but I was confident no bones were broken. I would have been capable of crossing to the loggia in order to speak to Geoffrey, had it not been for the frightful appearance of my swollen, discoloured face. I was well accustomed to strangers baulking at first sight of my prominent birthmark, crossing themselves in case I was the Devil's progeny, but such alarm would be compounded by my new accessories of half-shut eyes, a blackened jaw and jaggedly split lip. I sent Rendell to explain my circumstances to the apothecary and to ask Geoffrey to call on me. He came at once and rushed up the stairs two at a time.

'Great heavens, Harry! Who did this? Rendell said the villains were taken in the nick of time to save your life.'

'They were. I'd never seen them before and they wouldn't explain themselves last night.' I had been pondering how to ensure our conversation was not overheard by ever inquisitive ears. 'Perhaps while Geoffrey is with me, Rendell, would you go to the Palace of the Commune and enquire what news there is of my attackers? See if they've named their paymasters and when they are to be brought before the justices. I need to know who my enemies are and whether I will be required to attend in court.'

Rendell beamed with pleasure at this commission and hurried off full of self-importance, for once not suspecting my motives in sending him away.

Geoffrey thrust a jar of ointment into my hands. 'That will soothe your bruises. It's one of my own concoctions.' He waved a hand to silence my thanks. 'I hear you were masterful at the disputation. Could your opponent have been looking for revenge?'

'I find it difficult to believe it merited murder, though I've no doubt Berthold and his cronies think me an upstart. Maybe that's how scores are settled in Bavaria. It's a common enough occurrence in England.' I gave a weak laugh to show I was not deeply troubled. 'That's not what I need to speak to you about. I'm in an awkward spot and I don't want to do anything which you might misunderstand. I've no wish to mislead you.'

Geoffrey read the gravity in my look and settled on the window seat while I explained that I had been taken aside after the debate by Professor Bonalini and Gasparo da Friuli who offered me an opening to practise as a physician in the apothecary's shop on the Molino Bridge. 'I delayed my reply until I could speak to you. You told me that Messer Clemente regards Gasparo as a rival and I've no wish to offend Giorgio, still less you. But I confess I'm tempted to accept.'

'It's a great opportunity. Thank you for explaining.' He stood and stared out of the window for a short time. 'What would you do if I persuaded Giorgio to make you an equivalent offer? He has spoken of engaging a physician to hold consultations in the shop.'

'If it was left to me I'd seize the chance to work with you. But I require the agreement of my Professor to work as a physician while I'm studying. Gasparo da Friuli is his friend. I don't know that permission would be forthcoming to work with Giorgio.'

A glimmer of relief seemed to cross Geoffrey's face. 'You're beginning to understand how things operate round here.'

I ignored his ambivalent look. 'Why are Giorgio and Gasparo such rivals? There are a score of apothecaries in the town. Does it really derive from conflicting allegiances?'

Geoffrey seated himself again. 'Not simply but it goes back a few years. Gasparo was expecting to hold a junior position in the Guild but Giorgio was chosen instead. He offered bigger bribes I expect. Now it's come alive again because one of the main offices is to be filled before the end of the year. Giorgio is nervous Gasparo will outmanoeuvre him this time.'

'How would you feel if I took up his offer?'

'I'd be glad for you and I'd try to persuade Giorgio you were not conspiring against our interests.'

'I'm grateful.' I noted the way he associated himself with the older man. 'Will he make you a partner in the shop?'

'We've talked of it. I respect Giorgio. He's a skilled apothecary. And I think I could settle in Padua. There's only one drawback.'

I waited expectantly but he said no more and, perhaps because I was less clear-headed than usual, I risked an incautious question. 'Madonna Antonia?'

He shot to his feet, flushing from throat to temple. 'What nonsense have you heard? Is he spreading scandalous lies?'

I thought he was referring to Rendell and didn't know how to reply. 'Giorgio?' I asked with assumed innocence.

'No! Not Giorgio. His son. Pierpaolo, came home from Bologna a week ago. He's taken against me. He has no interest in the shop himself. He's studying law and wants to hold office with the Commune. But he sees me as some kind of threat. He hates Antonia as well and he made some snide remarks linking our names.'

'But there's no truth in these remarks? You refer to her with familiarity.'

Geoffrey sank back onto the window seat. 'I admire her more than any woman I have ever met. I think you would recognise my feelings.'

I was annoyed that he should remind me of my peccadillos with the woman who married Lord Walter Fitzvaughan. 'I felt only lust for Maud Warrenne.'

'I did not mean Lady Maud but Bess, whom you say you love.'

I was shaking with indignation. 'Bess is unmarried and I would wed her tomorrow if I could.'

'And so would I wed Antonia if she was free.'

I was so angry it took a moment for his words to register and I was aghast at them. 'Dear God, Geoffrey, what are you saying? Does she know?'

He crossed his legs. 'I have said enough and will not drag Antonia's feelings into this confession. They do not concern you.'

'But they concern Pierpaolo?'

'He has returned to Bologna and I trust will be sufficiently occupied there to divert his scurrilous imagination from his father's wife.'

'Are you wise to remain in the Clemente household?'

'Wisdom has nothing to do with it. I have no desire to leave. I've told you I respect Giorgio and I can be patient. I wish him no harm but he is forty-five years old and his health is not perfect.'

'Christ, that's appalling! How can you live like that?'

'You should know we do not choose our circumstances in this life.' He rose and moved to the door. 'I must go back. Use some of my ointment, physician, and send word to Gasparo da Friuli that you accept his offer. I will not hold it against you and Giorgio will understand.'

*****

When Rendell returned I was sitting with my head in my hands, wishing I had never heard what Geoffrey had told me, but I was determined to give no hint of it to the boy. Fortunately he was full of his own news and danced about the room as he shared it with me.

'They're gone. They ain't there, in the prison. The officer tried to pretend at first there'd never been men arrested for affray but when he realised who I served he said them villains were wanted in Venice for crimes of violence. They've been taken there under escort.'

'So won't they be brought to court in Padua?'

'Don't look like it. If they've got evidence enough in Venice, they'll be strung up there, I reckon. Can't be put on the gibbet twice, can they?'

I was relieved at the thought that I might not need to testify in court, although I could have wished Rendell showed a little more refinement in his expressions. I told him to eat some bread and sausage while I wrote and sealed two short notes, addressed to Gasparo and Professor Bonalini; then I sent the rascal off to deliver them. I heard his cheeky voice greeting someone as he ran down the stairs and a second afterwards René erupted into the room.

'I met Rendell earlier when I was going to my lecture. As soon as it was over I ran all the way to get here. Are you badly hurt? Who did it? Were they thieves?'

'Sit down. I'm all right, just more hideous than usual. It seems they were common rogues wanted in Venice for some misdeeds. They've been taken there to face justice.' These were convenient truths for I did not want René accusing Berthold or his friends, without better proof than we were likely to get, and the idea that my fellow students would seek to have me killed seemed preposterous. I chose to change the subject. 'I was rescued by that stranger who

53

came to the disputation. Professor Bonalini called him "Commendatore".'

To my amazement René turned pale. 'Are you sure?'

'He said his name was Matteo Maffei. Luckily he had a strong escort with him and they tackled my attackers just as one of them drew a knife. I passed out and, when they brought me round, Signor Maffei was wiping his own weapon clean of the scoundrel's blood. He must be quite handy with a dagger himself.'

'What are you saying, Harry? Don't you know who he is?'

'He said his cousin was married to Enrico Capello. That's Carlotta Schioppa. I met her once but I didn't tell the Commendatore that.'

'Matteo Maffei is one of the most renowned soldiers in the Venetian *Terrafirma*. He's a condottiere with a private army at his command and he sells his services to those who offer the best price. He fought for Venice three years ago when there were uprisings in Padua and Verona and helped put them down with some ferocity. But he's just as likely to take service with the Visconti in Milan or the Gonzaga in Mantua and fight against the Venetians.'

'Goodness, I am honoured that he should stoop to save a foolish student who'd had too much to drink.'

'Don't be so light-hearted about it. He watched you eagle-eyed during the disputation. I saw him. He'd have known who you were right away when he saw you again, however sozzled you were, and he has a reputation for deviousness. He's not credited with acts of charity. I can't imagine why he was concerned for your welfare but he'd have known what he was doing.'

'He said something of the sort himself, about rarely acting without a purpose. No idea what he meant. I admit he intrigued me.'

'Don't be drawn into his orbit, Harry. He's dangerous. Be thankful he left the town at dawn. Some at the university saw his troop ride out, full of swagger and bombast. They act as if they own the place wherever they go. You've had a lucky escape.'

'Thanks to him,' I said, intentionally misinterpreting René's meaning. I thought it best not to tell him that Matteo Maffei had assured me we would meet again.

*****

I settled easily into my weekly role as practising physician, welcoming the stream of patients who attended Gasparo's shop with their petty ailments or injuries. The apothecary was appreciative of the extra custom I brought him, as he mixed the potions I prescribed and increased his stock of dressings for abscesses and wounds, while Gabriele soon showed himself a bright lad, anxious to learn and capable of understanding much of what I did. Young Leone was eager to help as well, although he needed careful instruction, but Gregorio was aloof at first, uncertain whether my arrival was a challenge to his position as senior apprentice. He made it clear to me that I should not meddle with the contents of the boxes and jars, on shelves and counter, which held an extraordinary range of ingredients.

'I shan't try to make up my own remedies,' I said to reassure him. 'I'm able to do so, and have done in the past, but the idea of having me here is to offer a service to your customers and bring your master increased business.'

He ignored my attempt to soothe his ruffled self-esteem and pointed to a chest set on a table by the back wall of the shop. 'Only Messer Gasparo and I have the keys to the coffer. If you wish to carry out some procedure and judge the sufferer would benefit from sedation, apply to us and we will provide something suitable.'

'You have hemlock?'

'And opium, among other things. I imagine we are better equipped than the apothecaries who served you in England.'

'Even while in that benighted land, I heard of the vast assortment of herbs and powders used by Italian apothecaries.'

He smiled with an air of superiority, missing entirely the mild sarcasm in my comment.

Gregorio expressed scepticism when he observed my treatment for infected cuts, which I had learned from my old master in Duke Humphrey's service. Contrary to the practice of those physicians who encouraged the secretion of pus by keeping wounds wet, my method relied on cleaning and drying the gash, spreading it with honey and binding it tightly with a bandage. Grudgingly, Gregorio recognised that this process was usually successful and after a while he brought his mother to the shop, explaining that she was nearly crippled with her ulcerated leg which other physicians had failed to cure. I administered my treatment, explaining that it would take some time to achieve significant improvement in such a long-standing condition, but the old lady was soon singing my praises for easing her pain and Gregorio, as a respectful son, was bound to acknowledge I was not entirely useless.

*****

Several weeks after I began working with Gasparo, I was at the university one day when we were informed the expected lecture was postponed and we were to attend the dissection of a man executed that morning. By then I had viewed several such demonstrations but on this occasion I entered the chamber nervously because it occurred to me that the victim might prove to be one of my attackers, perhaps returned to Padua for trial and sentence without my knowledge. I held my breath as Professor Bonalini lifted the cloth covering the wretched fellow and let it out in a silent groan, for I did indeed recognise the man lying on the stone slab. Emaciated and twisted, he had not attacked me, nor did I think he had been capable of using violence on anyone. The lesions on his neck had grown worse since I saw him outside the church of S. Niccolò and I blamed myself for not seeking him more diligently to give him the ointment I had obtained. René looked at me enquiringly. 'You know him?'

'I saw him begging once. I wanted to help him but I never came across him again.'

'There're beggars aplenty in Padua. Half of them end up under Professor Bonalini's knife. He'll have stolen a crust of bread or spoken rudely to one of the town guard. That's enough to earn a noose.' René grinned then assumed a straight face as the Professor cast a disapproving glance in our direction.

After the Professor had completed his exposition and we were leaving the room, Berthold approached me and held out his hand. He had kept his distance from me since our disputation and my injuries but he had shown no open animosity. Now he smiled affably and after gripping my fingers he waved his arm towards his group of friends. 'Professor Bonalini has spoken to me and suggested I might have been involved in the attack you suffered. I assured him and I assure you that neither I nor any Bavarian was responsible for it. I bear you no ill feelings after the debate and would not stoop to involve myself in petty-minded revenge. I trust you will accept my word.'

I did so eagerly, feeling a weight of anxiety had been lifted from me and for a short while I was cheerful but I could not forget the sight of the pathetic beggar, whom I considered I had failed. As the days passed it was his face I saw when I closed my eyes and his distorted limbs featured in my dreams. Knowledge of his cruel death, doubtless for some trivial offence, intensified the sadness which had been seeping into my mind in recent weeks.

*****

As autumn spread its chill, dank murkiness over the town and cutting winds whipped up the sodden leaves between torrents of rain, the dismal season reminded me that nearly a year had passed since my flight from England and there had been no news for months to encourage me with hope that I might return. For all the pleasure I gained from my studies and the work at Gasparo's shop, I was overcome with loneliness and nostalgia for all that I had lost. I saw little of Geoffrey at that period and, with my permission, Rendell had taken employment in the kitchen of a fine mansion on the edge of the town. He still prepared my food and gave me attendance as needed, but in my lodgings I was often alone and I missed his company.

René recognised my melancholy state and urged me to accompany him on his frequent visits to the house where his Maria and her sister received their nightly visitors, but I always refused, without allowing myself to dwell on the attractions he described. Then, one day on my way home, I encountered Madonna Antonia Clemente crossing the piazza with her maid servant and I was struck again by her beauty. Her pregnancy was well advanced and visible under her fur lined mantle, but her face was radiant and I wondered anew how Geoffrey, feeling as he did, could bear to live chastely in her house – if indeed he did. I cursed myself for my vile suspicions. The following week, when I attended my patients at Gasparo's shop, I was consulted by the daughter of a neighbouring shopkeeper, a perky little minx who urged me to examine a sore place at the base of her throat. As she lowered her bodice to reveal an inflamed but harmless spot, she ran her tongue round her opened lips and it was all I could do to prevent myself leaning forward and kissing her. Next morning I told René I would be content to meet Samaritana if she would receive me.

I gathered that the mature, over-dressed woman, who bade us welcome and plied us with good wine, was the mother of the two girls René knew. They were not the only ones working in the house but he insisted the others were common whores whereas Maria and Samaritana were more fastidious in their tastes and their mother exercised discretion regarding their clients. He had already secured agreement that I, as a physician, was a suitable visitor for the younger daughter but I felt acutely uncomfortable while we waited. Maria was first to appear and the sight of her blowsy charms unnerved me while René winked and followed her out of the vestibule with a vulgar gesture. I was tempted to turn tail but the mother was regaling me with a long anecdote about frescoes she had commissioned to decorate the room where Samaritana would greet me and then the girl herself came down the stairs.

She was extremely thin, almost waif-like, and with a cloud of pale blonde hair wafting over her slight frame she looked nothing like her sister, with a delicacy of movement that held my attention. She escorted me to the upper chamber and offered me more wine while I stared in amazement at the brazenly explicit paintings on the wall. Padua was renowned for the frescoes of sacred stories in its chapels, by the Masters Giotto and Menabuoi, but I had never seen depictions of men in a state of arousal and scenes of copulation. The painter lacked the finesse of the great artists but the crudeness of his style was balanced by his liveliness of presentation. I gulped.

Samaritana giggled at my astonishment. 'Mother thinks I lack Maria's seductiveness and so the gentlemen who come to me need a little encouragement. I'm not offended. The pictures make me laugh. They are hardly realistic. Look at the length of that fellow's cock! Not to be found in nature – unless you are about to prove me wrong, English physician.' She came close and her subtle perfume inflamed my senses as she eased the gown from my shoulders. Her fingers travelled to untie my points and I gripped her fiercely, charmed by the mischievous sparkle in her eyes. She let her bodice fall open to reveal her small breasts with their firm, tinted nipples before she drew me to her bed. I took my pleasure of her shamelessly.

*****

Two weeks before Yuletide, I was about to leave Gasparo's shop after attending to my patients, when he called me into the inner room and invited me to sit on a cushioned chair. I was puzzled by this unusual behaviour but he looked on me benignly and complimented me on the custom I had brought him.

'My establishment has achieved such renown that I am confident I shall be chosen at our meeting this evening to fill the vacant position as President of our Guild. I am grateful for what you have contributed to this success and I should like to recognise it.'

'I receive pleasure from practising my craft,' I said.

'But I am concerned that you do not receive fulfilment enough, as a young man of great promise.' I was unclear what he meant and so did not reply. He put the tips of his raised fingers together and regarded me in silence before continuing. 'You are of course a single man so it is understandable, but I am told you frequent a whore.'

'I have done so of late. There's a woman who pleases me.' I was intent on not showing annoyance but my voice sounded hoarse. 'Do you consider it inappropriate for one working here?'

He laughed loudly. 'Of course not. Gregorio visits one of the harlots at the house where you go and I have no objection. But you are an older, professional man, likely to receive your doctorate within the year.'

'Not so soon, sir.'

My protest was brushed aside. 'My Friend, Bonalini, thinks highly of you and he is able to expedite the qualification of suitable students. I think you can be sure he will do so for one of the family.' He laughed again. 'You look bemused. Let me explain. A young man with your prospects should be married, as soon as you have completed your studies, and I have found you a winsome bride.' I gaped at him, speechless with shock, and he continued. 'My cousin has a daughter, fifteen years old, pretty and sensible; she can write her own name. She would make you an excellent wife. You would be part of the family then and you would benefit from Professor Bonalini's sponsorship.'

'He is related to you?'

'My cousin's wife is niece to the Professor. It will be a most useful connection to you. I don't expect you to answer at once but after the festival I will introduce you to my cousin and his household. If you agree, the wedding can take place later next year, when you complete your doctorate. You will reflect on this opportunity?'

I returned to the university reeling from the unexpectedness of Gasparo's proposition and what I had learned of his family relationships. I could not bear to imagine abandoning all hope of marrying Bess, and taking a wife he had selected for me, whose name I did not even know, but I acknowledged I was trapped by the offer of favours and the inevitable reaction if I spurned them. I did not visit Samaritana that evening, choosing to sit alone, torn by indecision. Had the time come to dismiss my dearest longing as a fantasy? What real prospect could there be of being united with Bess or even returning to England? With influential backing I could build a satisfactory life in Padua and, if the girl was pleasing, it was as much as most men in my situation could look to find. I hated myself for my cold logic and the potential betrayal of my love but I could not dislodge the temptation from my heart. The years of my youth would quickly pass and here was the chance to abandon past failures and start anew.

When Rendell came bounding home as the town clock struck the ninth hour, I let his ebullient chatter pass over my head until I realised what he was saying and sat up straight. 'That can't be right. Who told you this nonsense?'

'I just said: Geoffrey. I met him outside the Apothecaries' Hall. He'd come straight from the meeting of his Guild. He was full of it. Giorgio Clemente has been elected to the highest office. Your mate, Gasparo's got his nose right out of joint. Thought he was going to win, he did. But he lost by two votes.'

For a moment I speculated if this blow to his esteem would render void all he had said and offered me but then I realised it would make no difference. In fact it might make it more difficult to refuse because it would be seen as churlish to reject kinship with one who had suffered a disappointment. I went to my bed in desperate confusion and slept only fitfully until daybreak when, belatedly I fell into exhausted slumber.

*****

Rendell had left for his scullion's work by the time I dragged myself awake that morning, well past the hour I should have set out for my lecture. He had left me a basin of water and I was glad to refresh my face with it before pulling on my gown. Professor Bonalini would require a reason for my absence from the lecture-hall and I was considering how to excuse myself when I heard my landlady shrieking, followed by a thudding on the stairs. I flung open the door to see what was amiss as Geoffrey staggered into the room, white-faced and trembling, his cap awry, almost incapable of speech. He pointed vaguely at the window while he breathed deeply. I gripped his shoulders and sat him on my stool,

62

putting a goblet of wine in his hand. He shook his head and grabbed my wrist.

'Come. You must come. Please. Giorgio is dead.'

Chapter 5

He was lying on the floor of his shop, with his hands clutched to his chest and throat, his knees drawn up and his mouth screwed into a horrible grimace as if he had suffered intolerable pain. Geoffrey was trembling when he knelt beside me and we gently turned Giorgio's plump body to take in these details and confirm that there were no marks of injury on the corpse. My friend raised frightened eyes to mine. 'A seizure?'

'So it seems. He has something on the corner of his lip.'

'He always bought a pastry from the pie-man in the market-place in the morning, on his way to the shop. Look, there are chunks on the floor. He must have been eating when the fit took him and he dropped the rest of it.'

I thought quickly of the proper procedure to be followed. 'In a case of sudden death a Paduan physician should see him before he is moved. I would be regarded as a mere student. There's a doctor who practises in the Piazza della Frutta. I met him once. I'll go to fetch him. The priest must come as well. Then Madonna Antonia will have to be told. Would you wish to do that?'

Geoffrey shut his eyes. His voice was only just audible. 'I'll go as soon as the physician has been. Dear God, she isn't far from her time. She shouldn't be distressed.'

The priest and the doctor came at once and the formalities did not take long. The cleric agreed to make arrangements for the removal of Giorgio's body, so it could lie in the chapel of the Apothecaries' Guild, and Geoffrey was then free to go to Antonia. He begged me to stay at the shop while the Guild officers took Giorgio and he removed the key from his employer's purse so I could lock up the premises. 'Call over with it tomorrow,' he said. 'I've my own key and the shop will stay shut until the poor man is buried.' He sounded weary, his voice coming from far away as if he was only half-conscious of what he was saying.

'You'll send word to the son in Bologna?'

A shudder ran through him. 'Of course,' he said and he staggered off into the street.

It was not only the dead apothecary for whom I grieved as I kept my vigil: I worried for my friend. Geoffrey had hinted once that in his mind he nurtured the possibility of the older man's death but there had been no realistic likelihood of it occurring. Yet now it had happened and he was free, after a decent interval, to court the widow – who might already have given him improper encouragement. I believed Geoffrey an honourable man, even if besotted, and I suspected his look of devastation embodied his sense of guilt and shame. I wondered how Antonia truly felt and was glad I could not observe the scene between them. Perhaps for her, flirtation was simply a game and the amusement it provided would vanish as soon as her marital bonds were released. If that proved to be the case, Geoffrey's misery would be extreme.

I called on Professor Bonalini to explain my absence from the day's lectures and returned home a little before Rendell. He was irritated to have missed the excitement, as he saw it, and implored me to take him to the apothecary's shop so he could at least view the place where the body had lain. I saw no harm in this, so we set out across the piazza and I unlocked the heavy door to the shop.

'Where? Where was the body? Was it there?' He saw the direction I was looking and moved forward. 'Ugh! Did he fall on top of the mice?'

'The mice weren't there.'

'But they're dead too.'

I nodded but held Rendell back as he went to kick them aside. The little creatures were lying, just as Giorgio had lain, with their legs folded and their mouths open, and on the claws of one was a hunk of pastry. Rendell pulled free and bent to pick up another fragment of pie.

'Don't touch it.'

He looked up at me with a quizzical grin. 'Have they been poisoned?'

'I expect the pastry was too rich for them but it won't be very wholesome now.' I kept my voice calm. 'Sorry to disappoint you, but Messer Clemente showed no sign of poisoning. He hadn't been sick and he wasn't clutching his stomach. The doctor who came confirmed he'd had a seizure. Anyway that's where he fell. Now fetch that broom from the corner and we'll sweep this debris out of the shop.'

While Rendell's back was turned I slipped a piece of pastry into my pouch. I wasn't sure why I did this and certainly didn't intend to encourage the boy's gruesome imagination but I was as puzzled as he was by the dead mice. After he'd disposed of the rubbish in the gutter we left the premises and, to humour him, I put my finger to my lips. 'Just in case, don't mention the mice to anyone. Do you understand?'

'Rendell tapped the side of his nose and winked. 'You know me, Doctor. Silent as the grave I am when there's a mystery to be solved.'

Perhaps too apposite an expression for comfort, I thought.

*****

I had pondered how Gasparo da Friuli would react to the news of his rival's death and was impressed by his obvious sense of shock and the complete absence of any triumph or satisfying retribution. Along with his fellow Guild members he attended Giorgio's funeral service, as soon as Pierpaolo Clemente had arrived from Bologna, and I heard him speak with sympathy and respect to the bereft son. No one questioned the assumption that he would become President of the Guild without further formalities but he bowed his head modestly and shrugged off such speculation as premature. Gregorio was less reticent on his master's behalf and I overheard him speaking excitedly to other apprentices about the ceremonies he would attend at Giorgio's side and how he had been promised a partnership with the apothecary at the end of the year.

As dusk fell that evening after the obsequies, I sat alone at my window, reflecting on the vicissitudes of life and the lesson they offered: that opportunities should be taken when they presented themselves because there could be no expectation of a second chance, no certainty when the hand of Death would beckon. I heard the hurrying footsteps on the stairs and sighed; I did not welcome the prospect of company to interrupt my contemplations.

Geoffrey burst into the room and flung a bundle onto the pallet he had occupied when he shared my lodgings. He was ashen faced but his jaw was red and swollen. 'Harry, I beg you to let me stay here tonight.' He rocked on his feet and I supported him as he sat on the window bench.

'Of course you can stay. What's happened?'

'Pierpaolo has thrown me out of the house – his house. He made that clear. There were fisticuffs but he is a good deal nimbler than I am and he landed a blow which knocked me into the wall. Antonia was screaming but he ordered her to go to her room and stay there. He called her a whore. For her sake I had to leave. And he's forbidden me to go to the shop. He's having it bolted and barred.' He waved his arms about in agitation.

'Here sip this wine. Let me look at your head. You've quite a bump. You must rest.'

He had begun to shake. 'I should have stayed to defend her. What would Giorgio have said if he knew his son would call his wife such a name? The fiend would turn her out of the house if he could but he knows his father's will may require him to let her live there – unless she marries again. Dear God! He called the child she carries a bastard.'

I groaned inwardly as I sat beside him, recognising that I must engage with his problems and set my own aside. 'Geoffrey, as your friend, I must ask you. Is it your child she will bear?'

He looked at me blankly and shook his head. 'It isn't possible.' Then a steely look came into his eyes. 'She must have been already pregnant when we lay together. It was only once and we swore afterwards never to dishonour Giorgio again.'

I rose and leaned on the windowsill, staring out onto the darkened piazza. 'Pierpaolo knows you are Antonia's paramour?'

'Suspects, not knows. And I don't like your description. After her child is born and a few months have passed, we shall marry.'

'But until then she must remain under her stepson's protection.' I stood over him and, despite myself, my voice sounded accusing. 'You must have longed for Giorgio's death.'

'I never believed it likely. Christ, Harry! You make it sound as if, in my heart, I was a murderer.'

My knees began to wobble and I sat down quickly. 'No more talking now. You are injured and I am your physician. Lie on your bed and get to sleep. You can lodge here as long as you want but now you must rest.'

He nodded gratefully and did as I instructed. Soon he was sleeping and when Rendell came home I indicated in dumb-show that Geoffrey had returned. The boy gave a broad and mischievous grin, miming with vulgar accuracy what he deduced had happened, before turning to his own pallet. In our chamber that night, I alone was sleepless, beset by horrible doubts and speculation. Was the worst of my imaginings credible? I did not know.

*****

On the following Sunday morning, after attending Mass, I crossed the Molino Bridge, past the floating windmills where Leone's father had been killed, and along by the river, beyond the last buildings, until I came to the marshy bank beside the reed beds, where wading birds nested and water rats made their homes. I found a secluded pool overlooked by a shelf of flat mud, hidden by tall grasses, and here I laid out the fragments of pie I had taken from Giorgio's shop. Then I nestled into a depression in the ground a few feet away and kept as silent as I could. For a long time only the melancholy call of the birds and the beating of their wings disturbed the peaceful scene and I despaired of hearing any other movement. My hiding place was damp and cold but, in spite of my discomfort, my eyelids began to close and I must have dozed briefly. A rustle in the reeds startled me and I peered up, across the boggy ledge, and saw, with excitement, a water-rat sniffing the pastry and then, after a moment's consideration, devouring it. The animal sat back as if content with its meal and I was on the point of abandoning my observation and concluding that my fancy was an idle one, when all at once it began to twitch and then to convulse. Torn between self-congratulation and dismay at what it portended, I watched the wretched creature roll over, its front legs gripped to its chest and its back legs bent, while tremors shook its body until all motion ceased.

I staggered to my feet and ran, splashing through the soggy ground, suddenly frantic to get far away from the murderous trial I had conducted. I had no doubt now that the pastry was poisonous but with a toxin I had never encountered and could scarcely credit. Expert apothecaries might instruct my ignorance but expert apothecaries were the very people with the greatest reason to want Giorgio Clemente dead. Gasparo da Friuli, with whom I worked, was to be instituted as President of his Guild, in Giorgio's place, and Geoffrey, my friend who shared my lodgings, was infatuated with the poor man's widow. Vainly I longed to forget what I had discovered.

*****

If others had died suddenly and in similar fashion on the day of Giorgio's death, it would have merited gossip which I would surely have heard. The absence of such rumours suggested the lethal pie had been specially prepared and given to its intended victim, presumably by the pie-man from whom Giorgio regularly bought his pastry. I also patronised the pie stall in the market- place and thought the vendor an amiable fellow, unlikely to harm anyone. Yet if someone paid him well, he might have acted under instruction and, if so, it could be dangerous to challenge him on the subject. Nevertheless, although I dreaded what I might discover, I could not let the matter rest and next morning I made my way to the booth where trays of succulent-looking pies were laid out to attract passers-by. I engaged the man in conversation and worked the subject round to Giorgio's fate.

'He was a customer of yours, I believe.'

'That he was. Bought a pie regular as the sun rising.' He smiled in happy recollection.

'He'd been eating something when he was found. Your pie must have given him one last pleasure.'

'No. Strange that. When he passed me that morning he was carrying a sweetmeat. He showed me it and said he was sorry not to need a pie that day. I can't remember quite what he said but I gathered a woman gave it to him. It did happen sometimes, that his wife baked him a sweetmeat to take to the shop.'

I froze but collected myself in order to let the conversation drift on to other topics, so as not to arouse

70

suspicion, before continuing on my way. If what the man said was true, Antonia had been complicit in her husband's murder; maybe even its instigator, although Geoffrey must have been aware of the mysterious poison. I found it hard to imagine the illicit lovers as assassins but, in any case, if only Giorgio had known where he obtained the sweetmeat, nothing could be proved. Two dead mice were of no significance and I alone had seen the water-rat die. The murder had been craftily contrived and I had no firm evidence on which to base an accusation. Given the chance, Pierpaolo Clemente would doubtless be all too anxious to hound the pair as far as the gallows, but I would never provide him the means to do so without certain proof of their guilt.

*****

A few days after the Feast of the Nativity I went to call on Samaritana. I had not visited her since before Giorgio's death and René told me she had looked unwell when he last saw her, so I was prepared when her mother stated she was unable to receive me. I offered my physician's skill to suggest treatment, if I could. The older woman leaned towards me and her gold chains jangled on her substantial bosom. Her lips curled unpleasantly.

'Fine physician you are, not to have noticed how the disease was eating her. Coughing blood, she is now, and likely to be laid in her grave before many weeks are gone. A doctor's seen her – another of her callers – and he says she'll soon be in God's hands. So I have to give her house room until then, with her not bringing in any income. Mind you she's only got a mouse's appetite.'

I shivered with distaste and thrust some money into the woman's open palm. 'Care for her,' I said, 'and tell her I am concerned for her.'

She clenched her fingers over my coins. 'One of the other girls would be glad to pleasure you, physician, and their services are cheaper. If you like them skinny, Elena would suit you.'

I fled from the house before the girl could be summoned, mortified by my failure as a doctor and ashamed that I had used Samaritana for my gratification without noticing how ill she was beneath her artifice.

I returned home miserably, unfit for any other company, but Geoffrey was waiting for me in our lodgings with two glasses primed full of good wine and Rendell was beaming over a smaller beaker of the same liquid. 'You were quick,' the boy giggled. 'All done in a trice, was it?'

I ignored his obscene gesture and let Geoffrey take my gown and hand me a goblet. 'Pay no notice, Harry. I'm afraid I've got him tipsy. But with good reason! I've splendid news!' He pulled forward a stool for me to sit on. 'I was required to attend the office of Giorgio's notary so I could be informed of what concerns me in his will. What do you think? He has bequeathed the shop to me! Pierpaolo receives the house and money, of course, and Antonia is to remain in her home as long as she chooses: but the shop and all its contents are mine!'

I shuddered, wondering if Geoffrey had already known the provisions of Giorgio's will. If so, his motive for murder was all the stronger. I smiled weakly. 'Won't Pierpaolo challenge it?'

Geoffrey chortled. 'He's already engaged his own notary to have the will struck down as void. He's claiming I put pressure on his father to make a new will. Either that or Giorgio's mind was possessed when he wrote it. It's hardly likely the second suggestion will be upheld when he'd just been chosen as President of his Guild. The brotherhood of apothecaries would scarcely elect an imbecile or a weakling!'

I downed my draught in one and held my glass out to be refilled. If I was to celebrate the good fortune of my friend, the apparent murderer, I would try to drink myself into oblivion.

*****

The following Sunday I joined Gasparo da Friuli at his shop where he had two horses waiting so that we could ride into the countryside to the estate of his cousin, the father of Giovanna Lendro, my potential bride. I had ridden very little since coming to Padua, and was never comfortable in the saddle, but the journey towards the Euganean Hills was short and my mind too preoccupied for me to pay much attention to the soreness of my bottom. My situation, a prey to unprovable suspicion, was becoming intolerable and I could see no chance of escape unless I could make a new life for myself, so growing despair led me to contemplate favourably the drastic course of action Gasparo had put before me. Still I had heard nothing from England and my hope of seeing Bess again was fading irretrievably. She had probably abandoned any expectation of my return and, self-serving as the thought was, I argued to myself that she would have been advised by her friends to accept another suitor.

I was nervous of meeting Giovanna's family and sought assurance from Gasparo that the girl knew of my disfigurement, which distressed so many on first acquaintance. 'She knows you're ugly as the Devil,' he said cheerily as we rode into the courtyard of an impressive house. 'She's the youngest daughter and won't bring a large dowry, although you'll welcome a hundred ducats, I'm sure, and she'll be glad to net a husband with reasonable prospects.' As I dismounted with an ungainly jump, he slapped me on the shoulder and guffawed. 'She's a bonny filly. You'll find it easier to ride her than this nag.'

Her parents were affable but appraised me carefully and asked questions about my professional status before they sent for Giovanna to join us. She came into the room timidly, a short, neat little person, with unbound black hair falling straight over her shoulders, and she looked directly at my face. She did not blanch and I accounted that to her credit as I bowed. We exchanged a few words of courtesy but then fell silent as Gasparo and her parents led the conversation and she lowered her eyes meekly to the floor. Later, after the family meal, we were allowed to walk onto the terrace, from which there was a fine view of the hills, and to speak to each other more nearly in private.

'Your father has consented that I may pay court to you,' I said with awkward formality. Her eyes were very dark and her expression serious. I wished I could make her laugh.

'He has explained. I am happy to receive your attentions.' She pressed her lips together firmly as if there was no more to say.

It crossed my mind that she had learned her part by rote, so stilted did it seem. 'I put no claim on you. You must make your own choice. We don't know each other and I am a foreigner. I will wait until you are satisfied that your answer can be given with confidence. We would not marry until I have received my doctorate and am free to practice medicine in Padua.'

'I am content to become your wife, Doctor Somers.'

'It is too soon for you to be so certain.'

'It is God's will,' she said, concluding our conversation and turning back to the house.

'Can you be sure?'

Over her shoulder she cast me a glance of withering piety. 'It is God's will,' she repeated, 'and he will send his angel to bless us. We shall be enfolded in the angel's wing.'

'That is a beautiful thought,' I said as she disappeared through the door, although she had made it sound as much of a threat as a comfort.

*****

74

When I entered the lecture hall some days later, Professor Bonalini took me aside and expressed pleasure that I was soon to be counted among his relations. 'It will bring you good fortune, I assure you. I will be able to facilitate you setting up your physician's practice in the town, and I could add a little to the dear girl's dowry.' He patted my arm with avuncular familiarity which I found unnerving.

'We are not yet committed,' I said. 'Giovanna is very young and I fancy she has a solemn sense of duty. I don't wish her to bind herself without reflection. I've asked that she respond by the end of next month and, if she is then agreeable, the contract will be signed.'

'Is this some English nicety? You must be master in your house and not give her reason to believe she can cajole you as she wishes.' He laughed. 'Get her with child on your marriage night and she will give no trouble.'

Our conversation was curtailed when my fellow students trooped into the room for a discussion the Professor was to lead on symptoms and diagnosis. He gave the usual instances of beneficial practice to follow, involving examination of urine, determining what feverishness might denote and checking for breathlessness. Then he invited questions and soon someone asked how to establish if a patient had been poisoned. I edged forward on the bench, listening intently, but his answer related to vomiting, stomach cramps and diarrhoea, all to be expected.

I summoned my courage. 'Are there no other forms of poisoning,' I asked, 'which do not affect the gut?'

The Professor pursed his lips but Berthold intervened, eager to display his knowledge. 'The bark and leaves of the yew tree can bring about a seizure. I learned this from a wise woman of Regensburg.'

'I hope that, as physicians, we are not dependent on the whims of old women.' The Professor pulled on the lappets of his gown. 'It is said that the seeds of the yew are most potent and cattle have died from eating them. It's improbable a man would do so.' His lofty tone expressed disdain and he moved on to other topics.

After the discussion I caught up with Berthold as we left the hall and sought more information about the wise woman of Regensburg. He was indignant that the Professor had belittled his contribution and anxious to demonstrate he had made a serious point. He drew me into a corner. 'Pieces of yew are used to bring about abortions of unwanted brats. Old Gretel makes cakes and sells them at a price to wives who have enough infants at home or, more likely, have conceived one outside the marriage bed. It's a risky business though, – the quantities must be exact – and often enough the wretched woman herself dies.' He punched my chest lightly. 'It's not something honourable physicians should engage with; unless you've a mind to dispose of the maidens you get with child.'

I grinned weakly while he roared with laughter. 'And it kills by bringing about a seizure?'

'That's the beauty of it.' He slapped me on the back. 'No one could ever tell it was poison.'

'But wouldn't the victim spit out the cake? It must taste bitter.'

'Old Gretel swore it only took a few fragments to kill and she added a lot of honey.' He looked at me sideways. 'Is that whore of yours causing trouble? Do you want to be rid of her?'

I swallowed. 'She's dying as it is. No, I was just intrigued because I'd never heard of this form of poisoning before.'

'I'm sure that apothecary friend of yours could tell you more,' he said with a wink. 'Apothecaries know all sorts of tricks.'

'I've no doubt they do,' I murmured and a shiver passed through my body.

Chapter 6

Pierpaolo Clemente had returned to Bologna to complete his studies, leaving his challenge to Giorgio's will in the hands of his notary, and he cannot have been best pleased when that gentleman agreed with Geoffrey's representative that the interests of all parties would be served by keeping the apothecary's shop open. Under strict conditions, therefore, Geoffrey was permitted to run the business, which he claimed was his legal right, and he set about bringing in new customers by offering a range of cosmetic lotions which Giorgio had spurned. He maintained a proper gravity when he spoke of his dead benefactor but it sickened me to see him prospering from what it seemed certain was a criminal act – albeit one which could not be proved. I thought at times that my head would burst from the disgust I felt at sharing my lodgings with a pitiless murderer, a man who had been my trusted friend.

My agony of mind intensified when Geoffrey announced that Antonia Clemente had borne a son, a healthy child, to be named Giorgio. I could not bring myself to go to admire the infant, although specifically invited and despite assurances that his chin greatly resembled his late father's prominent jaw, but I felt bound to attend the baptism for fear my absence would lead to unwelcome questions. I wondered if Pierpaolo would arrive at the font to denounce his step-mother and proclaim the boy baseborn but the ceremony was conducted with decent propriety, and no one but me was outraged by Geoffrey standing sponsor for the baby. I made an excuse to escape the celebration at the Clemente house and wandered the streets during the evening until I resolved to call and enquire after Samaritana's condition.

Her mother eyed me frostily. 'Laid her in the grave this morning, we did. A week ago she would have been glad to know of your concern for her. Quite a soft spot she had for her physician, as she called you. God knows why.'

Tears of regret came in to my eyes for I knew I had failed the pathetic girl who had given me comfort and I muttered apologies. Remorselessly, her mother waved me aside. 'You have no business in this house, now she is gone, unless you will take your pleasure with one of the others. My time is valuable and I can't bandy words any longer with an ungrateful wretch.'

I fled to the nearest tavern to lose myself in drink once again but as I staggered homeward I was overcome by a feeling that my existence was worthless. I had squandered what youthful successes I achieved and was incapable of upholding the cause of justice which I honoured. It needed only the basest degradation to complete my ignominy and I deserved no less. This was my frame of mind when a common whore accosted me, lifting her skirts to show her privates, and, relishing my squalor, I dragged her into an alley and had congress with her against the wall. As soon as it was done this sordid act added to the revulsion I felt for myself and I arrived back at my lodgings, dishevelled and soiled, incapable even of remorse. Geoffrey, who was home before me, said nothing and helped me to my bed.

Next evening, when he returned from the shop, he was not so reticent and demanded to know what was ailing me. 'You've not been yourself for some weeks, and I can see things are getting worse. What is it?'

'Nothing!' Battling an insistent sore head, I pulled myself together; a fuller explanation was required to disguise the truth. 'Perhaps the wait for Giovanna to decide whether to accept me has made me tense. But that's over now. This morning Messer Gasparo handed me a letter from her father, conveying her agreement, so I've authorised the drawing up of the contract. Within a week I shall be committed to wed her on completion of my doctorate.'

'Is this true? It's very sudden. Is it what you want?'

'Of course it's true. Why should I commit myself if I didn't want to?'

'I'm sorry. I didn't mean to pry. I was just remembering Bess.'

'Well, don't! Bess is far away and probably someone else's wife. You've got your concubine! Why begrudge me a lawful bride?'

He hit me then and called me a foul name but I did not retaliate. I turned to the window, wiping blood from my lip, while he spluttered with rage.

'I've told you I shall marry Antonia. Are you such an unworldly innocent that you can't understand how such things happen?'

'Messer Clemente's death was very convenient for you both.'

'You said something like that before. Do you think we used witchcraft to procure it?'

I stared at him, not daring to speak. 'My entanglement with witchcraft in England led to my exile,' I said at length.

'Christ, Harry, I think you do believe we conjured up Giorgio's seizure? You, a rational physician?'

The apparent sincerity in his expression and words staggered me and I sank down on my stool. 'I'm not wholly ignorant. There are poisons which can mimic a seizure.'

Geoffrey started to take things from the chest where he stored his possessions and rolled them in an old gown. 'I can't continue to live under the same roof as a man who suspects me of murder. I will find my own lodgings. You have been my friend but some devil has twisted and perverted your mind. I trust you'll find contentment with your Giovanna but, if you are so obsessed by rancour and jealousy, I doubt it.'

I made no move to stop him as he left.

*****

79

Geoffrey's departure brought me relief although Rendell pestered me with questions and I was brusque with him, causing a tantrum of threats that he would soon be old enough to go for a soldier as he had always wanted. In a day or two he simmered down and I tried to set aside all that had happened concerning Messer Clemente, his shop, his wife and his death. I resolved to rise from the depths, into which I had allowed myself to sink, and I determined to concentrate on securing my own future as a respectable married physician. When my dreams were invaded by distorted visions of a sorrowful Bess, I dismissed them as idle and outdated illusions.

On the following Sunday I went again with Gasparo to visit his cousin and I knelt at the altar of the village church, beside Giovanna, to confirm our betrothal in the sight of God. Despite the momentous pledge I made, I felt numb, devoid of thought or sensation, but later when we were able to speak, out of earshot of the others, I tried to find appropriate words, for it was not the girl's fault that I lacked a lover's ardour.

'I hope this day's business brings you joy. Our marriage should take place before next winter comes.'

She raised her large eyes and I saw a hint of fear in them. 'I shall study to be ready to do my duty.'

My heart gave a jolt as I realised how greatly the child needed my protection. 'Don't regard our marriage as a mere duty. I trust we shall make each other happy.'

'We shall live in Padua?'

'Yes. I shall practise as a physician there. You know the town, of course?'

'I have been there once. It was unfriendly and noisy and dirty and I did not care for it.' She snapped her rosebud mouth shut.

'As mistress of your own house, you'll find it more agreeable, I'm sure.'

'I do not expect it to be agreeable but I shall accept God's will.'

She was so stiff and nervous that I wanted to take her in my arms to comfort her but I judged she would not approve of such intimacy. 'When we met before you spoke of us being sheltered by the angel's wing. I thought that was a lovely idea.'

'I said 'enfolded', not 'sheltered'. I pray daily for God's blessing on our union and that I may bear you sons.'

'Or daughters, Giovanna. If they are as pretty as you, I should like daughters.'

She stared at me. 'I did not know you were a flippant man.' There was no mistaking the disapproval in her voice. 'Excuse me. I should like to join my mother.'

I watched her walk steadily across the chamber and swallowed my disappointment that she was so unresponsive. Yet her vulnerability had its charm and, as I remembered Professor Bonalini's prescription for mastering a wife, I suppressed an indecorous and unworthy smile.

*****

When I was next in attendance at Gasparo's shop, the proprietor himself was absent on Guild affairs and had taken Gregorio with him. This happened frequently nowadays but there was no problem in leaving Gabriele in charge as he was fully competent to dispense the usual orders from customers. I was consulted by a few patients with straightforward ailments but then the door flew open and a woman rushed in carrying a screaming child with a blood- soaked cloth around his arm.

I examined and cleaned the nasty gash along his forearm while she explained how he had slashed himself playing with a knife in his father's butcher's shop. 'I told him often enough not to touch the knives,' she said, 'but he takes no notice.'

The boy continued to scream as I attended to the wound and blood dripped onto the table where I sat him. I beckoned Gabriele. 'The cut will heal better if it is stitched.'

'Can you do that?'

'I've seen it done and know what to do but it will be painful. Have we something to give him that will deaden the pain?'

Leone was peering over my shoulder. 'There's stuff in the chest.' He pointed to the locked coffer. 'But we can't open it.'

Gabriele gave a superior grin. 'Messer Gasparo has left me the key, now he and Gregorio have to be away from the shop quite often. Only to be used if the physician orders it, that's what he said. What would you like?'

I told Leone to pinch together the jagged edges of the boy's torn arm while I crossed to inspect the contents of box as Gabriele unlocked it. I quickly selected a mildly sedative powder and handed it to the older apprentice to mix with a little wine; but my attention was held by another packet in the neatly arranged tray. Each ingredient was clearly marked and this one read: *Seeds, bark and leaves of the yew tree, ground.* I concentrated on my task of soothing the patient and, as he became drowsy, put two careful stitches in his soft flesh. I told the weeping mother to contact Gasparo immediately if the wound became inflamed but otherwise to bring the boy the following week for me to remove my stitching. After they left I was showered with congratulations from Gabriele and Leone, who had been riveted with interest in my small operation, but my mind was distracted with other thoughts.

Did all apothecaries keep supplies of yew? Was it simply my ignorance that meant I had not known of its properties? Was it possible I had jumped to a mistaken conclusion about Geoffrey's guilt? Had I allowed myself to become obsessed by that idea? Had some demon truly taken possession of my mind and driven away my normal good sense? Was there another candidate for the role of murderer? Must I suspect my employer as well as my friend? What had really happened to Giorgio Clemente? What was happening to me? I made my way to that afternoon's lecture in a whirl of uncertainty and confusion.

*****

Rendell was waiting for me when I returned to our lodgings, at a time when he should have been at his scullion's work, and I knew immediately from his face that the explanation for his presence would not be welcome.

'They've kicked me out,' he said and his face reddened with truculence. 'Cheeked the cook once too often, I suppose. He's got no bloody sense of humour, stuck up prick.'

I sighed, thinking of prosaic matters. 'We'll be hard pressed to manage without your earnings, now Geoffrey's gone.'

'Whose fault is that? Why do we have to stay in this stinking town?'

'Stop ranting. We must find you some other employment. By the end of the year, when I'm wed, I'll have a household of my own and you can help to run it.'

'No I bloody won't! I'm not taking orders from your prissy little wife. There are companies of soldiers roaming the countryside, fighting for whoever pays best and I'm going to join one. You can't stop me.'

I controlled my annoyance. 'Don't do anything rash. If you're resolved on being a soldier, let me make enquiries to find a reputable band. Whatever your sister in England might say, I won't hold you back.'

His eyes became round with surprise. 'You mean it?'

I nodded. 'I owe you a chance to try your hand at soldiering as you're so keen on the idea.' I did not tell him that letting him go would break one more bond with the earlier life I had determined to abandon.

On the following Sunday I rode out, alone and unannounced, to call on my betrothed bride and I picked a posy of wayside spring flowers to give her. Her parents were flustered to see me but sent for Giovanna to come from the Lendro family chapel where she was praying, although there was a considerable delay before she complied. Her father started to chide her but I insisted I had been content to wait and held out the drooping spray as she approached.

She looked severe. 'Flowers are prettiest while growing in the ground,' she said.

'Then when we have our home I shall ensure you have a small garden where you can grow what you like best.'

Her mouth softened. 'I should like that. I had not known you were coming but I couldn't interrupt my prayers.'

'I understand. I hoped to give you a pleasant surprise.'

'I don't like surprises.'

Her father huffed with displeasure and walked away so I took the opportunity to go closer to his daughter. 'I'm sorry to have pulled the flowers from their roots but I meant well. Will you reward me for my good intentions?'

'How?'

'Like this.' I leaned forward and kissed her gently on the lips. 'It is permitted,' I said as she pulled away from me.

She lowered her eyes meekly. 'Please do not come again without announcement.'

'What must I do to make you smile, Giovanna?'

'God does not require me to smile. That is why I am happy in his service. You have contracted to use my body for carnal purposes. You do not possess my heart.'

Her father reappeared as she glided from the room and he spat angrily into the hearth. 'Don't worry, my boy, her mother was that way disposed before we wed. Take her by force and beat her regularly. She'll soon come to obedience and lose her wilful ways. That's all you look for in a wife, isn't it?'

I nodded but, far away in my ill-disciplined mind, came the recollection that once I had looked for far more – and found it.

*****

I arrived at Gasparo's shop earlier than usual, tormented by worry that the newly installed President of the Apothecaries' Guild had won his position by foul means, and I came upon Leone sitting outside the door munching a large pie. 'Gabriele's not come yet to unlock.'

'Are Messer Gasparo and Gregorio not here today?'

'Off on Guild business half the week, they are. Fair enough for the boss, he's President, but Gregorio's become so self-important, preening himself as the President's aide, dressed in the fine new tunic Gasparo bought him. It makes me sick.'

'So long as that great pie doesn't,' I said with feeble wit.

'It's not bad, the pastry's quite good.' Leone held out the pie for examination. 'But it's not like the sweetmeats Gregorio's mother used to make.'

All around me the sounds of bustling passers-by faded and I felt an ominous thud in my head. I struggled to focus my eyes on the apprentice. 'Gregorio's mother makes sweetmeats?'

'Used to. She's ailing now and anyway Gregorio's too grand to bring titbits for his inferiors.'

'Is her bad leg troubling her again?'

'It's not that. I think she's got a fever. Gregorio seems to think she won't last long. Not that he's bothered.'

At that moment Gabriele turned the corner, flourishing the key of the shop, and our conversation ceased but while I consulted with my patients that morning I knew that, as soon as I had completed these duties, I would visit the old woman. The weight which had been crushing me for weeks had shifted slightly and my mind began to function freely. When I left the shop instinct led me to secure Gabriele's agreement that I take Leone with me and this proved to be the most sensible thing I had done for a long time.

Leone knew where Gregorio's mother lived and led me into a densely inhabited area of ramshackle buildings where he banged on the door of a small hovel. A quavering voice enquired who was there and hearing the boy's name, bade him enter. I followed him but, as soon as the invalid, huddled on her pallet, saw me, she let out a piercing scream. 'Go away. Go away.'

I approached her, noting her flushed cheeks and frightened eyes. 'It's all right. You know me. I tended your leg. What's amiss now?'

'You're not to come! Gregorio said so. No physician – not needed, he said. And he won't let me have a priest. It's a priest I want. Can you get me a priest?'

'Of course I can. But what do you mean Gregorio won't let you have a priest?'

'He says I don't need to make my confession. But I do. I'm mortal ill. I'm sure of that. He knows what I shall say. He'd let me die unshriven. He'd help me on my way, more like.' Tears began to roll down her wrinkled cheeks and I took her hand.

'We'll fetch a priest directly. Don't worry. You shall ease your mind of whatever troubles you.'

Her wizened fingers clasped mine. 'Before Gregorio comes. It must be before he comes. I have to tell my sin, even though I will put him in peril.'

My heart was in my mouth. 'Is it some evil your son made you commit?'

A tremor passed through her frame. 'He stood over me and threatened to beat me but I knew it was wrong. The powder was foul but I had to put it in the sweetmeat. To kill the rats, he said, but I knew it was for a man – the man I had to give it to.'

I looked across at Leone. 'Take careful note of what she has said and run to the Palace of the Commune to bring an officer. Ask them to send a priest as well, but hurry.'

Leone's intelligent eyes were bright with understanding. 'The two-faced pompous lout! We'll get him!' He shot out of the door and I heard his rapid footsteps along the cobbled lane.

'You remember how I helped your leg get better,' I said, stroking the old woman's hand. 'I can help comfort your mind too. When there's no priest to hand, a physician can serve instead. I'd like you to tell me everything. I don't think you'd be held to blame if you were forced to do what your son ordered.'

She looked at me with pathetic eagerness. 'Is it true? Would God forgive me? I made the cake, like Gregorio said. Using the mixture he gave me. He said I must clean my hands afterwards and not put them to my mouth so I knew it was bad. And I didn't believe his story about the rats. He was too excited, too keen for me to take the sweetmeat to the man he pointed out. I don't know who he was. Did he die?'

'I'm afraid so, but it's not your fault. I'm sure the priest will tell you so and give you absolution.'

She sighed contentedly but then she seized my wrist in renewed agitation. 'Will Gregorio hang if they find out? My son – how could he do such an evil thing?' She clutched her stomach. 'The pain has come back. Give me my potion. There, on the stool.'

I took up a phial of liquid and sniffed it. 'Did a doctor give you this?'

'No. Gregorio made it specially. He said a physician prescribed it.'

I held it away from her. 'I'm afraid it will only do you harm. I'll get you something better.'

'Why? Why can't I have Gregorio's medicine? What do you mean?' Her voice rose to a shriek while her arms flailed the air and in trying to soothe her I missed the sounds outside, until the door crashed back against the wall.

'You interfering quack!' Gregorio launched himself upon me with his knife already drawn and drove the blade into my shoulder as I squirmed to the side. Then, when I sank to the ground, with blood spurting through my hands as I clutched the wound, he wrenched the hilt free and raised it above my chest, pinning me to the floor with his foot on my belly.

I caught at his ankle while he thrust downwards but, most remarkably, his mother managed to haul herself up to grasp his arm and the blade slewed into the pallet, spilling straw on his feet and putting him off balance. I struggled to my knees, gripping his legs, but he hurled me across the room and, although I crawled back, I lacked the strength to prevent him turning in fury to slash at his mother's throat. Her head fell back as a bloody cascade fountained from her neck and she slid down onto her bed with a groan of protest. Immediately he rushed to my side brandishing the weapon but, to my amazement, instead of stabbing my heart he seized my hand, together with the knife, as if he was wrestling to take it from me, and at that moment Leone and two officers burst into the room.

'Murderer!' Gregorio shouted. 'Arrest this murderer. He has killed my mother.'

At first the officials looked from one to the other of us in bemusement, while Leone protested my innocence against Gregorio's frantic accusations, but then a faint sound from the bed caused us to turn. 'My... son is the... murderer. God forgive...' She groaned as the last breath hissed from her ravaged throat and Gregorio took his opportunity to dash towards the door, while the rest of us were distracted, but Leone tripped him and in an instant the officers had him in charge. By this time I was crouched in considerable pain, with blood running down my chest and arm, and I was only dimly aware of the activity around me until I realised newcomers had joined us. A priest stood on the threshold observing the desolate scene and crossing himself, while Gasparo hurried to my side and started to rip up my tattered shirt to bind my shoulder.

*****

Gasparo carried me to my lodgings on his saddle and he summoned the nearest physician to treat my injury because I had lost a good deal of blood. Leone escorted us and explained to the apothecary what had led me to question Gregorio's mother and how I had pieced together the full story of the apprentice's perfidy. Gasparo was mortified to realise that the murderer had committed his crimes in order to profit from his master's good fortune. He made me drink a potion he had mixed to lessen my pain and he insisted on remaining with me until he was satisfied that the bleeding was staunched. He was generous in his praise for Leone's part in the villain's capture and admitted that the special compound, which he had suspected the boy of taking weeks earlier, contained a scraping of yew bark.

'I kept a supply but it was securely locked away. Gregorio had the key to the coffer. He must have helped himself over time, little by little so I didn't notice. My compound is favoured by the ladies who find themselves embarrassed by an untimely pregnancy.'

'So Gregorio built up a stock of it. He always planned murder!' Leone was indignant.

'I imagine he wanted to be prepared in case Giorgio Clemente thwarted his plans to bask in Messer Gasparo's success.'

The apothecary patted my arm. 'You must be right. You won't hold it against me? My family will be doubly proud that you have consented to join them, now you've exposed the perfidy of a wretch who would have besmirched my good name.'

I suppressed a sigh, which he interpreted as weariness, and I was indeed beginning to feel quite light-headed, with difficulty in focusing my thoughts. Shortly afterwards Rendell came home and expressed deep offence that I had been wounded and a murderer apprehended without his participation in the entertainment. He glowered at Leone, who had fulfilled the role of my assistant, which he saw as his own, but Gasparo soothed his battered self-esteem by giving instructions about the care of my shoulder and leaving him a pot of balsam which would help the injury to heal. I was glad when the apothecary and Leone departed and I could lie back on my pallet to rest but Rendell was not to allow me peace.

'A messenger from Venice came while you were out this morning. There's a letter for you – from England.'

He held out a shabby packet which I grabbed and, seeing the seal used by the Duke of Gloucester's chamberlain, I ripped it open, concentrating hard to read properly. I was surprised to see the manuscript was written in a scribe's hand and not that of my old friend himself, but surprise was soon dissolved in stark misery.

I hope you are prospering in your studies, dear Harry. It is my sad task to let you know of my beloved husband's death, most suddenly and cruelly. He always thought so highly of you and I share his affection for you. I shall be leaving the Duke's palace soon and will go to live with my daughter, Lady Blanche, so I will have the pleasure of your mother's company once again. I understand she is well. I trust it will not be long before you can return home but there is no encouraging news of your pardon so far.

90

There are some tidings which may give you pleasure, however. The Duke received a visit recently from Lord Walter Fitzvaughan and his lady. With them was her tiring maid, Bess, whom I think you will remember. She asked me if I knew how you were faring and I told her what we last heard. She begged that when my husband next wrote to you, he would give you her greetings and assure you she is waiting. Alas, it falls to me to discharge her request, now God had taken the chamberlain into his rest. I hope you have not forgotten the sweet young woman who prays for your safe return and that this will not be unduly delayed.

May the Mother of God bless you, Harry, and bring you this letter I have dictated.

It was signed with Dame Margery's shaky signature and dated a full three months previously.

As the sense of the message penetrated my clouded brain, it was as if something in my head burst open and all my stupidity and worthlessness gushed forth. Bess was true, waiting in hope and trust, while I had tied myself to a girl for whom I felt only a faint protective regard. I had doubted Geoffrey's integrity when I should have known better and I had conveniently assumed Bess would have looked elsewhere by now, because it suited me to seek an alliance which would further my prospects. I dragged myself from my bed, babbling incoherently, and, before Rendell could prevent me, I ripped the dressing from my arm and flung the pot of balsam to smash against the wall, leaving its contents hanging in blobs on the mottled plaster. I thrust the boy aside and rushed down the stairs, out into the piazza, blood pulsing down my arm with renewed force, and as a cart rounded the corner at speed, I flung myself in front of its wheels.

Chapter 7

In my delirium I saw a creature bending over me, spreading a vast wing which fluttered and blocked out the light, but I understood it was not an angel's wing shielding me, rather a demon's pinion, extended to bear me to its evil master, whose despicable acolyte I had become. I was content to go to my doom for it was what I had sought and I merited nothing less. Whatever else I had forgotten or chosen to ignore, including my unjust suspicion of Geoffrey, my treachery towards Bess was vivid in my fragmented comprehension and it was unforgiveable. Yet release was not to come at my bidding and, as I realised this, it seemed another proof of my bungling.

The skill of the carter in turning his horses meant I had been flung to the ground but not trampled or crushed by the wheels. I fell on my injured shoulder, ripping the wound wider and breaking my collar-bone, while a blow to my head left me insensible, but it was the fever that followed my insane effort at self-destruction which nearly accomplished my objective. When at last I regained my right mind, I did not know where I was until I distinguished Geoffrey at my side wiping my brow and Antonia Clemente standing in the background with a bowl in her hands and tears on her cheek.

'Welcome back, foolish hero. You are not allowed to opt out of your responsibilities. You are the toast of the apothecaries' Guild.'

'I don't want...'

'Quiet. It's too soon for conversation. The physician says you're to rest. You are in Antonia's house and Rendell is with you. I come every day.'

'You know that...'

'I said quiet! We know the whole story and I've seen Dame Margery's letter. When you're stronger we'll talk more. For now it's enough that you're out of the fever.'

I soon dropped into deep, untroubled sleep but in the following days numerous visitors called and were allowed to stay briefly at my bedside. From them I pieced together weird rumours which were circulating in the town, that I had not merely solved a murder but then had risen from my pallet, with blood pouring from my arm, and rushed into the street to save an infant from the wheels of a cart – at the expense of my own injuries. I protested that this was inaccurate but was loath to explain my actual intentions and my objections were brushed aside as modesty. My acquaintances wished to celebrate my heroism and nothing I could say would disabuse them.

I mentioned my discomfort with this fable to Antonia when I joined her at dinner as my recovery progressed. 'If they knew the truth, everyone would say the Devil had possessed me and I fear that may be so. I've suffered acute distress before but never been tempted to destroy my life. I am ashamed.'

'No one else needs to know anything except the version the town has chosen. It is true you were not in your right mind but it was not the Devil's work. Geoffrey says the potion Gasparo gave you was intended to make you sleep and when you resisted its effect, because of Dame Margery's letter, its power made you irrational.' I stared at her without speaking and she nodded. 'There was nothing wrong with Gasparo's potion, only your refusal to give way to it. Mind you, Geoffrey was rude about the balsam Gasparo left to treat your knife wound. He sniffed some on the wall of your room, where you threw it, and said the concoction was quite inappropriate for your injury.'

I felt my mouth quiver. 'Two apothecaries will never agree.'

'Good, I have made you smile. Now I know you are getting better.'

'To face the impossible situation I've made for myself.'

'What will you do?'

I shrugged. 'I don't know. I'm contracted to Giovanna Lendro. I can't honourably retract my solemn vow and her family would destroy my reputation as a physician.'

'She sent you a message while the fever had hold of you. I should have told you before but it didn't seem helpful. Now you can cope with her piety. She offered the solace that if it was God's will, you would live, and if His will was otherwise, she would pray for your soul.'

'She is young and innocent of the world's ways.'

'I've no doubt she would prove a devoted wife but she will not stimulate your intellect. Forgive me; it's not for me to give such an opinion.'

'I value your opinion – and Geoffrey's. I'm not worthy of his concern. Has he forgiven me?'

'For believing him capable of murder? He's still a little hurt by it but he has tended you with all the care a friend can offer. He knows what it is to be seized by dreadful imaginings.'

During those days in Antonia's house I came to appreciate her wisdom and to realise that my mistrust of Geoffrey had been coloured by jealousy of his relationship with her and my misunderstanding of its nature. By the time I returned to my lodgings I had strengthened my bonds of friendship with both of them and longed to repay them in some way for all they had done. Pierpaolo continued to harass his step-mother with threats to expose her adultery and to pursue his challenge to Giorgio's will. I could not see what I could do to thwart the vengeful youth but if an opportunity occurred I would gladly seize it.

*****

I returned to my studies at the university and there too I encountered extravagant descriptions of my heroism, not least from Professor Bonalini. While in body and mind I still felt fragile, I welcomed the opportunity to fix my thoughts on medical matters and I was pleased to be nominated to take part in a further disputation. This was to concern the virtues of treating the whole man, rather than a specific malady, but my opponent was to be a less experienced debater than Berthold and I considered the subject more straightforward than the desirable quantum of sleep.

I prepared my arguments and on the prescribed day I deployed them to the best of my ability, in front of a sizable audience of town worthies. I appreciated that many of them had come, not to listen to our erudition, but to view the subject of widespread, if blatantly erroneous, gossip. Among them, as before, I made out the swarthy features of the man who had saved my life, the Commendatore Matteo Maffei, and as the discussion rambled on, I wondered what it was that drew him to such learned events where he cut an incongruous figure. I remembered him coolly wiping my attacker's blood from his dagger and his promise that we would meet again. Perhaps, if he regularly attended disputations at the university, that was not so unlikely a prediction. At the end of the debate he made no overt attempt to claim my acquaintance but, as his party rose to leave the chamber during applause from the onlookers, he turned quickly towards the rostrum and it seemed to me that he winked in my direction. I could not be certain whether I merely imagined the rapid movement of his eyelid but the idea of such familiarity was disconcerting.

*****

There was no disguising Rendell's excitement when I entered our room after attendance at a lecture, for he bounced towards me with a menacing grin. It was two weeks since the disputation and I was so much restored in health that I could no longer delay the visit I was bound to pay to

Giovanna and her family. Yet I had no answer to the conundrum which faced me and it was made no easier by knowing that Bess, while grieving for my inconstancy, would urge me to fulfil my obligations to the innocent girl to whom I had betrothed myself. Thoughts of this duty soured my mood and I snapped at the lad who was jigging up and down in front of me.

'What?'

'Ooh, temper! Whatever it portends, it's due to me.'

'Don't talk in riddles.'

'All right, master grouchy physician. A servant came from the Capello tower asking you to call there on Saturday morning. Intriguing, eh?'

'Why? What have you done now? I told you not to go there.'

'Nor I ain't. Haven't been near the place. It's you they want to see, not me.'

'Who? Who's the message from?'

'He didn't say. Just that you're to call. I suppose Signora Schioppa-Capello is back. Perhaps she's going to ask that I go and play with little Signorina Carlotta. I'm a bit old for games with children but I'll oblige if they want me.'

Despite my peevish mood I smiled at the air of condescension Rendell was adopting towards an aristocratic household, but I also rejoiced that this request would prevent me riding out to see Giovanna on Saturday. I had already accepted that visits to her on a Sunday were inadvisable because they interrupted her devotions, so I had won another week before needing to embrace my betrothed once more. 'If the Signora asks for your inestimable services, I shall agree,' I said, more amicably than before.

Rendell beamed. 'That's the least you can do. It's all due to me that you can hobnob with the nobility in Padua, not just paltry apothecaries and professors.'

I gave him a half-hearted cuff and turned to the bowl of broth he had ready for me. 'Hobnobbing with nobility in England landed me here, remember!'

*****

I was greeted at the entrance to the Capello tower with the utmost courtesy and shown into a well-furnished antechamber with tapestries similar to those I remembered in the great hall. There was no sign of the boisterous little girl or her mother but in the distance I could hear music, probably from an upper room. An attendant told me I would not be kept waiting long and he poured me a goblet of delicious wine, which I sipped carefully as I did not want its unusual strength to go to my head. I brushed fluff from my gown, smoothed my lappets and tried to dislodge something sticky from the heel of my boot without depositing it on the tiled floor. After a short time the music ceased and I heard resolute footsteps approaching along a corridor. I rose and set down my glass as the door was held open by a servant for a lady to enter.

It was not Carlotta Schioppa although there was something in her carriage which reminded me of Enrico Capello's wife. This was a much older woman, magnificently but tastefully dressed in black silk threaded with silver filigree, wearing a single exquisite chain of gold and crystal draped across her bodice, and a headdress swathed in the finest white lawn. She moved gracefully, with an upright posture, but it was her face which held attention with her sharp nose and penetrating dark eyes, belying her years with their lively intelligence. Overawed by her grandeur, I bowed low.

'Doctor Somers, I have the advantage of you. I am Orsola Guarienti-Schioppa, widow of Sandro Schioppa. You have met my daughter and granddaughter.'

'Signora, I am honoured.'

'I have heard of your servant's merry exploit on the tower and your own more solemn achievement in bringing a villain to justice. My granddaughter still remembers the rescue of the cat, which is remarkable as she is such a scatterbrain, and the fame of your bravery echoes across the town.'

'More than I deserve. Some of the gossip is wide of the mark.'

She dismissed my comment with a wave of the hand. 'Gossip is always wide of the mark but if it is to your advantage it should be welcomed. You are also progressing well with your studies, I understand, and making quite a name for yourself in disputations.' I must have looked surprised at her improbable knowledge of my situation and she gave an unexpectedly throaty laugh. 'I make it my business to be well informed on matters that interest me.' She laughed again and I did not dare to ask how I could possibly interest her. 'In England you already practised as a physician, despite your youth, in the household of Duke Humphrey of Gloucester.' It was unclear whether this was a statement or question so I confirmed her assertion.

'He is a learned man, I am told. It is sad that his wife's foolish activities have brought him disgrace.' She poured herself some wine and seated herself on a settle. 'Of course it was that wretched business which brought you here so perhaps I should not regret it. You miss your country?'

'In many ways. Mostly I miss those I hold dear.'

'You do not have a wife?' Her tone was sharp but, as I shook my head, she continued her interrogation more gently. 'There is a woman for whom you feel tenderness? You are not affianced to her?'

'There is and I am not,' I said, feeling like a boy before his schoolmaster.

'The duration of your stay here is uncertain and your beloved is too far away to be allowed to impede your success. Have you been celibate in Padua?'

I gulped but felt unable to refuse an answer. 'Not entirely, Signora.'

She gave another deep and rather vulgar laugh. 'I should hope not! You frequent whores, I presume?'

'One whore. She has died.'

'Your fatal influence? Does untimely death come to most of your acquaintances?' As I opened my mouth to attempt a reply, she waved her hand again. 'That was unfair, I grant. But you are a free man?'

'I am contracted to a young woman of the house of Bonalini, kin to my Professor and to the apothecary, Gasparo da Friuli. I am to marry her when I have received my doctorate.'

Orsola Guarienti-Schioppa drained her glass and set it down on the table beside her with a thud. 'That is the first foolish thing I have heard of you. Do you fancy you love this girl or simply lust for her?' She rose. 'Ha! I see you do neither. Her relatives have offered you favours? To advance your career? Not a good enough reason to bind yourself to such a mediocre family. You should keep open your options until you are firmly established.'

'It's done now,' I said in great embarrassment.

'It is not done! You are free until your doctorate is completed. So, the solution seems obvious: don't complete it!'

'Signora, a doctorate from Padua would be a privilege I long to possess.'

'More than you long to possess this girl, I imagine. Never mind, there's time to remedy matters. A delay in finalising your studies can be utilised to unravel the tangle you've created. There are ways of arranging these things. And there will be no requirement for you to remain celibate. You must take an acknowledged mistress, of decent breeding. I could suggest one or two candidates but you will wish to choose you own. Do not gape at me, Doctor Somers, with that bemused expression. I am offering you a position –

a position in my household. You will leave Padua and reside in my house in Verona. You will care for the health of all my servitors and dependants and you will sometimes visit my estates outside the city, where I have a large workforce. I have always kept a physician and old Doctor Morano died a month ago. You will come?'

Her presence was so compelling that, even if she had been offering something I wanted to resist, I doubt I could have repulsed her. As it was, she was suggesting a role I coveted, similar to the one I had held in England, and she was giving me the faint hope of release from the contract binding my future. I had no idea how that might be achieved but Orsola Guarienti-Schioppa gave the impression of invincibility. 'I'm flattered, Signora, and honoured. It's most unexpected.'

'Of course it is; you need not state the obvious. But you will agree? I shall leave for Verona tomorrow and you will travel in a week's time. I shall be generous in rewarding you for your services, you may be sure, and you may bring your servant but I will not have the boy scrambling up the outside of my tower.'

I was grateful that she had lightened the tone of our discourse. 'Rendell talks of going for a soldier. I wouldn't stop him. It's what he wants and he is nearly thirteen.'

The corners of the lady's mouth curled downwards and she twirled the chain around her neck. 'That could be arranged,' she said. 'You will come then?'

'I shall have to explain to Professor Bonalini...'

'You need do nothing of the sort! I shall inform him that I have engaged your services. That's all there is to it. Do not imagine difficulties where there are none.' She swept her skirts round with a commanding gesture and fixed me with her piercing black eyes. 'I am not accustomed to asking a question three times. For the final time, Doctor Somers, will you join my household in Verona?'

I lifted my hands in surrender. Fate had contrived to offer me the new start for which yearned. 'Yes, Signora. I'm overcome with amazement but I will join your household in Verona.'

'Good.' She extended her right arm so that I could kiss her slender fingers, freighted with dazzling rings. 'This is a contract you will not slip out of, physician. I should perhaps have mentioned that some of what I have learned of you comes from my dear nephew, Matteo, whom you have encountered.'

She had the power of overwhelming my common sense and obstructing my memory, because I ought to have remembered the relationship. 'The Commendatore?'

Amusement gurgled in her throat. 'Some do call him that. He visits my house occasionally. You will find him interesting.' She gave a little trill on her last word.

The door opened, without me noticing how she had signalled to the attendant who stepped forward to escort me from the Capello tower. It seemed appropriate to move backwards from her, as if she was royalty, and I stepped carefully to avoid tripping on my gown. On the threshold I bowed with all the dignity I could muster.

'Oh, Doctor Somers,' she said as I turned. 'Your propensity for investigating puzzles has not of course passed unnoticed. In addition to engaging your medical expertise I expect to receive the benefit of your intellect. I can promise an intriguing mystery for you to solve in Verona. Arrivederci, physician, until next week.'

Part II – Verona: 1443

Chapter 8

The entrance to the Casa delle Arche was blocked by a long wooden chest straddling the full width of the doorway. This circumstance, which could not be accidental, held my attention and I did not note the elegant façade, with its colonnade of ornate arches decorating the ledge between the ground and first floors, giving the house its name. I was preoccupied, because it would be difficult to reach across the obstacle while on horseback to bang the knocker, shaped as a leering face, and it was unclear how access was to be obtained while the coffer remained in position. I looked round at the leader of the escort who had met us at the city gate but he was engaged in lively conversation with his four colleagues, pointing and laughing at our predicament. They did not seem surprised or unduly put out and after some murmured comments, among which I caught the name 'Iacopo', five pairs of eyes turned in unison to stare at me, as if interested to see how I would respond to the situation. Rendell, at my side, wheeled his pony and glared at our attendants. 'Tell them to move it,' he hissed.

Ignoring this advice, I slid from my saddle, and stood looking down at the chest, studying its elaborate bolts and hinges and the small round hole between them. For a moment I considered scrambling onto its lid, to reach the knocker, but I knew this should not be necessary for an invited guest. I was expected, I had been received by Signora Orsola's escort with proper courtesy, and it would be normal for the door-keeper to be waiting attentively to throw open the portal of her house when I arrived. I bent over the box and sniffed; then I took the knife from my belt and banged on the top with its hilt. I heard a faint squeak and banged again, stepping back quickly as the lid flew open. A velvet cap appeared crowning tousled curls and a pudgy, indignant face. I assumed the owner was on his knees until I realised this was a very short person with stubby legs.

'How did you know I was inside? Which of them told you?' He asked in a high-pitched voice, scowling at the five men accompanying me.

'No one told me. I noticed the bolts on the chest were not engaged and, if you make a practice of such jests, I counsel you not to eat such heavily spiced food. Your breath betrayed you. Messer Iacopo, is it?'

'You're a sharp one, Doctor Harry Somers! I'll have to look to my laurels.' He cackled unpleasantly and put his hands on his hips. 'I'm Madonna Orsola's dwarf and fool. The two conditions don't go together. I happen to be one and have the talent to be the other.'

I bowed and held out my hand which, after a pause, he grasped with surprising strength. 'You've brought your own dwarf, I see. Is he a fool too?'

I slapped a restraining hand on Rendell's arm. 'He's still a boy. He'll grow taller. As to whether he's a fool, you'll have a chance to find out.'

'He's the boy who rescued the cat on the tower?'

I gripped Rendell's wrist more tightly. 'His fame has gone before him.'

Iacopo scowled. 'Damn silly thing to do. I'd have leaned over the parapet and shoved the moggy off its perch. It must have snapped at little songbirds often enough, so I'd have been pleased to know it made a feast for their scavenging brethren when it was all mashed up at the foot of the tower.' He looked at me assertively as if defying me to disagree.

'As a matter of interest,' I said, ignoring the challenge, 'if I had stepped up onto the chest, what would have greeted me through your peephole?'

He looked even angrier and whipped a long-handled poniard from under his tunic. 'This, doctor. If you were

103

lucky, it would have sliced your boot leather but if you'd stood directly over the hole, I'd have tickled your genitals.'

'A novel form of welcome! Does your mistress know what you planned?'

'Do you mean the harlot who opens her legs for me or Signora Orsola who will have me beaten for effrontery? I like precision in language, Doctor Somers. It is my stock in trade.'

To my relief the door behind Iacopo had opened quietly while he was speaking and a burly official seized the little fellow under the armpits and swung him clear of the chest, setting him down on a bench in the passageway. At the same time he barked at my escort to remove the obstruction. 'Doctor Somers,' he said as his order was obeyed, 'on behalf of the Signora, I apologise for your reception. I am her steward. I was detained elsewhere and didn't realise this unruly wretch was up to his tricks.'

'Detained with cock in cunt, doctor, a nasty ailment that; do you know how to cure it? Which of the maids was it this time, Messer Sandrino? The pale one with the mole on her tit? I sucked it last week.' He ducked as the steward aimed a punch at his head and scuttled off towards the inner courtyard, yelping merrily.

Sandrino clapped his hands and a bevy of attendants appeared in order to lead away our horses, unload our packs, brush the dust from our clothes, offer us refreshment and generally greet us as befitted new members of the household. Iacopo was not mentioned again during these ceremonies but Rendell's expression had softened from the fury he had displayed earlier and, as we were led along a corridor to our rooms, he looked at me sideways and winked. 'That stunted bastard's got a neat turn of phrase. I might learn something from him.'

I did not rise to the provocation for I was mulling over the fact that, among Iacopo's outspoken mockery and vulgar jibes, he had made no reference to my all-too-obvious disfigurement. My birthmark had been the butt of my childhood persecutors and Iacopo might disdain such an easy target, yet it was also possible that, with his impaired stature, he had the delicacy not to refer to physical imperfections. He was a puzzling little rascal and I knew I must be wary of his caustic wit but I also found him strangely endearing.

*****

Messer Sandrino explained that Signora Orsola was engaged on business with her notary but would receive me during the afternoon. In the meantime he was assiduous in checking that I had all I needed in my chamber and personally escorted me on a tour of the principal rooms in the magnificent mansion. I noted that he was addressed with easy respect by the servants we encountered and saw nothing to suggest he was regarded as a tyrant who abused his position in the household. I concluded that Iacopo's taunts might have had little foundation and this affable steward was compelled to tolerate the mocking of a favoured jester. Such a situation was not unique. Some of the nobility in England gave clowns licence to tell vile lies as entertainment but Duke Humphrey of Gloucester, whom I had served, always preferred the conversation of learned men to such crude amusements. I shrugged away momentary nostalgia for the intellectual refinements of his palace at Greenwich and greeted my new companions and potential patients in friendly fashion.

Sandrino insisted that I join him in the midday meal, served to us privately in his study. As he clearly relished the tender mutton and capons, piled onto his platter in quantities at which I marvelled, we ate in silence until we were mopping up the delicious sauce with our bread. With globules of the liquid gleaming on his chin, he beamed at me. 'Signora Orsola keeps a good table. Indeed, everything

105

in her household is of the highest standard. You'll savour living here. I can vouch for the good nature of all the attendants under my direction and they will make you welcome.'

I noted the emphasis in his words. 'There are others you do not direct?'

'I speak of the people in the Casa delle Arche. I have no remit towards those on my lady's many estates but in the house there are only three who are beyond my bidding: the Signora's two principal women and her notary. The sisters, Constanza and Diamante, think themselves too superior to be guided by me but I fancy you'll have no problem in winning their approval. Constanza has a bad back and will plague you for simples to soothe her aches but, if you can persuade her that your remedies bring relief, she will treasure you like a cherished lapdog.' I raised my eyebrows at this unappealing prospect but Sandrino flicked a crumb from his upper lip with his tongue and continued. 'Diamante is the younger and, like her sister, unmarried. You will make up your own mind about her charms. They will certainly be on offer. She is possessed by the demons of wantonness.'

I tried to cover my embarrassment. 'Who is the third person you mentioned?'

Sandrino grunted and pushed his dish aside. 'Signora Orsola's notary is a law unto himself.' He smirked at his feeble pun. 'I have little to do with him but he assists her in managing the estates she has inherited and those of her brother, over which she has control. Guglielmo Guarienti is detained in Venice, you understand.'

I nodded although I did not understand at all. Sandrino had fixed me with a stern eye and it seemed best to leave his meaning to be clarified later. 'Is Iacopo in your charge?'

He cleared his throat. 'Insofar as anyone except the Signora can constrain his antics, I can. He can be a pestilential nuisance but he is indulged, for his former master's sake.' Sandrino rose from the table and summoned a servant to clear away the remnants of our meal. 'I'm delighted to make your acquaintance, Doctor Somers, but you must excuse me now as I have arrangements to make with regard to the Signora's journey. She will send for you shortly.' It did not seem appropriate to ask where or when the lady was going.

As promised I was in due course summoned to attend Orsola Guarienti-Schioppa in the chamber where she conducted business. This was situated on the corner of the first floor with windows facing across the street and, at right angles to them, others which looked towards the magnificent Scaligeri tombs outside the church of Santa Maria. I had glimpsed these fine memorials to the former rulers of Verona when we approached the Casa delle Arche and I had been looking forward to inspecting them more closely, until the complications of my entry into the house drove them from my head.

When I was shown into her room the Signora was accompanied by two men in legal robes and she introduced the elder, a sharp-nosed, thin-faced fellow, as her notary, Messer Bernardino Biagio. He greeted me with stiff courtesy but showed no pleasure at our meeting and made no attempt to present his assistant who peered at me through half-closed eyelids. Shortly after the formalities were concluded the lawyers gathered up their papers and left us. I was conscious of a pair of female attendants, sitting with their needlework to the side of the smaller windows, eyeing me silently while I conversed with their mistress. The atmosphere in the room seemed tense.

'Doctor Somers, you are welcome.' Signora Orsola wafted her hand in the air, dispelling the mood. 'I gather Iacopo greeted you in characteristic manner. He means no harm. Your accommodation is satisfactory, I trust, and Sandrino has done the honours? I should have acknowledged your arrival sooner but some inopportune developments have intervened and detained me. I have oversight of considerable estates and must visit one of our manor houses to settle a tiresome dispute. In due course you will see my lands and the people who serve me in vineyards, fields and pastures but first you should acquaint yourself with the members of my household here. I don't doubt Sandrino has told you something of them?'

I heard the rustle of stiff material behind me and presumed one of women had shifted position but I noticed that Signora Orsola looked quickly and, I thought, angrily towards the source of the slight sound. 'You need not regard Sandrino's views as Holy Writ, nor necessarily as representative of my own opinions. I wish you to exercise your own judgement and suggest you use the days of my absence to familiarise yourself with the ailments, real and imagined, which afflict my servants. However, I would ask you to allow my principal woman, Constanza, to consult you now, before we take our leave.'

'Of course, my lady,' I stammered as the older attendant was beckoned forward and I turned to bow to her. The woman I took to be her sister fluttered to her feet, intent on following her, but their mistress pointed to the door.

'Your presence will not be necessary, Diamante. Attend to the packing of my things. I will myself remain while the doctor speaks with Constanza, so you need have no fear that he will assault her virtue.'

I gulped silently as the slightly younger woman, who moved gracefully like a faded sylph, pressed her thin lips together and curtsied, her eyes all the time appraising me. Meanwhile Constanza swept forward until, after a few steps, she slowed and clamped her hand to the small of her back, grimacing. She was more heavily built than her sister and looked unfriendly.

'Doctor Morano prepared me a brew to lessen the pain in my spine but I have finished it and he has died.' Her tone was accusatory as if my predecessor had intentionally caused her inconvenience.

'You have suffered with this ailment for some time?'

Her bulbous nose twitched. 'It comes and goes. Over many months.'

'A shooting pain which moves about?' She stared at me suspiciously and gave an abrupt nod. 'Is it worse when you have been lifting things?'

'I am not a housemaid,' she snapped but then she relented. 'However I do lift the Signora's gowns from the chests sometimes. Perhaps it is true the pain returns when I do so.'

'A good friend of mine, an apothecary, concocts a tincture to rub into the area affected by such discomfort. I have a small jar of it in my room. You may like to try its effect.' I wished Geoffrey was at hand to mix more of the balsam if she found it useful, because I did not know the exact ingredients, but I remembered how Dame Margery had benefited from applying it years earlier at Greenwich.

Constanza sniffed. 'I hoped you would give me more of Doctor Morano's potion. He never suggested I rub it into my skin.'

'No, indeed. This is a different remedy – to be used as a poultice. You mustn't think of trying to drink the ointment.'

Her lips curved into a sneer. 'Do you think me stupid, English doctor?'

'Certainly not, madam, but I am now responsible for advising you and must take no chances that my foreign tongue is unclear.'

Orsola Guarienti-Schioppa fidgeted behind me as Constanza inclined her head slightly. 'If the Signora is content, I will use your tincture but I have no confidence it will reduce my pain.'

'I'll fetch the jar immediately.' While I was still speaking both mistress and serving woman turned to the door and, as it was opened, I noticed Diamante hovering outside. She favoured me with a coy smile and for some reason I shivered. Signora Orsola looked back over her shoulder. 'Study my household well, physician. I think you will find them of interest and when I return we shall discuss what is needed to ensure their well-being.'

*****

The lady left the house later that afternoon, accompanied by her two principal women, the notary, his assistant and an escort of six armed men. I saw them ride out of the courtyard and observed that a small figure on a pony, which scampered in a cloud of dust to join the group, was not sent back by his patron; at least I would be spared Iacopo's dubious merriment while I familiarized myself with other members of the household. My first impressions were confusing and I did not think I had the measure of anyone I had yet met in Verona.

Sandrino ensured my chamber was equipped with every item I requested and he described the location of the best apothecaries in the city, urging me to mention his name when introducing myself to them. He seemed to welcome my company and I was happy to take a glass of wine with him after the communal meal in the main hall. I already appreciated that the produce of the Signora's vineyards was of unsurpassed quality.

The evening was warm and our disposition mellow as we exchanged anecdotes, until the steward rapped his temple with his knuckles and shook his head with mild annoyance. 'There has been so much activity today I am become forgetful. Signora Orsola insisted that I should concern myself with your young servant's ambition to become a soldier.'

I was amazed the lady remembered Rendell's aspirations but did not admit it. 'I've asked the cook if he can help in the kitchens for the time being. It's work he knows. There's no urgency for him to become a warrior.'

'The Signora suggested he might see something of a soldier's life before he commits himself to leave your service and I can arrange that. My nephew, Alberto, is a captain with the Venetian garrison here in Verona, based outside the inner walls of the town, in the Cittadella. He's a good fellow and I'll take you to meet him. He's ready to let your lad spend some time each day helping with the horses and learning swordplay. The boy can return to the house here to attend to your needs in the evening and we'll see how he gets on. There's no real fighting at present in the Venetian lands on the mainland, the *Terrafirma* they call it, since the failed assault four years ago. The main problem for the garrison is boredom, I'd say.'

'That's a generous offer. Rendell will relish the swordplay.' I swirled the ruby liquid in my glass. 'The Signora is most thoughtful. I was afraid she might suggest sending him to join the armed band which I understand her nephew, the Commendatore, Matteo Maffei, commands.'

Sandrino cleared his throat. 'The Commendatore is her late husband's nephew but we don't mention him often in this house. He is a freebooter with no settled loyalties. He fought for the Most Serene Republic in the troubles four years past but he is as likely to draw his sword against the Venetian Doge if an enemy offers a greater sum to buy his services. It is an uncomfortable position for a family constant in their allegiance. Madonna Orsola's daughter is married to a nobleman of Venice and her son serves in the Venetian embassy to the King of France. I am surprised you know of her relationship with this mountebank.'

'I heard of him in Padua,' I said. 'He knew my Professor at the university.' I did not deem it wise to mention my own encounter with the Commendatore, when he saved my life, or the fact that the Signora herself had referred to him in perfectly cordial terms. 'You mentioned that the lady's brother is also in Venice.'

Sandrino rose and set down his glass. 'I think I told you so,' he said with irritation. 'Guglielmo Guarienti is detained there and Signora Orsola administers his lands. Do not probe too deeply, Doctor Somers, into what does not concern you.'

As I prepared for bed and parried Rendell's jubilant impertinence, after I told him what was being arranged for his benefit, I reflected that I must tread carefully until I understood the sensitivities lurking beneath the civilised veneer of Signora Orsola's household. I had much to learn.

*****

Sandrino did not appear to bear grudges and next morning there was no trace of awkwardness between us when he accompanied Rendell and me to the 'city within the city', the Cittadella, where the soldiers were accommodated. We crossed the open space beyond the ancient, ruined arena, to pass through the Porta Rofioli and were at once in a world dominated by horses and cavalrymen. At the point where we crossed the channel from the River Adige, which had been constructed so that supplies could be delivered directly to the garrison, porters were unloading bales of fodder from the craft moored by the bank and our path was strewn with wisps of hay. Along our route the clank and crash of farriers and blacksmiths beating metal in their smithies rang in our ears and posses of riders trundled past with jangling harness. In the distance, Sandrino pointed out, shouting against the noise, were the meadows of the Abbey of Santa Trinità where dozens of military horses grazed on the lush grass nurtured for generations by the monks. This sensible arrangement benefited both the health of the animals and the coffers of the Abbot who had negotiated very favourable terms for allowing access to the meadows with the army's Superintendent of Victualling.

Rendell could hardly contain his exhilaration at the sight of mounted soldiers tilting at the quintain in an exercise yard and I had to yank him away from this diversion to follow Sandrino into the headquarters building nearby. It stood in the middle of a garden which once belonged to a convent, according to the steward, and he put his knuckle to his nose when he explained that the nuns judged it prudent to remove themselves from the vicinity of the garrison while securing six hundred ducats for their property. 'A happy conjunction to preserve chastity and augment wealth', he murmured.

Alberto was only a year or two older than me and he impressed me favourably from the beginning. He questioned Rendell with affable perception, before sending him off with a sergeant to visit the stables, and he shook my hand to confirm the arrangements we had made for the time the boy would spend in the Cittadella. After this Sandrino explained he must return to his duties but the young officer invited me to stay so he could show me round the camp and I readily agreed. I was not greatly interested in military deployments but I was anxious to learn more about the city which was to be my home and to meet people from outside the Casa delle Arche. I soon found Alberto was good company and had unexpected connections.

We were walking parallel to the walls between the Cittadella and the river when he made his surprising announcement. 'I'm glad to meet you, Doctor Somers. I'd heard of you before you came to Verona though I never thought to meet you.' He grinned at my startled look. 'Oh, I've heard nothing but good, don't worry. My mother came from Padua, you see, and her sister's family still lives there, though not in happy circumstances. It's my cousin who sings your praises: Leone.'

'Gasparo da Friuli's apprentice! He's a bright lad. He was a great help to me.'

'I'm glad to hear you say so. He's had to carry a heavy weight as breadwinner since his father died. I'd like to see him away from the master he serves.'

I remembered the apothecary's attempt to rid himself of the boy's services but I thought those difficulties had passed. 'I understood Messer Gasparo offered him indentures to learn a trade after his father's death.'

'But you don't know why, I imagine. Messer Gasparo was responsible for my uncle's accident. He was riding by the river and became angry when he found the roadway blocked by a cart my uncle was loading with sacks of flour from the mill. He shouted at him to move it, while the poor man was balanced awkwardly stepping into a boat. Uncle slipped and was swept under the sails. He was knocked on the head and carried away while Gasparo was still raging at him.'

'I never heard that. Does Leone know?'

'Oh yes. The miller saw everything. I think it was his intervention that persuaded Gasparo to be so generous.' Alberto's lip curled on the last word but he stood still and extended his arm to point up at the walls. ''I'm neglecting my duty as guide to the Cittadella. Do you see where the repairs have been carried out? That's the place where the insurgents broke through the defences to take the gate four years ago.'

'Were you here then?'

'I was. Newly appointed and serving in my father's troop. I saw him sliced in two by a Gonzaga sword.'

'Dear God! I'm sorry. The Gonzaga of Mantua were leading the insurgents?'

'Mantua has always been Verona's rival and when there was a chance to cause trouble they took advantage of their involvement. They joined the alliance against Venice and took the opportunity to attack Verona but their success only lasted three days. Francesco Sforza led a counterattack and recaptured the city. Looking back it was a petty episode but there were casualties, my father among them, and it exposed divisions among the citizens. I'm certain the attackers would not have breached the Porta Rofioli without the treachery of some inside the city walls but it's never been proved.'

'Was no one arrested by the Venetian authorities?'

'No charges were laid but one or two suspects have been removed from Verona and forbidden to return.'

I stared at the young officer, recalling the phrase which had puzzled me. 'Detained in Venice? Was Signora Orsola's brother one of them?'

'You're a quick learner, Doctor Somers. Guglielmo Guarienti was suspected of sympathising with the Gonzaga faction although I don't think there was proof he did anything treasonable. No action was taken against him but then, a couple of months past, he was confined to the islands of the Venetian lagoon until further notice. The Guarienti and the Schioppa have a proud history of support for Venice's enemies, right back to when the Scaligeri ruled the city, but Signora Orsola has dissociated herself from her family's traditions. She's been adept at demonstrating her loyalty to our Venetian overlords.' He wrinkled his nose. 'I speak with the greatest respect of my Venetian paymasters, you understand.'

We laughed and shook hands again as we parted at the gate of the Cittadella with a promise to meet again when the captain was off duty. Then I went on my way pondering what Alberto had told me, conscious that the events of four years previously were fresh in everyone's memories and I was grateful to have been made aware of tensions still festering beneath the surface of Veronese life.

*****

Signora Orsola was absent from her home for longer than expected and Sandrino told me she had travelled to Venice, no doubt to see her daughter and grandchild as well as her errant brother. This gave me the opportunity to acquaint myself thoroughly with the members of the household and their ailments, enabling me to judge that my task as their physician should not be too onerous. I had taken the precaution of writing to Geoffrey du Bois to request that he send me another jar of his tincture, in case Constanza found it useful, and I was delighted to receive a reply within days, enclosing the ointment, but the letter which accompanied it contained surprising and strangely troubling news.

We learned that Giorgio's irksome son had been strongly advised by his notary to drop his challenge to his father's will. The evidence given by Giorgio's brother apothecaries in the Guild unanimously affirmed his clarity of mind and his affection for me as his partner, so no one doubted the sincerity of his intention to bequeath me his business. Rather reluctantly, I fancy, Pierpaolo has accepted his notary's advice – probably concluding that no lawyer cedes the chance to earn fees unless it is a truly desperate case. This joyful outcome strengthened our resolution to delay no longer and Antonia and I were married last Saturday. We have moved into the small lodgings behind the shop, which are cramped but will suit us, for the time being, until we can take our own house. We cannot even offer a roof to Antonia's maid but the girl comes in daily to help with little Giorgio, as does Leone who has left Gasparo and come to help me. He is a valuable assistant. I hope to inform you shortly of our move to a more suitable residence. We remain your loving and grateful friends.

I stared at the words and reread them. After what I had learned of Gasparo's role in the death of Leone's father I was glad the lad had moved from his old master to one who would value his services. Less happily I mulled over that, from what I knew of Pierpaolo Clemente, his docility in withdrawing the challenge to Giorgio's will did not ring true. I found this unsettling, but I was as much concerned by the rashness of Geoffrey's precipitate marriage with the late apothecary's widow. It defied convention to wed during the period of mourning and would be held to confirm the existence of a liaison pre-dating Giorgio's death. It would have been wiser to wait decorously, as Geoffrey had previously intended, in order not to give a rancorous stepson further grounds for nurturing a grudge.

At length I folded the letter and put it in my chest. It was nothing to do with me and I was more than forty miles away, in a different city and with new preoccupations. I wished the newly-weds well and hoped the passage of time would quieten malicious gossip but I could do nothing to help.

*****

That evening while I strolled across the courtyard as the light faded I noticed a door in the angle of two wings which I had not observed before. It was in shadow but the lowering rays of the sun picked out the carved architrave above it and drew my attention. I was studying the design of the decoration when the door opened slightly and a richly dressed woman appeared on the threshold. I glimpsed the gold braiding on her turbaned headdress and the brocade of her sleeveless over-garment, as she caught my eye and quickly retreated, shutting the door behind her, and I guessed she fled from my too obvious interest. A light fragrance hung upon the air. I was certain I had not seen her before among the female attendants and she had neither the bearing nor the clothes of an inferior. I had heard nothing of a visitor to the house and was bewildered by her presence but I resolved to make enquiries for I knew I would like to see her again, however grandly above my station she might be.

Next morning when I began to question Sandrino about the unknown lady he grew irritable and assured me I was mistaken, suggesting it was one of Signora Orsola's serving women, who had remained at the house and dared to try on one of her mistress's robes. This seemed to me highly unlikely and I was sure I would not have overlooked that incomparable face, even if I had seen it above a servant's garb. I remembered Iacopo's gibe about the steward's priapic behaviour and wondered if the lady was a courtesan who granted him her favours. It saddened me to think that was the explanation for her presence and felt a surge of foolish anger to imagine their coupling. I berated myself for becoming so disturbed by the momentary glimpse of a beautiful stranger but when I closed my eyes it was her face that shone in my darkened mind.

*****

On the afternoon Orsola Guarienti-Schioppa returned to the Casa delle Arche her retainers reported that she was in a foul humour so I was disconcerted to be summoned to attend her within an hour of her arrival. Constanza met me at the door to her mistress's chamber, looking flustered, but she gave me the faintest of smiles as she stood grasping the handle.

'How is your back? Was the journey painful for you?'

'It may have eased a little, I cannot be sure. If you had more of the ointment I would continue to use it.'

'I have another jar. I sent to my friend in Padua who mixes it.'

She raised her eyebrows. 'That was thoughtful. I am obliged. You'd best go in. The Signora is restless.'

Signora Orsola did not look restless. She was sitting at her desk and, although her expression was severe, she appeared quite calm. Unexpectedly she was alone and I feared she wanted to consult me on some delicate medical matter, which she did not wish even her principal attendants to overhear. This was irregular but I already knew the Signora was her own woman and no slave to custom. I held my breath as I bowed but she gave me no time to frame an astute question.

'Doctor Somers, you are prompt and I appreciate that. I need your services, in a personal capacity.' I composed my features into a suitably serious expression and was startled by her peal of laughter as she rose from her seat. 'Dear God, man, do you think I am about to describe some agony in my belly or groin? I assure you I have no malady of the body that I know of, although my mind is deeply troubled. Don't look so worried. I would not permit you to examine me unchaperoned – I have too much respect for both our reputations, implausible as it seems. I am unattended because of the nature of what I wish to say and have taken steps so we are not overheard. I have a task for you, outside your immediate professional sphere but within your capabilities, if what I have learned of your skill is true. When we met in Padua I indicated there might me an investigation you could make for me.'

'I remember you spoke of a puzzle, Signora.'

'It is now more than a puzzle. It is a matter of monstrous treachery. I have established with certainty that a member of my household has betrayed my family, no doubt to the villain's own advantage. You, Doctor Somers, will find out who it is and bring the wretch before me to receive just retribution.'

Chapter 9

I felt the warm flush rise from my throat and colour my cheeks, as I sought the appropriate response to the Signora's command, but she showed no sign of noticing my discomfort.

'You will make your enquiries without arousing the least suspicion that you are doing so, or that you know anything of the relevant circumstances. All members of my household are to be accounted suspects until disproved. Only an outsider, unfamiliar with the background can investigate the issue effectively.'

'This is why you brought me here?' A sudden suspicion that I had been tricked caused me to stumble over my words.

'Your worth as a physician is unquestioned, Doctor Somers. I have no doubts on that score but it is not the point. What I need now is your experience in ferreting out mischief and applying your intelligence to what you discover. Have you heard of my brother, Guglielmo?'

I stiffened and clasped my hands together to stop them trembling. 'I have, although Sandrino is loath to speak of him.'

'I imagine he is. You must decide if it is significant. Guglielmo had some foolish sympathy for the uprising four years ago but he did not take part in it. There was nothing solid to connect him with the insurgents – or so I understand. The Venetian authorities mistrusted him but, perhaps in deference to my son and son-in-law's devoted service to the Most Serene Republic, they took no action against him when they arrested others. Until a few months ago. Suddenly he was forcibly removed to Venice and is now compelled to reside there, under strict conditions, although no charges have been laid. I was puzzled how this came about and, when I invited you here, I thought you might help me look into the circumstances. However, the situation has become more serious. I needed to visit his estates and while there I heard rumours suggesting he had been betrayed by someone in my household, so I travelled to Venice to question Guglielmo myself. He confirmed that when he was detained the Venetian officials had in front of them a letter bearing the seal used by those who serve me at the Casa delle Arche. Not my personal seal, you understand, but one used for ordering supplies and trivial business conducted on my behalf. Find the traitor, Doctor Somers. I cannot countenance maintaining such a person in my service.'

I was moved by the passion in the lady's voice and knew I could not refuse her request. 'How many in your household can write, Signora?'

'All my principal attendants and, if the letter was dictated to another, the clerk is equally guilty.'

'Who keeps the seal?'

'There are three copies. My notary, Sandrino and Constanza each has one.'

'Then I must start with them – and others with access to the seal: Diamante, I imagine, as well as Messer Biagio's assistant. I don't know his name.'

'Alessandro. He is Bernardino's nephew.'

'Would the seal be readily available to others?'

'I think it would be unusual.'

'What about Iacopo?'

Orsola Guarienti-Schioppa spread her hands on the desk top, pressing hard so that the blood flowed from her fingers and the skin turned white. 'Iacopo can write and I accept you should, in equity, question him as he has often been with me here. Nevertheless you should understand he has always been my brother's servant, unlike the others. Bernardino Biagio, of course, has served us both as notary.'

'Do you have any suspicions yourself, Signora?'

Frowning, the lady rose and faced me. 'Prejudice rather than suspicion. Messer Biagio feathers his own nest

121

nicely from the proceeds of Guarienti transactions. Guglielmo and I are well aware of this and recognise it is the practice for notaries to augment their percentages by privy means. We do not complain while he serves us loyally but acquisitiveness can shade into greed and greed can lead a man along unsavoury paths.'

'You have charge of your brother's affairs while he is away? Does he have a wife and family?'

'He is twice widowed and has no living children. Will you do what I ask?'

'Signora, I cannot promise to find the proof you would like but I will do my best.'

'I am grateful, Doctor Somers. You may take your time, so as to be sure of your conclusion. I shall not press you for early results. By the way, on my travels I encountered my nephew, Matteo Maffei, and he sends his regards. Sandrino will not approve but I expect him to dine with me before long, so you will see him again.' I bowed my head, accepting this inevitability, but did not tell her what the Commendatore had foretold. 'As a matter of interest also, Messer Biagio has put in hand negotiations to free you from your inopportune betrothal. Giovanna Lendro's family will drive a hard bargain but I shall accommodate their claim.'

I could not hide my embarrassment. 'Signora, I beg you not to waste your resources on my account.'

'Really? I can't believe you wish to mate with that pious infant. If she breeds at all she would bear you devout eunuchs.'

The implication was clear. 'Have you seen her, Signora?'

'I visited the petty Lendro estate. I shall extricate you from this ridiculous entanglement and you will repay me by bringing me the serpent in my nest. You have leave to go, Doctor Somers.'

122

I understood the tacit bargain which had been made and, outside the room, I leaned against the wall, breathing deeply as I fought down nausea, until I became aware of a figure creeping to my side. Diamante brushed against me.

'She has bought you, body and soul, physician, has she? As she has all of us. But we must seek consolation. God will care for our souls, if we entreat him but, for our bodies' ease, we must fend for ourselves.' Her heavy perfume hung in the air after she entered her mistress's chamber and I found it necessary to spit a mouthful of bile into my hand.

*****

The first stage of my task was clear: to establish which, if any of them, had sufficient motive to betray the Signora's brother; and, in view of his mistress's comment, it seemed sensible to have an early conversation with Bernardino Biagio. I sought him alone, after we had dined, on the pretext of enquiring about his health, and he waved Alessandro aside when the younger man rose to accompany us. Bernardino grudgingly humoured me, as we walked in the courtyard, answering my basic questions and volunteering that he sometimes suffered with gripes in his stomach and constipation of the bowels. His thin-lipped smile, after sharing this confidence, was not encouraging.

'Doctor Morano kindly administered an enema from time to time and I may call on you for such a service but I consider myself in excellent health, Doctor Somers. I trust I shall make no other call on your professional services.'

'I'm delighted to hear it but, as I'm still learning about the household, I should be glad to ask you some other questions.'

He folded his hands on his round belly and looked at me with curiosity. 'What is it you wish to know?'

'How long have you acted as notary to the family?'

'By family I take it you refer to Signora Orsola and her brother. My father was notary to the Schioppa and, when I became qualified, the lady's husband, Sandro Schioppa, brought me to the Casa delle Arche to serve him. By extension, I assumed responsibility for the affairs of the Guarienti siblings. There is a third: Signora Orsola's sister is Abbess of a convent not far from Verona, at San Bonifacio, but her inheritance was mostly paid to her Order when she took the veil so I have little to do on her account.'

'I've heard how Signor Guarienti is detained in Venice. Does that make extra work for you?'

He steepled his fingers against his chest, as if in prayer, and answered me smoothly. 'A thoughtful question, Doctor Somers. I do carry greater responsibility for safeguarding his interests but the Signora has oversight of what I do.'

I was anxious to break through his reserve and risked a personal comment. 'You should take care not to exhaust yourself, Messer Biagio. The family obviously depend on you. I hope you are treated with respect by everyone in the household.' He raised his eyebrows as if I had exceeded my remit and I hurriedly continued. 'It's my belief that the strain of handling difficult situations can be deleterious for health.'

Bernardino nodded. 'A shrewd observation. I find it plausible. Alessandro assists me, of course, but he is inexperienced as yet, so a considerable burden falls on me. I do not regard Sandrino as a worthy steward for the Signora but he occasions me no trouble and her women are tedious but can be swatted aside. In the house only one person causes me irritation – the fool, Iacopo. He passes beyond the bounds of decorum in his mirth.'

'I've already suffered from that myself. He exposed me to physical injury. You think him dangerous?'

He licked his lips. 'I cannot understand why he should threaten those with whom he serves but I do not trust him.'

'Does he resent having had to join the Signora's household? Would he have preferred to go to Venice with his master?'

'Not at all. That's what is strange.' Bernardino pulled at his chin, showing the only sign I had seen him give of uncertainty. 'Iacopo declined to accompany Guglielmo Guarienti in his exile, after some disagreement between them, and the Signor permitted him to stay in Verona, with Signora Orsola. It's Iacopo's own ill temper that makes his foolery malicious.'

I thanked Messer Biagio for this information and we parted cordially but I had the impression he was relieved to end our conversation. I wondered how much he had withheld from his confidences and what he hoped I would fail to discover about his business activities. I doubted I would obtain much more information from his nephew.

*****

I ventured to the servants' hall after leaving the notary and was pleased to find Iacopo, cross-legged on the floor, regaling a group of retainers with his wit. During dinner he had moderated his language in the Signora's presence but now his vulgarity was unrestrained and when he caught sight of me he pointed and screamed with laughter. 'Why does this physician remind me of a horse's loose arse?' I braced myself as he answered his own question. 'His face looks as if it is covered in shit.'

So much, I thought, for my impression that the dwarf would not mock my disfigurement but the servants shuffled, uncertain whether to enjoy the joke at my expense, until I forced a grin. 'I've heard worse descriptions. Those born with disadvantages learn to ignore what cannot be

125

remedied. I cannot clean the stain from my face any more than Iacopo can add inches to his stature. I'd welcome a word, esteemed jester, if I could tear you from your audience.'

Iacopo slapped his knees and dismissed his admirers, while beckoning me to sit beside him. A fragrant scent rose from the herbs scattered on the floor which I crushed as I sank down, carefully avoiding the branch of thorn hidden under them. I lifted the prickly stem and waved it in front of him. 'Were you expecting me?'

'You're too sharp in your head, physician, so you save yourself from sharpness in your rump. I saw you talking to the notary and guessed he would defame me.'

'So here's your opportunity to retaliate. I imagine there's no love lost on your side?'

'He's a money-grubbing parasite who tricks those he serves.'

'He doesn't look as if he's very successful. He scarcely has the appearance of a wealthy man.'

'You're wrong, learned doctor. You haven't seen his vineyards and rich pastures, or the elegant furnishings in his house on his estate, or the silk flounces on his wife's fancy gowns. They lack for nothing except children – the rat-faced Alessandro is his heir.'

'I didn't know any of that. Do other members of the household have their own property outside the Casa delle Arche?'

'Only Sandrino. He has a modest house in the Borgo San Zeno, just outside the city walls. His wife and seven brats live there. You'd not believe it, would you? Hardly anyone knows. It might cramp his style if they did. The unmarried serving maids wouldn't be so willing to let him bed them if they knew there was no chance of him wedding them.'

'Is this true?'

'You can never trust what a fool says, can you? But most of it's true though there are only five children, so far as I know. He's a filthy hypocrite at any event.'

I whistled to show my surprise. 'You make it your business to know men's weaknesses?'

'And women's. They're pathetically amusing. Hasn't Diamante offered to open her legs for you yet?'

'Not exactly.' I was embarrassed but wanted his indiscretions to continue. 'She's given the impression that she would if I gave her the least encouragement.'

'It's a tragedy men run from one so eager. I've heard she was betrothed once but nothing came of it. Sandrino's had her of course. I think it turned her brain when she realised he wasn't offering marriage but naturally she doesn't know his little secret. She probably still nurses hope of winning him round, although she's rolled her eyes at Alessandro despite his sallow face and the fact his tastes lie elsewhere. But now you've come to the house and you're young and, despite that mark on your face, you're fairly presentable. You'll find her in your bed one night, believe me.'

'I promise you I won't!' I didn't attempt to disguise my horror at the idea.

'Oh, you'd fuck her if she promised to tell you what you want to know.'

I stared at him. 'What do you mean, what I want to know?'

Iacopo stood up in one smooth movement. 'I think you understand, physician. A good fool studies his masters and can foresee what they will do. I wish you success.'

I stayed crouched beside him, looking up at his complaisant smile. 'Why didn't you go to Venice with your master, Iacopo?'

He stamped his foot, grazing the side of my hand with his shoe, and scowled at me. 'That's one question too many. It has nothing to do with your commission. Keep to your charge, if you know what's good for you.'

'Did you accompany her when the Signora visited her brother last week?'

'You're as persistent as belly ache after eating unripe plums. Madonna Orsola took only Diamante and an escort of armed men when she went to Venice. The rest of us stayed at her country house until she returned.'

'Even Constanza?'

'She was suffering from a surfeit of unripe plums.'

I could not tell whether this was invention or the truth and I felt uncomfortable when I left him, suspecting that he could tell me much more. Despite his outspoken brashness, in his own way he was as reticent as Bernardino but he had certainly looked furious when I mentioned Guglielmo Guarienti.

*****

After learning what I had, it was necessary that I make an approach to Diamante but I decided it would be preferable to speak to her in a public setting, so I secured a place beside her at the noontide meal next day. She lowered her head and looked up at me through her pale lashes, in an attempt at coyness which did not convince, but when I asked how she had enjoyed the journey to Venice she assumed a bland expression.

'Well enough, Doctor Somers, but the heat was oppressive and there were storms. I've been there before of course and it is quaintly built with water lapping at every door, although I favour firm land beneath my feet. Signor Guarienti was not in an agreeable mood but I suppose it is not to be wondered at, given his circumstances.'

I pretended ignorance. 'Is he poorly housed?'

'Oh, not at all. He's not in one of the foul Venetian prisons. He is accommodated lavishly. He's a rich man and can purchase all the comforts he wants. He isn't constrained at all in his movements inside the city but he may not cross to the mainland and it is there, in the *Terrafirma*, that all his properties are situated. He's dependent on that rogue Biagio and the creepy Alessandro to manage his affairs. It's not an enviable position to be in, however much he may have brought it on himself.'

'You hold him blameworthy?'

She gasped in surprise and spoke hurriedly. 'I forgot you would not know his story. Four years ago he voiced support for the attack on Verona, even though he played no part in it. He was always more bluster than action but he antagonised Venice and invited punishment. I fancy the greatest penalty he suffers is the knowledge that Biagio is milking the profits from his estates.'

She spoke airily but there was something unconvincing in her levity. 'Doesn't the Signora have oversight, on his behalf?'

She shot me a rapid glance of annoyance. 'She does what she can but I counsel you not to underestimate that double-dealing notary. He's as devious and slippery as the fool, without Iacopo's merriment to temper his ill will.'

I tried a different tack. 'I was sorry to hear of your sister's ailment. Is she recovered?' I looked along the table, confirming that Constanza was not present.

Diamante began to protest but checked herself. 'It was only the rheum. She is much better and will not require your services, Messer physician. Would you reach me the platter of figs?' She pressed against me as if to demonstrate that she could not reach the dish herself and I forced myself not to cringe while I handed her the fruit and she simpered thanks. 'You deserve a reward for your courtesy, Doctor Somers. Here, open your mouth.'

Deeply embarrassed, I allowed her to place a fig between my teeth as Iacopo capered to my side. 'See here,' he carolled loudly, 'the physician is taking his medicine.

What will you give the lady in return? What prescription will satisfy her itch?'

Apparently unconcerned by his lewd gesture, Diamante gurgled with pleasure and snuggled up to my shoulder, while I became aware of Sandrino grinning broadly and Bernardino Biagio glaring.

*****

I encountered Constanza later that day on the narrow landing, near her mistress's bedroom. She was carrying three of Signora Orsola's dresses and a swatch of coloured ribbons, together with a reticule made of net containing sewing threads, and she stood back against the wall so that her encumbrances should not impede my passage. It was not the most convenient of places to meet but I welcomed the opportunity to speak to her alone.

'May I help you carry anything? You are laden.'

'Thank you but I can manage. I am taking my needlework to the hall where the light is stronger at this time of day.'

'Are you feeling better? I heard you were unwell while you were away from Verona.'

I detected momentary alarm in her eyes but she quickly controlled it. 'It was nothing. I wrenched my shoulder and it was painful but I needed only a few days' rest to recover.'

I nodded solemnly, while reflecting that if this had been an ailment of convenience, it had been badly contrived, unless she had suffered a surfeit of plums, the rheum and a wrenched shoulder in rapid succession. Moreover she had not mentioned it in our brief conversation on her return when she spoke of her bad back. 'I'm sorry to hear about it. You must take care not to aggravate it; but the balsam may ease your shoulder as well as your spine. Was it a disappointment to you, to miss visiting Venice?'

130

She hugged her burden to her chest and bit her lip. 'Not especially. I am familiar with the city.'

'And of course you know the Signora's brother. I have learned a little of his unfortunate history.'

The colour left her cheeks but again she seemed to master whatever caused her distress. 'His alleged treachery at the time of the uprising? It's an embarrassment to the Signora and I cannot forgive him for causing her pain. Excuse me: I must attend to my duties while the sunlight holds.'

I stepped aside to let her pass but one billowing dress in her arms caught against the newel post and, with a worried gasp, she leaned down to free it without damaging the material. As she did so the swatch of ribbons slipped from her hand and spread itself in a semicircle at her feet, like a depiction of the sun's multi-coloured rays in a painting. I moved to retrieve the fallen braids but she thrust the gowns into my arms and bent down awkwardly, supporting her belly with one hand, in order to lift and brush the swatch free of dust and tangles. It was quickly done; then she took the dresses from my grasp with a grateful nod and scurried to the stairs.

As I watched her scuttle down the staircase, I mused that none of the Signora's senior attendants felt much sympathy for Guglielmo Guarienti but only Bernardino Biagio might gain monetary advantage from his master's absence. Even so, the evidence was vague and I was no nearer determining whether anyone in the household had betrayed him. At any rate, Constanza seemed no longer impeded by her back, shoulder, stomach or nasal tubes.

*****

In the days which followed I questioned other members of the household, including the taciturn Alessandro, but learned nothing of significance to assist me in my search and I began to fear I would fail in my task. It came as a relief when Rendell brought me an invitation from Captain Alberto for us to meet the following day, so that he could show me parts of the city I had not yet visited. I readily accepted the chance to escape from the Casa delle Arche and was unconcerned by the dank, dull weather when I met him by the fountain in Verona's Piazza delle Erbe, a wide marketplace like the one of the same name in Padua. We stopped for a stoup of wine at a nearby hostelry and agreed on a route to take in some of the sights which he recommended and I had not seen. Alberto showed an unexpected appreciation of artistry, especially the wealth of frescoes and carvings in various churches, which I found somewhat overwhelming. He reeled off information about named masters and unrecorded painters in such numbers I could not hope to remember them, but I relished the freedom to explore Verona and concentrate on matters unconnected with the Schioppa and Guarienti. Early in our tour my heavy mood lifted when Alberto pointed out an impressive hanging tomb inside the upper church dedicated to San Fermo and I exclaimed in amazement as I read the inscription.

'I thought only great rulers and soldiers were honoured with such memorials – like the Scaligeri tombs. Was – what's his name – Aventino Frascatoro – really a medical man? I've never seen a physician with such a magnificent monument. I can't believe he was so esteemed.'

Alberto punched my shoulder playfully. 'Verona's a good place to practice medicine. They'll recognise your worth when you're dead.'

'That's very cheering!'

'Wait until we get to San Pietro Martire so I can prove my point. You'll see another fine funerary record there. It may even make you laugh.'

We visited so many other buildings and shared such enjoyable good humour, that I forgot this promise and

Alberto insisted we keep until last the basilica of Sant'Anastasia, which he believed to be the finest in the city. Nevertheless, as we approached that superb edifice, he drew me aside to see the little church of San Pietro nearby and he pointed up to a carving on the outside wall. 'This is the funerary urn of another admired physician and there he is in stone, lecturing to his students.'

I stared in delight at the solemn face of the lecturer and the riveted gaze in the eyes of some in his audience but I grinned at the expressions of others whose thoughts were clearly distracted, far away in day dreams. 'I've seen such faces when my old Professor was lecturing. Not everyone concentrated on his wise teaching. What do you think that fellow in the middle was contemplating when the sculptor captured his abstracted look: shortage of cash, what his next meal would be or his mistress's sleek thighs?'

Alberto laughed heartily. 'The same set of choices any soldier would dream about. What pathetic creatures men are!' His mouth straightened as he spoke in a more serious tone. 'Have you encountered any pleasing female company in Verona yet?'

'I haven't looked for it. There's none I'd care to pursue in the Signora's house.'

'I didn't necessarily mean carnal pleasure although that's not excluded,' he said with a wink. 'Gentle charms have their own delight.' Then he took my arm and drew me towards the imposing façade of Sant'Anastasia. 'The church is old but work is always going on inside and I think the newest fresco is the fairest I've ever seen. Its conception is so original and its execution marvellous.'

I did not know Alberto well enough to tease him on his unsoldierly appreciation of art but it endeared him to me and I followed him into the vast basilica and along its nave. We passed red marble columns, richly carved altarpieces in side chapels lining the aisle and multi-coloured terracotta tiles decorating the walls. There was no doubt of the fine workmanship my companion admired. Then, suddenly I stopped, speechless with disbelief and embarrassment, staring where Alberto's extended arm was, quite unnecessarily, pointing upwards to the arch spanning the south aisle beside the chancel.

'Isn't it glorious? It was only completed a few years ago. Have you ever seen such painting? It's so real you could slap the horse on its flank and expect it to trot, while the elaborate gilding would make a goldsmith proud. Messer Pisanello spent several years on the work when he returned from Rome. The subject is Saint George in Trebizond. The dragon's over there, you see, on the other side of the arch, and the knight's just setting off to cross the water and kill it. Isn't it remarkable to show his stallion with its back end to the viewer, so unusual? And that's real lapis lazuli the artist's used to make the sky so blue.'

'The woman?' Despite myself, my voice sounded reedy and I could only manage to speak the two words.

'The princess. She's come to see her rescuer off across the sea to destroy the murderous beast. Look at the gleaming metalwork on her robe. Magnificent!'

I gulped. 'Would the artist have used a model for the lady?'

Alberto pursed his lips. 'Fancy her, do you? She may have been a real woman. Painters often use whores to act as models. It's clever how she's half-turned, only showing her face in profile. She's not the main player in the scene, of course. Saint George, with his golden hair and armour, is the centrepiece. And see how well Pisanello has caught the line of the hound beside the knight. He's taut with quivering anticipation, all alive, unlike those poor, slaughtered creatures over there, at the entrance to the dragon's cave.'

Alberto burbled on but I had ceased to listen, as I stared more intently at the gold braiding on the princess's turbaned headdress, the brocade of her sleeveless upper-garment and, above all, the purity of her lovely profile.

Without a doubt it was the woman I had glimpsed in the Casa delle Arche, the woman Sandrino said did not exist. I had wondered then if she might be a courtesan who served the steward's lust and, from what Alberto told me that might be true, but her bearing was so regal it was difficult to believe. I didn't want to believe it but, more importantly, in that moment of shattering, terrifying revelation, I knew I could be certain she was a real, living woman, not an imaginary paragon. I knew also, against all common sense, that I would not be at peace until I had found her.

Chapter 10

The incarnation of Messer Pisanello's princess continued to
haunt my mind and she was there in powerful recollection, a
few days' later, when I crossed the courtyard, passing close
to the concealed doorway where I had seen the strange lady
during Signora Orsola's absence. I had been across to the
kitchen to attend to a scullion, who had scalded his arm, and
was carrying a bundle of surplus bandages, but I was not
alert enough to notice the large slick of oozing material on
the threshold of the entrance to main part of the house,
where I was bound. I would undoubtedly have skidded on
the greasy surface myself if the person throwing open the
door from the inside had not reached it first. With a flurry of
disordered shirts and a terrified shriek, Diamante lost her
footing and sat forcefully on the doorstep in a pool of
glutinous jelly.

'Are you injured?' I called as I ran forward. 'Don't try
to get up for a moment. We need to be sure no bones are
broken.'

'My dress is ruined,' the lady wailed. 'It's covered in
this sticky mess.'

'If you think it's nothing worse than bruises, give me
your hand and I'll help you up. Step forward beyond the
puddle.'

She winced as she stood but was able to draw herself
to her full height. 'I'm only bruised, I think. I will have
Iacopo thrashed for this.'

At that moment a crestfallen little fellow emerged
from the shadows. 'It wasn't meant for you, sweet lady. A
thousand apologies. I was waiting for the physician here.
How was I to know you would come first and slip with such
aplomb? I merely aimed to entrammel the doctor's feet in
the gluey stuff. I got it from the stableman. He has it to shine
the harnesses.'

Diamante snorted indignantly and removed her soft shoes in order to step back into the building, across the obstacle. 'I shall report you to the Signora. You go too far.'

'That was a dangerous prank,' I said as she departed. 'You're lucky she isn't seriously hurt. You'd better get hot water and clean the step before anyone else comes to grief. Bring a broom and I'll help you.'

At first we scrubbed the flagstone in silence but after a while Iacopo winked at me. 'You're not a bad sort, Doctor Somers. Have you found the one you're looking for yet?'

I hesitated in my brushing, dreading that he had somehow discovered my guilty desire for the nameless model in Pisanello's fresco. 'What do you mean?'

'Madonna Orsola believes she is harbouring a traitor, doesn't she?'

I swallowed with relief. 'Do you think it likely?'

'I wouldn't call it treachery to ensure a villain gets his desserts. More power to his elbow, I say – if there is such a person.'

'No one has much regard for your old master but there must be a stronger reason for betrayal than dislike.'

Iacopo emptied the remaining water in his bucket over the step. 'She's a wise woman to have sought your help. You won't be satisfied with the obvious.' I detected a sneer in his voice.

'And what is the obvious?'

'Whatever causes hatred – jealousy, lust, revenge, acquisitiveness, rarely finer instincts. Lawyers are grasping scum. Young and old. Still, it's hardly a matter of great importance that you're called on to investigate. You've no body with a knife through its heart laid at your feet.' He picked up the brushes and marched away, whistling.

*****

Alberto had suggested that I accompany him to Mass on the forthcoming Sunday at the church of San Lorenzo, which had not been on the route of our earlier tour, and once again I was pleased to escape from the Casa delle Arche. It was a pleasant enough small church, its exterior banded with courses of red brick, stone blocks and cobbles, and it had an unusual round tower at its south-west corner, but I could not determine what was so remarkable about it that my artistic friend should insist I visit. Inside it had high columns, similarly striped in red and white, but its decorations were ordinary and it lacked the frescoed magnificence of other churches we had seen. I did not notice the gallery above the west end of the nave until Alberto looked quickly over his shoulder and whispered to me.

'Do you see the matroneo, where the women sit? There are stairs in the tower leading to it. We shall wait at the doorway after the service. There's someone I should like you to meet.'

I opened my mouth to ask an excited question but the crucifer was leading in the procession of priests and acolytes so I kept silence but I could not pay attention to the liturgy. I trembled at the idea that Alberto had tracked down the nameless beauty who had captivated me and, hidden among the women in the crowded gallery, might be Pisanello's princess, a whore no doubt, but one whose favours I desired passionately. The very thought of meeting her made my manhood rise and I drew my gown about me carefully as we stood at the foot of the tower, watching the women emerge, growing every moment more nervous with expectation. Then Alberto moved forward and greeted a pretty, modest young woman dressed in widow's garb.

'Margherita, this is the English physician I mentioned, Doctor Somers. Harry, this is my sister, Madonna Fratta. She has invited us to eat at her house, across the road there.'

138

I struggled to hide my disappointment and to behave courteously, as we crossed to an elegant, narrow-fronted mansion, but soon realised it was no hardship to accept the widow's hospitality as she was both charming and intelligent. When we were seated in her comfortable solar and she had removed her hooded mantle, I saw a slight, shapely figure and a pair of bright mischievous eyes which reminded me, with a guilty pang, of my dear Bess. I learned she had been married to a merchant haberdasher, an older man, and widowed eighteen months previously, but she spoke of her late husband with obvious affection. She had an easy, teasing relationship with her brother and, while a serving man brought in the victuals, they had me rocking with laughter.

'Margherita lives here in spacious magnificence, as you can see,' Alberto said. 'I could billet half my company in this house.'

'Yet you oppose me taking lodgers. I'm sure some indigent gentlewomen would welcome sharing my accommodation.'

'They'd sponge on your generosity and prove unpleasant parasites. You always were too open-handed to the untrustworthy. Remember that urchin who made off with your purse when you stopped to give him bread?'

Madonna Fratta smiled sweetly as she turned to me. 'Alberto was such an unkind, rascally boy,' she said conspiratorially. 'He would balance on the parapet of the stone bridge above the Adige, when the river was in torrent, and then drop down to hang by his hands over the swirling water. It always gave my mother a fright but I would say to her, push him off and let him fall: he'll cry for help soon enough.'

'No wonder Rendell reveres the captain! My servant is cut from the same cloth and yearns for adventure. Alberto is training him to be a soldier.'

139

She giggled. 'Oh, I've heard about the redoubtable rescuer of cats from the tops of towers. But he cannot be as tiresome as this wretch was to his older sister.'

'Rendell has an older sister too.' I paused, remembering lively Grizel in Duke Humphrey's palace at Greenwich. 'She is married to my friend, Thomas, far away in England.'

'You miss your country and your friends.' It was statement not a question and her tone was compassionate.

'I do but there's so much of interest and such demands on my time here, I can't indulge nostalgia for long.'

Alberto tore a strip of flesh from the succulent capon in front of him. 'We're doing our best to ensure Verona works its magic upon Doctor Somers and binds him to us.'

'Yet he will not forget those he has left. Do your parents live?'

'My mother was well when last I heard. My father died when I was a lad.'

'You have no wife?' I saw Alberto's rapid glance at his sister as I shook my head but, unconcerned, she fingered the stem of her wineglass. 'Nevertheless, you have left someone dear to you, I suspect.'

'I have but nearly two years have passed since I left London and I receive little news.'

I faltered, unwilling to be drawn too far into the realm of reminiscence, and Margherita Fratta seemed to understand. 'Signora Schioppa's household makes many demands on you, I expect,' she said gently. 'You know of course that her steward is our uncle? If our father had lived we would have been even more closely bound to the Casa delle Arche.' Alberto coughed but she flapped her hand at him to wave aside his concern. 'I'm sure a physician needs to know all the underlying passions of the folk he cares for. That sad scarecrow, Diamante, was to have become our step-mother but was denied by a Gonzaga sword in the uprising. She would have cared well for our father, in gratitude for him taking her to wife when she was past her prime and shunned by others, and at his time of life he was content with her devotion.'

I must have looked surprised and Alberto shrugged. 'Sandrino says that when our father was killed demons took possession of Diamante's wits.'

'Such things can occur. It could account for her eccentric behaviour.'

My mind was racing, as I realised how antagonistic the poor woman must be to the house of Gonzaga and their alleged supporters, such as Guglielmo Guarienti, but then Madonna Fratta added to my distraction. 'If the marriage had taken place before father was killed, she would now have the status of a respected widow. That grasping notary delayed matters while he settled the contract to his own advantage.'

'Bernardino Biagio?'

'No. It was beneath his dignity to tangle with such a petty matter. His nephew, Alessandro dealt with it – or, rather, he didn't. He was angling for an increase in fees by prolonging the business. A greedy fellow, he seemed.'

Iacopo's words came back to me, when he castigated all lawyers, young and old, and I wondered if I had missed an implication. Perhaps I had too readily dismissed the younger man from consideration in my enquiries and I determined to question Alessandro in more detail about his dealings with Guglielmo Guarienti. This train of thought reminded me that I had been absent from the Casa delle Arche for some hours, without advising anyone I would miss the midday meal, but I was reluctant to leave my delightful hostess and her brother. Our pleasant discourse was brought to an end not on my account but by the arrival of a messenger with a sealed note for Alberto. When he read it he whistled and put the paper down on the table, pushing back his chair.

'You must excuse me, Margherita. I am needed in the Cittadella in case orders come through from headquarters. There is news from Mantua. The Marquis Gianfrancesco Gonzaga is ill and it is believed to be serious.'

'Does that affect us in Verona?' I asked.

'It remains to be seen. If he dies his son, Ludovico, will be proclaimed his successor and he has been no friend to us in the past. He was fighting for the Visconti of Milan while his father still pretended to support Venice. Mantua has suffered for its allegiances and what Ludovico will inherit is a poor shadow of the City's former power but we need to watch the position there carefully.'

I left with Alberto and quickly put the affairs of Mantua from my head. What I reflected on, while I trudged back towards the Piazza delle Erbe, was that I had not felt so contented or enjoyed such honest, entertaining company since I arrived in Verona.

*****

As I hurried into the piazza I realised that a figure in front of me, dawdling his way in the same direction, was none other than Alessandro and this fortuitous opportunity seemed too good to miss. I increased my pace, battling a way through the crowded marketplace, and caught up with him before he turned off into the network of smaller streets leading to the Casa delle Arche. When I drew level, I hailed him but I had no intention of making him jump in the way he did, as if I was a ne'er-do-well wielding a dagger. An official wearing the lion of Venice was coming from the opposite direction and I guessed he had been delivering messages to Signora Orsola from her daughter and son-in-law. Alessandro flinched as the man passed us, clasping his hands to his chest, and it took him a moment to calm his breathing while I made apology for alarming him.

'Sorry! I thought I recognised it was you I was following.'

'You followed me?' He was trembling but he sounded angry.

'Not intentionally. I'm returning from visiting friends near the church of San Lorenzo. I only spotted you as you came to the piazza.'

He gave a weak smile. 'Ah! I see. I've been out to the Borgo San Zeno. I go to Mass there most Sundays.'

I nearly referred to Sandrino's family living in that district but remembered in time that I was not supposed to know of their existence – and perhaps Alessandro was unaware of them. 'I haven't visited that great church yet. I've seen its fine tower from the riverside.'

Alessandro shuffled his feet. 'My brother is a priest and I visit him,' he said. He sounded wary but there was a hint of smugness in his tone.

I wanted to encourage him to speak more freely and it seemed best to change the subject, so I mentioned the news which had come of the Marquis of Mantua's illness. I hadn't expected him to react particularly to this information and I was surprised to see his mouth clamped shut as if he was unwilling to comment. I concluded that as a conscientious young lawyer he thought it injudicious to observe on such a matter. Thwarted in this attempt to draw him out I decided to risk a more pointed enquiry.

'Your name was mentioned over our meal. Captain Alberto and his sister, Madonna Fratta, were telling me of the misfortune which befell Diamante when their father was killed.'

A vein was throbbing at his temple and, although he clutched his gown tightly, Alessandro's hand twitched. 'A sad business indeed. We don't speak of it in the Signora's house. Diamante has never recovered from her loss.'

'I understand.' I paused and took a deep breath. 'I've been learning other things about the household and the

Signora's family. Did you know her brother when he was in Verona?'

He gave me a sideways look. 'Of course. My uncle and I handled his affairs – we still do.'

'That must give you a great deal of paperwork. I've heard rumours he was difficult to work for.'

Alessandro stood still. The blood had drained from his naturally insipid face. 'What do you mean? What paperwork? Who has told you such a thing? Some say he is a badly misused gentleman and we should disregard malicious gossip.'

'I'll be happy to do so. I'm simply piecing together a picture of the Signora's family. I had the honour of meeting her daughter when I was in Padua.'

A little colour came into his cheeks. 'Signora Carlotta Capello is a most gracious lady. If you found favour in her eyes, it is much to your credit. Was that how Signora Orsola came to know you?'

I confirmed that it was and intended to follow up this promising thaw in his reserve but, as we rounded the corner by the Scaligeri tombs, a youth hurtled towards us, shouting my name.

'Thank Christ you're back! We didn't know where you were and he's going on something terrible.'

I grabbed Rendell by the shoulders and forced him stop dancing about in front of me.

'Who? What are you talking about?'

'Mister du Bois. Your mate, the randy apothecary.'

'Geoffrey's here?' I ran forward to the entrance of the house, with Rendell scampering beside me, and to my shame I thought that my friend's precipitate marriage had proved a disaster, causing him to abandon his new wife. Only when I crossed the threshold and saw him hobbling towards me, did I appreciate that he was injured and in deep distress. One side of his face bore scorch marks, his left arm was strapped across his chest and he leaned on a heavy stick,

144

dragging his right leg. I held out my arms to embrace him. 'Dear God, Geoffrey, what has happened?'

'We're ruined, Harry. We've lost everything. We only escaped with our lives because the baby woke and cried before the smoke enveloped us.'

I gripped his upper arms for he seemed in danger of falling. 'Your wife is safe?'

'And little Giorgio: terrified and destitute, but safe. They are following more slowly in a wagon. Leone is with them. He insisted on coming though I can't provide for him. Antonia's maid refused to leave Padua and, with our predicament, she couldn't be greatly blamed. I rode on ahead to see if I could find shelter for my wretched family. They will be in Verona tomorrow. At least the villain failed to kill us.'

'Someone intentionally fired the shop?'

Geoffrey pulled away from my grasp, leaning on his stick. 'Pierpaolo has done all he could to harm our trade and undermine our standing in Padua but he didn't succeed. It would have been galling for him to see our business prosper, so it's obvious where to place the blame when flaming, oily rags are flung through a broken shutter at dead of night. He'd know there's much in an apothecary's shop that's flammable and the fire took hold in seconds. Glass shattered in the heat while liquids sizzled and powders blazed. I doused a blanket in water and flung it over Antonia and the baby. It saved them from the worst. We had to run through the flames to get out.'

'Holy Virgin! But is there proof against Pierpaolo?'

'Of course not. You may be sure no one saw anything. It was all a dreadful accident. We are held guilty of carelessness, failing to cover the embers of our fire properly when we went to bed. Pierpaolo has asked the magistrates to have me arrested for endangering the lives of his beloved step-mother and little brother. Vile hypocrisy. We couldn't stay in Padua. We have nothing. He has won.'

Geoffrey began to totter and suddenly Sandrino was beside us, helping him to a stool which Iacopo had carried from the gatekeeper's lodge. I became aware of half a dozen whispering onlookers clustered across the courtyard and Constanza squeaking that the unfortunate victim must be the apothecary who mixed her precious balsam. Then the ranks of attendants parted and, from their midst, Signora Orsola sailed forward, with Bernardino Biagio at her elbow.

'No more! The poor man is half-dead from exhaustion. Doctor Somers: you will cease to interrogate him and dress his wounds. Constanza: have rooms prepared to accommodate the apothecary's wife and child. We shall grant them a resting place. Sandrino: send a man to await the poor woman at the city gate and escort her here. I am appalled to hear of such villainy.'

I smiled in relief at the indomitable lady and took a step to follow Geoffrey into the house but she grasped my sleeve. 'Who is this Pierpaolo?' she asked.

'The adult son of an apothecary, the late Giorgio Clemente, and his first wife who died years ago. Messer du Bois has married Giorgio's young widow and taken care of her infant son, Pierpaolo's half-brother. Giorgio bequeathed my friend his business, quite lawfully. Pierpaolo tried but failed to challenge the will and believes he has been cheated of part of his inheritance.'

'Pierpaolo is also an apothecary?'

'No. He attends the university at Bologna. He studies to become a lawyer.'

'Hah!' The Signora's eyes flashed as she swung round to address Messer Biagio. 'Bernardino, have the facts checked. If what is alleged seems credible, that unworthy villain must never wear a notary's gown. Destroy him. See to it, my good man. Diamante, the poor woman will need a change of clothes. Look out one of my older gowns which will serve a turn for her. Come, come, physician, your services are required without delay.'

146

When I reached the pallet where they had laid Geoffrey, Signora Orsola could still be heard outside the room issuing orders. Despite the pain he was in, my friend smiled as I crouched beside him. 'She's a rare martinet, the lady of the house. She has you all under her thumb, I'm thinking.'

'You never spoke a truer word,' I said as I stripped the hose from his suppurating leg. 'But you seem to have won her good opinion and are in no position to complain.'

Geoffrey closed his eyes as I started to scrape the wound clean with my knife. 'God bless you, Harry. I had nowhere else to turn.'

Chapter 11

The household was in turmoil for the rest of the day and it completely escaped my notice that Alessandro was not present when the menfolk assembled for a draught of wine before retiring, as was their custom. It was not until next morning, after I had satisfied myself that Geoffrey was making progress and not feverish, that I encountered Bernardino, looking even more trouble-worn than usual, and he asked me if I had seen his nephew since the previous morning.

'I came back to the house with him in the afternoon, just after Messer du Bois arrived. We met as we were crossing the Piazza delle Erbe.'

'I never saw him. He's not in the house now and his bed has not been slept in. It's a damnable nuisance. I wish him to go to Padua to pursue the enquiries Signora Orsola has ordered.'

'Sandrino has arranged an escort to meet Madonna du Bois on the highway from Padua. Perhaps Alessandro went with them.' I felt sorry for the young man always at his uncle's beck and call.

Bernardino ran his tongue across his lower lip. 'Perhaps you are right. I will enquire.'

He nodded and hurried away as Rendell emerged from a doorway, tapping his nose. 'Naughty nephew, absent without permission, eh! He never came into the house yesterday, you know.'

'What do you mean? He was with me when you ran up to us in the street.'

'Right enough but he never followed us past the entrance. He must have heard the commotion going on in the courtyard and I guess he had better things to do than get caught up with it.'

I shrugged. 'He seemed quite jumpy when I spoke to him.' The bells of the Lamberti Tower had begun to ring the hour and I realised it was already ten o'clock. 'Why aren't you in the Cittadella, wielding your sword and learning to be a warrior?'

'Mucking out the stables, more like. Sandrino got his nephew to send an armed escort to meet Madonna Antonia and Captain Alberto decided to go himself. He gave us lads the morning off. He thought he'd return around noon so we're to reassemble then.'

'I'll walk down to the city gate by the castle to meet them. Leone's with her and he's the captain's cousin but Madonna Antonia won't know anyone here and she must be anxious about Geoffrey. Come with me.'

'Still got a soft spot for the apothecary's widow or the new apothecary's wife, should I say? Reckon you're in the wrong profession, physician. She likes their lusty potions better than your arid book-learning.'

I cuffed his head lightly. 'You're spending too much time listening to Iacopo's vulgar wit.'

'Christ's blood, I could teach him a thing or two! Did you know he had Diamante over in the hay store last night? One of the scullions saw them at it. Can you imagine their coupling? Grotesque!'

'I doubt it took place. All scullions are scurrilous liars.'

'Hey! I was a scullion.'

'Exactly.' He dodged my raised arm but trotted by my side as we left the house. I did not choose to pursue his distasteful line of speculation but I felt momentarily sorry for that wretched, lonely serving woman.

*****

As I had planned, we reached the gate long before Antonia's party was due to arrive, and to Rendell's surprise I suggested that we proceed into the Borgo beyond the walls and visit the basilica of San Zeno. I could not ignore the extraordinary bronzes on the great west door and studied with fascination the various panels depicting the saint's life and other less identifiable scenes, but on this occasion I had not come to enjoy the artistic treasures of the church. Instead I greeted one of the Benedictine monks leaving the portal and enquired if he knew where I might find the priest who was Alessandro's brother.

'This is a monastic church,' he said. 'Built on the burial place of our revered saint who watches over the city's fortunes. The priest you want does not serve here.' He turned to re-enter the church and flung open the door.

'His brother told me he was a priest at San Zeno.'

'Enquire at the minor church of San Zeno Orador along the quayside,' he snarled and slammed the door shut in my face.

'I'd guess he don't like this bloke you're looking for.' Rendell cocked his head and winked. 'He knew who you was talking about though, I could tell.'

We retraced our steps to find the little church near the city gate, across the way from the castle which guarded entry to the city and the bridge over the river. I was pleased to encounter the sacristan sweeping the nave and I made the same enquiry of him. His reply was more accommodating but it puzzled me.

'Father Mario certainly serves this church but he isn't here. He left at daybreak on some urgent business. I expect him to return tomorrow.'

'Do you happen to know if his brother Alessandro was with him?'

Unkempt eyebrows shot up into the man's narrow forehead. 'Father Mario left alone. His brother was here yesterday. He usually comes to Mass on Sundays. Now I remember he came back in the afternoon. That was unusual. He must have forgotten something. But he was gone at dusk. I saw him walking towards the gate. Quite misty it was.'

'Did Father Mario seem disturbed after his brother's visit?'

'I couldn't say. Why should he? He spoke his evening office and retired as usual. He didn't tell me he'd be absent until this morning. Before you ask, I've no idea where he's gone. He does pay visits away from the city from time to time. I'm not privy to his business.'

'Do they – the brothers – have family they might visit?'

'Only an uncle, the notary Alessandro serves. That's all I know. Excuse me.'

I let him go with thanks for his help while Rendell looked up at me quizzically. 'What's all this about, doctor?'

'I don't know but I have an uncomfortable feeling something isn't right.'

'God help us and keep us safe from Somers intuition,' he intoned.

*****

It had started to rain heavily when we left the church but we were not allowed to shelter in the gatehouse as the guards said we would impede travellers entering Verona. A contingent of Venetian troops had taken up positions outside the guardroom, in addition to the normal custodians, and it looked as if extra precautions had been put in place to control entry to the city, perhaps because of uncertainty about the situation in Mantua where the Marquis was said to be dangerously ill. We wandered onto the bridge and peered down into the leaden water surging over the stone bases of the castellated towers which supported the huge structure. The level was so high the archways on each side could accommodate only the flattest of boats beneath them, but this was a situation familiar to those using the river and, through the vaulted central arch, a string of barges was bringing timber from the forests in the hills.

My hood had become saturated and I dragged Rendell back to the gate, ready for a confrontation with the surly sentinels, but to my delight I spotted Alberto riding imperiously towards us with a bedraggled lady seated behind him, clinging to his waist. After them trotted the escort and the trundling wagon in which Leone, an improbable and unhappy-looking nursemaid, sat clutching an irritable infant who struggled and screamed.

Madonna Antonia looked up as I hailed them and it was pleasing to see the smile of relief she gave me. 'Doctor Somers! Oh, I am so glad you are here? How is Geoffrey?'

'He's recovering well and needs only a little rest to make him whole again. Did the captain tell you Signora Orsola has offered you shelter?'

'Indeed, he did. I shall be mightily embarrassed to intrude on the great lady's household. I know of her, of course, from her visits to the Capello tower. She is so kind – but her intervention is due to you, I'm sure, our true friend.'

Tears were streaming down her cheeks and she began to sob while the formalities were completed and the guards waved her small entourage through the gate. Alberto slowed his horse to a walk, so I could shuffle along beside them, and he leaned over to speak in my ear.

'She needs time to rest and compose herself. She's grimy from the journey and distressed, as you can see. I propose we stop at my sister's house so she can prepare herself for the entry to the Casa delle Arche.'

It was an excellent idea and I was sure Madonna Fratta would make Antonia welcome and soothe her anxieties. It seemed her brother had already sent warning of the impending visit and Margherita was duly waiting on the threshold, full of gracious concern to put her guest at ease. She sent her woman to help Antonia bathe and find her a fresh gown and she summoned another maid to relieve

Leone of his squalling burden. Looking uncomfortable in the midst of this female activity, Alberto decided he had fulfilled his duty and suggested that he and Rendell might depart to the Cittadella, leaving me to escort Geoffrey's family the rest of the way. I was quite content with this arrangement and, when Antonia reappeared, clad in a simple but spotless dress, with her hair coiled under a pristine veil, she smiled brilliantly and expressed her gratitude to everyone, but especially and unjustly, to me.

'I know it is all due to you, dear Harry,' she said. 'Geoffrey was certain you would stand beside us in our hour of need.'

Inevitably I flushed with pleasure at her undeserved words and I noticed Margherita Fratta standing rigidly upright as she looked from one to the other of us. She seemed to become more abrupt in manner and sent orders for the men of the escort, who had been given refreshment in the kitchen, to rouse themselves and be ready to set off again. Leone drew me outside to inspect the horse which had been provided for me, with Antonia riding pillion, and he winked at me in a way that reminded me uncomfortably of Rendell.

'My cousin didn't like Madonna du Bois calling you by your baptismal name.'

I stared at him until I remembered that Leone was mother's sister's son to Alberto and Margherita but I was still mystified by his meaning. 'Why should Madonna Fratta be concerned by that?'

'Oh, Doctor Somers, you are innocent in the ways of women. My cousin, the winsome haberdasher's widow, has her eye on you, I'm thinking. She doesn't approve of you flirting with a married woman, who is not her.'

I insisted the lad's fancy was rubbish but I was startled by the notion and, as I conveyed Geoffrey's wife to join her husband, I began to wonder if there was truth in his idea and, if there was, how I should respond. I recalled that,

153

when we first met, Margherita had made me think of Bess, which was much in her favour, and there was no doubt she was attractive. She was a respectable widow, not to be trifled with without serious intent, but she was real and close at hand. She was neither the nameless courtesan of my tumescent dreams, nor the beloved maiden I had not seen for two years, in a land far away. Nor, indeed, was she Giovanna Lendro, who I had nearly forgotten but to whom, presumably, I was still formally betrothed.

*****

Once Antonia had been made welcome and re-united with her husband, Sandrino drew me aside and offered me a glass of wine which I gratefully accepted, for the sake of its warming properties, as I was chilled from my soaking. I enquired if Alessandro had returned.

'No and Bernardino Biagio is furious. His nephew was due to travel to Padua to complete the revocation of your marriage contract – damn fool that you were, to bind yourself to a silly girl with no significant dowry. Signora Orsola is so indignant about your friend's plight that she has insisted the journey take place at once, so that action can be initiated against this Pierpaolo Clemente at the same time. Because Alessandro is nowhere to be found, Bernardino has had to go himself and he's not pleased to be on horseback in this weather.'

'Oh dear, I'm glad his mission is not solely on my account. But where do you think Alessandro is? Has he gone missing before?'

'Never. But he's a strange fellow, doesn't chat freely with anyone as far as I know. Perhaps he's got himself a doxy and is infatuated with her charms. He risks a beating from his uncle when he does return.'

I shrugged and changed the subject. For no real reason I felt uncomfortable about the young lawyer's disappearance, fearing that something in our conversation the previous day had led him to behave in this unaccountable way. Later I went over in my mind what we had talked about, remembering that he had seemed edgy, but I could not identify what we had said which might have disturbed him. I concluded it was at least equally likely that, while we walked together, he had thought of something he had forgotten to say to his brother and this explained his return to San Zeno Orador. Whether there was a link with Father Mario's subsequent and unaccompanied departure from his church, I had no idea, but if it related to some matter of interest to the pair of them, they might well have arranged a rendezvous. The theory was feasible but it did not satisfy me.

*****

The Signora seemed to enjoy the role she had assumed, as benefactress to my homeless friends, and she had already instructed Sandrino to make enquiries as to whether an apothecary's shop in the city was vacant or expected to become so shortly. Geoffrey and Antonia, although still weary after their ordeal, were cheered by the prospect of starting a new life, free from Pierpaolo's hostility, and almost everyone in the house appeared delighted to be assisting the agreeable couple. Little Giorgio, however, did not settle in his new surroundings so easily and continued noisily fractious. A baby's loud wailing was an unfamiliar disturbance in the Casa delle Arche and, although most members of the household, tolerated it, Constanza seemed to find it particularly distressing. I fashioned for her use two plugs of felt which she could insert into her ears, in an attempt to ensure she would get to sleep, and next morning she told me the devices had proved successful.

At first light I had been summoned to see the Signora and discovered that, while she continued to seek a resolution of her guests' difficulties, she had business of her own which needed attention. 'It is necessary for me to visit a property outside the city once again,' she said. 'I shall depart tomorrow and I have decided you should accompany me, Doctor Somers. We shall be away for two or three nights and it will give you an opportunity to meet the servants at the estate. I'm sure they will regale you with details of their ailments so you had best bring a selection of your potions and liniments. I shall take only a small escort, with Diamante to attend me. Sandrino will pursue the interests of your friends while we are absent. Speak to the stableman and he will provide a packhorse for your baggage.'

I retired from my audience breathless from the lady's energy and pleased at the chance to travel outside Verona, but as soon as I started to descend the stairs from her room I heard loud voices in the courtyard. I continued down to the ground floor to see what was happening and was startled to recognize, from their livery, three men of the Communal Guard standing over a muddy bundle on the ground. Sandrino and Iacopo were crouched beside it, peering at its contents, but as soon as he saw me the jester broke away from the group and bounded to my side.

'There's no knife through his heart but you have your body now, physician. Prescient, wasn't I, to mention a body? Can you identify the assassin? All his legal arguments couldn't save him from a vagabond's attack.'

Dropping to my knees by the corpse, still wrapped in the sodden sack which had concealed him, I confirmed that it was indeed the wretched Alessandro. I concluded that he had been dead and under water for perhaps twenty-four hours. His face was marked, presumably by flotsam it had crashed against, and one of his arms was broken in two places. I looked up at the guards. 'Where was he found?'

'Caught against the stanchions of the old stone bridge in the centre of the city. He'd been carried down the river with a couple of uprooted trees loosened by the downpour. Probably he was thrown over the parapet of the castle bridge. That's what usually happens when the cut-purses kill their prey.'

I shuddered at the man's casual manner. It was all too likely that villains would dispose of their victims in the waters of the Adige; I had nearly suffered a similar fate once, in the flowing tide of the River Thames. I drew back the sack to disclose more of the body. 'He's been robbed, I suppose? There's no purse on his belt. Did he wear a ring?'

Sandrino nodded. 'A simple signet. That's gone too, has it? His fingers are bare.'

I rolled down the neck of Alessandro's jerkin which had ridden up, under his gown, and I examined his throat, trying hard to keep my detachment. Then I shook my head. 'He was throttled. See the marks here – a knotted rope was used, I should think. Poor fellow. But he was probably already dead when he was put in the sack.'

Sandrino rose and took charge of the situation, issuing orders for care of the body, instructing a man to ride after Messer Biagio to tell him of his nephew's fate and then striding off to inform his mistress of the calamity. The guards were directed to the kitchen for refreshment before they resumed their duties and I was left alone with Iacopo.

'I would not consider that Alessandro offered an attractive proposition for a thief intent on enrichment.' The dwarf compressed his lips. 'Was it that straightforward, physician?'

'Who can say?' I murmured. 'We know of no reason why he should have been targeted otherwise. Do we?'

'That's a question for you to answer, Messer inquisitor. I wish you good luck.'

He sauntered away but his words echoed in my head. I had no idea why Alessandro had been murdered but it did seem unlikely the motive was simple robbery and, even if it had been, I felt a nagging responsibility for him being in the vicinity of the castle bridge when darkness fell two days earlier. I was more than ever convinced that the explanation for his return to the Borgo of San Zeno lay in something spoken between us and, although I was completely at a loss as to what that might have been, I felt it incumbent upon me to solve the mystery.

Chapter 12

I was gratified to find Geoffrey on his feet again and free from the fever which might have developed after an infected wound. I explained that I was to be absent from Verona for a few days and, when he pulled a face at his enforced idleness, I suggested he might go through the collection of bottles and basins which my predecessor had left in the physician's room.

'Doctor Morano died suddenly and he left a vast collection of powders and liquids which I haven't taken the time to inspect fully. At first glance I couldn't even identify some of them. I'm loath to throw away mixtures which might be useful so it would be a great help to me if you'd look along the shelves and tell me what there is.'

My apothecary friend raised his eyebrows. 'Did he make up his own potions? I can't approve of that – a physician taking the crust from my fellow guildsmen. If I manage to get established with a shop in the city, I'll insist you come to me for all your remedies.'

'Certainly, I will. You already have one faithful acolyte in the household. Constanza swears by your balsam for her aching back.'

'So she's told Antonia, with profuse paeans of praise for my skill. Mind you, my credit with that lady may have been cancelled out by the noise of Giorgio's crying. Old maids can be sensitive to unfamiliar screeching.'

I made a selection of dressings and unguents to pack in the satchel supplied by the stableman and put a clean gown and linen undergarments in the roll which would rest behind my own saddle. When I was satisfied everything was ready for my departure next morning, I slipped out of the Casa delle Arche and made my way once more to the church of San Zeno Orador. Some instinctive reticence had prevented me mentioning Alessandro's brother to Sandrino, and I knew the priest might still be absent from his charge, but Father Mario had the right to know of the young notary's murder and it was the least I could do to tell him. Other enquires would have to await my return from the Signora's country estate.

At the gateway beside the castle officials in Venetian livery were still watching travellers leaving and entering the city, alongside the usual Veronese guards, but they looked bored and their presence did not seem to signify any particular emergency. I had heard the Mantuan Marquis was recovering from his malady so perhaps a larger Venetian presence at the gates of Verona was no longer necessary. The custodian recognised me and I parried his jibe about becoming an habitué of the Borgo and his knowing wink which suggested the nature of the delights I might sample there. Impressed by his memory for faces, I stopped and enquired whether he remembered Alessandro, describing his appearance and his visits to the church.

'Bless my soul, of course I remember him. Regular every Sunday he comes. Never asked his business, mind you, if you get my meaning. Funny thing about last Sunday though.'

I pretended ignorance. 'What do you mean?'

'Came back after he'd gone home. Never known that happen before. What's more he's never re-entered the city. Must still be at the church or travelled on somewhere.'

I thanked the man for his information but I found it unsettling. It suggested that Alessandro had been attacked in the Borgo, then trussed up in the sack and bundled into the river from the nearby bridge, as the guards who discovered him had suspected. Yet his brother's church was only a stone's-throw from the gate and it was difficult to imagine a robber operating so near armed watchmen. Besides, the sacristan had told me he saw Alessandro approaching the gate when he left Father Mario on Sunday. I crossed towards San Zeno Orador and was surprised to see a cluster of clerics and servants crowding the entrance. Among them was the sacristan and I tried to attract his attention without interrupting the discussion among his superiors.

'What do you want?' he asked aggressively as he sidled away from his companions.

I reminded him of my previous visit. 'I thought Father Mario might have returned by now.'

The sacristan made a strange sound, between a squawk and a roar, and he crossed himself. 'What's left of him is back and the rest never will be.'

'Please tell me what has happened.' I could not keep my voice from shaking.

'He was set upon on the road to Brescia and done to death. His body was found this morning in a thicket beside the track. A woodman brought it here.'

Words would not come to me for a moment, so profound was my horror, but my presence had attracted the attention of a priest who strode to join us. 'Why are you enquiring for Father Mario, physician? What is your business with him?'

I rallied myself, wondering if they already knew of the notary's demise. 'I am a friend of his brother, Alessandro.' I was unprepared for the ferocious response.

'Bah! Don't name that foul sodomite. He is not brother to our sad departed colleague. They fabricated the reason for their familiarity. He pandered to Father Mario's weakness of the flesh and, because of their vile coupling, our true brother in Christ has died unshriven, with all his sins upon him.'

'They were not blood brothers?'

'You are another of the same persuasion, I fancy, come to lure Father Mario from the paths of virtue. Shame on you, disfigured foreigner, for such abominable filth!'

'No! No, I'm not. I only know Alessandro because I serve in the household of Signora Guarienti-Schioppa. His uncle, Bernardino Biagio, is her notary.'

'You bandy the names of influential citizens, to whom respect is owed. So did that perverted animal when I challenged him about his visits. He denied the nature of his relations with Father Mario but I knew better.'

I struggled to keep my temper. 'Are you breaking the sacred trust of a confession, priest?'

'Get out! Leave this place and return to your physic. You may tell his purported relative that Father Mario is gone to his reward in the nether parts of Hell.'

I left without another word, without saying that Alessandro was also dead, without asking all the questions I should have liked to pose about the circumstances of Father Mario's death. Clearly the information I had been given so unpleasantly offered a possible explanation for the double murders, by someone who presumed to consign their souls to perdition, but I speculated whether there could be some other link between their destinies. It seemed improbable that these were simply the result of coincidence, an ominous twist of fate. I knew I must await my return to Verona after the visit to Signora Orsola's estates, and that of Bernardino from Padua, before I could pursue these troubling questions further.

*****

It was not the best time of year to journey along the waterlogged valley of the Adige and both horses and riders were thoroughly bespattered with mud and fragments of dank vegetation by the time we turned towards the foothills of the mountains to the north. In normal conditions it was a comfortable day's journey from the city but the heavy going was wearisome and I was delighted when a member of our escort pointed out the building on a small hill, which was our destination.

'See the walls climbing the slope. They lead up to the castle. It's just coming into view.'

For no real reason I had expected a large farmhouse or a crumbling mansion and I must have looked surprised. 'A Guarienti castle?'

'No. It's the Castel Schioppa. Belongs to the lady's son but he's at the French court on Venetian business so Signora Orsola has charge of the estate. Decent wine they make here.'

We lumbered up the hillside along by the castellated wall and entered the courtyard of the small but sturdy castle, where we were greeted by an assembly of deferential attendants who welcomed their overlord's mother with ostensible enthusiasm. They quickly took charge of our horses and baggage and led my companions to their quarters but Signora Orsola, who seemed the least tired of our party, insisted I accompany her to the parapet to admire the view across the valley. I noted the areas of flooding in meadows which flanked the river and clumps of dismal, drooping trees lapped by ripples of the still spreading water.

'Do you see the settlement in the distance and the enclosed edifice beside it? That is the convent of San Bonifacio where my sister is Abbess. It is there that your unlamented, soon-to-be former, betrothed will spend the rest of her life.'

'Giovanna is to become a nun?'

'A highly suitable outcome, in my opinion. She can indulge her passion for prayer to her heart's content. Heaven knows my sister will welcome a devout novice. Most of the girls sent to her house have become an inconvenience to their families and would rather be in the arms of a lusty admirer. Bernardino says Giovanna positively purred when he suggested she take the veil and I have offered a generous dowry for her to settle on the nunnery.'

I curbed the ironic comment which came to my lips about Guarienti wealth going full circle. 'I think it is an appropriate outcome and I hope Giovanna will be happy in her vocation.'

'A letter from Bernardino was awaiting me here, saying that the final agreement will be signed tomorrow. You will then be free, physician, to consider a more fitting liaison.'

'I shall not hurry to contract myself again, Signora.'

'I understand that.' She leaned back against the low wall and gave a knowing smile. 'But I do suggest you think through the advantages of a marriage with my dear Diamante. She is of gentle birth and still capable of child-bearing, if you are speedy in impregnating her. She has suffered several disappointments in her life and misfortune has corrupted her mind but a husband would cure her of her transgressions. I have no doubt she would be a devoted slave to any man who took her in matrimony. I should be pleased to see you united with her and would provide for you both liberally.'

I tried to hide my astonishment and distaste. 'I'm grateful. I will consider your suggestion seriously but I beg you to allow me a period of reflection after my previous error.'

'That is reasonable. You are judicious.' She flicked an insect from her sleeve. 'On another matter: I promised not to press you for a conclusion to your enquiries, but have you made progress in seeking the person who betrayed my brother?'

'I've learned much that may be relevant, Signora, but nothing conclusive. Many in your household do not esteem Signor Guarienti.'

She gave a throaty laugh. 'Such nicety of expression! They have good cause to dislike him, but I would expect their dependence on my favour to outweigh their abhorrence of my brother's misdemeanours. It is time to expedite your investigation, Doctor Somers. Bring me the villain by the Feast of the Nativity and by the same Holy Day let me know your decision with regard to Diamante. I urge you to review your options carefully.'

My mouth dropped open. She swept up the steps to enter the castle and I followed more slowly; once again I felt unpleasantly trapped.

*****

We retired early to our beds after the rigours of the journey. Most of the Signora's male attendants were squeezed into a single guest room and I was surprised to be allocated a pallet in a tiny garret all to myself, but assumed this was due to my superior status among her followers. Such was my self-satisfaction and naiveté.

I discarded my gown and sat down on the bolster, in shirt and hose, to check the contents of my satchel, setting out on the coverlet the various potions and powders which seemed to have travelled without damage. I was starting to replace the packets in their container, and had not yet extinguished the taper, when I heard a light footstep outside my room and in that instant I was disabused of my innocence and knew I must forestall mischief. I set down the bundles and flung open the door just as Diamante raised her hand to knock. She wore only a shift and her hair was unbound, falling forward over her shoulders in greasy coils. She gasped and seized my wrist.

'Doctor Somers, you were expecting me!'

I pushed her back into the corridor and closed the door with my free hand. 'Certainly not. It's very wrong of you to come here.'

She brushed her fingers against my blemished face. 'You are lonely, are you not? As I am. I am not a green girl. I won't deceive you. I know how to give pleasure – and to receive it.' She pulled on the ribbons at her throat so that her shift fell open and she clamped my hand onto her left breast. 'Let me suckle you. See how my nipple stiffens in your hand.'

I broke her grasp and stepped back against the door. 'No! You must go at once.'

'Don't pretend, physician. You share my longing.'

She lunged for my privates and I gave a cry as I struggled to escape her sharp nails. A door opened in the distance and, as we both froze, she nestled against me, sliding her hand between my legs. 'I may be more faded than Sandrino's niece but I am nothing lacking in lust,' she whispered.

'Be quiet.' Someone was walking along the passage below us and I heard them pause at the foot of the spiral staircase up to my attic.

'We had best go into your room if you don't want to be caught appearing to coerce me to your will against the wall.' She leaned back on the stonework and lifted her skirt.

Reluctantly I opened the door and pushed her inside, clamping my hand over her mouth until the footsteps receded. Then I gripped her shoulders, holding her away from me. 'What did you mean about Sandrino's niece?'

She smirked. 'Madonna Fratta has entertained you at her house, has she not?'

'With her brother at her side. What filth are you suggesting?'

'Your friend the apothecary's sweet wife says the widow desires you as her bedfellow. Perhaps you have already mounted her.'

'I have not and these are slanderous lies.'

'Which I shall tell to one and all unless you pleasure me. Do you wish the virtuous widow to become the butt of men's ribald mirth?' She slithered away from me and flung herself on my pallet, kicking out her legs from underneath her skirt. Her thighs were surprisingly smooth and slender. 'Come, English devil. I don't believe I am altogether repulsive to you.'

'You will hold your tongue, you foul-minded bitch. You disgust me.'

'I think not. Look down for your proof. The price of my silence is your swollen prick. My mouth will be sealed if you possess my other secret lips.'

I took a step towards her and she reached out for my hand, trying to draw me down into an embrace, but I hauled her upright and dragged her, with shameful force, out of my room. I hurled her against the newel post and slammed the door, heaving a chest across it to block access. After a few moments I heard her footsteps descending the stairs and then I slumped on my pallet, breathing heavily and gradually controlling the urge which had come upon me, of which she, all too evidently, had been aware. I cursed my susceptibility, while rejoicing that I had resisted such ill-advised carnal temptation, but I was deeply worried by her threat to traduce Margherita Fratta's reputation.

*****

Signora Orsola gave no indication that she knew what had occurred but next morning she told me Diamante would be escorted back to Verona, whereas I was to remain at the castle to meet the servants there, whose health was in my charge, and to attend a small private dinner later in the day. My relief was so great I enquired no further and set about acquainting myself with the ailments of the various attendants, dispensing potions and advice liberally. I was aware that visitors arrived in the courtyard somewhat after midday and I assumed they were local gentry invited to dine with the Signora. I duly brushed my best gown and straightened my cap so I was neatly arrayed when summoned to join them in antechamber to the great hall.

The lady beckoned me to stand beside her by the elegantly carved overmantel, alongside a crackling fire, and I noticed with surprise that a table had been set up in the small room, furnished for only four diners. I had expected hospitality for a larger company, served in the hall itself, but the display of golden vessels and Venetian crystal indicated that the guests for this intimate meal must be eminent. The Signora nodded approvingly at my appearance and, encouraged by this, I was about to ask who I was to meet when the door was opened by a lackey and two people were admitted. Dizziness swept over me and I think I must have staggered slightly but, at that instant, the attention of the newcomers was concentrated on their hostess and my eyes were beginning to focus properly again when Matteo Maffei strode forward to grasp my hand.

'We meet again, Harry Somers, as I foretold. You look a trifle strained. Does my dear aunt impose onerous duties on her physician?'

I struggled to form a polite denial but the Commendatore pulled me forward. 'Sweet, this is the impressive Englishman I met at Padua. Doctor, may I present my companion, Madonna Beatrice.'

She bestowed a lovely, heart-rending smile on me and I bowed low in appalled disbelief and ridiculous elation. The apparition I had seen at the Casa delle Arche, the model for Messer Pisanello's frescoed masterpiece at Sant'Anastasia, was standing before me, more beautiful close at hand and in the flesh than I had dreamed. I was incapable of speech and rooted to the spot but she was entirely calm.

'Doctor Somers, we glimpsed each other when I stayed unobtrusively at the Signora's house. I was not then at liberty to greet you.'

I found my voice, although uncertain how much to say. 'I enquired of the steward who you were but he denied I had seen you.'

She trilled with laughter. 'Sandrino was sworn to secrecy about my visit on that occasion, although I have an open invitation from the Signora to stay with her. More importantly, Sandrino resents my presence at any time and wishes I did not exist.'

'Madonna, I find that improbable.'

Matteo Maffei took his lady's arm. 'I told you he was smooth-talking and perceptive. The only reason our good Sandrino would prefer me to have a different friend is that Madonna Beatrice is of the house of Gonzaga.'

I started to bow again but she put her hand gently on my wrist and she must have felt me tremble at her touch. 'I am the bastard of a Gonzaga bastard,' she said. 'Not deserving of much respect or indeed worthy of animosity on that account, but Sandrino's brother was killed by my Mantuan kinsmen.'

Signora Orsola had been observing our exchange with amusement but now she clapped her hands for the servants to attend and show us to our seats. Rich wine was poured into our goblets and a succession of exquisitely cooked dishes brought to the table. I ate and drank with a mixture of ecstatic enjoyment and miserable comprehension, but I remained oblivious of what I swallowed. All I was conscious of was that Pisanello's princess was a living woman, seated across the table from me, speaking merrily and with confidence, beguiling me in earnest with her wit and charm – and that she was the Commendatore's mistress. The perfume I remembered wafted into my nostrils and the flutter of slender ringed fingers, delicately taking food from the bowls in front of us, distracted my attention from everything else. Luckily for me my hostess and her guests were content to savour their meal before the conversation turned to serious matters and by then I had managed to thrust aside my useless self-absorption, to concentrate on information which might be valuable to me.

Matteo Maffei raised his glass. 'Doctor Somers, you should know how pleased I was that my aunt took my advice and engaged your services. You will appreciate by now that it is not your medical acumen alone which she seeks but your intelligence and knowledge of human frailty.'

Despite the wine my mouth was dry. 'It has been much exaggerated.'

'That is for us to judge. I know the Signora has asked you to expedite your enquiries relating to her brother. I think you should know why the matter has become more urgent and, although it pains me to mention something so indelicate, I feel bound to remind you that you are in my debt for the little matter of your life. Alas, it sounds vulgar to put it in these terms, but I trust you recall the pledge you gave me. The moment has come for me to seek redemption of your promise.'

My stomach churned as one unlikely event followed another and I felt I was in the middle of a nightmare, no longer a tantalising dream. 'I acknowledge my debt,' I said. 'Without doubt, I owe you some service.'

'Capital! I am obliged.' He swivelled in his chair and stretched out his elegant legs, crossing his ankles. 'You will comprehend that, by sharing this with you, we are demonstrating our faith in your discretion.' He smiled with his lips but his eyes were frosty as he sipped his wine. He was no longer the composed patron of learning I had met in Padua. 'It hardly needs saying that, if you betray our trust, your neck will be broken and your entrails strewn in the gutter.'

I was aware of Madonna Beatrice's soft sigh and nearly lost my concentration. 'I understand. I won't break your trust but I can only do my best to fulfil the task. I can't promise success.'

He grunted. 'We are reasonable in our expectations.' He spoke with most unreasonable joviality while I was trying to dismiss the idea of my entrails floating among the slops of night-soil in a drainage channel. 'My aunt commissioned you to find a traitor in her household because we believed her brother had been exiled solely as a result of that person's malignant lies.' He paused and quaffed more of his wine. 'Now we know the position is more serious. It seems that

170

fool of a Guarienti – excuse me for speaking frankly, dear aunt – Guglielmo Guarienti did more than nod approvingly towards the rebels against Venice. Four years ago he gave money to support them and wrote letters making clear he would declare allegiance to the Gonzaga Marquis of Mantua and, even worse, the Visconti of Milan, if the insurgents were successful.'

At the mention of the Gonzaga, I could not prevent my eyes straying in embarrassment towards Madonna Beatrice and she registered my concern on her account. 'You needn't be troubled, Doctor Somers. I feel no family obligations to the Mantuan lords.'

Matteo Maffei waved his hand dismissively as if her sensitivity was unwarranted. 'We are given to understand some incriminating letters still exist. They must be found and we must destroy them or Uncle Guglielmo will be executed and our family honour tarnished.'

I wondered which outcome he feared most. 'You hope I can trace these papers?'

'No, Doctor Somers, we require you to obtain them and give them to my aunt or me. That is the reparation I seek in return for saving your life in a Paduan alley. You will be well rewarded when you succeed but we cannot afford failure. If your mission is discovered, we are bound to regard you as expendable.' The harshness of his voice and the unconditional nature of his demand gave the lie to the earlier assurance of reasonable expectations and when I did not reply he banged his fist on the table. 'Do you understand?'

'Very clearly.' I nodded unhappily.

'Capital. We drink to your success.' The Commendatore lifted his glass once more.

I tried to hide the panic sweeping over me. 'But I must ask you to tell me everything you know about these papers and how you learned of them.'

'Of course.' Matteo Maffei leaned back in his chair and raised one leg across the other knee. 'Marquis Gianfrancesco of Mantua was the recipient of these imprudent communications and, being a wise and unscrupulous ruler, he kept them in case they should prove of use but he did nothing when Guglielmo was removed to Venice a few months ago. Last week the Marquis suffered a seizure. He has rallied but the shock turned his thoughts towards his own mortality and he resolved at once to set his affairs in order. He is a diligent man and he ordered his secretary to check all his papers against the inventory he maintained, so they could be passed to his son, Ludovico, in a methodical manner when the time arose. Naturally my dear uncle's letters had been stored securely with other documents but when the chest was unlocked the Guarienti items were missing. The secretary swears they were there during the spring of this year when he made his annual check of the records he held. Certain of the Marquis's trusted servants have access to the chest and all of them are being questioned – rather roughly, I suspect – but the letters remain absent. They may have been taken at any time over the last few months and Gianfrancesco is of the opinion they are no longer in Mantua. Since the discovery of the theft, all travellers and goods leaving the city have been searched rigorously.'

I glanced uncomfortably towards Madonna Beatrice. 'May I ask how you know this?'

The Commendatore chuckled. 'The noble Marquis told me every word himself. Don't look so startled, good doctor. I have come from Mantua. He invited me there to discuss the possibility of employing my troop of men in defence of his city, should his son have need of support. Ludovico has been a condottiere, as I am, and I am acquainted with the whole family. The Marquis hopes to draw me away from my previous commitment to Venice and has offered very good terms. I said I would consider his proposal, which pleased him, and as we relaxed over a flask of wine he told me of his predicament. He knows, of course, that I am related by marriage to the Guarientis and I think he gave me the information by way of a warning, to be passed to my dear Aunt Orsola, in case her adherents had been responsible for the theft. Needless to say, she has no knowledge of the matter but she is concerned to ensure that her brother's foolish writings should neither fall into the hands of the Venetian authorities nor return to Mantua.'

'The Marquis has his own men seeking the papers, I presume.'

The leader of mercenaries lolled languidly in his chair. 'You grasp the point immediately, as I was confident you would. You will run the gauntlet of the Mantuan soldiers and, as I believe they already have wind of Guarienti's indiscretions, the Venetian officers who will also seek to seize the documents.'

'An appealing proposition,' I said.

Matteo sat forward, ignoring my rueful comment. 'The Most Serene Republic's interest in your commission is no idle threat. I have received intelligence suggesting they have been made aware of the stolen papers.'

A wave of annoyance at the unreasonable risks I must run made me testy. 'How do you suppose I am in a position to fulfil this task?'

'Haven't you already made some progress in your investigations? My aunt believes you have.'

I rose from my seat. 'Are you suggesting that the person who betrayed Signor Guarienti to Venice initially has obtained the papers?'

For the first time Maffei looked surprised. 'Isn't that a sensible assumption?'

'I think not. We must suppose that the original traitor was driven by hatred of Signora Orsola's brother, for whatever reason. In that case, if he already possessed the papers or knew he could acquire them, surely he would have passed them to the Venetians at the time he denounced Signor Guarienti. Such evidence would have guaranteed that his enemy was executed, not merely exiled.'

I was gratified to hear a faint murmur of appreciation from Madonna Beatrice and the Commendatore guffawed. 'You see, sweet, I told you the fellow was uncommonly bright.'

I followed up my advantage quickly. 'Am I still to look for the person who first betrayed the Signor?'

It was Signora Orsola who replied. 'I should like you to complete that commission. I cannot rest easy with my servitors until I know who has failed in their obligations. Besides, although what you say is good sense, you may find a connection between the two enquiries.'

I turned my gaze on the older lady. 'You set me a challenging task. I must ask for freedom to concentrate on it, untrammelled by other commitments or concerns.'

'You'll need to keep up the appearance of acting as my aunt's physician otherwise you'll incur suspicion.' Maffei sounded impatient.

Signora Orsola held up her hand to silence her nephew. 'That is not what Doctor Somers means.' She turned to me with a thin smile. 'I understand and I shall not press you for a reply on the suggestion I made until this trouble has been resolved.'

'I ask more than that, Signora. I need to be certain I shall not be diverted by the fantasies of others.'

She bowed her head with a semblance of humility. 'I shall arrange it. The fantasist will not trouble you during your enquiries.'

Matteo Maffei clapped me on the shoulder. 'I have no idea what that exchange meant but I'm impressed if you can bend my formidable aunt to your will. Now, go about your business. Remember all that I have said. You will report progress to the Signora but if you should require to contact me, my men are encamped on the nearer shore of Lake

Garda, to the west of Verona, below the mountain ridge, outside the Scaligeri Castle at Torri.' He swung away from me and held out his arm to Madonna Beatrice. 'Come, sweet, we must be on our way. We have a distance to cover before nightfall.'

The young woman rose and, as she took her lover's arm, she extended her other hand to me. I shivered as I kissed it and then she lightly touched the mottled stain on my cheek, wiping away the sour memory of Diamante's similar gesture the previous evening. 'You are courageous, Doctor Somers.'

'I have little choice, Madonna.'

'Choice! That is not a luxury women know. Indeed few people can select their fate but some can rise above the compulsions put upon us.'

Her words rang in my ears as they left the room and long afterwards I mused on what they were intended to convey.

Chapter 13

We had not progressed far along the track towards Verona when the Signora reined in her dappled mare to fall back, allowing most of our escort to pass in front of her, and called me to join her towards the rear of the column. Her attendants recognised this move as signalling that she wished to conduct a private conversation and they took up defensive positions around their mistress but at a distance out of earshot. It was neatly done, without the need for words, and I admired the ease with which she controlled her followers.

The convent of San Bonifacio lay around two miles to the south of our route and she stretched out her hand to indicate its sombre walls. 'Diamante has been taken to reside with my dear sister for a few weeks, to benefit from a period of quiet contemplation, away from the fleshly temptations to which she is a victim.'

I knew I was meant to express gratitude for this device, which freed me from the importunate woman, but a different reaction was overpowering. 'She will meet Giovanna?'

'Undoubtedly.' Signora Orsola urged her mare into a trot and I was forced to do likewise, as she turned to glance at me over her shoulder. 'Intimations of your past and of your future! What would you give to eavesdrop on their comparisons of your character?'

'I shudder at the thought of it. Couldn't Diamante have gone elsewhere?'

'Nowhere else could provide the facilities to keep her under surveillance. Rest assured, my sister will ensure every word of their conversation is reported to me.' I sighed audibly but the lady laughed. 'Passable physician you may be, but you lack the capacity an Italian would have to keep your women in order.'

'I have not noticed that all Italian women are biddable.'

'Well observed but we are a minority. Do you suppose my husband's nephew allows his woman a free rein? Gonzaga blood may flow in her veins but Matteo is not deterred from taking his whip to her beauteous breast when it pleases him.' She was looking at me closely and saw me gulp back a protest. 'Do not involve yourself with matters beyond your remit, Doctor Somers. He would cut you to pieces if she so much as smiles on you out of turn. I speak by way of friendly warning – he is a dangerous man.'

My mind raced with the thoughts which her words provoked. Was my fascination so obvious? Was Madonna Beatrice wanton in her affections? Did the Commendatore really treat her with brutal violence? If she suffered at his hands, how could I hope to dismiss her from my heart, as I resolved I must? I fought to control myself. 'Signora, if I am to have any chance of success in the commission I have been given, I need your help.' She slowed her pace to amble beside me, raising her eyebrows. 'I believe your principal attendants have not been open when I spoke to them. I have sensed that most, if not all, have kept back information they did not want to share with me.'

'You think I can compel them to reveal their inmost secrets? You disappoint me. Have you concluded nothing from their confidences?'

'They all speak ill of Bernardino Biagio but I am not convinced he stands to gain from your brother's exile. I suspect he had a freer hand in administering the Guarienti estates when your brother was in Verona than he does now you have oversight of his work.'

'Shrewdly put, physician.'

I realised she would not offer me more without prompting. 'I am not ruling out Messer Biagio as the possible traitor but his reason would be more complex than greed. The motive for any of the others to betray Signor

Guarienti is likely to be a sense of enmity, hatred or revenge. There may be such feelings among them but I've not been able to establish strong evidence. You may know something they are unwilling to tell me.'

Her mare had come to a halt, hooves pawing the ground, and she lowered her voice as the escort pulled up in a circle around us once again. 'I know of only one factor you may consider pertinent and it grieves me to declare it. But you are right, he will not explain himself. It is too painful for him.' She paused and I held my breath, judging it unwise to press her too far.

'Iacopo's father was my father's fool,' she said at length. 'He served my family well and I dandled his little, stunted son on my knees the year before I was married. They both remained in Guarienti service and in time Iacopo took his father's place as a witty, ribald entertainer.' She clamped her lips together and I feared she would say no more.

'You told me Iacopo was your brother's fool but I don't know why he came to join your household.'

She bent forward to pat the neck of her restive horse. 'A year ago my brother had incurred some paltry debts which he could not readily repay. Bernardino urged patience on his creditor but the rogue bore a grudge and threatened to expose Guglielmo, calling him a man of straw whose bond was worthless. My brother could not tolerate such ignominy and sought a way to raise the money he owed without delay. Iacopo's reputation as an inventive jester was widely known and a nobleman had already enquired whether he might purchase the jester for his court. In the face of his impending disgrace, Guglielmo retracted his earlier refusal of this proposal and offered Iacopo for sale.'

'But it didn't happen?'

'Iacopo appealed to me to save him from humiliation. He flung himself at my feet, sobbing and swearing he would never return to serve his master. It was the first I had heard of my brother's embarrassment – he hadn't wished me to know of his prodigal behaviour. At once I redeemed Guglielmo's debts and offered Iacopo a place in my house. He is a proud little fellow and, after a lifetime of loyal service, he did not deserve to be treated as a mere chattel, to be put up for sale. He took my brother's perfidious intentions very badly and I think his wit has been more barbed and cruel since that time. In all truth, I cannot blame him.'

The mottled mare began to move forward slowly as the lady completed her story but I could not let her escape so easily. I pulled my horse flank to flank with hers. 'Who was it, Signora, the nobleman who wanted to buy Iacopo?'

She stared at me coldly, gripping the reins with clenched fingers. 'Gianfrancesco Gonzaga,' she said. 'The Marquis of Mantua.'

Then she kicked her mount into a gallop and I let her go.

*****

Throughout the rest of our journey I contemplated the information I had been given, recognising that Iacopo had a powerful reason to hate Guglielmo Guarienti and, with what I had seen of his malicious nature, I must now regard him as the likely traitor, responsible for his former master's exile. I wondered why, knowing what she did, Signora Orsola had not accused him directly and, with discomfort, I concluded that if the favoured prankster was to be disgraced, she wanted someone else to carry the responsibility. I served her purpose and could be regarded, in Matteo Maffei's words, as expendable. If all went well I would be rewarded with generous payment and the sadly disturbed Diamante as my bride; if I failed my doom had been described concisely by the Commendatore. In the past I had found myself in the power of an unscrupulous Englishman and narrowly escaped following him to the gallows; now I was at the mercy of a scheming Italian family and my future prospects were scarcely less dismal.

I decided I would not challenge Iacopo immediately, for I had no proof of his guilt, and it would do no good to alert him prematurely and incur his hostility. I hoped I could avoid contact with him, while I pursued other enquires I felt it necessary to make, but I had no sooner dismounted and unhitched my saddlebag when he bounded across the courtyard towards me, waving an tangled contraption of cords and webbing. Other attendants stood back, hiding mischievous grins.

'Welcome home, dear Doctor. Have you ever seen so large a cat's cradle? It is most cleverly constructed. Let me hold your roll so you can take the web in your hands. Here!'

He seized my burden and reluctantly I held out my hands to humour him but, when he had fitted the cords over my fingers, he pulled on a loose end and the device tightened around my wrists so that I could not free them. While I protested and struggled to rid myself of the cordage, he bent down quickly and fixed loops to my ankles, again tugging them taut and causing me to tumble to my knees. With a cry of triumph he jerked the strings and, helplessly assuming the role of his puppet, I crumpled on the ground, doubled up like a new-born baby. He screeched with laughter.

'Trussed as capon for the spit. My own invention. I think the justices might welcome it to constrain their more troublesome prisoners. Will you write me a testimonial, Doctor Somers? It could be hooked onto a robust tree and save the need for cells.'

I tried not to show my anger. 'I respect your ingenuity and acknowledge the effectiveness of your trap but I should be glad to go to my quarters. I have been in the saddle for many hours.'

'Then be grateful you can rest lying down, better than sitting on a sore arse.'

He skipped away from me, ignoring my shout of annoyance, accompanied by a titter of amusement from the onlookers who were not disposed to assist me but, across the courtyard, a door was flung open and Sandrino emerged flourishing a heavy pole which he brought down heavily on Iacopo's shoulder. 'Take your tricks elsewhere, wretched clown. You go too far. Be off!'

Iacopo waggled his thumb on his nose as he ran into the house while the steward, ignoring the gesture, produced a knife from the sheath on his belt and slit through my bonds. 'You're too trusting, Doctor,' he said. 'You should know better than to play along with that knave's games. You'll risk serious injury if you encourage him.'

While murmuring thanks for my release I pondered that, if Iacopo was indeed guilty of treachery to the family he served, with his cunning and skill he could prove a dangerous enemy. It would be sensible to heed Sandrino's warning.

*****

When I entered my room I was greeted by an ebullient Rendell, brandishing a short sword and burbling of the competition to be held in a few days' time between Captain Alberto's pupils. He executed some fancy movement with his weapon, whisking it close to my ear and within an inch of my nose, and shrieked excitedly that he was one of the boys tipped by their peers to win the prize. 'You must come and watch me! You should be proud.'

I did not hide my annoyance for I wanted only to refresh myself and change my travel-spattered clothes but I dared not shift my position in case I suffered injury. 'I'd rather see you learn some peaceful trade, as you well know. Put down your sword and get me water to wash my face.'

'Why, do you think you can wash off your birth stain?'

It was unlike Rendell to turn his resentment into personal offensiveness and I should have recognised how disappointed he was by my offhand response. He flung down the blade, clattering against the table leg, and flounced from the room. Several minutes later, when he had not returned, I went down to the well to fetch my own bucketful of water and laboriously brushed the grime from the bottom of my cloak.

My appearance was more presentable when Geoffrey put his head round the door to greet my return and he was altogether more cordial and placid than my occasional servant. When I asked after Antonia and little Giorgio he chuckled and assured me they were well.

'They've won the hearts of the Signora's household. Antonia helps the other women with the spinning and needlework while the baby propels himself between their feet, on all fours, at remarkable speed. He's spoiled by half a dozen aunties.'

'Not including Constanza, I presume?'

He tapped his nose and winked. 'That's where you're wrong. She's quite captivated and coaxes him onto her knee whenever she can.'

I expressed astonishment that this change had occurred in just three days but to Geoffrey it seemed nothing exceptional. He pointed to the alcove where my physician's remedies were neatly stacked. 'I've done a good job for you, I think. I threw out the mouldy mixtures and liquids with scum formed on their surfaces. What's left is serviceable and labelled so you can tell one jar from another without needing to summon an apothecary every time you want to distinguish a poultice from a laxative.'

'Outrageous!' I threw a friendly punch. 'A physician's calling is far superior to that of a mere potion-mixer.'

'Debatable,' he laughed. 'But you might be interested to know the quantity of pennyroyal, wormwood and juniper berries old Doctor Morano kept. I hesitate to name the purpose of the concoctions he could have made from them.'

I raised my eyebrows. 'They are used to procure abortions, among other things, but I doubt the mixture was much needed for that purpose in this house.'

'Sandrino told me young women from the town would visit the doctor from time to time.'

'Sent by Sandrino himself, I suspect! The old goat!'

We chuckled and our merriment dispersed the bad temper I had displayed to Rendell. I was further relieved to learn that Bernardino would not return to the house until later the next day. He had been informed of his nephew's death, of course, but it was my duty to speak to him about it and there were other matters I wished to ask him. His continued absence meant I could postpone that testing conversation and concentrate on less arduous tasks, to which I was more suited: treating scalds and abrasions and removing an impressive splinter from a stable-boy's forefinger. During the evening I joined the company of senior attendants, with Geoffrey and his wife, and listened to Iacopo, in unaccustomed solemn mood, singing gentle refrains of loss and unrequited passion. Constanza had taken the citole to accompany him and I noted the unusual softness of her expression as she plucked the strings until, as she laid down the instrument, she wiped a tear from eye.

I returned to my room much pacified and found Rendell bundled up on his pallet, pretending furiously to be asleep, with his mouth in an angry pout. I judged it wise not to disturb him, even to make an apology, but acknowledged to myself that it was incumbent on me to attend his exhibition of youthful military skill, however much I disliked it.

*****

Next morning I told Rendell of my intention to be present at the competition and admitted I had been unreasonably grumpy on my return to Verona. He accepted my confession with lordly disinterest but the quiver at the corner of his mouth told me he was satisfied to receive it. Then he set off for the Cittadella with a jaunty step and I went to see Geoffrey to put in hand a plan I had devised while I lay sleepless for much of the night. He readily agreed to lend me Leone's services for a few days and did not enquire the reason. The youth himself was eager to be away from the Casa delle Arche and usefully employed, for the time hung heavily on his hands while Sandrino continued his enquiries to find premises for the apothecary's business. I asked him to dress in his shabbiest clothes and, as we walked towards the city gate by the castle, I outlined to him what I wanted him to do but I did not tell him of the concerns I had been turning over in my head.

Something about Alessandro's death had been troubling me and I could not find an explanation for the discrepancy. It had not been until the second day after his disappearance that the body of Biagio's unfortunate nephew had been spotted, caught on the buttresses of the ancient stone bridge in the heart of Verona, but at the time the river had been rushing along in spate and the distance from the brick bridge beside the castle was not much more than a mile. If the notary had been attacked and killed in the Borgo San Zeno soon after visiting Father Mario, he would surely have been thrown into the Adige without delay and, if so, it did not make sense that his corpse had not been found by the men of the Communal Guard until two days later. Was it possible he was not murdered immediately after leaving his friend? If so, what was he doing in the meantime and where was he? I recalled the injuries to head and arm which he had suffered and an uncomfortable thought came to me.

As we passed the church of San Lorenzo, Leone pointed across to Madonna Fratta's house and he grinned at me. 'My cousin likes you,' he said. 'She blushes when she speaks your name.'

'Nonsense! But she's a charming lady.' I glanced briskly at the façade of her residence and was relieved to see there was no one at the windows. Happy though I would be to encounter Margherita Fratta again, I did not wish to be diverted from my purpose at that moment.

We passed through the city gate and approached the church of San Zeno Orador. The sacristan was alone, crouched on a stool under one of the arches dividing the nave from the side aisle, polishing a large salver. He did not look welcoming but I gave him no chance to express his misgivings, launching into the explanation I had contrived and shared with Leone. 'I am sorry to intrude on you but this lad is a relative of the late Father Mario. He has been sent by his mother to make small donations to this church and to the fellow who found her cousin's body and brought it here. She knows Masses will be said for the repose of the unfortunate priest's soul but she feels it is the least she can do, as a poor woman, to pay respect to the dead man.'

At the mention of donations, the sacristan's features relaxed and he nodded. 'A worthy intention. The church will be grateful, however small the offering.'

Leone had adopted a hangdog expression as in silence he drew from his pouch a few coins which I had given him. 'It isn't much,' he said with a shrug. 'Please keep something for yourself. You must have been inconvenienced.'

The sacristan smiled. 'God bless you and your mother, boy, and have mercy on the soul of your wretched relative.'

'Do you know where he can find the woodman who brought the body here?'

The man shook his head. 'I never heard where the fellow came from.'

'Surely he can't have come from far away? How else did he know Father Mario belonged here?'

'The Father carried a token of San Zeno which the peasant recognised – as I hope all Christians would. He took the body first to the basilica but the priests there knew where their brother in Christ officiated. They brought him home.'

I thanked the sacristan and gave him another small coin which he slipped into his tunic rapidly. 'It was on the road to Brescia, I understand?'

He nodded and I did not prolong our conversation, shepherding Leone from the church and walking with him until we were on the outskirts of the Borgo San Zeno. 'I don't think the woodman can have come far. I was told he'd found the body the same morning it was brought here. Ask in every village but take care. Remember you're poverty-stricken and have nothing worth stealing. We don't want you attracting the attention of thieves.'

'You think that's what happened to Father Mario?'

'It's one possibility and it may be true.'

'But it may not?' Leone grinned. 'Leave it to me, Doctor Somers.'

I slapped his shoulder and waved him on his way. Then I retraced my steps and re-entered the city, hoping all the time that I had not done wrong by sending the youth on this apparently innocuous expedition. Only as I approached Madonna Fratta's house once more were my thoughts diverted and I wondered whether I might knock at the door to wish her well but I dismissed the idea, perhaps from delicacy. Then, as I entered the market-place in the Piazza delle Erbe, I was rewarded with the sight of the lady in person, accompanied by her maid, both carrying baskets of fresh produce from the stalls. Her lips curved into a glorious smile and the blush spread from her cheeks to brow and chin.

'Doctor Somers! This is most fortunate. I had intended to send a message to enquire whether you would be able to come again to service at the church of San Lorenzo, with my brother, and then to dine at my house.'

'Madonna, I'd be delighted.' Her face, encased in its widow's wimple, was prettier than I remembered and her voice was melodious.

'Would this coming Sunday be possible?' She smiled again as I agreed. 'I'll tell Alberto and he can arrange to meet you. Until then.'

There was a new spring in my uneven gait as I went on towards the Casa delle Arche.

*****

Bernardino Biagio was seated in his study amid rolls of parchment and heavy legal tomes when he agreed to receive me, some hours after his return. He looked haggard, which was not surprising, and I thought it best to get my business with him done quickly. I gave my commiserations on his nephew's death and told him I had examined the body when it was brought to the house.

'I am obliged, Doctor Somers.' He clamped his mouth shut as if there was no more to say but then seemed to think better of it. 'He had been robbed, I understand. There's a nest of scoundrels in the Borgo beyond the city walls. It is ill advised to venture there by dark, especially with a full purse. Alessandro was a competent notary but he lacked discretion. I shall require a new assistant.'

'I imagine your nephew handled a good deal of business on your behalf.'

'He was a reliable aide in routine matters. I did not entrust significant paperwork to him and I certainly did not send him to deal with important contacts. Hence it proved a wise decision that I went myself to unscramble the foolish entanglements of others near Padua.'

Something in Messer Biagio's words gave me a momentary misgiving, as if he had evoked some memory that I could not pinpoint, but his final allusion was not lost on me. 'I must thank you for releasing me from my commitment to Giovanna Lendro. Signora Orsola has told me of your success. I am indebted to you.'

Bernardino grunted and flexed his fingers. 'She'll do well as a holy votaress although her prayers with regard to some of her acquaintance may not be charitable. Her family are deeply offended by the insult to their honour. Still, you are rid of them and her.' He gave a self-satisfied smirk and smoothed his robe before continuing. 'I went from Padua to Bologna to meet the inestimable Pierpaolo Clemente. A nasty little rat. He'll prosper in the law.'

I was uncertain whether to grin at a witticism or ignore the irony. 'I don't imagine he confessed to involvement in the fire at Geoffrey's shop.'

'There was no need. As it happens his Professor in the School of Law at Bologna is an old crony of mine. We called in the pathetic schemer and made clear he was liable to be dismissed from the university and barred from ever being received into the notaries' Guild. It had a salutary effect.' Biagio paused and licked his thin lips as he recalled what had clearly been a satisfying encounter. 'The young idiot protested at first but quickly changed his tune and begged us to save his career. He promised to do whatever we asked in recompense. I have a signed bond from him swearing he will do nothing to inconvenience, harass or injure the lives, interests or connections of Messer du Bois and his family, now and forever.' While I expressed delight, he stretched out his legs and sighed. 'In return it will be useful to me to have a notary in Padua who can be trusted to follow my instructions. Messer Clemente is a promising student and will qualify next year. He will practise in the town of his birth and, when appropriate, I will send him directions. The relationship will not be formal, of course, and will not need to be declared.'

I inclined my head, unwilling to comment on these arrangements, as Bernardino rose to his feet. 'I toyed with the notion of bringing Pierpaolo here to serve as my assistant in the absence of my nephew but I concluded that would be inadvisable. I should not wish to threaten the integrity of his bond by placing him near his step-mother and her husband.'

'I'm sure that was prudent,' I said with a bow.

'The professions of medicine and law should respect each other, I believe, Doctor Somers, don't you agree? I am glad to have been of some assistance to you and your friends.'

I left the notary's study with an uncomfortable feeling of obligation to a man I did not like but I was truly pleased for Geoffrey and Antonia. I went to tell them what Biagio had contrived to neutralise Pierpaolo's hostility and found them already rejoicing that Sandrino had located premises, just off the Piazza delle Erbe, which might serve as an apothecary's home, with living accommodation above the shop. I wished that my own predicament might be so easily resolved and I could not rid myself of an uneasy feeling that something Bernardino had said carried a significance I should have recognised.

*****

Next morning dawned more brightly and colder than the previous rain-soaked week and it raised my spirits. It was Friday, the day before Rendell's swordplay and two days before I was to dine with Margherita Fratta and her brother. I decided to be enthusiastic in praising my servant's exploits, however well he did, and looked forward with gentle anticipation to seeing that sweet face shyly blushing across the table from me. I examined a groom who had developed a fever, but concluded he should soon recover, and I strapped the ankle of a kitchen maid who had turned her foot when she slipped on the stairs while carrying a platter of sweetmeats. I was surprised, when I emerged from the steamy bakehouse, to find Bernardino waiting for me and when he drew me aside I feared something had gone awry with his schemes.

'I did not mention it yesterday but I may have to call on your physician's skill before long. Oh, don't look concerned. It is nothing unusual for me. A touch of constipation, you know. I think I mentioned how Doctor Morano would administer an enema from time to time. I may have need of your services to do likewise if things do not resolve themselves. You will oblige?'

The prospect was not pleasant but I agreed and he went on his way, humming tunelessly, while I returned to my room. At the sight of a sealed letter by my door I banished the improbable hope that it might be news from Leone and opened it with interest. Then I sat down in alarmed fascination as I read the carefully written words.

Dear Doctor Somers, forgive my effrontery. I am in desperate trouble and implore you to help me. I can only explain if I see you and this cannot be at my house. I beg you to meet me by the tower at the church of San Lorenzo, this evening at dusk. Please do not fail me. Your grateful friend, Margherita Fratta.

I stared at the extraordinary message and recognised the inconsistency of its urgency with the lady's modest composure earlier in the week and the fact that we were to meet, with her brother, in two days' time. It made no sense. I enquired of an attendant where the letter had come from and was assured that it had been delivered to the house by a respectable looking maid-servant who was insistent it be brought to my attention without delay. I had to conclude that something serious had occurred to distress Madonna Fratta and for some reason it was not a matter she could share with Alberto, her natural protector. For a dreadful moment I remembered Diamante's threat to besmirch the lady's reputation but that was surely no longer a real danger. Then it came to me that Margherita's anxiety probably concerned the captain himself and, as she knew me to be his friend, it was logical for her to appeal to me for assistance. Why our meeting needed to be away from her house, I could not understand but I did not doubt her sense of decorum or for a moment question her motives, and I was flattered that she had turned to me. I waited for the daylight to fade in a ferment of anxiety and delight that she had sought my help and prayed I might be able to ease her mind. I was unclear whether it was simply because she reminded me of Bess that I felt concern for her welfare or because her own charms attracted me. At all events, as soon as the sky reddened in the west, I donned my best gown and short cloak and my hand trembled as I placed my cap on my tidied hair.

At the entrance to the Casa delle Arche I encountered Rendell in animated talk with Geoffrey and I guessed he was trying to persuade the apothecary to come with me to observe the martial competition in the Cittadella next day. They called out to ask the cause of my hasty departure but I brushed aside their enquiry and set out as briskly as I could for the church of San Lorenzo. I suppose I thought of myself in the guise of a knight errant but I scarcely looked like San Giorgio in Pisanello's mural – and Madonna Fratta was not the model for his princess whose beauty I could not forget.

*****

I followed the same route I had taken with Leone, while I explained what I wanted him to do, and I was beginning to be troubled that he had not yet returned. There should have been no danger in his task but if he had come to harm, I knew the burden of responsibility would be hard to bear. There were few wayfarers about, except a servant bearing a lit torch as he escorted his master into the city, and when Madonna Fratta's house came into view I noted flickering lights in two windows. Although the day had been bright night was falling quickly and, when I turned along the rutted street towards the church, its tower stood starkly against the darkening sky. A cat ran mewling across my path but I could see no human figure by the portico. I felt a frisson of alarm and brushed it aside; strange though my assignation was, there could be nothing sinister about it.

I neared the door at the foot of the tower and became aware of a faint movement further round the curved wall, so I took a step in that direction, catching my breath as I glimpsed a slight form huddled against the stonework. She was enveloped in a hooded wrap and her dusky skirts merged into the gloom. Hearing my step she half-turned and, without speaking, held out a hand to beckon me; a ring twinkled on her finger. The crack of a twig behind me caused a moment's hesitation, for the lady's reputation was at stake, but I concluded it was the skulking cat and moved forward into the deeper shadows.

The ruffian was upon me before I reached her. The squelch of a boot in the soggy ground alerted me too late to avoid his blow but, as the sword flashed in the corner of my eye, I twisted and ducked to protect my head. Instead, the blade sliced through the material of cloak and gown, into the top of my left shoulder, opening my old wound, and I heard myself scream a useless warning for Madonna Margherita to run. While I staggered from this first impact and searing pain shot down my arm, my attacker raised his weapon once more and I saw its damascened edge, already viscous with my blood, driving towards my chest. I flung myself sideways, conscious of a shrill cry nearby, but I was defenceless against the cudgel that crashed onto my skull and felled me to the ground before the sword lodged itself against my ribs.

Chapter 14

I thought it was Bess's face I saw at first when I lay in fever and then Matteo Maffei's lovely mistress, at which point I believed I must have left this earthly life. Only as my mind cleared did I realise it was Madonna Fratta who tended me, under the guidance of an elderly physician, and I concluded I was in her house. As my recollection of the events outside the church of San Lorenzo returned, I gave Heaven thanks that she was safe and had somehow escaped my attackers but I could not comprehend why I was still living. My head was muzzy, dressings swathed my shoulder, arm and chest and I knew I was being given substances to deaden the throbbing of my wounds, but the swordsman had known his business and his second thrust should have found my heart. My nurse and her medical instructor fiercely forbade me to speak or worry myself about such matters until I was strong enough to hear the explanation and I had no choice but to obey. I drifted in and out of sleep.

At length, after a few days which seemed to me incalculable weeks, I was allowed visitors and Rendell, Geoffrey and Alberto came to my bedside, with grim faces but a hint of triumph in their eyes. I was proud that, despite my injuries, I remembered my grievous sin of omission so far as my servant was concerned.

'I missed your swordplay, Rendell. I was unwillingly detained. How did it go?'

'I missed it myself.' He sounded extremely self-righteous. 'My forearm was slashed so I couldn't take part. It's mending well.'

I stared, uncertain whether the improbable connection could be true.

'You owe your life to Rendell,' Alberto said, 'and to Geoffrey.'

'And to the captain,' Rendell added. 'If he hadn't been at Madonna Fratta's house, you'd be in your grave.'

My mouth dropped open and I felt very weary. 'Explain,' I said as the lady herself entered the room.

Rendell assumed the tone of an adult speaking to a rather dim child. 'You may remember, when you left the Casa delle Arche, I'd just returned from the Cittadella. I'd walked with the captain as far as his sister's; she'd invited him to call because she wanted to speak to him. He was giving me some tips for the competition next day and I had my sword at my side, ready to practise what he told me. I saw Madonna Fratta as he went into the house; she waved at me. Then, when I saw you rushing off in a right tizzy from Signora Orsola's, I wanted to know what was up – so did Messer du Bois – and after I got to your room I saw the letter.'

'You can't read,' I muttered.

'Messer du Bois can! I knew it must be a trick and we ran to catch you but, even with your crooked leg, you got to the church before we could. We saw a fellow lurking behind you in the shadows and guessed you were in danger. Messer du Bois was unarmed so I told him to fetch the captain but I had my sword and I drew it.'

I closed my eyes. 'The man was an assassin. He towered over me. You stood no chance.'

'So why am I still here and he's dead?'

Alberto took up the story. 'Rendell was incredibly brave and sensible too. He remembered what he's been taught and didn't try to fight hand to hand but he distracted the man, so his murderous strokes went astray, and that gave me time to get there and finish off the rogue. If the fellow's accomplice hadn't whacked you on the head, you'd have seen it all and avoided the befuddled state you've been in these last few days.'

'The woman hit me?'

'The woman who wasn't me!' Madonna Fratta came forward. 'It could have been a youth in disguise or a woman with good muscles. She fetched you a hefty blow.'

194

'Was she caught?'

Alberto shook his head. 'Sadly, no. We haven't been able to trace her but the Communal Guards are still searching. The dead man was well known to them – a cut-throat for hire to anyone willing to pay. He's eluded justice for ages. The woman was probably his sister who's acted as decoy for him in other cases.'

I was overcome with gratitude to my friends and, in my weakened condition, felt liable to burst into tears. I forced myself to hide my emotion and looked at Rendell. 'I'm sorry you lost the chance of winning the prize at the sword play competition.'

He shrugged with exaggerated nonchalance. 'Me mates all cheered after they heard the tale and the Captain gave me a public commendation. Anyway, I wouldn't have missed the scrap for worlds. Crossing swords with a real bloody fighter was miles better than a pretend tussle.'

After this Margherita Fratta hustled Rendell and her brother out of the room, insisting I must rest, but I begged Geoffrey to stay a little longer. When the others had gone I leaned forward to grasp his wrist and, in my anxiety, I could only manage one word. 'Leone?'

Geoffrey's smile freed me from the burden of guilt I carried. 'He came back three days after your rough encounter. He's in fine fettle – and he's waiting outside. Shall I bring him in?'

In an instant Leone was beside my bed. 'Are you well enough to hear my news?' he asked. 'It's not what you expected. I don't know if it's significant.' I urged him to go on. 'I visited umpteen scruffy hamlets and slept in barns and ditches before I found the woodman who'd discovered the priest's body. I was beginning to think you'd been given duff information – and so you had, but I'll come to that. Then I met a fellow who'd heard the story of the corpse in a thicket and knew where the woodman lived. It wasn't on the road to Brescia at all but on a track that runs off it to the south. So I came to him and he was grateful for the coins. He told me two things you'll find interesting.'

I must have looked eager and Leone grinned, enjoying the suspense. 'First, your priest was on his way back from wherever he'd been. A peasant at the next village a few miles to the south had seen him riding towards Verona, on the previous day. He'd happened to tell the woodman when they were gossiping after the body was discovered. Second, Father Mario's saddle-pack had been ripped open and the stuffing pulled from his saddle, as if the attacker was looking for something other than small change in the priestly purse. The horse was grazing nearby and every bit of its harness had been torn off and split apart. If Father Mario was carrying ducats or something else of value, he'd have hidden them of course, but there's no way of knowing what the thieves found, if anything.' Leone paused and I could tell he had more to reveal but I did not hurry him. We held each other's eyes until he giggled. 'The fellow told me where the track led.' He paused again, chuckling at my, by now, obvious impatience. 'It connects with the road to Mantua. It's a longer way round than the direct route but it would be quite handy if you wanted to conceal where you were going or where you'd been.'

I lay back on the pillow, intrigued but unable to judge what this might mean, and Madonna Fratta, returning to the room, clapped her hands to dismiss my remaining guests. 'You must sleep after such excitement,' she said to me severely. Her face was pale and without the hint of a blush. 'I'll not have the care we've taken of you wasted.'

I called out to Geoffrey. 'I need to get back to the Casa delle Arche as soon as possible. Can you arrange it? I might need an arm to lean on when I walk.'

'You'll not go on foot,' my nurse declared. 'Alberto will take you on his horse – and not for two more days.'

Geoffrey stepped back from the doorway. 'You'll be in danger, surely, at the Signora's house? Whoever hired the assassin must have been a member of her household, to know of your friendship with Madonna Fratta and the church where you'd met her first, with her brother.'

'Would many at the Casa delle Arche have known this? Sandrino, of course, but who else?' I was puzzled.

'Any of them, I'd guess. I'm afraid Antonia has babbled about the pretty widow she met when you escorted her into the city. Pardon, Madonna, my wife admired your charm and meant no harm.'

I noted that Margherita Fratta gave a tiny, contented sigh as she ushered Geoffrey out of my chamber but there were so many perplexing developments for me to consider that I did not give that phenomenon further thought. Above all I felt vindicated in pursuing my suspicion that the deaths of Alessandro and Father Mario were not casual, unrelated occurrences, although whether they had any connection with the fortunes of Guglielmo Guarienti I had no evidence. There was more to be uncovered, I felt sure. I also wondered whether the attack on me had necessarily been arranged by a colleague at the Casa delle Arche. The Commendatore had warned that I faced danger from the officers of both Venice and Mantua. They were not attractive alternatives.

*****

Next day the physician who attended me accepted the urgings of a fellow professional and confirmed that I would be fit in the morning to make the short journey to the Casa delle Arche. Madonna Fratta questioned him closely as to the wisdom of my departure and, when he left the room, having repeated his opinion, he winked at me as if we were part of a conspiracy. After escorting him downstairs, the lady returned, plumped up the cushions in my chair and then seated herself to face me, across the blazing fire in the hearth. She looked at me sternly.

'Doctor Somers, I wish I could trust your judgement as much as I recognise your resolution. I cannot be confident of your safety when you leave my house. You clearly have powerful enemies.'

I inclined my head to acknowledge her concern. 'I'm not at liberty to explain why that may be the case but it is important for me to identify those who wish me ill. I'm sorry you should have become embroiled in this unpleasantness but I'm deeply grateful for the care you've shown me.'

She leaned towards the heat of the fire, stretching out her slender hands. 'It was on my account that you walked into the trap which had been set. I can't forget that. You believed I needed your help and you came.'

I tried to hide my embarrassment in banter. 'You were right to question my judgement. I should have known the letter could not have come from you, Madonna. It was a preposterous idea.'

She folded her hands in her lap and the way she looked at me captured some quality of Bess's frankness, causing me to clench my jaw. 'Yet I'm flattered that you were ready to help me. Your enemies relied on your generosity of spirit.'

'Or my gullibility.'

'I don't believe you are gullible, Doctor Somers, but I think your good nature puts you at risk amongst the crafty and rapacious men who rule our land.' I could feel my colour rising and I was tempted to tease her by asking whether I was also at risk from her lovely countrywomen but some fragment of good taste prevented me. As if reading my thoughts, she shook her head and gave a slight gurgling laugh. 'Although we don't know each other well, it doesn't become us to bandy words for I believe we both understand our true sentiments. I am glad that I have met you, Doctor Somers.' She paused for a moment, noting my confusion, and then she lightened the atmosphere between us, letting irony creep into her voice. 'At least you are privileged in your ability to act on your own behalf. You can't imagine how greatly I would like, just for a single, transitory moment, to play a part in an adventure.'

'Madonna...' I stared at her, at a loss for words.

'A shameful fancy, is it not? I am not a gentlewoman, only a respectable haberdasher's widow who will comply with convention and live her life in quiet pursuit of virtue, but if the chance came to flutter free for a brief time, I would rather enjoy the frisson of excitement. You look surprised.' She was utterly composed but her tone became serious. 'Did the young woman you told me of, who captured your heart in England, never admit to such unwomanly ideas?'

She had an uncanny knack for drawing me back to thoughts of Bess.

'She had the opportunity you covet and took it wholeheartedly. My escape from London, securely embarked on a ship for the Low Countries, owed everything to her resourcefulness and daring. She confronted villains and saw them off, masquerading as her mistress and defying a host of perils.'

'A fortunate young woman indeed.' Margherita Fratta's voice dropped to a whisper. 'Can you really believe that, after she had shared this experience with you, her resolution could be broken by two years of absence? I think she is constant and still waits for you.'

I owed her the truth. 'Perhaps I dare not share that faith because I have not been so constant.'

She did not succeed in hiding a hint of annoyance as she stood up and smoothed her skirts. 'But, as I think we have established, you are a man and the expectations are different. I am happy that we understand each other, Doctor Somers. In other circumstances I might flirt a little with so kind and gallant a defender but I know your heart truly lies elsewhere and I respect that.'

I struggled unsteadily to my feet. 'In other circumstances I would be honoured to...'

'But I have known since we first met that my role was to raise an echo of your love. Still,' the mischievous twinkle returned to her eyes, 'if you should discover an occasion for me to find the tiniest adventure, as a friend, I should be grateful.' Then with a swirl of silk, she left the room, leaving a faint fragrance in the air and uncertain emotions in my heart.

*****

Alberto paid me the courtesy of providing a horse for my use, rather than expecting me to ride pillion, but because my left arm was still strapped he insisted on gripping my bridle as well as his own. I must have cut a pitiable figure when we skirted the bustling market stalls in the Piazza delle Erbe but the appearance of the captain's crest showing the lion of Venice was enough to ensure some deference from hawkers, shopkeepers and bystanders, while we were passing. When we had escaped from the throng and rounded the corner by the Scaligeri church, Alberto was as surprised as I was to see a posse of horsemen drawn up outside the entrance to the Casa delle Arche, bearing on their chests and their unfolded pennants the self-same symbol of the Most Serene Republic. Immaculately trained, they recognised an officer with the Venetian garrison, albeit one stationed in this dependent city, and they saluted smartly.

'Signora Guarienti-Schioppa has visitors,' Alberto murmured. 'She may not invite you to be presented to them. Don't be offended. Your battered features would not do her household credit.'

I swore genially at him as we rode through the gateway but, knowing what Alberto could not, I concluded that, despite my blemishes, it was highly likely I would be summoned forthwith to Signora Orsola's presence. And so it proved. Despite Sandrino's urgent wish that I should visit a stable-lad whose face and neck were covered in a rash, I was whisked upstairs, at the lady's express command, to pay my respects to her guest. Iacopo tried to delay me with malicious allegations about Bernardino's impending disgrace, which he claimed was the objective of the Venetian visitation, but the steward cuffed him aside with a vicious blow. Nervousness and acrimony seemed to ripple through the air in the Casa delle Arche.

Chapter 15

The lady was magnificently dressed, in a gown of splendid brocade I had never seen before, with a veil of silver tissue cascading from her elaborate horned headdress. At her side was a thin, austere-looking man, clad in a doublet of black silk surmounted by an opulent sable robe. He wore a collar of gold links, bearing the crest of the Venetian lion, and his only other adornment was a large emerald in his velvet cap. There was no mistaking his status and the steady focus of Signora Orsola's eyes as she fixed them on me made clear that I was to behave with the utmost circumspection.

'Signor Giustiniari, this is my physician, Doctor Somers. Signor Giustiniari is a member of the Venetian Council of Ten. We are greatly honoured by his visit.' Honoured and troubled, her eyes spoke as I bowed.

'Ah, the amorous English physician! I have heard of your misfortunes. Was it a furious husband who treated you so roughly, in order to satisfy his abused honour?'

'I never saw my assailant's face but I admit there was a gentlewoman in the case.'

A tiny twitch at the side of Signora Orsola's mouth showed that she approved my response, giving no suggestion that a Venetian cut-throat might have been employed to kill me.

'I am relieved any murderous intentions were thwarted but you must appreciate that the virtue of our Italian women is sacred to us.'

I did not respond to his sardonic provocation. 'I owe my life to my friend, Captain Alberto, from the garrison in the Cittadella.'

Signor Giustiniari held my gaze. 'You choose your friends wisely,' he said at length. 'Captain Alberto is a fine servant of the Most Serene Republic. You will do well to be guided by him. When you are not gallivanting in pursuit of our tradesmen's wives, do you find your employment with Signora Guarienti-Schioppa congenial?'

'It is a privilege to serve her household and its members provide me with a variety of maladies and minor hurts which test my skills.'

His lip curled aggressively. 'Smooth-talking and astute, as I have heard. I counsel you to concentrate on these proper matters for your professional judgement and not to fritter your time in less noble pursuits. It has come to my ears that you may be diverted from the practice of medicine by fanciful ideas of solving mysteries which are not your concern. This would be most inadvisable. The Most Serene Republic and its dependent *Terrafirma* value your experience as a physician and I have received good reports of your capability from the esteemed Professor Bonalini in Padua. I trust your recovery from these present injuries will be rapid.' I bowed, expecting him to dismiss me after these acerbic words, but he continued to regard me in silence. 'Did the aggrieved husband flay the side of your face, to cause that dire eruption of the skin which disfigures your cheek?'

I clenched my fists, determined not to show my fury at his discourtesy. 'I am a dutiful son of Holy Church,' I said guardedly. 'I give no credence to the ignorant who have suggested the Devil put his stain on me but it did not come from any mortal intervention.'

A curl of the lip again. 'Your composure in adversity does you credit. Take care not to become complacent and venture beyond the limits of your capacity.' He moved closer and glared coldly at me. 'The Signora is unfortunate in having two of her followers set upon by ruffians in the last few weeks. I am told the young lawyer was brutally attacked. Did you know him well?'

'No, sir. He was not a colleague who encouraged familiarity. Speaking as a physician, I thought he suffered a disturbance of the humours which made him of a nervous disposition with others.'

The Venetian nobleman sneered. 'You may well be correct, Doctor Somers.' Then, at last, he dismissed me and I was gratified to see the flicker of Signora Orsola's eyelid, signifying that I had acquitted myself acceptably. Yet that knowledge brought me little comfort, for Signor Giustiniari's detailed information about my activities and the implicit threat he had given me were both deeply disturbing.

*****

After this subtle battle of wits I wanted only to get to my chamber, change into fresh garments and spend a restful half-hour before resuming my duties and visiting the spotty stable-lad. Instead, along the corridor from the Signora's solar, Bernardino Biagio was waiting, clutching his gown across his chest and stooping as he advanced upon me crabwise. His face was pinched and his complexion unhealthy.

'I thank God you did not suffer fatal injury, Doctor Somers. I have great need of your services.'

'What is it, Messer Biagio? You look in pain.'

'Shrewdly discerned. My guts are torturing me but my arse will let nothing free. Several days have passed without passing a stool. I pray you administer an enema without delay.' His breath was noxious. 'That pompous Venetian fellow has not helped my condition. He started by asking whether he could see any papers which my nephew was working on and I assured him I had taken charge of everything Alessandro left. He then dared to question whether I had in my possession papers relating to the Signora's brother which I should disclose to the Most Serene Republic. I expressed my outrage at such a suggestion that I should breach my lord's confidence, while giving my lawyer's oath that I have never seen anything treasonable in his correspondence. I am insulted that the Council of Ten should imply I might condone treason or betray the family I serve. That high and mighty Signor actually asked that I open my strong-box in front of him, to reveal the papers inside it. I refused absolutely. The box is triple locked and no one has access except me. I am a notary of unimpaired reputation. How could they treat me like a common vagabond? Their foul insinuations have brought renewed agony to my belly. The gripes are intolerable. I beg you to give me relief.'

Biagio's account of his professional indignation was muddled but the attempt to broach his strong-box was intriguing and, with reckless disregard for the warning Signor Giustiniari had delivered, I formed a rapid conclusion. Clearly the servants of the Most Serene Republic were aware of, but had failed so far to identify, any documents incriminating Guglielmo Guarienti and sending one of the Council of Ten to pursue the matter openly bespoke a degree of desperation. Nevertheless I could not allow myself to be distracted from my immediate responsibilities.

'I'll do what I can of course but Sandrino wishes me to confirm whether a boy from the stables has brought corruption of the flesh into the household, by way of suppurating pustules.' Bernardino shrank back and I patted his shoulder. 'Lie on your bed in whatever position gives you relief and I'll come to you as soon as I can. I'll ask Messer du Bois to fashion a suitably gentle substance to purge your constriction without burning your anus. He'll have it ready for when I can come.'

Bernardino expressed unusually humble gratitude and shuffled towards his room but I did not move away at once, waiting until I was certain I had not imagined movement in a shadowy alcove along the passageway. I strode forward and dragged the eavesdropper into the light, shaking him angrily. 'How dare you listen to a consultation between a physician and his patient? Even you should recognise that a man's health is no matter for jest. You go too far, Iacopo!'

'The Venetian's fingered you as well, has he? Properly riled, aren't you, Doctor Somers? I shouldn't care to be a patient in your care while you're in that mood. Poor old Bernardino! Let go of my ear; you're hurting me.'

I was surprised to realise I was squeezing the little fellow's lobe with unnecessary force but as I pushed him aside I slapped his cheek to compound the injury. He squealed and glared with a fury he not previously directed towards me, before stumping off with an aggrieved wail. 'Fucking physician! You'll be sorry for this.'

I leaned against the wall to recover my composure, ashamed of my behaviour towards the despicable dwarf. I was in no state to show the forbearance which was my duty in dealing with the afflicted, but that was no excuse, and I promised myself I would apologise as soon as I had completed my duties. Then I called on Geoffrey to seek his assistance in mixing a suitable substance for an enema and, briefly, in my friend's company I found relief in shared and private laughter. Geoffrey was improperly mirthful at the idea of poor Bernardino being put at my mercy and made factitious remarks about the opportunity to add something unpleasantly astringent to the mixture. We exchanged vulgar jests on the subject, which were unseemly but soothing to my harassed mind and aching body, so my equanimity was pleasantly restored by the time I descended to the outhouse where the wretched stable-lad had been confined.

As I hoped and expected the boy's flushed face displayed a particularly fierce case of that youthful affliction in which scabby flakes and discharges of pus besmirch an already blotchy complexion. There was no danger to others and I promised to send him a balsam to reduce the itching. I called on Sandrino to assure him there was no cause for panic and was pleased to hear from him that Signor

Giustiniari had left the Casa delle Arche. He was to be entertained that evening by the Podestà, the senior nobleman who represented Venice's interests in Verona, but he was to call again on Signora Orsola around noon the following day. I trusted I would not be required to encounter him on that occasion.

Heavy with weariness I left Sandrino and climbed the stairs towards my own chamber to prepare for my encounter with Bernardino's posterior. I had reached the first landing and turned to the upper flight when Constanza emerged from the women's room, clutching a gurgling infant to her chest. I stopped in surprise at the sight of such unexpected mutual contentment and she looked no less taken aback by my appearance.

'Doctor Somers! Oh, how you have been battered! The villain meant to take your life. I thank the blessed Virgin you were spared.' Her concern seemed genuine.

'Amen. It's kind of you to be anxious on my behalf. Despite my bruises, I am much recovered and within the week I should be able to use my left arm again. But you, Madonna, are looking very well. Has the ache in your back eased? You must be careful lifting the lively bundle in your arms. Master Giorgio is growing apace.'

She gave a contented sigh. 'He has brought me delight that I never thought to find. I marvel now at my distaste for his wailing when he first came here for I am privileged to help care for him and give his mother respite.' The child was becoming restless and squirmed, pulling at her necklace. 'There, there, my poppet, we will go to find her at once but here is the kind doctor to whom we are so grateful.'

I did not want to detain her but I was puzzled by her words. 'What have I done to deserve your gratitude?'

For a moment she lowered her eyes and, had she possessed a different nature, I would have considered her manner coy. 'Signora Orsola has told me – in confidence of course – about your commitment to marry my dear sister. I am overwhelmed with joy that your marriage will restore her disturbed senses and drive away the demons which have plagued her.'

'I've given no commitment, Madonna. The Signora has charged me with duties which must be performed before I can think about my own future.'

'But the Signora has offered you Diamante's hand and a jointure to provide generously for you both?'

I acknowledged this was true and forced myself not to recoil when she leaned forward to plant a kiss on my cheek. 'You shall be my dearest brother,' she purred. 'All things may yet be remedied – and by a physician. It is fitting. There is bounty still to be found in my cruel life. If only you could cauterise the last lesion in my heart.' She pulled back from me sharply as if alarmed that she had said more than she intended and the movement displeased Master Giorgio who let out a furious yell. I was glad of his intervention.

'You'd best take the child to Madonna Antonia and I have medical duties to fulfil. Please keep these subjects close from others until they are resolved.'

'Assuredly. But if I thought that when you become my good-brother, you might offer sympathy for my loss, the hope would brighten my days.'

The baby was now exercising his powerful lungs to their fullest extent and I was not sure if I heard her correctly. 'If there are issues you would wish to discuss more fully, let us seek a better time and place.'

'Dear Doctor Somers, perhaps it should be done but my courage is feeble. You shall advise me. God bless you.'

I watched her move off towards the apothecary's quarters with relief but considerable perplexity. I was too weary to burden myself with seeking the meaning of her strange allusions. I longed for my pallet and an hour's recuperation but first I must attend the constipated notary so I gritted my teeth and smiled grimly at the prospect.

*****

The dish lay ready for me on the table in my room and Geoffrey had been generous in the quantity of material he had provided. It was singularly unattractive, shiny and grey with specks of white dotting its glutinous surface, and for a moment I wondered if my friend had actually carried out his jest to put something unappealing in the mixture. I noticed a splodge of the substance on the floorboards beside the table and was surprised that a diligent apothecary should have left a spillage without wiping it clean but my attention was quickly diverted as I gathered my implements. Only as I balanced the pouch of tools, with the dish, in my one good hand and struggled to open the door at the same time, did I realise that I might face some difficulties in carrying out the treatment unaided. So, while passing along the corridor to Bernardino's room, I instructed a page to solicit Messer du Bois's assistance with the procedure.

Bernardino greeted me with faint moans and implored me to administer the enema without delay so I carefully scraped a curl of the concoction onto my spatula and began to shape it for insertion as best I could. I was reassured to hear the tap at the door and Geoffrey moving to my side. 'Your timing is perfect. I hadn't thought how awkward it would be to do this one-handed. I shall need another pair of hands to hold the basin to receive the consequences.' I held out the empty receptacle for him to take.

'Stop!' He grasped my wrist. 'Don't use that.'

I rounded on him angrily, although I could scarcely credit he would play a practical joke at such a time. 'What do you mean?'

'That isn't the mixture I made. Where did you find it?'

'In my room of course. On the table where you left it.'

'It isn't right. Something's been added. Those white flecks shouldn't be there.' He snatched the dish from my hand and his sudden pallor convinced me this was no prank.

Despite his discomfort, Bernardino twisted on his side to face us. 'What is it? What has happened?'

Geoffrey had taken the dish to the window to peer more closely at its contents and he spoke quite calmly. 'My simple mixture has been adulterated and I'd stake my reputation that this white powder is arsenic.'

'What?' Bernardino and I exclaimed simultaneously.

'Someone is attempting to poison Messer Biagio in an unusual way, although I am not confident it would have succeeded. The arsenic would not be ingested normally and so it might not be efficacious...'

'The Visconti of Milan were said to have used this trick against Rupert of Bavaria years ago.' Bernardino's voice had gained strength. 'It did not succeed then. I read of the case when I was studying the law with regard to poisoning.'

'Nevertheless this must be considered a serious attempt to kill you.' I turned to Geoffrey. 'Do you have any more of the original compound?'

The apothecary nodded and produced a small box from inside his gown. 'I took the precaution of bringing a little in case it was needed. See how smooth it is. The murderer has sprinkled the arsenic into my mixture and crudely stirred it.'

I fixed my eyes on my patient and stilled my shaking hand. 'Bernardino, I will administer the correct enema in the hope that you will rapidly benefit but when that has been done I suggest we consider how to proceed in the face of this murderous attempt. I suspect your intended death is part of wider mischief. We must seek to turn the situation to our

210

advantage. It may even be prudent to pretend the poison has taken effect.'

The notary smiled thinly. 'Doctor Somers, you are a man after my own heart: innovative in the face of adversity. Pray commence.'

*****

As evening fell Sandrino announced to the household that Messer Biagio was very unwell and, after treatment I had given him, he was languishing on the verge of unconsciousness. Geoffrey reported to me that the implication I might have harmed Bernardino hung in the air and, when the steward added that I was suffering from exhaustion and had taken to my bed, there was much muttering about my competence. I was certainly glad of a period of rest but would have chosen other circumstances in which to enjoy it. Nevertheless, crouched in the unfamiliar chair by Bernardino's desk, I managed to doze lightly.

There was only the sliver of a dying moon that night and it did little to illuminate the narrow bedroom through the open doorway from the notary's study. With wayward symbolism the beam picked out the metalwork on the lid of the strong-box, standing on the table beside his bed, and showed the three keyholes which needed to be engaged to open the chest. Further away from the window all was darkness and the house was silent, not least because Sandrino had insisted Bernardino must be undisturbed and blankets had been laid in the corridor to deaden any sounds.

I had no way of gauging the hour when at last I was roused by a groan from the bedchamber. In the stillness I fancied I could hear the intake of breath as the intruder entered from the passageway and waited to see if the invalid would rally and discover he was not alone. I prayed that the would-be thief would hold his nerve and the notary would sustain no injury, while I listened carefully until I detected the tinkle of the keys, lifted from Bernardino's belt which had been flung aside to give his belly greater freedom. I was disconcerted to realise how quietly the interloper moved and, had it not been for Bernardino's pre-arranged whimper, I might have been unprepared for the next crucial stages of our contrivance.

To my surprise the visitor slipped out of the sickroom, back into the corridor, and then, with the slightest click, I heard the door from the passage into the study being locked. The villain was leaving nothing to chance for, even if the invalid was capable of rallying, Bernardino could not now escape through the adjoining room. I feared the action also implied that my presence in the study might have been detected, for I too was now trapped.

Shrouded by one of Bernardino's gowns, I crept into the darkest corner behind the communicating door while the rogue re-entered the bedchamber. I felt certain that my breathing was thunderous and my legs were trembling uncontrollably. I heard him approach the strong-box and fiddle with the keys as he determined which fitted each of the locks and I peeped from beneath my cloak to confirm it was as I suspected. My anxiety was unnecessary and he concentrated on his task, adroitly mastering the catches, until when the lid flew open he audibly suppressed a sigh and drew out several packets of paper. He held them to catch the light of the moonbeam and chuckled as he set one aside. In that instant of turning away from the window, with his eyes more accustomed to the gloom, he must have caught some faint movement from the shadowed doorway and suddenly he leapt towards me with his knife unsheathed.

I shouted as I grappled one-handed with my attacker but I could not have held my own for long and I was deeply grateful when the door into the bedroom from the corridor was flung open and friends rushed to my assistance. Geoffrey and Sandrino quickly restrained the dwarf while

212

Bernardino, gaunt and pallid as his nightshirt, leapt from the bedclothes brandishing a cudgel and bellowing about treachery and theft. Iacopo spat in my face, as I sank on the floor dabbing at a thin gash across my wrist and he poured out a stream of abuse and curses.

Undaunted, the notary picked up the packet of papers taken from his strong-box and examined it. 'These relate to the proposed transaction between Signor Guarienti and Marquis Gianfrancesco of Mantua. There is nothing treasonable here. It was merely a commercial sale which was never put into effect.'

'Who said there should be more? This is what I wanted to see. These papers record my lord's intention to sell me, after a lifetime of service, in order to redeem some measly debt. How much? How much was he to receive for casting aside my lifetime of devotion?'

Bernardino fingered through the documents. 'Since you ask, the sum was one thousand ducats, an uncommonly large amount for a jester. It is the value of a wealthy diplomat's ransom. You should be flattered.'

Sandrino intervened and beckoned into the room three armed men waiting in the passage. 'Enough of this. Put this villain in chains and set him in the storeroom until morning. He will appear before the Signora and receive justice at her hands. We have apprehended a thief and murderer.'

'Scarcely a murderer,' Iacopo snarled. 'I see no one dead, more's the pity. You think you're clever, English physician, don't you? But you know nothing. You'll reap your reward soon enough and it won't be pretty. The Venetians will curdle your guts and shrivel your manhood. I'll dance on your grave.'

His enraged screams echoed along the corridor as he was dragged away but it was not his imprecations which worried me. Exhausted and perplexed as I was, I thought it possible that he was speaking the truth when he claimed to be interested only in the papers which related to him. For the sake of his offended honour, he had been prepared to commit murder and to tarnish my reputation as a physician but it did not necessarily mean he knew of the documents for which the nobility of both Venice and Mantua were searching. One thing seemed certain, however: there were no such papers in Biagio's strong-box.

Chapter 16

By the time I was escorted to Signora Orsola's room, shortly after daybreak, she had already been made aware of the night's events by Sandrino and Bernardino. I was pleased to see the notary looked less pinched and sallow and he assured me my treatment had proved efficacious but the lady raised an imperious hand to check his expression of gratitude.

'I do not care to hear these intimate details, Messer Biagio. Suffice it to say that you are both relieved and alive. Iacopo is being fetched from the storeroom where he has been imprisoned and I need to determine his fate before the Venetian embassy returns. Doctor Somers, is it your view that he is the traitor who originally betrayed my brother?'

'Signora, I think you should put the question to Iacopo. I am not convinced the timing supports that idea.'

She nodded. 'It had occurred to me. Bring him in!'

She had heard the clank of chains as Iacopo was dragged towards her door and in a moment he was hurled at her feet. His face showed bruising which had not been there at the time he was taken in charge and when he opened his mouth it was clear two of his teeth were newly missing.

'Signora,' he snivelled, 'I have been beaten.'

'And you think you do not deserve it? You are likely to incur a far worse fate. You will answer my questions truthfully or you will be put to the torment. When did you tell the Venetian authorities that my brother had been in communication with Mantua?'

I noticed Sandrino and Bernardino exchange quick glances of surprise but Iacopo's attention was wholly on his mistress. 'When you took me to Venice two or three months ago.'

'Why did you do that?'

'Because I hated your brother for his willingness to sell me, like a horse or a parcel of land. I, who had served your family loyally all my life.'

Signora Orsola bit her pale lip and beckoned me to take up the questioning. 'Signor Guarienti was already detained in Venice at that time. Did you think he was not being punished sufficiently?'

'Oh, wise physician! If you had not interfered with what did not concern you, nothing would have thwarted me.'

'Answer the question!' Sandrino prodded the prisoner with his foot.

'Guglielmo Guarienti is living in luxury. I had imagined him languishing in a Venetian prison, starving in an underground cell, suffering the exquisite agonies for which the Most Serene Republic is noted. I was infuriated to hear how he is living – lacking nothing, indulging every carnal whim, with a string of mistresses in tow.'

'So you suggested to the Council of Ten that he had been in communication with Mantua, pledging support for the uprising four years ago? That there was written evidence of his treachery?'

'And so there is! Messer Biagio had it all the time.'

Bernardino drew his gown across his chest and cleared his throat. 'What you discovered last night, when you were intent on murder and theft, merely concerned the Signor's proposal to sell your services to the Marquis of Mantua. You may see that as insulting but it was not treachery to Venice.'

For the first time Iacopo looked at a loss. 'I did not specify to the Council of Ten what papers there might be, only that I knew there had been written communication with Gonzaga.'

I caught Signora Orsola's eye and she nodded. 'Iacopo,' I said, 'why did you not tell the Venetians about the papers when you first laid evidence against Guglielmo Guarienti and caused him to be arrested?'

216

His heavy chains clanked as he twitched in anger. 'I never did any such thing. I never laid evidence against him until we went to see how he fared in Venice. I was delighted someone had accused him and led to his arrest but it was not me! You are trying to entangle me in things I know nothing about. My anger has festered since we went to Venice but I did not put him there. I wanted to see what value he set on my services in bartering with Gonzaga but I know nothing of other papers.'

'Why should we believe you?' The Signora's sharp question cut across his protests and he turned to face her, as a wave of confused emotions passed over his haggard face.

'You will indict me for attempted murder, Signora, and my life is forfeit. Why should I deny other transgressions? How will it advantage me?'

The lady rose from her chair and drew herself up with all the inborn dignity of her noble ancestry. 'What you say has the ring of truth and your life is indeed forfeit. I do not propose to execute sentence on you immediately, however, as I want our Venetian visitors far away from Verona before I take action that may annoy them. Sandrino, you will arrange for Iacopo to be taken at once, under guard, to the Castel Schioppa and there incarcerated securely until I am ready to declare his fate. Go, wretched, ungrateful clown, you have betrayed my house.'

Signora Orsola indicated that Bernardino and I should remain after Iacopo was taken away and, while his cries faded along the corridor, she resumed her seat. 'Do you accept my judgement?' she asked.

'It is your prerogative, Signora,' the notary said and he gave no hint of any resentment.

'I think it judicious,' I added. 'Iacopo may need to be questioned again but I also thought he spoke the truth. If so, it remains to be resolved who first betrayed your brother and who knew of any written evidence of his alleged treachery towards Venice.'

Bernardino peered at me before transferring his attention to the lady. 'Signora, I swear I have no knowledge of paperwork between your brother and Gonzaga other than that relating to Iacopo.'

'I accept that.' She turned to me. 'Doctor Somers, what is it? You have become quite pale. You are still weak from your wounds. We have tested you too greatly.'

'No, no, Signora. It was something that Messer Biagio said that has echoed in my head and brought back a memory I should have remembered sooner. He spoke of paperwork and it was this that featured in the conversation I had with Alessandro on the afternoon before he vanished: the day news came of Marquis Gianfrancesco's illness. Alessandro seemed extremely nervous, shaking at the sight of a Venetian messenger coming from this house, and when I mentioned paperwork he rounded on me unexpectedly, asking what I meant. I can hear the alarm in his voice when he asked me "what paperwork?" He must have turned on his heel then and I believe he returned directly to the Borgo San Zeno.'

Signora Orsola tapped the arm of her chair. 'Bernardino, could your nephew have been aware of correspondence with Mantua without your knowledge?'

The notary shuffled his feet. 'It is most unlikely but I cannot say it is impossible. Are you suggesting that the foolish young man's death was other than common assault?'

'I think it possible,' I said. With your permission, Signora, I should like to ask Messer Biagio what he knows of his nephew's friendship with a priest, Father Mario, who served at San Zeno Orador and Alessandro spoke of as his brother.'

Bernardino looked uncomfortable and twisted his fingers together. 'They had known each other since boyhood and Alessandro insisted on keeping up their acquaintance although I advised him against it. The priest had a dubious reputation for matters I should not care to name before

Signora Orsola.' The lady snorted derisively but the notary hurried on with his account. 'Father Mario was well thought of in some quarters, I understand, despite his weaknesses.'

'You speak of him in the past tense,' the lady said.

'I heard he met an untimely end at the hands of bandits, or possibly men offended by his un-Christian behaviour.'

'As did Alessandro.' Her comment hung in the air for a moment before I intervened.

'Messer Biagio, you say that Father Mario was well thought of in some quarters. What did you mean?'

Bernardino looked down at his taut, bloodless fingers. 'He was a native of Mantua. He held some kind of honorary position in the city and was invited there from time to time. Alessandro once told me he continued to act as confessor to some of Gonzaga's henchmen whom he had known years earlier.'

'You never thought to tell me this, Bernardino? Your nephew was consorting with a priest who served Gonzaga!'

'Signora, I did not think it signified to that extent. I tried repeatedly to disassociate Alessandro from the priest's pernicious influence but there was nothing to suggest a more sinister link with Mantua.'

In the distance the bells of the Lamberti Tower rang the hour and Signora Orsola stood. 'Signor Giustiniari and his Venetian cohorts will be returning soon. They must hear nothing of these disturbances in the house and you had best both keep out of the way. Bernardino, you have leave to return to your close-stool. Doctor Somers, please consider carefully the implications of all that has occurred, what you have remembered and what we have just heard. Wait on me after we have dined this afternoon and we will discuss the matter further.' The notary and I bowed and moved to the door and only then did she add icily, 'I am obliged to you both for your services, even if some disclosures are somewhat belated.'

*****

I was not summoned to meet Signor Giustiniari again and had time to mull over all that had been revealed in the last twenty-four hours, before taking my place at the household's communal meal. The atmosphere was subdued and I fancy I was not alone in regretting the absence of Iacopo's annoying but distracting japes although Sandrino did his best to lighten the mood. He announced the happy news that he had concluded negotiations for the premises which were to provide a home and apothecary's shop for Geoffrey and Antonia, so Bernardino would now draw up the necessary legal documents with a view to Messer du Bois opening his business before the Feast of the Nativity.

I leaned across to my friend and slapped him on the shoulder. 'Watch out for the terms the notary inserts. You'll be in debt all your life, paying back the Signora's loan if he has anything to do with it.'

Geoffrey winked. 'She's given clear instructions that no advantage is to be taken of us. After all usury is an abomination, even in dealings with a foreigner. Antonia has charmed her, as she does everyone, and we are sincerely grateful to the lady.'

Signora Orsola had risen so, although I was still chewing, it was time for me to leave the table and attend her but I made my way to her room full of misgivings. I had decided what I must do but I relished neither the need to explain my intentions nor the prospect of implementing them. Constanza admitted me to the solar, where her mistress was standing in front of the window which faced towards the Scaligeri church but the darkness outside was uninterrupted. The room itself was dimly illuminated by a single candle set in a sconce on the wall and the thought came to me that the lady wished to obscure the subject we must discuss as profoundly as the gloom surrounded us.

220

Constanza withdrew to a stool in the corner by the empty hearth and, in defiance of the shadows, pretended to sew.

I could not make out the Signora's expression as she turned but her voice was full of regret. 'Well, Doctor Somers, what have you concluded?'

I took a deep breath to outline the theory I had developed. 'I believe the secret of the stolen letters is somehow bound up with Alessandro and Father Mario. I don't suggest that they were complicit in the original allegations which led to your brother's arrest – that may or may not be so – but it seems to me probable they obtained the documents missing from Gonzaga's strong-box. I believe both men died for their presumption, at the hands of dangerous enemies, but there is no evidence the papers have been retrieved, either by Venice or Mantua. Quite to the contrary: we know the Council of Ten is still searching for them and your nephew must have been told about the unresolved theft, by the Gonzaga Marquis, after the wretched pair had been murdered. Alessandro's body was battered and he may have been tortured before he was killed, perhaps to secure information about the papers' whereabouts. Then the priest may have been set upon in the hope he was carrying them.'

'But it seems he was not. If your premise is correct, how do you explain that?'

'The Commendatore told us that, following discovery of the theft, travellers leaving Mantua were being searched rigorously, so I wonder if it is possible Father Mario had stolen the papers but secreted them in Mantua itself until he could safely retrieve them. Then, when he was warned by Alessandro the Marquis might be on his deathbed, he deemed it prudent to remove them from the city but in the event decided he could not do so without risking capture. I think he was returning empty-handed when he was attacked.'

'In which case the papers are still in Mantua?'

'It is possible.'

Signora Orsola inclined her head slightly. 'So, in the absence of living witnesses, what do you propose?'

'To go to Mantua myself.'

I heard the rustling of material from Constanza's corner and sensed, although I could not see, the rigid set of the Signora's mouth. 'That is foolhardy, is it not?'

'I shall try to mitigate the dangers. I have no wish to throw my life away on a fool's errand but a visit to Mantua seems necessary. I will appeal for help to the Commendatore.'

I did not add "and to his Mantuan mistress" but I knew Signora Orsola understood my intention. 'You may think this will mitigate the danger,' she said, 'but it could place you at worse hazard. Matteo may give you advice but he will abandon you to your fate if your mission fails.'

'He made that clear, Signora, but I have no other choice if I am to pursue the commission you gave me and cancel my debt to him. I need your permission to absent myself from the household. I should also like to know whether you believe the servants of Venice are likely to track my movements.'

She sighed and moved to stand below the lamp, so that shadows streaked her face, highlighting the wrinkles normally concealed by cosmetic paste, and she appeared years older than usual. 'You have permission to do what you judge needful. As for Venice, I have no doubt the Council of Ten regard you with suspicion. Indeed Signor Giustiniari suggested that you might be seized and taken to the Most Serene Republic. An embassy from England is expected to arrive there before the mountain passes are closed for the winter and it would be an earnest of good will towards your King Henry if the Council were to hand over a wanted criminal who fled from justice in his realm. You are a marked man, Doctor Somers, and if your leave the

222

comparative safety of Verona, you may never reach the walls of Mantua.'

It was worse than I feared and I caught my breath. 'I understand, Signora.'

She pulled herself upright and, as she moved, the contours of her face resumed their natural shape. 'Then I shall wish you God speed, physician. I set only one condition. If you are successful in finding incriminating papers, you will deliver them to me and no one else. I wish to destroy them with my own hands. Do you accept that?'

It was a reasonable request and I knew I would rather hand any documents to her, not the Commendatore. 'Yes, Signora.'

'Thank you, Doctor Somers. You may go.' I bowed but she checked my departure as I moved to the door. 'I counsel you one thing more. Do not take unnecessary risks. You face innumerable obstacles. Do not add to them by incurring the wrath of one who could prove your nemesis.'

I had no doubt of her meaning but the possibility she referred to seemed remote. 'Thank you, Signora,' I said lightly.

*****

Constanza followed me from the room and her mistress made no attempt to call her back. She accompanied me along the corridor and, as we turned a corner towards the stairs, she put her hand gently on my arm. 'The Signora does not believe you will return alive from this expedition.'

I grunted to conceal how startled I was by this declaration. 'How much do you understand of what we discussed?'

'Enough. I do not comprehend why you are bound to obey Matteo Maffei's orders.'

'He saved my life in Padua. I gave him my pledge although I scarcely expected I would be called on to redeem it.'

'You know little of the family's honour. I beg you to take care. My sister's well-being rests in your hands.'

Marriage with Diamante was far from my thoughts at that moment but I was touched by Constanza's continuing concern for her sibling. 'Do you hear how she fares in the convent?'

'No. She would not be permitted to write to me. It is always the same when she is at San Bonifacio.'

'She has stayed there before?'

'Twice, each time after she had been ill. The place has harsh memories for her.'

'That's unfortunate. When I've gone from the house, you could ask the Signora to let her return here.'

'You are considerate.' Constanza fastened her fingers on my wrist. 'I wish you had been here years ago. Things might have been different.'

'What do you mean?'

'I do not speak now of Diamante's troubles but my own loss.'

I was reluctant to hear her confidences but I was compelled to listen. 'You referred to your loss before. You have been bereaved? Were you betrothed to someone who died?'

Her voice was scornful. 'No: that is Diamante's story. I was never betrothed.' We had reached the staircase and she pinned me against the banister. 'I am sworn to silence but my heart bursts to speak out and now they are sending you to your death, I shall do so. I know you will not reveal my secret. Six years ago, Doctor Somers, I bore a child.'

A recollection came to me of the way she had supported her belly when bending to retrieve a swatch of ribbons, by the very newel post against which I was leaning, – a common enough gesture but one instinctive to women

224

who have carried a child to term. It seemed so inconsequential to remember this detail.

'Do you wish to tell me more?'

She nodded and her eyes were glistening in the darkness. 'The man was not free to wed me. Signora Orsola knew I had been seduced and forgave me; it was then she took me into her household. Doctor Morano suggested means to destroy the fruit of my sin but I refused to consider it and, with my lady's blessing, I was put away to bear my child secretly. I bore a daughter, Doctor. I saw her sweet face but she died, as babies do, within two days of her birth.'

'That is a sad tale, Constanza. I'm sorry.'

Her fingers tightened their grip on my sleeve. 'Six years I have lived with my grief. I understood before she was born that I must part with my infant, if Signora Orsola was to keep me in her household, but the little one would have been reared at in the convent at San Bonifacio and I would have known her safe. I don't even know if they gave her Christian burial there. I should have liked to shed a tear on her grave but they bundled me back to Verona.'

'Does Diamante know your history?'

'Of course. She has little sympathy for my sorrow. She chose a different solution. I have long since ceased to speak to her of my loss. I made confession years ago, of course, and my confessor has bidden me dismiss the transgression from my mind and concentrate on a life of repentance, chastity and service. Do you think it wrong, Doctor, that despite his counsel, I have yearned to tell another of my disgrace?'

I was puzzled by her reference to Diamante but I owed her a reply. 'Not at all. I think it most natural. I am no priest but as a physician I feel sure you should remember your child with love and not try to deny your grief. I don't seek only to treat occasional ailments but the whole person. That is my training and I believe it is the key to the balance of humours in our make-up.'

225

She released my arm and stepped back. 'God bless you, Doctor Somers. You have brought me comfort. I shall treasure your words and I shall pray for you, in life and death.'

'That is most heartening,' I murmured as we parted. I had much to reflect on before morning.

*****

I sent Rendell with a message to Alberto and was delighted that the captain agreed to meet me at his sister's house an hour before midday. This gave me time to pack my saddlebag and seek Geoffrey's agreement to borrow Leone's services once more. Then I made my way to the house where I had recuperated after the attack outside the church of San Lorenzo and Madonna Fratta was pleased to note how well my injuries were healing. She and her brother listened intently to a brief account of my own plans and I outlined what I had come to ask them. A mischievous smile played round her lips as she grasped what I was proposing and she waved her hand dismissively at the hint of unpleasantness which she might encounter. Oblivious to the implication his sister had speedily recognised, Alberto found my request surprising but he was no less puzzled by the enthusiasm Margherita displayed in agreeing to my suggestion without waiting for his advice.

'Well, I can see no harm in it,' he said, 'but are you sure you want to make the journey? It's hardly the time of year for a lady to venture out of the city.'

'It's only a short distance, brother dear, and you may ensure I am well attended. It will relieve the tedium of my daily life and offer a small diversion which I shall welcome.'

I hid my grin of appreciation and mirth at his bemusement. 'I was wondering, Alberto, if Rendell could be one of Madonna Fratta's escort? He would see it as an honour – and one that he deserves after all he did for me.'

'A fine idea. But won't you need a servant yourself in this journey you're to make?'

Madonna Margherita gave a wicked, knowing giggle. 'I fancy Rendell may not be the Doctor's preferred assistant on this occasion.'

'He is still rather young and I trust it will not be a swordsman I need at my side.'

'You will take Leone?'

How easily she read my mind. 'Your young cousin has proved his worth before. I value his cool head and intelligence.'

Madonna Fratta served cold meats, bread and cheese and we drank toasts to the two ventures on which we were to embark. Then Alberto set off to arrange his sister's excursion and I lingered for a moment on the threshold to say goodbye to her. 'I hope you will find interest in your mission,' I said, bowing over her hand.

'I'm grateful you have found me a means of entertainment.'

'It is a kindly act but take care not to put yourself in a disagreeable position.'

She held my eyes and the laughter left hers. 'You have not told us much of your own assignment but I deduce it involves danger.'

'Leone will not be at risk,' I said.

'I don't doubt it. But it is your safety which concerns me. May the blessed Virgin protect you, Harry.'

Her use of my given name gave me joy and I lowered my eyes. 'Madonna, if I have your prayers to support me, I shall find courage to face whatever comes. It will be my goal to return and listen to the description of your own adventure. God keep you.'

Part III – Verona, the Veronese hinterland and Mantua: 1443

Chapter 17

We crossed the river by the stone bridge, over the arches where Alessandro's battered body had been found, and climbed the hill to the Castle of San Pietro which dominated the left bank of the Adige, overlooking the congested streets of the city. Like the Cittadella, this Veronese citadel was garrisoned by the Venetians and young Leone was carrying a message from his cousin, Captain Alberto, to a colleague in command of a division of soldiers based there. I had expected my departure from Signora Orsola's house to be monitored and was not surprised to note a sharp eyed gatekeeper on the bridge who looked at us with suspicion until reassured by sight of Alberto's communication. At the castle the obliging officer received the letter with a smile and was pleased to entertain us to a simple meal, before providing a knowledgeable guide to lead us on the first part of our journey northwards. Once again I was conscious of a watchman in Venetian livery peering at us with curiosity as we left through the postern gate, away from the city, until he learned the purpose of our journey and realised that we had his captain's blessing. Then, as the wintery sun reached its zenith, we set out on our route following the upstream curve of the river where it tumbled towards Verona from distant alpine heights.

The narrow, steep-sided valley ran between the bulk of Monte Baldo to the west and the remote Lessini Mountains north of the city. It was on the lower slopes of the latter hills that Signora Orsola's family owned vineyards and, higher up, rich pastures where sheep grazed in the summer and provided good quality wool for the cloth trade. The servants who had oversight of these interests were located in a farmstead and hunting lodge and our guide accompanied us along the uphill track to the complex of buildings, accessed under an archway bearing the Guarienti-Schioppa crests where he left us. Members of the household and their outdoor workers had been promised a visit from the lady's new physician and we were made welcome. Soon, with Leone's help, I was dispensing tinctures and balsams to ease aching muscles and creaking joints and, less happily, listening to symptoms of more pernicious medical conditions, which I might alleviate but could not hope to cure.

We spent two full days at the manor house so I was able to give ample time to accounts of ailments and offered eager patients the best advice I could. Leone meanwhile engaged shepherds and vineyard workers in conversation, drawing on their detailed knowledge of the neighbourhood and showing youthful inquisitiveness about life in the secluded countryside. He reported to me as we rested side by side on our pallets on the second evening of our visit.

'The frontier with the Emperor's lands is not far from here to the north but there's an ill-defined area in between where men do not venture without armed escorts. The people here look to the south, to Verona, to sell their merchandise but for the main part the workers in these hills never travel away from them.'

'Have you learned anything about routes to the west, over the mountain ridge, towards the Lake Garda?'

'Oh yes, they do exist but they're said to be treacherous for strangers unfamiliar with the rock-faces and ravines. The best are south of Monte Baldo, winding their way across to the lakeside castles of Torri and Garda. The peaks are already impassable with snow but the lower tracks are still open – to those who know the way.'

'We'd best not delay then, in case these overcast skies produce a blizzard in the next few days. Have you managed to get a rough idea of how to find one or other of the paths?'

In the darkness I could tell Leone was grinning. 'I've done my best. It'll be an adventure, right enough. The main problem may be fording the river but our worthy guide from the castle of San Pietro mentioned a spot the locals use. Do you remember? He pointed out the precipitous track which leads down to the shallows. It's a good bit further south from here.'

'That's no bad thing,' I said as I snuggled into the scratchy mattress and drew the coverlet around my shoulders. 'Everyone here has got to believe we are returning to Verona, so we should set off confidently back on the way we came. We'll be well beyond the Signora's estate before we need to divert to the west. If your route could bring us out to the lake near Torri, we shouldn't be far from the Commendatore's camp and that will be very convenient.'

'Snowstorms, wolves, wild boar and brigands permitting,' Leone murmured.

'As you say, an adventure, right enough.' I hoped I sounded more buoyant than I felt while my drowsy mind remembered Margherita Fratta who should be starting off on her own adventure in a few days' time.

*****

I did not admit to Leone how alarmed I was at the prospect of our expedition. I was unused to traversing barren country and remembered how uncomfortable I had felt on our journey into Italy across the mountains, even though Geoffrey and I had been part of a strongly armed party, led by experienced guides. Now the lad and I were alone, in uncertain winter weather, passing through unfamiliar terrain and forced to climb high over the shoulder leading to the rugged peak, Monte Baldo. Moreover although I was feeling stronger my left arm still ached and its movement was restricted by the injury I had suffered. I never thought myself a brave man and it was with the greatest reluctance that I imagined myself confronting the challenges to come but circumstances had conspired to dictate my actions. My sleep was fragmentary that night.

The river crossing proved more straightforward than we had feared, once we had made the difficult descent down the steep track, and it was clearly in regular use by local farmers. So, too, the first part of the ascent beyond the ford was on a well-trodden path but, as we climbed beyond the highest shacks, the mountainside became bleaker and the route less easy to distinguish. As nightfall approached we found shelter in a rough sheep-pen, hoping to rise with the sun and complete our journey in daylight, but when we roused ourselves in the morning we were enveloped in thick mist and could barely discern the way we had come the previous evening. We were still some way below the crest of the ridge so it was clear we needed to continue uphill but traversing the rough ground, devoid of obvious features, we had no means of knowing if we were heading along the recognised route. We dismounted and led our horses slowly, step by step, scanning the limits of visibility and dreading the moment when we realised we had strayed into impassable territory.

Sure enough that moment came, when I noticed the earth crumbling beneath cautious hooves and checked Leone's advance behind me. 'I don't like the look of this,' I said. 'There's a dip in the ground and there are loose stones but I can't see how far down it goes.'

We withdrew a few paces and I took the reins of Leone's horse while he reconnoitred carefully along the edge of the depression. He soon passed beyond the distance I could see and I urged him to keep calling out, to ensure we did not lose each other, but there was no mistaking the crunch as his foothold gave way and he tumbled down the slope. I froze with horror at the thought the lad had disappeared into some terrible abyss and my cry was more like a scream than a measured shout for reassurance. To my relief he responded with a muffled roar of annoyance and I held my breath while he dragged himself, hand over hand, back up the disintegrating scree to re-join me. Twice he slipped and dislodged a small avalanche as he scrabbled for a hold, digging his fingers into the earth to secure a grip, groping with his feet for a solid toehold, but eventually he heaved himself upright beside me.

'No good trying to go down here,' he said cheerily. 'There's a sheer rock-face a few feet down below the rubble. Luckily there's a narrow ledge where I managed to stop myself sliding. We'd best creep along the top of the precipice and hope it doesn't stretch too far.'

Good sense might have decreed that we hunker down until the mist lifted but it had become very cold and occasional snowflakes floated in the air, so we were faced with a choice of unpleasant fates. Without debate, we agreed that we should go on, following Leone's suggestion, and we went on tiptoe, testing each step for stability, keeping the horses away from the brink, while our sight-lines became even more restricted. I was aware that I had lost all sense of direction and thought it likely, if we succeeded in escaping a worse calamity, that we would find ourselves back in the valley from which we had come. I was beginning to reconcile myself to that outcome, as the best way to guarantee our safety, when I realised that we had started to climb again, still walking parallel to the edge of the ravine, and this prompted conflicting hopes. Further progress uphill might yet bring us to our objective, crossing the shoulder of the mountain, but it also offered the prospect of new dangers as we passed into unknown and unseen territory. In my weariness I scarcely knew which outcome to prefer.

After a short time the ground seemed to flatten and, where it did so, we felt an unfamiliar movement of the air in our faces. 'The wind's getting up!' I said and we paused, clutching our horses' bridles, staring ahead as, almost imperceptibly at first, the mist thinned and swirled in front of us.

'Look! Look below!' Leone yelled. 'We've reached the top. What's that streak of grey in the distance?'

I flung my arm around his neck. 'That's Lake Garda. That's where we're bound. We're on track!'

The vista was quickly obscured but it had shown us enough to know the direction of our descent and, still leading our horses, we began to pick our way down the irregular slope while the snow fell more steadily and settled around our feet. Fortunately the flurries were disturbed now and then by the strengthening wind, causing drifts to build up against boulders, but giving us glimpses of the lake and the wooded area we must cross to reach it. As we progressed, Leone began to hum a jaunty ditty in celebration of our success and, with tuneless enthusiasm I joined in, hauling myself back into the saddle as we reached the shelter of the trees.

It was gloomy under the overhanging branches but we found a trodden path which wound its way, skirting the undergrowth, towards the centre of the forest belt and, despite the worsening conditions underfoot, we rode with carefree relief, paying little attention to our surroundings. We passed a pile of felled tree trunks and I smiled to think we were in an area where woodmen worked and lived, enjoying the comfortable realisation that we had passed beyond the inhospitable terrain of the mountainside. Then, suddenly my benign thoughts were shattered as a rope whirred in front of me, causing my horse to shy, and Leone yelped as he was dragged from his saddle. I rotated to see what had happened and was caught off balance when a cloth was thrown over my face and I too was forced to the ground.

'Where do you think you're going and how did you get here?' a voice asked, evidently not expecting a reply from our blanketed mouths. 'Who are you fucking spies for?' A kick to my groin did not encourage a response and I was flung over my own horse while my captor mounted behind me.

*****

I shouted muddled protests which were ignored until I calmed myself to think rationally. Then I bellowed as loudly as I could. 'I demand to see the Commendatore. I am come to meet Matteo Maffei!' But my words had no discernible effect.

Our pace slowed and I heard the creak of a gate so I roared again. 'I am physician to Signora Guarienti-Schioppa. I have business with the Commendatore.'

The gate clanged shut and I heard voices as a bolt slid into place and someone took the reins while the rider behind me dismounted. Leaving me spread-eagled across the saddle, he pulled the blindfold from my head and lifted my chin to stare into my face. His ill-favoured features seemed vaguely familiar but perhaps I saw in him the personification of all evil ruffians. 'What's your name then?'

'Harry Somers, physician. I am known to the Commendatore.'

'Why have you come here over the mountain? Men on lawful business come by the lakeside.'

I had no wish to explain more than necessary to this fellow, especially as I was not certain he was one of Matteo Maffei's men, but prudence dictated I risk something of the truth. 'I needed to avoid Venetian agents who have been tracking my movements.'

His mouth twisted into an unfriendly smirk. 'Why should I believe you?'

'The Commendatore himself will vouch for me.'

He signalled to two men who dragged me from the horse and, while they held me upright, he punched my belly. 'Sadly for you, the Commendatore is not here. As you well know, I suspect. You're a liar and an imposter.' He landed a second blow on my chin and drew a dagger from his belt.

There was only one desperate and risky chance for me to take. 'Madonna Beatrice! She knows me. Is she here? She could speak for me.'

The rogue fingered his blade as if unwilling to be dissuaded from blood-letting but a second man strode forward and whispered in his ear; then he scowled and sheathed the weapon. 'If you're lying, I'll skewer your guts. Bind his hands and take him to the woman.'

From the corner of my eye I could see where Leone had been stripped of his jerkin and bound to a tree beside an angry lout who flicked a horsewhip in the air. 'Release my assistant. He is an apprentice apothecary and innocent of any ill intent.'

As I spoke the whip slashed towards the boy's back and, although he did not flinch, a line of red specks appeared through his torn shirt. I hurled myself towards his abuser but was brought to the ground by two men who roped my wrists together. My captor's knife was at my throat again and his eyes glittered with excitement.

'Unwise. You've interfered with the camp's justice. The boy was cheeky and must be flogged. You've tried to prevent his punishment and so your life is forfeit.'

'Stuff and nonsense! Is this the justice the Commendatore sanctions? Free them both at once.'

The voice that could have seduced me from all virtue and ravished me with a sigh rang out imperiously until the posse of men fell silent. She glided between them, wrapped in a furred mantle, holding a lantern above her head, and stood looking down at my huddled body. 'Lift him and untie his hands.' There was a new note of compassion in her words.

'Madonna,' I stammered in confusion. 'We are at your mercy. We mean no harm.'

'Of course you don't, Doctor Somers. This is all a perverse misunderstanding. Carlo, these men are friends of the Commendatore and should be received with honour. Return to your post and have a care how you challenge strangers. A mistake like this could cost you dear.'

The man who had seized and threatened me glowered at her but said nothing and I sensed that Madonna Beatrice did not feel free to upbraid him more forcibly. He gave a curt nod and turned back to the gate in the wall, beckoning his two acolytes, while the lady snapped her fingers to summon her own attendants. 'Bring these men dry clothes, give them food and drink and see to their injuries. When Doctor Somers is refreshed bring him to the Commendatore's chamber. I shall be pleased to hear his errand, on my lord's behalf.'

She moved towards the castellated building, darkly looming in the distance, and my eyes followed her with gratitude, admiration and, despite all good sense, desire.

*****

'You look considerably more presentable,' she said as I was shown into her presence an hour later. 'Matteo's robe suits you well. I apologise on his behalf for your reception. It was a misfortune that you encountered Carlo. He is an ungovernable thug. The leader of mercenaries has need of such men but they do not readily do the bidding of anyone other than their master. When his back is turned they look for cruel entertainments.'

'I am profoundly grateful for your intervention. I gather the Commendatore is not here.'

She gave a little gurgle of amusement. 'Between you and me, Doctor Somers, he is gone to Milan. The Visconti are trying to wean him from accepting Mantua's commission so they can employ his troop of men directly. Their terms are tempting.' I was still naïve enough to be startled by the

236

negotiable allegiances of mercenary bands and my surprise showed on my face. 'Don't judge too harshly, physician, men of the Commendatore's calibre, successful condottieri, are not to be rated against the moral code of other worthy men.'

The candles in the sconces lit her face with flattering highlights but they did not disguise the dull bruising below her eye. I clenched my fists but tried to speak equably.

'I am not familiar with such matters. I prefer a simplistic concept of honour and goodwill.'

She sighed and held out a goblet of wine. 'What luxury to indulge such dreams,' she said. Then her voice took on a sharper edge. 'Why have you come here, Harry?'

I felt myself blush at her familiarity but I summarised the reasons for my convoluted journey: my belief that the Venetian authorities had tried to have me killed because of the enquiries I had made, the explicit threat their representative had made against me and the knowledge that they were keeping me under surveillance.

'What have you discovered that so alarms the Council of Ten?' Her eyes fixed on mine and, for my own peace of mind, I looked away first.

'I lack proof but I think that Bernardino Biagio's nephew and the priest from San Zeno Orador were murdered because someone – probably Venetian agents – suspected they held the papers stolen from the Marquis of Mantua.'

'And you believe they did?'

'I find it plausible that the priest took the letters – he often had business at the Gonzaga court and he might have had access to the strong-box where they were stored. I imagine he consulted his lawyer friend, Alessandro, when he realised what he had found and the pair of them saw a chance to profit from Signor Guarienti's indiscretions – but they were inexperienced in handling such dangerous material and doubtless uncertain how to act. It's possible Father Mario never took the papers out of Mantua and simply hid them somewhere in the city. Then, when Alessandro panicked and urged him to retrieve them, it was too late because powerful men were already on their trail and both men were murdered.'

'Is this more than an ingenious guess on your part? I understand the pair indulged in perverted pursuits. Isn't that enough to explain the attacks on them?'

'That's true, Madonna; it can only be conjecture. But there are oddities about the coincidence of their deaths. When I first examined Alessandro's body I concluded he had been dead and in the river for about twenty-four hours but he'd been missing for two days. I attributed his injuries to the battering of the Adige in flood but I wonder now if he'd been tortured in the intervening period, tortured in order to prise information from him about the whereabouts of the letters.'

'He could have been tortured simply because he indulged in unnatural practices. There are men who would believe that justified.'

'Again, you are right. But if you'll allow me to develop my theory, you'll see there is logic to it. Father Mario went to some trouble to disguise where he was going – he took the highway to Brescia but diverted on to a track leading to Mantua and came back the same way. He left his church at daybreak after Alessandro rushed back to see him but he was not attacked until he was nearly home again from wherever he'd been. In the meantime the poor young lawyer had been strangled. He may have been forced to say what the priest intended to do but believed he'd given his friend time to retrieve the documents. Father Mario was killed on his return journey but it seems he had no incriminating documents with him and his assailants went away empty-handed.'

Madonna Beatrice strolled to the darkened window and ran a finger along the stone lintel. 'That's borne out by Venice's continued efforts to find the papers and I know from my Gonzaga relatives that they are still missing. But, if your supposition is true, how could we hope to trace where they have been secreted?'

'That is the crux of the matter, Madonna, and here I have only the benefit of a foolish hunch to guide me.'

She turned and gave me a radiant smile which convulsed my stomach with delight. 'Pray share this hunch with me.'

'I believe Father Mario was a man of some ingenuity but if we could trace his contacts and places he frequented, we might find a clue to the hiding place.'

Her beautiful face glowed with intelligence. 'In Mantua?'

'You follow my thought processes, Madonna.'

'Mantua is a busy city and the Gonzaga palace alone is vast.'

'I don't think the papers will be in the palace. I have come to beg your help in securing entry to the city, without exciting interest in my mission. That's why I am here, Madonna. I would have asked the Commendatore's assistance but it's your aid I was really hoping for and, in his absence, I make bold to ask you directly. Could you provide me with an introduction to someone to be trusted in Mantua?'

She put her forehead to the lintel, closing her eyes, and I felt my heart thud in my chest as I waited to see if I had offended by my audacious request. If Matteo Maffei had been present he might well have booted me from the room and I expected he would resent my direct approach to his mistress. Yet it was her response which mattered to me, both for the sake of the matter in hand and because her good opinion was precious, beyond reason. She stood without moving for so long that I began to fear I should take my leave, disgraced in her eyes and a failure in my own. Then a tiny movement of her wrist alerted me to stay a little longer and she put her arms across her breast, hugging her shoulders as if she was fighting to contain overwhelming passion.

She dropped her arms to her side as she came forward and her voice was calm. 'Doctor Somers,' she said, 'I find your theory credible. It should be pursued. But what you propose is dangerous. You will be risking your life. I can think of only one way to lessen the peril slightly.' She paused for a moment and I could not imagine what she was about to say. 'I shall visit my house in Mantua. It is some time since I was there. I shall take my woman and two of Matteo's trusted men as escort and I shall be accompanied by my personal physician and, if you wish, his assistant. Will you accept this role and, as a temporary expedient, enter my service – perhaps as my secretary as well as physician?'

A tremor passed through my body and my hand was shaking. 'Madonna, won't there be danger for you too?'

'Not great, I think. Will you do this, Harry? Will you come with me to the city of my birth?'

I dropped to my knees in front of her. 'It is more generous than I could have dreamed of but I will most willingly come and pledge you my service.'

She signalled that I should rise and, as I stood up, very gently with her fingertips she stroked the blemish on my cheek.

Chapter 18

We took a boat and were rowed down the lake until we disembarked on the southern shore where horses were waiting. It had not been easy to persuade Leone to return to Verona, although he appreciated there were messages to be conveyed to Alberto and Signora Orsola, but what finally convinced him was the promise that I would need someone outside the city to help me surreptitiously, when the time was right. At this thought he brightened and, with Madonna Beatrice's help, we arranged a method to keep in touch once he was lodged nearby. I waved him on his way, as he set off eastwards, in the reassuring company of some respectable and well-armed merchants travelling to Verona, before I resumed my place, riding alongside the lady, my heart full of excitement and nervousness.

While we waited to cross the causeway and bridge into the city I scanned the skyline of turrets and towers, marvelling at the strong position Mantua enjoyed, enclosed by walls and almost surrounded by its river and three sluggish lakes. It would not be an easy matter to slip away from its protection unobserved, avoiding the checkpoints manned at every entry, and I noted how wayfarers leaving the fortifications were being searched thoroughly, as Matteo Maffei had told us. It was daunting enough securing admittance to the city, by the gate beside the line of mills, where the soldiers peered at us with frosty politeness. Madonna Beatrice was treated respectfully but without any effort on the part of the guards to expedite her party's entrance and I was scrutinised with unnerving attention. I had no doubt my distinctive features were well marked and my presence, although not challenged, was a matter of suspicion. With some difficulty I tried to look unconcerned during the inspection of our baggage and it was not until we had been waved through and rounded the corner into a narrow lane that I began to breath more naturally.

The lady's house had a narrow frontage, three storeys high, with its first floor projecting onto a portico supported by antique marble columns. Between each storey, on the exterior, was a band of elegant arcading which was matched by the cursive pattern around the windows at each level. It faced a central piazza, not far from the Gonzaga palace and, without any flaunting grandeur, its appearance was impressive. I registered these facts as we arrived but was relieved to be shown to a modest garret at the back of the house where I could recover from the alarm I felt. The hostile appraisal of the Mantuan guards had filled me with foreboding and my mission had never seemed more foolhardy. I reflected that the dangers I faced in an unfriendly city were likely to be worse than the hazards of the mountainside and I was seized by involuntary shivering, grateful to eat in private when food was brought to my room.

After I descended to the main part of the house next morning I was told that Madonna Beatrice had already gone out but wished me to wait on her in the afternoon. I was advised not to venture into the streets before her return and this reinforced my discomfort, so I was on tenterhooks until I heard her voice in the vestibule. Soon afterwards I was summoned to the main salon where I found her flushed from the cold air but also, I discovered, with the pleasure of a successful visit to her Gonzaga kin.

She greeted me merrily. 'Who would have thought that the weedy youth who teased me as an infant would acquire such grave demeanour now he is near to becoming Marquis? Ludovico is grown pompous, full of his own importance, but he will not obstruct our purpose.'

'You have visited the palace?'

'I have been graciously received by my lordly and legitimate cousin, Ludovico, and, as always, propositioned most indecorously by his chamberlain.' She waved aside my burble of concern. 'Never fear, Harry, the fellow knows he has no prospect of satisfaction while I am protected by the

Commendatore and accorded courtesy by the Marquis. Alas, dear Gianfrancesco is a shadow of his former self since his illness and he has passed conduct of business to his son, so it is Ludovico who will receive us tomorrow morning. I have ordered a new robe for your use so you will be fittingly arrayed as my secretary.'

'I am to meet Lord Ludovico?'

'Yes. It will confer respectability on your presence in the city. I was outraged by the surly looks those guards threw on you at the gate. I've also ascertained the names of two retainers at the palace whom your Father Mario visited when he was in Mantua. I admit I needed to let the chamberlain fondle my hand more than was seemly to obtain the information but Matteo must remain in ignorance of my trivial dalliance. You will be able to interview the men once Ludovico has acknowledged your position as my secretary.'

'Madonna, I'm overwhelmed. I trust you will not have to engage in any further unwelcome dalliance.' The words escaped my mouth before I could check them.

She ran her finger along the seam of her dress, jogging the seed pearls with which it was decorated. 'It was nothing,' she said as she folded her hands in her lap. 'Dalliance is my trade and sometimes it is pleasurable.'

Her eyebrows rose as she smiled and pursed her lips; then she sent me away to prepare for the meeting with the Marquis of Mantua's heir.

*****

He was a thickset man, plainly dressed, and to my eyes he resembled a wealthy merchant rather than the denizen of a princely house. I knew he had fought as a condottiere in years past but his manner now better befitted the counting house than the battlefield. When we were shown into the painted hall his wife, Barbara of

Brandenburg, was seated beside her husband, a heavy-featured woman with one infant in her arms and another clutching her skirt. After I made my obeisance she and her attendants left us and as I noted the supercilious look she cast on Madonna Beatrice I was glad she would not be present for my interview with Ludovico. He ordered a low chair to be brought for his cousin but then sat appraising me in silence while I became increasingly uncomfortable.

'Doctor Harry Somers,' he said at length. 'You served an English Duke, of the royal blood?' I confirmed my status and he continued. 'You are now acting as secretary and physician to my sweet Beatrice? Matteo Maffei has recruited you?' I inclined my head and he guffawed. 'Then I must believe he has seen great potential in you. What have you come to Mantua to do?'

'To serve Madonna Beatrice,' I muttered inanely.

He laughed again. 'Not in her bed, I trust! Or that villain will split your belly and extract your entrails. So why have you come? I hope you are not here to look for certain papers.'

He shared his cousin's knack of changing the subject without drawing breath and, already disconcerted by his indelicate sally, I found myself wrong-footed by his challenge. 'Papers, my lord?'

'Papers which were stolen from my father's strong-box: a theft only discovered when we checked the inventory recently. Papers that incriminate Orsola Guarienti's brother and will put a Venetian noose around his neck if they find their way to the Most Serene Republic. Papers the Signora has probably asked you to find. Papers I require to retrieve for my father.'

Madonna Beatrice rose and sank in a deep curtsey. 'Ludovico, you may rely on my discretion absolutely. I would countenance nothing to impair your interests. Doctor Somers is here on an act of charity following the death of a man in Verona.'

244

'Sweet cousin, come here.' He beckoned and stood, grasping her by the waist, fastening his lips on hers in a long slobbering embrace. Crimson with embarrassment and fury, I watched and wondered if there had been more between them than family affection. He held her a moment longer and then pushed her away. 'I trust you with nothing but a man's cock, Beatrice,' he said and moved forward to confront me. 'Doctor Somers, you are welcome and have permission to pursue your charitable business during your stay in Mantua. It beggars belief that the papers I spoke of would still be in our city and I do not take that possibility seriously. However I must make clear that if by the remotest chance you should find them, you will deliver them to me and no one else. If you do that honestly, you will leave this city with honour and reward. If you find them and dispose of them to others or destroy them, you will first be placed in a cage for public display, so the worthy citizens of Mantua can hurl abuse and ordure at a traitor, and then your severed head will be set on a spike to look blindly across the Middle Lake as a warning to others while your body will be flung into a pit of lime. Do I make myself clear?' He gave a short laugh but, as before, he did not wait for a reply. 'Go!'

He reached for Madonna Beatrice's wrist but she stepped aside. 'Will you not stay, sweet cousin?'

'No, Ludovico,' she said, taking my arm. 'You have threatened my secretary and offended me. I believe you still hope to engage Matteo's services to fight your wars. You will not wish me to tell him how you insult me.'

'He knows you for a sneaky harlot, as I do, my dear. Remember what I have promised your physician if he disobeys my order. Think of that while you bestow your favours on him.'

I did not dare to speak as we were escorted from the palace, so overcome was I by her cousin's final taunting words. By contrast Madonna Beatrice seemed quite unconcerned but as we crossed the piazza she smiled at me.

'We have Ludovico's permission, Harry. He has always had a vicious sense of humour but he clearly does not believe the papers are in Mantua. He won't bother to have you followed. You may proceed with your enquiries.'

'But if I find the papers...' I faltered.

'Let us take one step at a time. Who knows what the next may be?'

Afterwards, as we stood in the entrance hall of her house, she touched my face lightly, as she had before, and gave me the names of the men I was to question.

*****

Next morning I was admitted to the palace without difficulty and I was impressed that the gatekeepers already knew my name. The men I was to see were two brothers, a deacon and a scribe who, I learned, had been acquainted with Father Mario since boyhood. They were polite but wary and seemed anxious not to claim close friendship with the priest, although they conceded they had made confession to him occasionally. They were adamant that they had not seen him since mid-summer and refuted any suggestion that he had visited them more recently. I did not sense that they were lying and reluctantly accepted their statements but I urged them to think whether there were others in Mantua with whom he kept contact.

The deacon shook his head but the scribe pondered before answering. 'We had another colleague. The four of us grew up together. Paolo was one of the Marquis's trusted messengers who travelled the countryside on his master's behalf. He used to join us for a flask of wine when Mario came to visit but in the spring he was struck down by a grievous convulsion and lost the use of his limbs. He moved away from the palace and his sister took care of him, Madonna Gabbia she's called. I don't know if he's still living. It's possible Mario kept in touch with him. Our duties have made it difficult for us find out what has happened to him.' He shuffled uncomfortably as he sought to excuse this lapse.

The deacon appeared irritated with his brother. 'There's no way poor Paolo could have survived this long. We shouldn't send Doctor Somers on a wild-goose chase.'

'I'd like to pursue any possibility,' I said. 'Where does Paolo's sister live?'

They shrugged and presumed it was outside the city walls, asking to be excused from further questioning in order to attend to their onerous responsibilities. I let them go, as it was clear they would tell me nothing more, but I regretted their indifference to this old friend's fate. I could not dismiss the chance of finding him and with some trepidation I begged a moment of the chamberlain's time to enquire if he had knowledge of Paolo's whereabouts. He was a suave, beautifully dressed official, with spotless nails and soft hands, and I looked on him with distaste, remembering his designs on Madonna Beatrice. He brushed my request aside, insisting he was far too occupied to recall an insignificant messenger who left the palace months previously, but when I offered payment to help refresh his memory his eyes gleamed greedily.

'It comes to me dimly that there was such a fellow,' he said after a pause. 'He could no longer be accommodated in the palace. We are too crowded here to cope with invalids.'

'I heard Paolo's sister took him to her home.'

He wrinkled his nose. 'It may be so. A widow, I believe.'

I jingled another coin. 'Do you remember where she lives?'

'Beside the walls, along by the upper lake, I seem to think. Next to a bakehouse. An inferior area. I can tell you nothing more.'

I thrust the money into his hand, expressing thanks, and hurried off, suppressing the instinct to punch his sneering face.

*****

A row of workshops and food stalls nestled against the walls where they curved away from the lake and the street swarmed with people buying and selling their wares. It was not a district frequented by the well-to-do but the atmosphere was vigorous, full of raucous cries by the hawkers and arguments between sturdy housewives and doleful looking salesmen. It did not merit the chamberlain's description of an "inferior area" but I was propositioned by a plump young woman when I rapped at her door next to a bakehouse. I soon discovered there were several bakers with premises along the strand and I called meticulously on them all until I identified the house where Madonna Gabbia was said to live with her brother who was deprived of movement and speech.

A scrawny woman of indeterminate age answered my knocking at what was little more than a hovel and I explained my business while she held the latch firmly as if ready to slam the door in my face. Her brow was puckered but when I mentioned Father Mario her expression softened.

'We've not seen that good man for several weeks,' she said. 'Is he unwell?'

I was forced to describe what had happened to him although I did not dwell on the details. She listened to my sorrowful news without showing emotion but then she held open the door and I entered the single room she and her brother inhabited, poorly furnished but neat and clean. She led me to the pallet where Paolo lay, under a jumble of blankets, staring with unfocused eyes, and in a quiet voice she explained to him what I had just told her. He seemed to understand what she said and grunted mournfully but he was incapable of speech.

'We were fearful he'd met with harm,' the woman said. 'His life was sinful but he was true to my afflicted brother – which is more than can be said of Paolo's old workmates at the palace. They're too full of their own importance to visit the sick. I thank God I have charitable neighbours who help me in my care, washing and feeding and turning the poor man. If I'd had to depend on the Marquis's servants, I'd be shredded with exhaustion and Paolo would be dead.'

From what I had seen of the scribe and the deacon, her strictures seemed justified and I murmured sympathy, praising the way she had supported her brother. She seemed grateful for my understanding and I ventured to ask her a direct question about the matters which concerned me. 'When did Father Mario come here last?'

She sat down beside the invalid, holding his hand, and I realised he was aware of everything we were saying. 'He made a hurried visit. It was already autumn weather. It must have been just before he was killed, from what you told me. He was only in Mantua for a short while but he found time to call and cheer my brother.'

'Did he speak to you of any papers he had or was seeking? I beg you to tell me what you know – it may help identify his murderers.'

'He didn't mention papers but I could tell he was afraid. All the time he was on edge and when I saw him off from the house he looked to right and left as if he expected to be followed. Paolo sensed it too, didn't you?'

The motionless man made a sound in his throat and she patted his wrist. Then he made a small gesture with one hand and she nodded. 'Paolo remembers he was carrying his satchel. He said nothing about it but it may have held papers.'

'Do you know where else he may have gone while he was in Mantua? Is there another person he may have visited?'

Paolo's mouth moved silently and he looked up at me with desperation but Madonna Gabbia understood. 'His mother is ailing. He was a devoted son.'

'His mother! She lives in Mantua?'

'Only a stone's throw beyond the city gate, by the mills. She's not in her right mind these days but he always went to see her. I can't think she'd know anything about papers. She's a confused old woman.'

'I'd like to see her nonetheless.'

Madonna Gabbia stood up and touched my arm. 'I can't be away from Paolo for long but I'll take you to her lodgings. I beg you not to tell her about her son's death. She's distracted enough and it will only cause her further grief. She doesn't need to know. She'll not long be in the world. Let her die believing Mario is prospering.'

With some misgivings I promised to keep silent on the priest's fate and bent to wish Paolo good fortune before I left. He spread his fingers on the coverlet and seemed content; the muscles of his mouth moved slightly into a ghostly smile.

*****

Madonna Gabbia accompanied me to the shed-like structure where the old woman lived and this was just as well because there was no answer to my tap on the door until Paolo's sister shouted that I was Mario's friend. As soon as a wizened little person opened the door my guide propelled me inside, before slipping away to re-join her brother, and I was left to stare into a pair of expressionless, milky eyes. The smell wafting from the interior, suggesting filth and urine, was repellent.

'I am come from Verona,' I said in the hope that this news would register among her scattered thoughts.

'I didn't know you bore the mark on your face,' she said. 'Mario never told me.'

I swallowed my denial that he had ever known me, realising that she took me for someone else, and a reprehensible idea came to me. 'After a time, when people know me, they cease to notice the blemish.'

'The flesher's son had a crooked nose. They said he fought with a demon who twisted it. Down on the bridge it was. I mind it well. I was a young thing then, before I was spoken for; you'd not believe I was so sprightly.' I feared I was to listen to a long rigmarole of events which might or might not have happened many years ago but suddenly she jerked up her head and peered at me closely. 'Who are you? What's your name? Why are you come?'

With silent regret for my falsehood I gave the answer I hoped would win her help. 'Alessandro, Madonna, Alessandro Biagio.'

She shuffled to my side and grasped my wrist. 'I knew it. God bless you. Mario calls you his friend. He's a lonely boy. They used to jeer at him, the neighbours' children. He's well away from here. Priest at a great church. Blessed Mary be praised! He sent you to me. He said he would.'

'He isn't able to come himself at present, but I bring you his love.'

'He said so. That he'd send you. If he couldn't get here. He made a great point of it. Said it more than once. As if I wouldn't remember. My memory is clouded these days but I'd not forget what my boy said. You don't think that, do you? I've got it safe for you, never fear. He said I was to keep it safe. If I forgot everything else, I was to remember that, he said. He's a good son. Priest at a great church. Blessed Mary be praised!'

251

I took her hand in mine and it was my fingers which were trembling as I struggled to find the sense of what she had said. 'You have something for me? You have papers?'

'Not papers, bless you, no. But the key is safe. He said I was to give it to you if you came. Now where did I put it?'

'A key? Do you know what lock it fits?'

She gave an improbable giggle, sounding almost as if she was a capricious girl teasing a suitor. 'Naughty boy! You know that, not me. Now where can it be? I put it somewhere safe.'

There seemed nothing for it but to help her search through her room, lifting bundles of unwholesome rags, scratching about on the dirt-encrusted floor and even swilling round pots of unsavoury water but there was no sign of a key. It was frustrating yet the old woman's growing distress was equally upsetting. She began to tear crusts of bread apart, poke her fingers into the droppings beside the mouse-holes and then to pour out the noisome liquid in a bowl, slopping it over her feet. All the time she was moaning to herself as her fury increased.

'The girl who brings me food has taken it. She must have done. Not to be trusted. She's a thief. Known her mother all my life but she's a thief.'

'What use would the key be to her?' I asked in an attempt to seem calm. 'Does she know the lock it fits?'

The frightened eyes fixed on mine in bewilderment. 'How could she? Only Mario knows. And you.'

'Then I don't think the girl would have taken it.'

'Must have done, must have done.' She started to tug at the thin coverlet on her pallet and I sought desperately for a way to stop her destroying her wretched possessions until inspiration came.

'Was the key on a string or ribbon? Did Mario ask you to wear it round your neck?'

252

She stopped her frantic attempts to tear the cloth and her mouth dropped open. Her hand flew to her throat and from beneath the pleated barbe under her chin she extracted a thin cord. 'It's here,' she said contentedly. 'You knew.'

I helped her slip the precious object over her head and she was happy to see me hide it inside my gown. 'Mind you take care of it. It's important to Mario.'

'And to me,' I said with sincerity. 'Did Mario say anything you were to tell me when you gave me the key?'

She shook her head several times. 'The angel's wing,' she muttered vaguely. 'Under the shadow of the angel's wing. He said you'd know.' Suspicion crept into her voice once more. 'Why do you have to ask?'

'Only in case there was a longer message. You've done wonderfully well. Mario would be... will be so proud of you.' She did not seem to notice my blunder. She had turned away to smooth down the bed cover and reorganise the things she had moved in her vain search. I tried one final question which might give me the information I needed. I could think of nothing else which might be helpful. 'Where is the church Mario attends when he in is Mantua?'

'Good boy, you should go there. Mario loves San Leonardo. Not far from the middle lake. He served there, you know, when he was a lad. He'd like you to go there. I haven't been there for years but he always went. Tell him I looked after his key. Never let anyone know I'd got it. Not till you came. He said to give it to you. God bless you. Tell him his old mother blesses him.'

I nodded and pressed her wrinkled hand. 'Of course. He sends all his love and prays for you every day.'

The joy that flooded into her worried eyes justified my invention, I told myself, and I left her wiping tears of happiness. My own mood was more troubled. It felt as if I was on the brink of a discovery, for surely the key would give access to the papers Father Mario had hidden, but whether their secret resting place would be revealed in the church of San Leonardo was doubtful and, if it was not, I had no idea where else to look.

I found the church without difficulty but it was growing dark and, when I peered through the door, there were several clerics gathered in the nave in front of the darkened roodscreen. If I was to explore the interior unmolested my visit would need careful planning, daylight and the help of a colleague to distract the attention of any who might query my searches. Pondering deeply, I made my way back to Madonna Beatrice's house and begged an interview with her.

*****

I told the story of my day's enquiries while she fixed her beautiful eyes on me and listened attentively, a slight crease on her brow reflecting her concentration. She praised my perceptiveness in conjecturing that Father Mario might have kept the papers in the very city where they had been stolen and, as I knew she would, she grasped at once my need for help when I returned to the church of San Leonardo. She offered all members of her household to do my bidding.

'You weren't followed as you made your enquiries today?'

'I don't think so.'

She nodded. 'It really seems that Ludovico does not suspect you. He sincerely believes the papers were out of the city weeks ago, before anyone saw they were missing.'

'That's reassuring.' I swirled the wine in the goblet she had given me. 'I've been thinking about the implications. It makes it unlikely Father Mario was killed by Mantuan attackers. The timing doesn't fit. Security at the gates, to search those leaving, had already been strengthened before his final departure and knowledge of this must have convinced him he should leave the papers hidden in the city.'

'So the assailants were more probably servants of the Most Serene Republic.'

'As I presume were those who sought my death outside the church of San Lorenzo.'

I did not want to dwell on that recollection and started to develop a plan to give me the opportunity I required next day. With her usual calm intelligence my confidante made various suggestions, and I expressed my gratitude, but I must have looked troubled because she leaned back in her chair, regarding me coolly.

'What is it, Harry? Something is worrying you, beyond the problem of finding the lock which will take your key?'

'You're too observant, Madonna. It doesn't signify in our schemes – it's merely a memory the old woman's words evoked. The pious young girl to whom I was briefly betrothed spoke of us being sheltered by the angel's wing. She was well intentioned, although our union would have been inauspicious, and I fear I served her badly. My problem is re-awoken guilt.'

'I heard something of your history from Signora Orsola. She extricated you from the engagement, I believe. I didn't think you had compromised the girl?'

'Not in any carnal manner but I deceived her into trusting the sincerity of my attentions.'

Madonna Beatrice gave a trill of laughter. 'I didn't know Englishmen were so proper in their attitudes. She is much better fitted for the nunnery.' She stretched her arms above her with languid elegance. 'You, however, Doctor Somers, are no stranger to carnal matters, I surmise.'

I knew I was blushing and found myself tongue-tied. She reached out her hand and grasped my arm. 'You have no serious entanglements at present?' I shook my head in blind confusion. 'Find those papers, dear friend, and we will see what other lock your key might open.'

I dared not credit what she seemed to suggest, nor question her meaning, but she relieved me from my vain attempt to speak by rising and moving to the door. 'God give you good fortune when you visit the church of San Leonardo in the morning. Tomorrow evening we shall meet again. I shall pray for your success.'

The service of Mass at Tierce was not usually so well attended as that at daybreak, when the pious heard the office of Prime before going to their labours. Nevertheless I arrived early at San Leonardo's and, while the candles were lit, I was able to walk down one side of the short nave, peering at frescoes and altar frontals, before selecting where to stand, on the opposite side of the church, when the priests entered the sanctuary beyond the screen. During the initial chanting and throughout the ceremony I cast searching glances along the walls, noting where there were depictions of angels. On the south side of the nave I could see the angel of the Annunciation and those of the Nativity, while on the north side stories from the Old Testament were illustrated, with a heavenly creature hovering over Abraham, to stay his hand from sacrificing his son, and a veritable profusion of angels were displayed ascending and descending the ladder above Jacob's head, as he slept on his stony pillow.

All these pictures needed close scrutiny in case, beneath any of the angels, a small keyhole was hidden giving access to a locked recess inside the wall. I looked round again and noticed a side altar, at the four corners of which gilded columns bore the figures of flamboyant angels, wings outstretched. These too must be examined although it was unlikely the poles were wide enough to accommodate a hiding place. For a moment I was seized with panic that Father Mario might have secreted the papers somewhere in the chancel of the church, where only clergy were admitted, until I calmed myself with the recollection that he had made provision with his mother for Alessandro to retrieve them if necessary. The young lawyer would have been barred from passing beyond the roodscreen, as I was. There could be no certainty that the papers were in San Leonardo's at all but, if they were, they must be in the public area. If they were not, I acknowledged to myself in despair that I had no idea where else to look.

The service ended and as the congregation made their way out I lingered, admiring the paintings and failing to discern any keyholes on the south side of the nave. I turned back towards the north wall but became aware of a priest approaching with an ingratiating but impatient air, as if he recognised his duty to give me spiritual succour, should I have need of it, but hoped he could hasten me out of the building. I raised my arm and immediately a loud wail arose from the vicinity of the west door, followed by a man's anxious shout, causing the priest to turn, exclaim and make his way towards the disturbance. I heard his sigh of frustration as I hurried to inspect the wall below the multiple angels who pounded the treads above Jacob's sleeping head.

I could find no keyhole, either near that fresco or the representation of Abraham's sacrifice, and, as I had surmised, the slender columns by the side altar were smoothly unpierced by any aperture. Desperately I looked around but could identify no other angels and I was at a loss what to do. The splendid Gonzaga maidservant at the west portal was in the full flow of hysterical sobbing and Madonna Beatrice's steward was shouting in fury as the unfortunate priest, whom they had distracted, tried vainly to quieten them both. They had won me all the time I needed to complete my examination but it was useless. My hunch that the church of San Leonardo was the hiding place for the Guarienti letters had been shown to be groundless. In genuine need of divine inspiration, I dropped to my knees in front of the side altar and bowed my head in prayer.

I heard the priest call for one of his colleagues to assist him in dislodging the disruptive pair from the entrance of the church and footsteps passed behind me as someone emerged from the vestry to answer his summons. I could not loiter in the nave much longer without explanation and when I opened my eyes my lashes were damp with tears of disappointment. Then a quiver rippled through my body and I caught my breath. The old woman's halting words came back to me as I stared at the wall. She had not used the phrase 'sheltered by the angel's wing', as I had misquoted Giovanna Lendro. She had said 'shadowed by the angel's wing' and there, on the plaster of the wall in front of me, some feet from the altar but in the candle-lit shadow of the wide wings of one gilded angel, aloft on its high pole, was a small mark. Frantically I waved my arm and was delighted to hear the swish of steel as the steward drew his sword and the priests squealed with horror. Balanced on a kneeling stool I stretched my arm to feel the outline of the keyhole and, on tiptoe, holding my breath, I inserted the key. It turned more easily than I hoped and a small door slid open, allowing my fingers to explore inside a narrow niche. The thin packet of papers slid into my hand and, despite the nervous flutter of my heart, I had the presence of mind to lock the tiny safe before I stepped down from my perch.

I sauntered to the door, one hand deep in the folds of my gown, while the distraught maidservant collapsed, as if in a faint, into the arms of one of the priests. The steward thrust his weapon back into its sheath and swept the girl across his own shoulder, while threatening to summon the Gonzaga guards to punish the uncaring pastors.

'Ignorant busybodies,' he shouted as he strode away with his burden. 'She needs to be managed by those who know her condition. I shall make report of your cack-handed interference.' I wondered how often Madonna Beatrice's resourceful steward and maid had acted out scenes like this on behalf of their mistress. Their talent and aplomb were undeniable.

I smiled sympathetically at the woebegone priests and slipped a generous donation into the hand of one, bowing my head at his words of benediction as I strolled off along the road. All the way back to Madonna Beatrice's house, by a roundabout route, I kept to my measured pace and fought to slow the racing of my pulse to a similarly gentle rhythm.

*****

She was at my side when I unrolled the folded papers and together we read the incriminating contents; for without doubt, if the Venetian authorities were ever to obtain this evidence, Guglielmo Guarienti was a dead man. His signature confirmed unequivocal and active support for the Gonzaga attack on Verona four years previously.

'I wish I could set a flame to them here and now,' I said.

She put her hand over mine. 'We mustn't do that. Signora Orsola is the one who should destroy them and she has to see the papers first. She deserves to know with certainty that she has saved her brother.'

I nodded. 'You've sent the messenger across the causeway?'

'All the arrangements are in hand. You will make your rendezvous tomorrow night.' She moved to the window and looked out at the growing darkness. 'You are sure you wish to do this, Harry? It's dangerous. You could make good your escape when you meet Leone and I would take my chance when your absence came to light.'

'If it was discovered that I'd absconded from the city your cousin would suspect you had dealt with him disloyally. I wouldn't trust him to respect your ties of kinship in such circumstances. I can't leave you to such an uncertain fate.'

'You are courageous. Yet I don't think you are by nature a man to encounter danger willingly.'

'You read me well, Madonna. I am no man of action. The terror I experienced when Leone and I crossed the mountain ridge would have disgraced an infant.'

'But you suppressed this terror and overcame the perils which faced you. I call that bravery.'

She glided towards me and took the paper from my hand to lock it in her strong-box. 'Let that incendiary document rest there until tomorrow. Your first victory is won. You need diversion.' I did not respond to her raised eyebrow for I was in no mood to be teased but she came to stand close to me and touched my cheek. 'Don't you recall what I promised yesterday?'

'Madonna, I beg you to excuse me.' I was bewildered by her apparent levity.

To my amazement she held my arm and brushed my birthmark with her lips. 'Do you not want me, Harry? I was under the impression you desired me? Was I wrong?'

'For Blessed Mary's sake, I beg you let me go.' I clenched my hands by my side to prevent them embracing her.

'I think you should have added "or" and gone on to tell me what would happen if I didn't let you go. Let us put it to the test.'

She clung to me and as I felt her warmth I could control myself no longer and kissed her with all the fervour in my heart. 'I desire you with the strength of my body and the passion of my soul. But you are not free.'

'I am a whore. Did you not mark my cousin's description?'

'It pleased him to taunt you.' I held her away from me, struggling to steady my voice. 'Why does the Commendatore not marry you?'

'Oh, Harry!' She snuggled up to me again. 'Are you so innocent? Matteo has a wife and sons, safely ensconced on his estate near Padua. That's why he was in the city when you studied at the university. He visits regularly to get her with child again. I am his amusement between whiles.'

I ran my finger along her cheekbone where faint bruising was still visible. 'He mistreats you?'

'Not seriously. I have experienced worse. Do you know whose mistress I was before Matteo carried me away? When I travelled to Verona I was in company with the artist, Messer Pisanello. You've heard of him?'

'I saw your likeness in the church of Sant'Anastasia. I loved you from that moment.' My voice was hoarse and I knew my attempts to act honourably were futile.

'Pisanello was good to me. He rescued me from a fellow artist who abused me more cruelly than Matteo has ever done.'

'Why did you leave him?'

'His fancies wandered and Matteo offered comfort an artist could not rival. I am a realist, physician, not a heavenly paragon. And it's you that I now desire. Will you not oblige me, chivalrous Englishman?'

It was a question I never answered with words for I lifted her into my arms and carried her to the daybed in the corner of the chamber. There I found ecstasy beyond my imagining and I lost all thought of dangers beyond the fear of losing this paradise which was now mine. For good or ill, I knew my life had irrevocably changed.

*****

When morning came and the winter sunlight glowed on her nakedness, I knelt before her to pour out all that I could express in language and begged her to marry me. She smiled silently and slid down beside me on the marble floor, stroking my hair.

'You are rather too liberal in your offers of marriage, physician. Are you not betrothed to the excitable lady, Diamante?'

'No, I am not. It is a poor joke. Can you think that I would let that travesty of womanhood keep me from wedlock with you?'

262

'I think you are cavalier with your affections.' She laid her head against my chest and slipped her hands to my groin.

'I've never known rapture till I lay with you. I will cherish you all my life. Say you will marry me.'

'We cannot speak of such things now. Dear Harry, you have dangers still to face.'

'If I know you are my promised bride, I'll do battle with the Foul Fiend himself.'

'I will not put you to such a test. Let my body be your surety. See how it responds to your touch – as you do to mine.'

'Then when this ordeal is over, I may ask you again and you will accept me?'

'Let this moment suffice for now,' she said. 'Body and soul, I am yours.'

It was enough and I was filled with joy.

*****

During the afternoon of that dreamlike day Beatrice's steward escorted me around parts of Mantua I had not previously seen and when we returned to the house the messenger had come from across the lake to confirm everything was ready for my night-time rendezvous. As darkness fell my love and I sat together saying little and in silent understanding touched only our hands, but we had no need for words to prove the power of the bond between us. When it was time for us to part she kissed me chastely and ran her fingers over my face as if to imprint my features in her heart.

'Come back safely, Harry, if you value my peace of mind. But if you are in too great peril, flee from the city. Make good your escape. Don't be afraid for me. If Ludovico threatens me, I shall deny knowledge of your mission.'

'He won't believe you. I shall return to you, living or dead, and the hope of our union will impel me to survive. When I leave the city it will be openly and at your side.'

It was a dark night, with a biting wind and short-lived glimmers of a crescent moon through the racing clouds. Clad all in black, with my hood pulled low, I was as well shrouded as possible and I had a fair chance of staying hidden. Only ne'er-do-wells were abroad at that hour and I must take care to avoid encounters with any vagrants, as well as with the city guards. Apart from the fleeting moonlight, occasional lamps were still lit outside entrances but I needed to count my footsteps to be sure where to turn, as I had been instructed when reconnoitring that afternoon. I took a narrow passageway away from the centre of the city and twice I flattened myself in a doorway at the sound of movement ahead of me.

Once it was only a rat clawing a heap of rubbish but the second time three noble revellers, brandishing a lantern, stumbled round the corner and gazed along the lane before one of them subsided onto the beaten earth and spewed into the gutter. His companions dragged him to his feet and noisily urged each other to keep quiet while I waited in dread for the watchmen to appear and discover both them and me. Arrest before I had gone a hundred yards would have been an ignominious end to my exploit and, if the papers I was carrying were found, I would soon be exhibited in Ludovico's cage until my head was severed to decorate a spike above Mantua's main gateway. Sure enough the flicker of torchlight heralded the arrival of two soldiers in the distance and they strode towards the raucous trio.

'Stop that racket! It's after curfew. What's your business?' they shouted but I detected uncertainty in their tone.

'Mind your manners.' The least unstable of the merrymakers drew himself upright. 'Seem to have missed our way. Returning to the palace. Devil take servants, we've lost our escort. Kindly lead us through these alleyways.'

One soldier was inclined to protest but his colleague put a restraining hand on his arm. 'This way, my lord,' he said and, to my huge relief, courteously propelled the staggering noblemen back in the direction from which they had come.

I leaned against the doorway until my palpitations ceased, then I crept forward again, step by step, street by street, towards the postern in the city wall which gave access to the middle lake. The steward had told me that when Mantua was at temporary peace with her neighbours, as she was at that time, the postern was not manned at night and left unlocked so that the guards could slip out for assignations on the lakeside with their doxies. The weather was unpropitious for such encounters but I could not be sure my exit would be unobserved so I moved cautiously to lift the latch and froze as the hinges creaked. Those who made use of the postern must be unconcerned by this sound, I thought, but I crouched on the gravel foreshore until I could be confident I was alone and identified the reassuring shape by the water's edge. My vigil was uninterrupted and I began to breathe more easily before I heard the distant tolling of a bell and knew midnight had come.

Almost numb with the cold I felt my way down the slope until the water lapped round my feet and I gripped the stern of the rowing boat to heave myself over the side. I groped for the oars and slid them into position, easing them into the shallow eddies without a splash. It was many years since I had rowed and I was never proficient as an oarsman but a boyhood on the banks of the Thames had given me some experience and gingerly I pushed away from the land. It was too dark to see across to the other shore and we had judged that using a blazing torch to signal to each other would be hazardous, so I had to trust to Providence and my assistant's skill that our meeting could be achieved. The spot for my departure had been chosen with care, screened by the curve of the lake from close observation by soldiers on guard at the gateways on both causeways. I was about equidistant from them and hidden also, for the moment, from sentinels on the roof-walk of the castle which overlooked the eastern causeway. When I had gained the middle of the lake my boat would be visible, if the moonlight picked it out, but it was not unknown for fishermen to put out on the lake at night and provided they did not stray too far across the water, they were left undisturbed. I knew well enough that what would cause the Gonzaga barges to be launched and pandemonium to break out was if boats from either side of the lake were seen to meet in mid-channel. Illicit trading, evasion of taxes and the stowing of contraband were rigorously controlled, for the sake of the Gonzaga coffers, never mind the handing over of secret documents.

I had pulled some way from the bank and, as the clouds became thicker, I could not see at all where I was. It seemed impossible that Leone would find me, for I might have drifted to right or left without knowing it and had no way of correcting my position. I made a cautious ripple with one oar so that, if he was at all near me, he might detect the boat but there was no response. A pinpoint of light appeared to the west and I realised it must be at the guardhouse beside the Porta Molina where the mills bordered the causeway. This meant I had passed the bulge in the shoreline by the city walls and must be nearing the middle of the lake. I ought not to go further so I shipped my oars and hoped I would not be carried too far in either direction. I sat despondently, aware how cold I had become, while all around me there was only the gentle movement of the water, intensified every now and then when a gust of wind caused waves to break against the planks of the hull. I felt horribly alone.

In a moment of calm there came a faint sign of movement on the water ahead. I could not be sure if I imagined it but I peered into the darkness and gave a slight cough. It seemed to be answered by a more deliberate beating of the waves and then a beam of moonlight gave a brief glimpse of the object skimming towards me. The furry creature rose and fell as it swam, its long tail streaming behind it, and only when it was within a few feet of the boat could I distinguish the darkened face beneath the improbable headgear and the young man's arms propelling him smoothly across the lake.

'Leone!'

He drew alongside and grasped the gunwale of the boat, grinning broadly. 'Do I make a good water rat?'

'Most convincing. Will your hat keep the papers dry?'

'I've a letter for you inside the skin, from Cousin Alberto. It's well wrapped in a leather pouch and I don't think many splashes have landed on my head anyway. Lift off my hat and take it out. If the letter's got here undamaged, I'll be able to get your papers back safely.'

He reached with one hand to untie the strap under his chin which held the "rat" in position and I took it from him. My cold fingers fumbled with the layers of protection but I succeeded in extracting the letter and, although there was insufficient light to read it, I could see it was undamaged. I substituted the Guarienti papers in the pouch and made sure they were securely enveloped in the padding.

'Brilliant! Well done. Did you find a remote place over the lake to hide your horse?'

'No problem. It's rough scrubland. Unfrequented. Wayfarers keep to the tracks leading to the causeways. I've two horses waiting. One's for you.'

'You know I have to stay in Mantua. When you're safely on your way to Verona, Madonna Beatrice and I will leave openly, through the main gate.'

'Do you trust the Marquis not to detain you? You could get away now, with me. Cousin Margherita said you should.'

It took me a moment to register that he was referring to Madonna Fratta and I was shocked to realise I had forgotten her. 'Has she arrived back safely from her excursion?'

'She only set out three days ago. The snowstorm delayed her departure and then she suffered from the rheum. She's better now and seemed excited but she wouldn't tell us what you asked her to do.'

'She should be home when you return to Verona. Tell her I'll wait upon her within the week and thank her for her trouble. You'd better return across the lake now. You're not too tired?'

He took the hat from me and, treading water, fitted the furry article on his head. 'Not likely. I spent half my boyhood in the river at Padua. You're sure you won't row across?'

'No, Leone. Get to Signora Orsola as soon as you can and don't give the papers to anyone else, even the Commendatore.'

'Especially the Commendatore?' he asked and I knew that in the darkness he was winking.

I had always recognised his quick intelligence and I gave him an appreciative cuff as he pushed off from the boat. I watched the water rat disappear into the gloom and then I rowed slowly back towards the city but I had some difficulty in finding the shore by the postern gate, as I had obviously drifted some way to the west without knowing it. Rain had begun to fall and by the time I tied the mooring rope to its post I was soaked. I hoped those precious and troublesome letters were effectively sheltered in their watertight package atop Leone's head but my mood began to lighten at the prospect of triumphantly re-joining the woman I loved. I made my way through the quiet streets without mishap and returned to Madonna Beatrice's house before the first hawkers from the countryside were let into the city with their baskets of eggs and pats of butter, to cry their wares, set up their stalls and waken the populace from enviable slumber. She had spent as sleepless a night as I had, waiting for me in the salon, but we were soon enfolded in each other's arms, forgetful of all else but our gratification.

*****

It was next morning when I read Alberto's letter and I stared at his message in surprise, trying to work through the implications of his unexpected news.

'The woman who masqueraded as my sister when you were attacked has been apprehended and put to the instruments. She quickly confessed. Her brother was not working for the Venetian or Mantuan authorities. He was engaged to despatch you by a Signor Lendro who lives near Padua. I think he may be known to you.'

Too well I understood. Signor Lendro, Giovanna's father, had ordered my death to avenge the offence to his family's honour I had committed by breaking off my betrothal to his daughter. It was nothing to do with the Guarienti papers, Signora Orsola or the Commendatore. I wondered if Giovanna had been party to the plot and realised she must have been: the woman outside the church of San Lorenzo had masqueraded as Madonna Fratta and the Lendro girl could only have learned of my acquaintance with Margherita from Diamante, ensconced with her in the Convent of San Bonifacio.

Then I was filled with serious misgivings. Alberto had not dated his note but in any case he did not know the significance of its contents for his sister's well-being. Leone said she had set out from Verona three days before he met me so she should now be at the convent, as my secret emissary, facing a vengeful young woman who sought my death. My thoughtless request for Margherita's help might have put her in danger and I would be able to do nothing to assist her – perhaps until it was too late. I prayed that her innate good sense would protect her from harm.

I confess I did not concern myself for long with Margherita Fratta's welfare, spending most of the day in company with Beatrice and my feverish delight drove away all other preoccupations. We planned our departure from Mantua for the following morning and, with reluctance, I recognised that she must re-join Matteo Maffei by the shore of Lake Garda while I journeyed to the Casa delle Arche.

'But you will come to Verona in a week or two?' We had discussed this likelihood previously.

'Yes. That is agreed. I am to represent Matteo at the Signora's celebrations for the Christ child's natal day. He has to travel to Venice before then and may not return in time to join us.'

This much I knew but I was broaching treacherous ground with my next entreaty. 'Leave him, Beatrice. Leave him and the restless, harsh life you lead with him. Let us set out together from Verona while he is away and take a road far to the south, where we won't be known. I can seek a position as a physician in some far off city and you can live respected as my beloved wife. Say you will do it.'

She moved to and fro across the room with her familiar gliding movement and her fingers entwined themselves in the jewelled fringe of her girdle. 'You don't understand what you are asking.'

'I know we will risk Matteo's fury but surely even his influence can't stretch throughout Italy into every state and realm.'

'Perhaps, but I didn't mean that.' She came to a standstill bedside me. 'Do you really think me fit to be a physician's wife?'

'If we love one another, how could you not be fit? You've said you love me.'

'I love you, Harry, but it's not so simple.' She turned away, looking out of the window towards the roof of her cousin's palace. 'I can imagine great joy as your wife but I know myself and I am not equable or constant. I should grow restive, discontented with my contentment. I am not made for quiet happiness.'

'You mean what I offer is not worthy of your position? You are a Gonzaga. I insult you by offering marriage with a foreign nobody.'

'No, Harry, no!' She flung her arms around me. 'It's the finest compliment I've been paid. It's I who am not worthy. Don't look so miserable. Perhaps I am wrong. I have no experience of what you propose. Perhaps it is possible.'

Her voice faded and I seized the slight opportunity of her hesitation. 'Promise me you will think about it while we're apart. Let the idea grow in your heart until it cannot be denied. Then, when you are in Verona, send me word that you're willing to come with me. We shan't need to discuss it further. Just say that you're ready and tell me a time to meet you. Give me twenty-four hours' notice and I'll make all necessary arrangements for our departure. Let's agree a meeting place now.'

'Where would it be?' Her tone was listless but her question filled me with hope.

'Where could it be but in the church of Sant'Anastasia, beneath your own portrait, where I fell in love with the dream of your perfection?'

'So be it,' she whispered and she clutched me fiercely as if physical contact gave her confidence to face the uncertain future which was all that I could offer her.

*****

It was as well that we had agreed our plan before we set out next morning to leave the city by the Porta Molina because we were stopped at the gate and escorted into separate guardrooms. I spent an anxious hour listening to movements outside the locked chamber and only breathed

271

more easily when I heard Beatrice's raised voice thanking someone and requiring that I be informed she would join the Commendatore's escort who were waiting for her across the lake. 'I trust Doctor Somers will be free to cross the causeway soon and I wish him an uneventful journey to Verona,' she added loudly.

I shared her wish but as time passed and I was kept without food or drink my anxiety grew. The bundle of my possessions had been taken from my saddlebow but eventually they were returned: unrolled and crumpled but intact. They had clearly been rummaged with great thoroughness and shortly afterwards I too was subjected to a body search by a stern-faced officer who made me disrobe to my undergarments and patted me all over to ensure I concealed nothing of interest to his master. At any rate, I reflected, it was reassuring that they were unaware of my night-time expedition on the lake. After these indignities I was given a hunk of bread and a flask of wine but my enquiries as to why I could not be released went unanswered.

I judged it was mid-afternoon when at last I was taken from my cell but I was not allowed to go free. I was to wait for a further period in a larger, more finely appointed chamber until I heard movements outside the door and deferential voices welcoming someone. I knew then what to expect and bowed respectfully as the door opened and Ludovico Gonzaga was admitted. He did not look pleased.

'Doctor Somers,' he said, 'you propose to leave our city. Where are you going?'

'To re-join the household of Signora Orsola Guarienti-Schioppa in Verona. Madonna Beatrice no longer has need of my services.' I tried to keep the annoyance I felt from my tone of voice.

'My men have sought to ensure you are not carrying the missing Guarienti papers.'

'So I imagined although you had told me you didn't believe they were in Mantua. I do not have them.'

'But you made various enquiries in the city and behaved suspiciously.' This seemed to be a statement, not a question, and I merely repeated my declaration.

'I do not have them.'

'I am satisfied they are not on your person or in your baggage but I do not trust your words, physician. Your horse trappings and saddle have been examined but, in order to be sure they will be ripped apart. I am not prepared to allow the animal to cross the causeway. If you are so anxious to depart, you will leave on foot, dressed as you are and with your bundle under your arm. A fresh horse will await you on the other side of the lake. You are forbidden to return to Mantua on pain of imprisonment.'

Annoyance got the better of common sense. 'Did you treat Madonna Beatrice and her attendants with equal discourtesy?'

He leered at me and licked his pendulous lower lip. 'In exactly the same way. Every jot and tittle of baggage was scrutinised and I had the pleasure of seeing my lovely cousin stripped naked. Before I enjoyed her incomparable favours, you understand. Now go!'

I could not guess if he was telling the truth or merely mocking me but I fought back my fury. I was aware of him standing outside the gatehouse watching, as I walked the length of the narrow causeway, along with a straggle of other pedestrians, dodging the hooves and whips of those permitted to ride over the water on horseback. My heart was tormented and my mind in turmoil but I had succeeded in escaping from Mantua and when I was once more in the saddle I set my course towards Verona.

Part IV – Verona, Padua and Venice: 1443-4

Chapter 20

I struck across country towards Verona finding chilly shelter for the night in a shepherd's shack. Next morning I was up at first light and, riding as fast as my numbed limbs and unfamiliar horse could manage, skirted the city to the south and east towards the track I had taken when I accompanied Signora Orsola to the Castel Schioppa. It was not long before the forbidding walls of the convent of San Bonifacio came into sight and I headed directly to its main portal, intent on securing immediate attention, however disruptive and inappropriate my arrival might be deemed. On the far side of the street a group of men clustered in the doorway of a scruffy hostelry and from their midst a short figure erupted, rushing to grab at my reins before I could thump on the door. I wheeled the horse as irritation changed to uncertain relief.

'Rendell! Have you news of Madonna Fratta?'

'She's not here. Her brother fetched her away two days gone. Gawd love us, Doctor, he was that angry. He said you'd put her in danger and left her unprotected. None of her escort could go into the convent with her. She'd understood the rules and wasn't bothered but Alberto carried on alarming about that Lendro girl you were fool enough to promise to marry. He swore he'd cut your throat if anything had happened to his sister.'

I slipped from the saddle and gripped Rendell's shoulder. 'Is Madonna Fratta unharmed?'

'Right as rain so far as I could see. She was annoyed her brother created such a fuss, insisting she leave the convent. She'd been here a couple of days and it looked as if she'd enjoyed her stay.'

I gave silent thanks to heaven for her safety and gathered my distracted thoughts. 'Why are you still here, Rendell? Did Alberto disown you?'

'Nah, he wouldn't do that. He knew I'd done my best and it wasn't my fault. I refused to go back to Verona. I gathered from his ranting that he'd sent to tell you the rogues who attacked you were paid by Signor Lendro and I knew you'd realise the lady could be in danger, what with Diamante being jealous of her too. Alberto had only found out later that Giovanna was in the convent. He thought it was just Diamante she'd come to see. I told him you'd ride here as soon as you gathered what had happened, that you'd never put Madonna Fratta at risk, let alone abandon her. So I said I'd wait for you – and so I have.'

I bowed my head and tried to disguise the tears in my eyes, overcome with tiredness and gratitude. 'You've become a mature young man, Rendell,' I said pompously, 'and you read your master very well. I'm touched by your loyalty.'

Rendell shuffled awkwardly. 'Are you going to try to see Diamante – or the other one – now you're here?

I shuddered. 'No. I'll hear what Madonna Fratta has to tell me. That's if Alberto will let me anywhere near her.'

'If I'm any judge – in my newfound maturity, you know – he'll not be able to stop her, if his sister wants to see you.' My tearful appearance clearly embarrassed him and he disengaged my hand from his shoulder. 'You look done in, Doctor. The inn has some passable ale as well as wine. Come and try some. I've got a good horse waiting for you, better than this nag you were riding when you got here. Reckon you need me to look after your interests.'

Choking slightly, I nodded and was glad to follow him into the suddenly appealing hostelry. I felt humbled to be so supported.

*****

275

Once back at the Casa delle Arche I subsided onto my pallet and slept undisturbed until next morning. This restored my spirits and I felt ashamed of my weakness outside the convent. I was glad Rendell had already gone to the Cittadella for the day and, as I bathed and dressed myself in fresh hose and jerkin, topped by a pristine gown, I readied myself for the inevitable meeting with Signora Orsola. I knew I could not answer all the questions she would have but I hoped I had done enough to satisfy the remit she had given me. I longed to return to my physician's mundane duties, to study the humours and ailments of my charges, to prescribe remedies and advise wise behaviour to encourage health – like maintaining an equable temperament, which I had so grossly failed to do. Yet, in my heart I was not hoping for a long period of quiet and commonplace service in her household for, despite all my resolve to stay calm, my thoughts turned insistently to the dream of Beatrice sending me word that she would meet me by Pisanello's masterpiece so we could embark on a new and sanctified life together.

The Signora received me in her solar and her face was rejuvenated by joy as she greeted me. I had no need to make my enquiries but I did so all the same.

'Leone brought you the papers, Signora?'

'Indeed he did and he has been well rewarded, a promising lad who should do well.'

'You have destroyed them?'

'Witnessed by Bernardino and Sandrino. I crushed the remaining ashes through my fingers and ground them into the flagstone of the hearth. You have served me with intelligence and bravery, Harry Somers. I shall not forget your achievement.'

'I trust I've done enough to be acquitted of the debts I owed you and the Commendatore.' There was still weariness in my voice which I regretted.

'Matteo is a law unto himself, as you must know, but I shall send him word of my gratitude to you. Who would have thought that sly reptile, Alessandro, was capable of such perfidy? How did he hope to benefit from it?'

'I've learned he made hard bargains with his clients in order to enhance his fees. He delayed completion of Diamante's marriage contract with Alberto's father until it was too late and the poor man was killed in the insurrection. I think Alessandro was driven by simple greed. We may never be able to prove it but I suspect he was attempting to bargain with the Venetians to secure a rich reward before he would hand over your brother's letters.'

The lady snorted. 'The Council of Ten wouldn't have been amused by such antics. So you think they ordered their men to take him in charge and force his hand?'

'I believe so. I noticed a heavy presence of Venetian troops at the castle gate on the day he disappeared, when news came of Gianfrancesco Gonzaga's illness.'

'They wouldn't have been gentle in their attempts at persuasion. Alessandro was well out of his depth in that negotiation. Silly young fool!' She spread her skirts and settled on an upright chair. 'So was it Alessandro who wrote the letter which Guglielmo glimpsed when he was arrested and taken to Venice?'

'I can't be sure but I suspect so. The letter can't have suggested your brother incriminated himself in writing or the Venetians would have put him in prison then and there. Alessandro probably believed he was being subtle in disclosing a small amount of information at any one time and intended only to produce the actual letters when he'd agreed a price which satisfied him. The Venetians would have considered that irksome and no doubt kept him under observation. They would have found out about Father Mario and very likely concluded that one or other of the pair had the letters in his possession all the time. When they lost patience they decided to use rough tactics to obtain the documents. My guess would be they tortured Alessandro until he confessed that his friend had gone to Mantua to retrieve them.'

The Signora nodded but her thoughts had reverted to her brother's situation. 'We cannot be certain Alessandro betrayed Guglielmo to Venice in the first place?'

'I fear not.' I looked at her blankly, dreading the renewal of my thankless task to identify all culprits and remove all doubt.

'Perhaps it is enough,' she said doubtfully. 'The worst villainy has been exposed and remedied. You may continue your enquiries at leisure, Doctor Somers, but you have already merited the recognition I promised you. I propose to bring Diamante back from my sister's convent and I recommend you to affiance yourself to her speedily.'

I shut my eyes and did not trouble to conceal my disquiet. 'I beg you to give me a few days' respite, Signora, to regain my strength more fully.'

'The Feast of the Nativity falls in a week's time,' she said. 'Diamante will join us on the eve of that Holy Day. Will that suffice?'

'I am grateful.' I struggled to find a way of asking what was most important to me and all the more urgent now. 'You mentioned the Commendatore, Signora: have you heard from him? Madonna Beatrice told me he was going to Venice.'

The lady smiled and put her hand to the jewelled clasp at her throat. 'I didn't know that. I trust it means he has decided to renew his commitment to serve the Most Serene Republic and renounce his dalliance with Mantua and Milan but I fancy he is still bargaining to find the highest bidder for his services.'

'The Madonna said she would be coming to Verona to join your celebrations for the Feast and the Commendatore would do so if he returned in time.'

'How gratifying.' I detected a strain of irony in her comment. Then, with further expressions of gratitude, she dismissed me and I concluded she found the subject of Matteo Maffei's mistress distasteful. Little escaped her shrewd perception and I dreaded that I had betrayed myself in speaking too earnestly of Beatrice.

⁕⁕⁕⁕⁕

When he returned from the Cittadella, I sent Rendell with a message to Madonna Fratta, asking if she would receive me, for I feared she would blame me for putting her in an uncomfortable and potentially hazardous situation which incurred her brother's anger. While I waited for the boy's return with her answer I visited Geoffrey and Antonia in their new home, to admire the spacious shop he had filled with jars, flagons and retorts and to commend the way his wife had made their living quarters so elegantly cosy. Customers were already examining the remedies he offered for sale but, in a lull between visitors and after Antonia had taken little Giorgio back to his toys, I drew Geoffrey aside and unburdened my heart to him. He had been driven by reckless passion for the woman he married and I believed he would sympathise with my predicament.

'You've taken a desperate risk,' he said, as he rearranged a row of flasks which a client had disturbed. 'Be satisfied that you've bedded her and leave well alone. She can't seriously intend to abandon her lover for a mere physician and, if she did, your life would be forfeit. Christ, man, I've heard about the Commendatore from Sandrino: he has a reputation for brutality, under a civilised veneer, and would never brook such an insult.'

I shrugged. 'You know well enough how difficult it would be to follow that advice when body and soul cry out for consummation. If she comes to me, I shall hazard everything to make her my wife.'

Geoffrey banged a pestle on the counter, making the glass jars rattle. 'You swore once Bess was your true love.'

I had not expected my friend would challenge me in this way and I felt a moment of shame. 'She was but she is a thousand miles away and I may never see her again. Most likely she is wed to a worthy admirer by now.'

'How convenient for you to believe that!'

I turned away from his sarcasm, hurt by the lack of fellow-feeing I had looked for, and I changed the subject. 'Leone was of inestimable help to me in my mission. I'm grateful to you for lending me his services.'

Geoffrey's tone kept its hostile edge. 'He does nothing but sing your praises. I fancy being an apothecary's apprentice is no longer enough to satisfy his ambition. He murmurs about becoming a physician.'

I ignored the note of criticism. 'He's quite intelligent enough. Signora Orsola appreciates what he did. I wonder if she would sponsor him to attend the university at Padua. I could give him practical experience in the meantime.'

'So you're after stealing my apprentice now, are you? Will you take him with you to share your love-nest with the whore? He's a well-favoured lad. You'd best beware she doesn't entice him into her bed while you're out tending an invalid. She might find his lusty charms attractive when she tires of you.'

Stung by his unforeseen bitterness, I rushed at him and my fist struck his jaw although he deflected the force of the blow by grasping my wrist. We stared at each other, frozen, suddenly appalled by what had happened, until I sank onto a stool.

'Geoffrey, forgive me. You goaded me too far but I've no wish to resort to violence.'

He moved to the inner door, rubbing his chin. With his hand on the latch he looked at me. 'You do love her, Harry, don't you? I can see it's no idle infatuation. God help you! I don't know what I can do but you have my goodwill. I won't stand in Leone's way either, if you can arrange something for him. I shouldn't have been so snide in my remarks.' There was a formality to his words which conflicted with their sense.

He stepped towards me and we clasped each other briefly before he left the shop and entered the house. I staggered into the street, moving as if I had been the one to be punched, but the injury was in my mind for I was horrified that I had damaged our friendship so thoughtlessly. I would be wary of Geoffrey now, and he of me. I hoped our old familiarity could be restored but I knew it would take time and meanwhile I felt bleakly isolated. I wondered if it was possible that I was purposely trying to sever the links which bound me to Verona and my past life, careless of the damage it might cause. Was this what it was like to be held in purgatory, not knowing the ultimate fate of one's soul?

*****

Rendell was waiting for me when I returned to the Casa delle Arche and he announced that Madonna Fratta had insisted I should call upon her without delay, disregarding all her brother's objections, so I set out again without even visiting my room. As I trudged towards the church of San Lorenzo I grew calmer and, despite my anxiety about what she might have to tell me, I understood it was the prospect of Margherita's soothing presence which brought healing to my distressed mind.

She greeted me with her usual easy charm and bade me sit with her in the window embrasure while her maid-servant took a stool at the far end of the room. I started to apologise for asking her to visit the convent of San Bonifacio without considering any potential danger but she waved aside my mortification with a laugh.

'But it was enthralling. I wouldn't have missed it for rubies. Alberto is being stuffy and too protective. His sister is proving an embarrassment and he thinks she should speedily wed a dignified merchant like a good, obedient little widow. I shall, I shall, I have promised him but, when I become a respectable wife once more, I shall treasure the memory of my adventure when I made enquiries on your behalf.'

'I didn't know my attackers outside the church were sent by Giovanna Lendro's family.'

'Of course you didn't. How could you?'

'They could only have known of your existence and used your name to trap me because Diamante had spoken to Giovanna at the convent. In Diamante's distorted mind you may have seemed a rival to be punished, or even eliminated, and Giovanna's kin have no compunction about the use of violence. I put you in dreadful peril. Alberto is right to hold me blameworthy.'

Again she laughed. 'Oh, you silly, silly men! I only glimpsed Giovanna from a distance. She is lodged with the novices and assiduous about her calling. I think she told her parents what she had learned from Diamante in all innocence and was horrified to hear it led to the assault on you. I was told she was undergoing severe penances to purge herself of her sin.'

'Thank Heaven. But Diamante's vindictiveness could be bad enough. She must have been abusive to you.'

Margherita's eyes twinkled. 'You forget: she should have become my step-mother. She was more concerned to preserve my virtue from your evil intentions. She told me at sordid length how you molested her and that Signora Orsola is compelling your marriage in order to salvage her tarnished honour.'

My cheeks were burning. 'It isn't true. The Devil puts delusions in her mind.' My protest sounded feeble.

Soft fingers gently brushed my hand. 'I know that, Harry. She imagines what she would wish to happen. But I discovered what you wanted to know and can bring some comfort to Constanza.'

'Her child is buried at the convent?'

'Yes. An obliging and diligent sister who maintains San Bonificio's records had no qualms about telling me the infant was buried there six years ago.'

'That'll be reassuring news for a bereaved mother but it didn't justify the risk you took in going.'

'On the contrary, my visit was opportune for Diamante and she was glad to share confidences with me in a way she could not with the nuns. I understand more of her torment, poor woman.'

There was something portentous in Margherita's tone and I swallowed my anxiety. 'Can you tell me?'

'I wasn't sworn to secrecy and I think it may be relevant to matters in the Signora's household which have concerned you. It's obvious that after my father was killed Diamante fell into a frenzy of despair. She behaved indecorously in her craving to secure a husband but all did not go well and she reaped the consequences. She spoke with hatred of your predecessor as the Signora's physician.'

'Doctor Morano?' Recollections of Geoffrey's discovery and Constanza's words thudded in my head. 'I had suspicions that he dealt in forbidden practices.'

'Yes. Diamante was compelled to accept his ministrations, in defiance of God's law, to rid herself of embarrassment and she became very ill. Sad lady, motherhood would have brought her supreme joy.'

Margherita fixed me with an unblinking gaze and I took her hand. 'Did she tell you who the man was who fathered the child she lost?'

She answered in a low voice, fingering the folds of her skirt. 'It was the Signora's brother. She knew that years earlier he had dishonoured Constanza but Diamante

283

persuaded herself that he was sincere in his protestations of love and would make her his wife.'

'Dear God! What you've discovered, Madonna, may be the key to all that has happened since Guglielmo Guarienti betrayed Diamante's trust.'

I lifted her fingers to my lips and caught a movement at the end of the room as the serving woman bowed her head lower over her sewing. Margherita withdrew her hand but smiled brilliantly. 'I hope so. You won't marry Diamante?'

I stood and turned away from her. 'I don't wish to cause her further pain but I can't.'

'Not because of this disclosure, I think.' Her tone was emphatic. 'The worry that wrinkles your brow has some other origin. It was evident when you entered the room.' I could not dissemble to her and I nodded. 'Something has happened, Harry, hasn't it?'

What instinct gave her the ability to read my mind? Once more I marvelled at her insight but I prayed silently that she would not question me further.

'Who is she?'

'I have no right to speak of her unless... unless she chooses to come to me and I don't know if she will.'

Margherita rose and moved to my side. 'Weeks ago I realised a malignant demon dictates your fate and you are powerless against his wiles. Now I appreciate whose guise the demon takes and I tremble for you. She is very beautiful.' She needed to say no more but she reached up to touch my cheek with her fingertips. 'I am cursed with good sense, Harry. Otherwise I could have loved you. It is as well I have resisted such foolishness, is it not? Leave me now.'

I think we were both choking with unspoken regrets as I departed.

To push aside my distress I rushed back to the Casa delle Arche and begged Signora Orsola to have Diamante fetched from the convent without delay. Now I knew I had brought pain to one I esteemed, I longed to break the final bond of obligation holding me to the house of Guarienti-Schioppa and to Verona.

Chapter 21

On the Eve of Christ's Nativity, Diamante returned to the Signora's household and was brought before her mistress, accompanied by her sister, to listen while I outlined my supposition that her actions had led to Guglielmo Guarienti's exile. She was remarkably self-possessed and stared at me with a hostile expression until I finished my accusation; then she stood up kicking away her stool.

'I have nothing to fear from you, Doctor Somers, nor the Signora. I have made full confession of my fault at the convent. I am bidden to make pilgrimage to the shrine of Saint Luke in Padua to complete my penance and will be purged in the sight of God. You can do nothing to undo that blessed absolution.'

'So you admit your evil acts?' Signora Orsola sounded unforgiving.

'Signor Guarienti used me grossly. He deceived me with false promises and then employed Doctor Morano to destroy his seed. He knew I was not like Constanza, that I would not bear my child quietly and see it taken from me to expire at San Bonifacio. He spurned me and taunted me with my shame, so I wrote secretly to the Venetian Council telling them how he had favoured the cause of the Gonzaga at the time of the rebellion. I was overjoyed when he was arrested and removed to Venice.'

'You vindictive slut! You threw yourself at a nobleman far above your station. What right had you to complain when he took advantage of your lecherous advances? Did you really believe he would make a serving woman my equal in our family?' The Signora's disdain rang through the chamber.

'They were his words, not mine.'

I intervened in this exchange of hostility. 'Madonna, I can see that your letter alerted the Venetians to the Signor's alleged treachery but he was placed in honourable detention, not imprisoned. I believe a second letter was sent to advise them specifically that papers existed incriminating him more seriously. Did you send that too?'

Her lip curled with contempt. 'You are clever, English physician, are you not? You were brought here to ferret out our misdeeds, intent on worming your way into the Signora's confidence. I knew all the time Signor Guglielmo had committed himself in writing to the Gonzaga Marquis. That great nobleman had no secrets from me, my lady, when he savoured my charms and thrust his seed into my belly. When I first wrote I did not tell the Venetians he had put his signature to papers which, I surmised, were probably still kept in Mantua. I was content that he should suffer the rigours of a Venetian prison and languish in their hands until he died.'

'But then you travelled to Venice with the Signora and saw how he was housed comfortably and not imprisoned.'

'I told Iacopo who had his own reason to hate Guglielmo Guarienti. The pathetic dwarf did not know there was signed proof of the Signor's treachery but he knew there had been correspondence with Mantua about selling his services to the Marquis. We fed each other's indignation that the traitor should be accorded a privileged life in Venice, surrounded by every luxury and bedding the most notorious courtesans the Most Serene Republic could offer.'

'Ha! There we have it. A woman's paltry jealousy, bent on destroying her superior in spiteful vengeance.' Signora Orsola spat out her words and then rounded on Constanza. 'You allowed your sister to use your seal, the seal of my household, to verify her traitorous letter.'

'Never! Diamante never had access to my seal.' Constanza sounded deeply distressed but Diamante said nothing.

'I think the case may be otherwise, Signora,' I said. 'I don't believe it was Constanza's seal which was used.'

Diamante gave me a venomous glare as I continued. 'There was a kink on the edge of the seal and only one within the household matches that flaw.'

'Whose? Name the traitor.'

'Signora, I believe it was Sandrino who gave Diamante his seal and that he was complicit in the approach to Venice.'

As the lady sank onto a chair with her hand to her mouth, Diamante hurled herself on me pummelling my shoulder until I grasped her arms and held her rigidly while her screams rang through the house. 'Perfidious intruder! Baseborn scum! May you moulder in the nethermost pit of Hell! May you die in excruciating pain! May the demons extract your guts and cause you to writhe in agony for all eternity!'

The Signora rang her bell to summon the attendants, already positioned outside the door, who hurried in to remove the distracted woman and keep her close confined. During the hurly-burly of their departure, Constanza was weeping silently and I went to her side.

'You are blameless of your sister's actions. Her wits are afflicted. You could do nothing for her. Let me give you some comfort. I have had enquiries made. Your little child is buried at the convent of San Bonifacio. After so long perhaps the Signora would ask the Abbess to permit you to visit the grave.'

Constanza clasped her hands to her breast in silence while her mistress registered what I had said. 'Is it possible you would wish to see the bastard's grave?' She sounded disbelieving. 'I never thought you would seek to be reminded of your disgrace. I am astonished.

Constanza ignored the lady's insensitivity. 'May I go there, Signora?' she asked softly.

'If you wish it. It will be arranged. Now leave me with Doctor Somers. Your sister will be put away where she can do no further harm. It would be best if you do not see her before she is taken from the house and say nothing to Sandrino of what has occurred here.'

Constanza curtsied and slipped out of the door while I waited for Signora Orsola to speak, uncertain what she would say.

'I didn't know you had examined my attendants' seals,' she said accusingly.

I bowed my head. 'Signora, I never did so.'

She took a deep breath. 'Then?'

'I conjectured Sandrino might have helped Diamante. Iacopo told me they were close. His rascally mind suggested they were carnally intimate but they simply shared a common grievance against Signor Guarienti. Sandrino's brother, the man she was to marry, was killed by Gonzaga soldiers in the uprising the Signor supported.'

'You are a devious investigator, Harry Somers, but you have resolved all the mysteries which troubled me. I am grateful. You are of course released from the commitment to marry Diamante.'

I bit back the comment that I recognised no such commitment. After the passion the Signora had shown in the exchanges with her demented attendant she looked exhausted, shrunk into herself, aged beyond her years.

'I would ask that Diamante is not kept in excessively harsh confinement. It is the infirmity of her wits which has driven her actions. The best chance of improvement in her condition would be to lodge her in a restful, kindly place.' The Signora looked at me with frosty disapproval and I hesitated to press the point. 'What will happen to Sandrino?'

She gazed at me for a moment as if the meaning of my words was lost to her, then she drew herself up and folded her hands together. 'I will upbraid him and castigate his betrayal. But I will agree to retain his services as steward if he pledges future loyalty. I shall also send for Iacopo to re-join my household.'

I hid my astonishment at this sudden change in attitude. 'Signora, I think you show great wisdom.'

'Hah! You presume to judge me, physician? You are impertinent but I forgive you, in view of your services. These underlings had no right to act so perfidiously; yet it has been borne in on me how inappropriately my brother has behaved. I have put myself and others to some trouble to save him from a worse fate than exile. That is achieved and I can now be magnanimous in restoring my retainers to their proper places. I know their misdeeds were not directed towards me. Enough! I have no need to bare my soul to you, Doctor Somers, but I have other matters to draw to your attention. They will not be welcome.'

I stared at her, nervously speculating that her news concerned my liaison with Madonna Beatrice, as she waved me to a seat. 'I have received a letter from my daughter, Carlotta, in Venice.'

She paused and I felt compelled to fill the silence. 'I trust Signora Carlotta is well and her little girl.'

'They are both in good health, I thank the blessed saints, and they remember you and your servant with gratitude – hence the letter. Carlotta sent it by personal messenger to make sure we received it in time.'

'In time?' I caught the ominous emphasis she had given the words.

'The Council of Ten has ordered your arrest. You are to be taken to Venice and, I imagine, put to their unrivalled torments. Clearly they have pieced together your activities on my behalf.'

I needed space to collect my thoughts. 'You are not in danger yourself, Signora?'

'I am far too well connected with the Venetian dignitaries for them to move against me. You will be my proxy. However, if you leave Verona by nightfall you may succeed in escaping them. I advise you to head south, out of the *Terrafirma*, towards Florence or Rome. The Venetian decree will be of no account there. I shall be sorry to relinquish your services but I cannot in all conscience reward what you have done by allowing you to meet your end in a Venetian prison. The fastest horse in the stables is at your disposal. Go and gather your possessions. I have no doubt the Council of Ten's agent will arrive by tomorrow morning. Every hour you gain is precious.'

*****

Numb with horror, I muttered my thanks to her and went to my chamber to put together a bundle of clothes and my physician's implements. There was no sign of Rendell and I concluded this was probably fortunate. I did not wish to place the boy in the invidious position of having to choose between accompanying me, which he might see as his duty, and staying under Alberto's charge, learning the military skills he craved. He would do well enough, seeking his future as a soldier in the Italian states where there was frequent fighting. I left a short note in simple English which I hoped Geoffrey would read to him.

I understood there was no time to make my farewells to anyone, if I was to benefit from Signora Carlotta's generous warning, although I particularly regretted leaving Geoffrey so brusquely after our quarrel. I was glad the Casa delle Arche was unusually quiet, when I made my way down to the courtyard but, as I mounted the sleek grey stallion which was ready harnessed for my use and a groom checked the straps fastening my bundle, Bernardino Biagio galloped through the entrance gate. His face was flushed but he took in the situation at a glance and reined his horse to a standstill beside me.

'God's blood, Harry, I'm pleased to see you've been alerted. I've just heard that Venetian devil, Signor Giustiniari, is expected here in the morning and his arrival bodes you no good. Get out of the *Terrafirma* with all speed.

291

He'll not quibble at pursuing you as far as he can. Your best plan would be to make for Mantua where he'd not be welcome.'

Despite the ache in the pit of my stomach I laughed. 'I'm under sentence of execution if the Gonzaga catch me in their lands. I'll have to find another route to safety. But I'm thankful to see you. Would you explain my rude departure to others in the household and beg forgiveness for my discourtesy?'

'Most willingly. You go with my heartfelt gratitude, Harry, you know that. If I could help you further, I would. God bless you and keep you from harm.'

He slapped my horse on its flank to send us speeding out of the courtyard and I shouted my goodbye over my shoulder. 'And you, Bernardino. Don't hesitate to consult Messer du Bois if you need relief in the future from constipation in your bowels!'

Despite all the injunctions to make haste, as I turned into the piazza in order to follow the street towards the castle gate, I came to a decision and trotted the length of the square towards the apothecary's lodgings. Whatever harm I had done to our long friendship, I resolved not to compound it by leaving without explaining my position to Geoffrey. It would take no more than a few minutes and I could still be clear of the city before nightfall. I tethered my horse to the ring on the wall outside shop and was about to push open the door when I heard my name called from across the marketplace as Leone came running towards me.

'What a bit of luck to catch you away from curious eyes! I thought I'd have to go to the Signora's house to find you. I've got this letter. It was delivered to me at my cousin, Margherita's, so I could give it to you privately.' He thrust the sealed packet into my hand while his eyes travelled to the hefty bundle behind my saddle. 'But are you leaving the city?'

Ignoring his question, I cracked the Gonzaga seal in half and unfolded the paper. The message was brief but it contained my whole world and I gulped for breath as I read.

Tomorrow at first light, after Matins, I shall await you at the appointed place. I love you.

I was trembling from head to foot, for it seemed to me that benevolent fate had intervened by providing me with an impeccable reason to leave Verona and the people I had known there, while bringing me my lover to share the new life I craved. I was not aware that the door had opened behind me until Geoffrey spoke over my shoulder.

'Harry! I'm so glad you're here. I've felt badly since our disagreement. I shouldn't have provoked you with my callous taunts. I should have seen how deeply you felt. Are you off on a journey? Come in before you go and drink a glass to our friendship.'

I followed him through to his living quarters where Madonna Antonia greeted me affectionately and poured wine. Little Giorgio had been clinging to her skirt but when he saw me he tottered a few steps before tumbling to his knees and crawling rapidly to my side. I lifted him onto my lap and made faces to amuse him before I outlined the warning I had received from Signora Carlotta Schioppa and the need for me to depart from the Venetian *Terrafirma*. 'I have no time to visit all my friends but I didn't want to go without saying goodbye to you both,' I ended lamely.

'I'm glad you came, Harry, but don't put yourself at risk by lingering,' Geoffrey grasped my hand.

'May the saints guide and protect you,' his wife exclaimed.

'Give me five minutes to get my things. I'm coming with you.' Leone's excited voice drowned the others. 'Signora Orsola gave me a rich reward which I've sent to Padua so my mother is well provided for and Messer du Bois won't keep me here if you need a companion on the road.' He turned expectantly to the apothecary who mouthed agreement.

I felt a glow of pleasure. 'If Geoffrey gives permission, I'd be happy for you to join me, although I can't promise a life free from peril and discomfort. But there's no hurry for you to make up your bundle. When I came here I intended merely to bid you all God-speed but now something has intervened and I beg shelter under this roof until first light. I can still be clear of the city before the Venetian posse arrives.'

'Why put yourself in unnecessary danger?' Antonia sounded anxious but Geoffrey was biting his lip in silence. I knew he had seen the paper in my hand when he found me on his doorstep.

Leone's intelligent eyes lit up and he smiled knowingly. 'We're not to go alone?'

I nodded. 'We are to meet at dawn and will take the road towards Brescia. The Venetians will not discover I have left the city until we are well away.'

Geoffrey strode across the room banging his fist into his other hand, obviously frustrated by my obtuseness but willing himself to refrain from criticism. Antonia watched him nervously without understanding the tension between us until he turned, his annoyance mastered, and gave me a feeble grin. 'Your heart is possessed by Cupid's beguiling cadences and it's useless to argue. I fear for your safety and peace of mind but you know that. May God have mercy on your besotted soul. Leone, you are joining a mad man. Make sure he makes provision for your studies in physic; then leave him!'

His wife started to frame a question but he shook his head and she never completed it. Instead he brought bedding from their chamber for me to rest on during the night, ensconced beneath the counter in the shop, and he sent Antonia to prepare food which we could put in our saddlebags for the journey. I gave Leone instructions and money to secure horses for himself and the lady, whose name was never mentioned, and to him alone I gave details

294

of our meeting place. He accepted the arrangements I described without a quibble but, after his return as darkness fell, he joined me in the shop and in a whisper told me of two matters which troubled him.

'I got the horses from the hostelry near the entrance to the Cittadella. As luck would have it Rendell was just leaving through the gate and he saw what I was doing. He guessed I was acting on your behalf.'

'He wouldn't have seen the note I left for him by then. I hope he'll be satisfied that I wrote to explain my departure. You didn't give him any details?'

'No, not a word. But there's another thing. Should I go to explain your departure to my cousin, Margherita?'

I shook my head. 'There's no need. She won't be surprised. She and I spoke of many things the other day. She will understand.'

'I think she loves you.'

'No, Leone, she is far too sensible. Don't worry.' I tried to sound matter-of-fact. 'I dare not say goodbye to Alberto to avoid putting him in a difficult position with his Venetian paymasters. Margherita will tell him as much as is necessary. Are you sure you want to come on this madcap journey to I know not where?'

'You'll take me as your assistant and help me become a physician like you said?'

'I'll do everything I can. Now get some rest. Tomorrow may be more testing than traversing the shoulder of Monte Baldo or swimming the Middle Lake at Mantua.'

'I enjoy such escapades,' the lad said as he rolled a blanket round him. 'They are monstrous fun.'

'Monstrous' seemed to me appropriately ambiguous but I feared I was taking advantage of his innocent excitement. He was soon asleep while hours passed before I found fleeting slumber. At first light I would cross the threshold into my unimaginable future where fate and Beatrice Gonzaga awaited me. Nothing else mattered.

Chapter 22

At dawn on the Feast of the Nativity there were few people abroad in the streets but a good number of the pious were already at their devotions in the churches. We waited with the horses a short distance from the portico of Sant'Anastasia, near the memorial to the physician teaching his inattentive pupils which had so delighted me on my first visit with Alberto. Worshippers were already trickling out of the great basilica and when I judged most must have departed I left Leone and slipped inside, making my way towards the high arch by the south transept. The towering portrait of Beatrice, in the guise of St. George's princess, made me catch my breath, as it always did, and for a moment it seemed inconceivable that the live woman it represented would soon be at my side ready to join our fortunes forever. I glanced around nervously, suddenly afraid it was all delusion, perhaps some trick played by a malignant servant forging her mistress's writing. Yet, the message I received was in Beatrice's hand: that I could swear.

I sank to my knees in front of a side altar, as much to calm the thumping of my heart as to satisfy my urgent need to pray. Christ crucified in agony looked down at me woodenly from his cross standing on the marble slab but I was so love-struck that the enormity of his suffering seemed at that instant no greater than my own. With half-closed eyes, I mumbled a supplication, trying to suppress my blasphemy and concentrate my attention on a plea for divine help, until I became aware of a shadow beside me and looked up in joyous disbelief. Shrouded in a hooded travelling cloak, she took a step back when I leapt to my feet and held out my arms, as if my exuberance embarrassed her; but she had come and I cared for nothing else, oblivious of bystanders staring and figures moving towards us along the aisle.

'Beatrice!' My voice cracked on her name. I could say no more.

'Harry.' She spoke in a whisper. 'Oh, Harry, I am so sorry.'

I did not hear the footfall behind us as I realised her cheeks were wet with tears. It was natural she should be distressed at such a supreme moment in our lives and my only thought was to enfold her in my arms and give her comfort; but I never did so. My arms were seized and my wrists forced together behind my back before I made sense of the movements around me and when I began to struggle it was too late for effective resistance. I twisted to face my assailants, kicking out instinctively as I registered the red and black of their livery, but the punch to my stomach winded me and I caught only a fleeting glimpse of the man at my shoulder before a sack was thrown over my head and I was dragged backwards towards the west door. Memories of that unpleasant face whirled in my mind as I heard Beatrice's cry of anguish.

'Forgive me, Harry. Forgive me. What I wrote was true. Remember that always.'

Her tremulous voice grew distant as the heavy door was opened and I was carried through it into the forecourt. I could not bear to think of what Beatrice had said, the pain of her part in my capture was too intense, but I understood with appalling clarity what the presence of that villainous wretch implied. It came to me that outside the Scaligeri Castle at Torri she had called him Carlo. He was Matteo Maffei's violent right-hand man – and he had attacked me before.

An icy blast of fresh air reminded me that Leone was waiting nearby with our redundant horses and it was imperative that my foolishness should not lead him to disaster. With all my strength I shouted into the hessian muffling my mouth. 'Run! Run! You have no part in this.'

I could not tell if he obeyed my call or whether he had already fled at the sight of my attackers. I was pulled from my feet, which were quickly strapped together, and I was flung, belly down, across a saddle while a rider mounted behind me. I felt his legs move as he spurred forward and we did not pause when a furore broke out nearby. I heard shouts and a woman scream, followed by the thud of a falling body and a ghastly groaning, while other hooves were clattering on the cobbles. I prayed it was not Leone who had been grievously wounded and tried desperately to convince myself that the moans of the injured man were not those of a youth. When I twitched with discomfort as we sped along the street the horseman at my back used his whip on my buttocks. After this I lay as still as I could, accepting that to protest or struggle had become meaningless shadow-play, for the woman I loved had betrayed me.

I heard the familiar sounds of bustle at the city gates, less on the feast day than at other times, and then we were galloping through the countryside, traversing rough terrain, jolting on uneven ground, occasionally bounding over some obstacle which bounced me about and threw me against the hard leather pommel. We were not alone. Several horses accompanied us and their riders shouted to each other with warnings about treacherous surfaces and occasional ribald jests. In time we slowed our pace and I assumed the men were satisfied they would not be pursued or intercepted – although I knew there was small prospect of that.

I had lost my bearings and was perplexed as to the intentions of my captors. At first, in my befuddled state, I assumed I was being conveyed to the Venetian troop sent to arrest me but this band of ruffians belonged to Matteo Maffei and it was still possible he had offered his services to the Most Serene Republic's enemies. Perhaps it would be on a Gonzaga gallows in Mantua that I would meet my end, a nicely ironic twist to my fortunes. As our journey continued, however, I concluded the Commendatore was probably going to execute me himself, with all the barbarity he could muster, for besmirching his honour and daring to bed his paramour. The ignominy of this fate was not lost on me but Beatrice's complicity was worse to contemplate. I dismissed her tears and words of regret as worthless travesties of grief.

I could not discern Carlo's voice among the cacophony of yells but I imagined him directing the actions of his men with fierce but taciturn authority which would be unchallenged. I knew now how faithfully he served the Commendatore and how dastardly his master was in manoeuvring to secure what he wanted. When I saw Carlo at Torri I fancied I had seen him before and now I understood the circumstances. His vicious expression as he glared at me in the church of Sant'Anastasia had made me recall the similar grimace he gave when he attacked me in the Paduan alley, at a time I thought him a footpad, just before I was 'rescued' by Matteo Maffei in person. I was wiser now in my interpretation of that incident and the reason no villains were ever brought to justice. It had been cleverly contrived but Carlo must have hated me for the slashed wrist he received from his master in order to make the charade more realistic. Inside the darkness of the sack I gave a wry smile.

*****

We rode for hours until we halted in a wood for the men to relieve themselves and take refreshment. My blindfold was lifted briefly and a skin of tepid wine was thrust into my hand, together with piece of dried fish: I reflected that this would probably be my last feast to celebrate Our Lord's Nativity, indeed my last meal of any sort. I glanced round and glimpsed the gleam of water in the distance but had no way of knowing whether it was lake or river and there was no sun in the overcast sky to suggest direction. As soon as my keeper saw me move my head he forced the sack back in position and we were quickly remounted and on our way again. It was growing dark.

As the condition of the road improved the rhythm of horses' hooves became steadier and, despite the discomfort of my body and the misery in my soul, I must have fallen asleep. I came to myself when we clattered to a standstill and after some peremptory shouts I heard the creaking of gates swinging open. Through the sack I could make out the glimmer of lights: torches, I presumed, to guide our entrance into some castle or town. Shortly afterwards the rider behind me bent forward to remove the cover from my head and I was dazzled by the sudden brightness as we entered a courtyard lit by blazing flambeaux in sconces fixed to the walls.

'Here we are, matey. You can look around now. Nothing here to let you know where we are.'

He hauled me to my feet and I stared at my surroundings, stifling surprise when I realised he was quite wrong. Above the wall beside the gateway, ghostly in the shadows beyond the lights, loomed the outline of a tower: a tower I recognised, albeit I was looking at it from an unfamiliar angle. A miscellany of memories and emotions flooded my mind as I remembered Rendell stepping cautiously along the narrow ledge below the battlements which I could not see properly but knew to be there. From our location I deduced we must be outside one of the mansions fronting the Piazza della Frutta. We were in Padua.

*****

They took me to a room on the first floor, richly furnished, with fine tapestries covering the walls and a Turkey carpet spread over the long table. Flasks of wine, goblets of Murano glass and bowls of fruit and sweetmeats stood on a heavily carved cabinet to one side and tapers in a free standing candelabrum gave brilliance to the opulent scene. A fire burned in the hearth beneath an impressive overmantel bearing an unknown coat of arms. I was offered a low chair to sit on and a cloth to wipe from my face the filth thrown up by hooves pounding into puddled mud. I sank down gratefully although pain shot through my stiff limbs when I bent my knees. I accepted a draught of the wine, careless as to whether it might be poisoned, reflecting that if I was to be summarily despatched, I was not over-concerned as to the method. A guard stood watching me impassively but I would give him no trouble; I had lost the will to resist.

I drank deeply and although it made me drowsy I did not collapse with apoplexy or stomach cramps. Instead I became aware of my hunger and wished there was more substantial food on offer, while I bit into an apple, but at that moment the door opened silently. It was the faint movement of air which alerted me, as the tapers fluttered, and I turned to see the guard bowing before he left the room while his superior strode forward to face me across the table.

'It would be unkind to remind you of Adam's fall when Eve plucked the succulent fruit and betrayed his virtue.' Matteo Maffei stood with his back to the fire, smirking at me with a cruel glint in his eyes.

'There's no need,' I said.

'You look so woebegone I should perhaps give comfort by telling you the whore was unhappy to play the part designed for her at the basilica. You have roused unlikely affection in her faithless heart. I had to use means of persuasion to ensure her compliance.'

I struggled to my feet. 'You beat her again. You are a barbarous brute.'

He laughed. 'It never ceases to astonish me what a fastidious fellow you can be. Or how unworldly you are. Did you really think Beatrice Gonzaga would leave my protection for life as a physician's helpmate? Could you imagine her

301

cutting up her old dresses to make bandages for your patients? Modestly biding by your fireside while you tended the delirious and dying? How could you let yourself be deluded by such a senseless dream?'

I did not respond for his questions were too shrewdly put and I was ashamed to give the answers we both knew to be true.

He twirled a tassel on the lacing of his shirt. 'Yet you behaved with courage and ingenuity at Mantua. Your latent talents were the reason for employing you and I am sure my aunt has given gracious thanks for what you achieved. It's regrettable that I must now vitiate that gratitude by making you over to those who wish you harm. I'm afraid I must trade you like a commodity in the marketplace for you are desired by the Venetians and, as I warned you, you have become expendable to me now you have fulfilled your task.'

'You intend to switch your allegiance back to Venice?' My words seemed to come from far away and I blinked, trying to clear my head.

He slapped his thigh, laughing heartily. 'Poor innocent, I have no allegiance, as you call it. My services have remained engaged to Venice throughout the recent escapade and I have received a generous retainer while I dallied with other rulers and misled them. The Council of Ten have been entirely content for me to deceive the Gonzaga and Visconti into thinking I might fight for them but that was never my intention. In the past I have fought for other paymasters but my contract with the Venetians is far too lucrative to put at risk. Unlike my uncle, I did not inherit wealth although I made a favourable marriage; all I possess I have striven for with my sword-arm and my mind. Venetian ducats purchased me this fine mansion and all its contents, together with the silks and brocades both my wife and mistress wear. Now I have negotiated a rich reward to deliver you to the Council and I shall not put that at risk by defaulting on my commitment.'

'I thought Signor Giustiniari had been sent to arrest me. Is it a competition?'

'Ah, English wit in extremis! Delightful. No, Harry, it was all contrived. We were confident you would learn of Giustiniari's expedition and that you would seek to escape from Verona. Sweet Beatrice's part was to delay you and ensure my men could intercept you at a convenient time and place. Giustiniari will return to Venice in a few days and we will drink together in his grand palazzo, toasting the success of our mission.'

'I've been a credulous fool. Right from the beginning. You even arranged for me to be attacked when I was studying in Padua so you could pretend to save my life and put me in your debt. I have recognised your henchman as my assailant.'

Matteo narrowed his eyes and clenched his fists, as if holding back sudden anger, and I wondered for a moment if he was about to hit me. 'You should be flattered that even then, after so brief an acquaintance, I discerned the possibility of using your skills for some purpose in the future.'

'So you wished to place me under an obligation. It is long since discharged.'

'I agree but it has been overtaken by a different debt. You owe me a life.' His words made no sense to me and I stared at him blankly until he pounded the table with his fist. 'In other circumstances I would congratulate you on working out the little masquerade that brought you under my influence but your servant's murderous attack has blighted any good will I felt towards you.'

I could not prevent a shiver down my spine. 'I don't understand.'

He moved closer, peering into my face from a distance of six inches so I could smell his meaty breath. I was glad I had enough self-control to hold my ground. 'Carlo was my valued lieutenant. He fought with me throughout my campaigns and his loyalty was absolute. Your servant cut his throat and so I demand his life as forfeit.'

'My servant?'

'Outside the church of Sant'Anastasia, as you were being bundled across a saddle. My men were remiss not to realise your attendant was waiting nearby with horses for your escape. He leapt upon Carlo from behind and severed his windpipe with a knife.'

I closed my eyelids for a moment. I could not imagine Leone acting with such ferocity and the idea of him taking Carlo unawares seemed improbable. 'I don't believe it. It's not in the lad's nature to kill.'

'It's in any man's nature to kill if he sees a threat to what he treasures. You are the boy's hero. Believe me; I have seen such things many times but his devotion does not excuse his violence. The youth has been apprehended and will be here tomorrow. I warn you I shall require a life for a life and will personally eviscerate him. You are responsible for him so you will watch every incision and hear every scream. You may consider my action barbarous but it is soldiers' justice. Then my men will escort you to Venice for your own lingering death at the mercy of the Most Serene Republic's unparalleled instruments of torment. I trust you will not feel uncharitably towards me. I assure you I bear you no ill will. It is the commerce I trade in which dictates my behaviour. Make yourself at ease while you can. Until the prisoner arrives you may use this chamber and enjoy its comforts. They will be the last you encounter in this life so I counsel you to relish them.'

He had hardly drawn breath as he switched from vicious ranting to hypocritical charm and the gracious offer of hospitality. Then Matteo Maffei turned on his heel and clapped his hands before leaving the room. At once a serving man appeared bearing a platter of spiced mutton and bread which he set before me, bowing as if I was some honoured guest. My hunger had dissipated in horror at Leone's fate and through the long night I left the food untouched. To my shame, guilt at ruining the lad's life gave way in my mind to pining for my lost love. Again and again I went over her entreaty for forgiveness. 'What I wrote was true,' she had said and what she had written was, 'I love you.' If I could believe that, if she had been coerced into betrayal despite her sincere love, it would mitigate the bitterness of my last hours; but I could not convince myself to accept even a fragment of comfort.

*****

Slumped in the chair, I must have slept a little before dawn came and on waking I forced myself to eat a few mouthfuls to give me strength for the ordeal to come. Later I walked across to the window and looked out. I could not see the Capello tower from that angle but below, in the courtyard, the shadow of its battlements fell distinctly over the flagstones. My life had travelled full circle, I reflected. I had first come to Padua, seeking a haven from the death sentence pronounced on me in England; now I had returned as a prelude to facing my doom in Venice – and must watch Leone tortured to death in the city where I had saved him from false accusation. In the sober clarity of morning I was seized by overpowering remorse.

I was left undisturbed and the winter sun had reached its feeble zenith before I heard shouting in the courtyard and the jangle of harnesses as horses were ridden through the gateway. I saw well-muffled men dismounting and then it seemed another party arrived, causing the grooms to run to the second group and a steward to march from the building, apparently to demand the newcomers' business. I could not hear the words exchanged but I saw them escorted into the house with ceremony and only after this did I realise a third troop was entering the curtilage. I caught my breath when the cart trundled forward, conveying its ominous burden, and Matteo Maffei emerged to lift a sheet covering the dead body and salute the cadaver of his wretched colleague. I looked in vain for poor Leone but he and his captors must have ridden into the corner of the yard screened from my view. After some while the funereal cart was driven away and the courtyard emptied so I sank back on my chair and waited.

The Commendatore looked angry when he paced into the room, accompanied by several attendants, and he threw a roll of parchment onto the table. 'Confound the interfering bitch,' he said, 'and all bloodsucking lawyers! Don't think you or your minion will escape justice, physician, but it seems we have to endure some legal platitudes before we proceed to action.'

A posse of robed officials crowded through the door behind him and, at the very back, I glimpsed soldiers with the lion of Venice on their surcoats. My attention was held, however, by the lean, heron-like figure who moved past Matteo Maffei, as of right, to take the central position. I shook my head, believing for a moment that my disordered mind had conjured up a vision from the past, but when Professor Andrea Bonalini spoke his sonorous tones wrested me into the present.

'I am pleased to see you again, Harry Somers, although these are not the circumstances in which I hoped to do so. I trust your unfortunate situation will be speedily resolved. My good friend, the Commendatore, can be a little hasty in his judgements and I am sure there has been some misunderstanding.' Matteo Maffei began to protest but the Professor held up his hand as if to silence a troublesome student. 'My business will be quickly accomplished and then the lawyers can proceed to their disputations. Harry, I have received a most effusive letter from Signora Orsola Guarienti-Schioppa. She lauds your skill most enthusiastically. She credits you with saving the life of her notary and performing innumerable other services which she does not itemise.' I opened my mouth to explain that most of the achievements to which she referred were unconnected with my physician's expertise but Professor Bonalini was not to be deflected from his purpose. He continued with the utmost solemnity as if making an oration to a vast assembly. 'The Signora makes the case for recognising your practical abilities as proof of your worthiness to receive the doctorate of the University of Padua which you did not complete when in residence here. I am fully persuaded she is correct and I am empowered, in suitably exceptional cases, to confer the award without the strict requirements of the statutes being met. It gives me pleasure therefore to present you with the scroll confirming your status and to greet you for the first time in Padua with all propriety when I address you as Doctor Somers.'

With a flourish he produced the roll of vellum from inside his gown and thrust it into my hands, before embracing me. I wanted to laugh at the preposterousness of the occasion but some spark of professional pride flickered and I thanked him with humble gratitude. It was satisfying to realise that the Commendatore was irritated by this petty ritual but Professor Bonalini was not ready to give him the floor.

'Signor Matteo Maffei, I understand from communications that you have taken in charge a young fellow who serves Doctor Somers and that you intend to pass sentence on him. I must advise you that your right to act in this way is challenged as this learned young lawyer will explain.'

The Commendatore's face had turned scarlet and he seemed momentarily dumbstruck when the Professor ushered forward a youthful fellow clad in the black gown and cap of the legal fraternity. Once more I stared in disbelief. He drew himself up and assumed a confident stance, as if about to lecture some malefactor. I had seen him only once before, at his father's obsequies, but I had no need of his introduction for I knew him – by sight and still more by villainous reputation.

'Signor Maffei, I am Pierpaolo Clemente, notary of Padua, representing before you my principal, Bernardino Biagio of Verona, with whom you are acquainted. He has instructed me to object to your actions in presuming to judge Doctor Somers' servant.'

The Commendatore could restrain his anger no longer and he let out a torrent of abuse. I reflected that I had never seen Matteo lose his self-control but a movement beside Pierpaolo drew my attention to the lawyer's companion, a slender young man swathed in a travelling cloak and hood who was clutching a small box. My mouth dropped open but sparkling dark eyes met mine, instructing me to show no surprise, and imperceptibly I nodded. In that moment the extraordinary events happening around me fell into place and I understood all the activity which must have been undertaken on my behalf since I was abducted from Verona.

'Signor Maffei,' Pierpaolo intoned, 'I shall be obliged if you would produce the prisoner so we may be certain of whom we speak.'

Matteo was happy to comply with this request, giving orders to an attendant, and while we waited I glanced again at the person accompanying the lawyer as if I still did not trust the evidence of my own eyes. Keeping his mouth downturned in serious contemplation, Leone winked at me.

The short and scruffy prisoner had been ill-treated: his face was swollen and streaks of dried blood ran from his nose to chin. His clothes were tattered and he walked with a limp but he held himself erect, as a soldier should, and he showed no fear. With a jolt I realised that, young as he was, Rendell had become a man, a fighter to be reckoned with who had killed an enemy and was not abashed by this rite of passage. He looked at me and grinned.

Pierpaolo resumed his courtroom posture. 'You are Rendell, servant to the English physician, Doctor Somers?'

'Yeah.'

'You are charged with the crime of homicide against Signor Maffei's henchman, Carlo. What do you say to that?'

Rendell chuckled. 'I say I done him in because he were carrying off my master and he intended to do the doctor harm. It were fair and square.'

Matteo let out a roar of triumph. 'You see he doesn't even trouble to hide his guilt. By Christ, I'll slice him open from crotch to breastbone!'

Pierpaolo smoothed his immaculate gown. 'I counsel you to do no such thing. The lad has offered a credible defence which must be tested but you are not impartial and have no right to determine its adequacy.' Whatever pressure Bernardino had put upon the newly fledged lawyer, it had achieved remarkable success and, despite all I knew of Pierpaolo's own reprehensible past, I could not but admire his crafty aplomb. After a pause, while the Commendatore spluttered, the lawyer continued. 'He is not within your jurisdiction.'

'I have the right to exact retribution from a foreign servant for the murder of my lieutenant.'

'Not from a sworn soldier serving the Venetian Republic.'

Professor Bonalini gave a satisfied purr, as if he wished to claim credit for the young exponent of a discipline other than his own, while Pierpaolo fixed his eyes calmly on Matteo.

'Nonsense. The boy is body-servant to the physician. They came together from England.'

'Captain Alberto took my oath to serve Venice a few days back. He'll swear to it.'

I was aware of bustle at the back of the room as the soldiers by the wall parted to let their commander come forward and, with considerable apprehension, I recognised this person as Signor Giustiniari, member of the Venetian Council of Ten who I was certain had no liking for me. He took Rendell's chin in his hand and tilted it upwards. 'If you are lying, boy, it will be the worse for you.'

'I ain't lying, guvnor.' Under intense provocation Rendell had reverted to his native language.

Leone stood beside Rendell and bowed low to the Venetian. 'It is true, my lord. Captain Alberto is my cousin and I know it is true. I was also witness to the events outside the basilica of Sant'Anastasia. Rendell had come unbidden to join me there. I was waiting with the horses for the doctor. I can vouch for what Rendell has said.'

'And you are?'

'Apprentice to Doctor Somers, my lord. My name is Leone. I am a native of Padua.'

Pierpaolo Clemente nodded. 'The lad is known to me, my lord. He acquitted himself worthily before he left this city. He is honest and well esteemed.'

'Cor blimey! I just realised who you are. You're Giorgio Clemente's bloody son!'

I closed my eyes in despair at Rendell's outburst, dreading the impression it would make on the austere Venetian, as Signor Giustiniari placed a hand on the young lawyer's arm.

'The apothecary, Giorgio Clemente, who was murdered just after he had been chosen as President of his Guild? I met him years ago. He was an upright man.'

Pierpaolo bowed his head meekly to receive the nobleman's sympathy. When he looked up I caught a glint of malice in his expression as he glanced towards me but he was Bernardino Biagio's creature now and he knew his part. 'Thank you, my lord. You should know that Doctor Somers was the man who identified the murderer.'

'Is that so? And his servant is become a soldier of the Most Serene Republic. Matteo, my friend, these matters are more complex than we might have imagined. It is not appropriate for you to pursue them. I shall take charge of Doctor Somers and the boy, Rendell, and convey them both to Venice so their cases can be heard in full by the highest authority. You have leave to return to your troop of warriors. They may be needed before long as the Visconti are reported to be restive. Men, bring the prisoners but treat them with respect; they are not proven malefactors.'

The soldiers jumped to attention and gave us time to make our farewells and give our thanks. Professor Bonalini patted me on the shoulder and wished me well, carefully avoiding any suggestion that he took sides between opponents, while Pierpaolo bowed coldly in response to my words of gratitude.

'I trust report will be made to Messer Biagio that I performed to your satisfaction,' he said. 'I am gratified to have been of help.' There was no sincerity in his voice but I knew Bernardino's hold over him was strong enough to prevent him causing mischief.

Finally Matteo Maffei joined me. He had recovered his supercilious air and brushed off any affront to his dignity from the Venetian noble. 'What an interesting life you lead, Doctor Somers. I fancy we shall not meet again. I don't envy you the next stage of your existence. You will either repine in a foul Venetian prison or they will deliver you to the English embassy which has arrived in the Most Serene Republic so you can be returned to your own land for execution. Which fate would you prefer?

I did not answer but, still clutching the roll conferring my doctorate, I allowed myself to be led away by the soldiers. At the door, Leone gripped my wrist. 'I'm coming to Venice too, Doctor. I'm keeping an eye on what happens to you and Rendell. But I must give you this. Madonna Beatrice asked me to get it to you as soon as I could.'

He held out the little box he had been clasping and I stuffed it into my gown before giving him a heartfelt hug. I had no wish to open the whore's gift and resolved to throw it into the gutter as we rode from Padua. Behind me Rendell was disputing cheerfully with his guards the possibility that Venice might surpass London in beauty and wealth.

Although under escort, I was allowed the dignity of riding a horse myself rather than being bundled in front of my captor in the manner Matteo Maffei's men had conveyed me to Padua. I learned Leone was permitted to ride at the back of Signor Giustiniari's troop but Rendell had been taken away and throughout our journey I worried about his fate. My own destiny seemed of little importance, given the destruction of all my hopes, but I feared subjection to the ingenious instruments of torture, for which Venice was famed. I dreaded the pain they would inflict and I dreaded also that I would be compelled to confirm the existence of the papers I had retrieved in Mantua, thus effectively sentencing Signora Orsola's brother to death and putting the lady herself in danger. She had been confident the Venetians would not take action against her but I knew that if my limbs were stretched unbearably or my fingers crushed, I might well scream out in agony, admitting she had destroyed the damning evidence they wanted. I could have no faith that I would withstand brutality without capitulating or that she would be spared the Most Serene Republic's vengeance.

In other circumstances I would have rejoiced at the first sight of the extraordinary city floating in its lagoon as we took to the sea. The low-lying islands, freighted with huddled buildings, rose improbably from the water, defying good reason which suggested they must sink. Then, as we entered the waterway snaking its way through the largest landmass, even in my despondent state I became absorbed in studying the variety and grandeur of the structures along its banks. Workaday quaysides, bustling with the paraphernalia of commerce, crates and cranes and vessels of all sizes, were interspersed with soaring churches and elegant palaces, ornately carved and canopied. Banners with the lion of Venice hung from balconies, together with elaborate crests which I presumed were those of the eminent

313

families in the Most Serene Republic, and I caught glimpses of richly dressed men and women promenading on galleries decorated with lace-like tracery. It was breath-taking and for a moment my anxieties faded in admiration of the scene before me, until I realised we were making for a jetty outside a mansion at the junction with a smaller canal.

It was not as splendid as other edifices we had seen but it would have put to shame most of the houses beside the Thames in the City of London. I wondered if its pleasant façade could really hide underground chambers where atrocities were carried out but I determined to resist such thoughts and stepped ashore with all the assurance I could muster. My show of bravado was weakened by the need to say goodbye to Leone, who was to be conducted to a hostelry where he could stay to await a decision on my fate. Signor Giustiniari gave him permission to visit me later in the week and I clung to that promise, giving me hope I would not be put to the instruments in the meantime. I was further cheered by the appearance of the room in which I was to be lodged; plainly furnished but with a high ceiling and a marble-tiled floor, it did not resemble a conventional prison cell despite the bars across the window. Nevertheless, when I was left alone and the bolts had been engaged outside the door, I sank onto the bench by the wall and a wave of terror passed through my body. I unrolled Professor Bonalini's scroll and as I read again the solemn words certifying I was a doctor of the University of Padua, tears streamed down my cheeks.

*****

I was treated with courtesy by the attendants who brought me food and cleared my slops but I could learn nothing from them of what was planned for me. I amused myself by gazing out of the window which overlooked the smaller canal, counting the narrow boats with curved prows which were punted skilfully into its channel. Sometimes they missed collisions by the width of a finger as they wove gracefully between each other, keeping their passengers and bundles of merchandise steady, but their sinuous passage was not achieved without expletive-laden shouting by the boatmen. I marvelled at the small groups of waterfowl which swam unperturbed amid this hubbub, hugging the bank until some unusual sound or movement alarmed them and they flew off with angry squawks.

I could not make out what kind of building it was, where I was kept, because the noises I identified were contradictory. Some suggested it was the residence of a family when I heard female voices and the scampering of children on the floor above. At other times, especially in the quiet darkness of night, I fancied I heard distant groans and, once, a gruesome scream echoing upwards from the cellars below ground. These occasions seemed to confirm the common rumours about ghastly deeds in subterranean chambers and I speculated whether there were hatches in the base of the walls giving on to the canal which could be opened to dispose of unwanted prisoners, dead or still living.

As the days passed and the horrors I suffered remained imaginary, I became calmer in my mind, although always anxious about Rendell, and I steeled myself to look inside the box Beatrice had given Leone and which, despite my earlier resolve, I had not jettisoned. I thought perhaps she had written me a note, full of hypocritical apologies, and I knew that would be difficult to bear but at length I yielded to curiosity and unclasped the lid. I was not at all prepared for what I found and could make no sense of it, for wrapped in a fold of crimson silk lay a single white feather. There was no message, no explanation, and all I could think of was that it signified by its lightness and fragility the transitory nature of our relationship. It was worse than a disingenuous apology from a careless mistress: it was a gratuitous insult, for she could have no doubts about the sincerity of my feelings.

At last, on the sixth day of my imprisonment, Leone was admitted to my room and I flung my arms around him, rejoicing that he looked well cared for and in good spirits.

'I thought Signor Giustiniari might have revoked his permission for your visit.'

'No but they've only allowed me a few minutes. I wanted to be able to bring you news and there were enquiries I had to complete.'

'There's news? Do you know what's happened to Rendell?'

'He's held in the prison near the Arsenal but hasn't been brought to trial yet. I'm not allowed to see him and conditions there are said to be stark but I bribed a warder who told me he's holding his own among the tough criminals he's lodged with. I've more definite news about you.'

He paused and I recognised reluctance in his fleeting frown. 'Go on.'

'You're to be brought before the Council of Ten in the morning. Signor Giustiniari is to present the evidence against you.'

'Am I to be put to the instruments before then?'

'I don't think so. That may follow if you are intransigent and don't confess.'

'I understand.'

I must have looked as miserable as I felt and Leone gave me an encouraging smile. 'At least one person in Venice is desperate for you to stay silent.'

Fear dimmed my intelligence and I imagined for a moment that Signora Orsola had come to the city.

'Signor Guglielmo Guarienti has sent you a present to demonstrate his good wishes.' Leone held out a basket which had been tucked under his arm. He lifted a napkin to show half a dozen sweetmeats. 'He must have heard of your arrest from Verona.'

I laughed. 'He certainly has every interest in my resisting the temptation to confess. It's his life as well as mine that's at stake.'

'Don't become too despondent, doctor. There are other people I'm trying to contact who might help you.'

The door creaked open and the warder entered jerking his head to indicate that Leone must leave. 'No more chatter now. Off you go, lad. What's that in the basket? Sweetmeats, eh? I'll try one of those.' He munched happily as Leone left and then he examined the wicker container more thoroughly, squeezing some of its contents. 'Don't reckon there's a knife or a file inside the little cakes but I better confiscate the basket, just in case. Enjoy your confections.' He tipped them onto my wooden platter and went off stroking the impounded receptacle, whistling a cheery tune.

I was impressed by the warder's diligence in ensuring I had not been sent a weapon but it served to remind me of another sweetmeat which had concealed a vicious ingredient and killed the apothecary, Giorgio Clemente, in Padua. That uncomfortable memory made me consider more thoughtfully why Signora Orsola's brother should send me a present. It was true he would wish me to stay silent in face of the fiercest torture but he would know it took an exceptional man to do that and a humble physician could not be expected to show unusual bravery. It would be safer to ensure that he was never put to the test. Was it unreasonably distrustful to be so suspicious? Certainly the warder had shown no ill effects of his nibbling but maybe it was too soon for any poison to have had an effect and, in any case, only one or two of the sweetmeats might have been contaminated. I resolved to leave them alone but, perhaps to divert my mind from the prospect of facing the Council of Ten, I decided to conduct a trial of their purity, as I had done on that previous occasion.

I stood at the window watching two ducks swimming beside the bank and, although I wished them no harm, I crumbled all but one of the cakes and tried to throw the pieces into the water. This was not easy as the bars were close together and I could not force my whole hand through them, so the morsels fell short, landing on the expanse of scrubby grass between the house and the canal. The ducks showed no inclination to fly up to take this offering and I sighed at the failure of my test as I sat down on the wall-bench. In an hour or two the warder returned to empty my slop-bucket, clearly in robust health, and he helped himself to the remaining sweetmeat. I concentrated on what I must say when questioned by the Council of Ten, while it began to grow dark, until I heard a plaintive screeching outside the window and roused myself to peer into the gloom. A large gull was writhing on the ground, its legs crumpled under it, with noxious, green fluid bubbling from its beak.

The case was proven. At least one of the confections, lying in fragments round the bird, had contained toxic matter and I had proof enough of what Signor Guglielmo Guarienti's good wishes really signified. I was fully persuaded now that Iacopo, Diamante and Constanza had been correct in their assessment of his self-serving character. Yet it was on his behalf that I had acted throughout the sorry saga of recent weeks and I was trapped. There was no reason on earth why I should protect his interests in front of the Council of Ten but to betray him meant betraying Signora Orsola and that I could not bring myself to do.

*****

I was taken by water to the Doge's palace and was sufficiently composed, when we disembarked, to look in awe at the masterful decoration of its frontage facing the lagoon. The walls of pink and white marble glowed in the morning

318

sun above an exquisite loggia, carried on slender columns, which surmounted an arcade with wider arches. I had never seen such delicate masonry but I was given no opportunity to study it as my escort hurried me along a vaulted passage, across a courtyard and into the building, where we climbed a back staircase to the second floor. Then I was marched through a succession of rooms until we reached a stuffy vestibule and waited outside double doors guarded by halberdiers.

I could hear faint voices inside the Council Chamber and concluded that the Ten were already assembled but before long two strangers presented themselves to the soldiers and were admitted. The older man wore the robes of a Venetian nobleman but his fair-haired companion was richly dressed in parti-coloured hose and a short tunic which showed off to advantage his shapely legs. I wondered if this was an occasion for onlookers to gawp while a prisoner was humiliated and condemned but my speculations were interrupted as the doors were flung open a second time and I was hauled forward.

There were far more than ten men seated in the great chamber and for a moment I was confused about where to stand and which dignitary to face, until I recognised Signor Giustiniari and realised that those clad as he was, in ceremonial gowns, must be the members of the Ten. They were grouped in a semi-circle, five and five, divided by an unoccupied gilded chair on a platform, and behind them were a dozen or more other men, with different insignia which, I learned later, indicated their rank as senators. Along one side of the room stood attendants and a handful of observers, including the pair I had seen earlier. Some of the noblemen were still conversing between themselves but most appraised me silently with hostile eyes. Facing them, clerks sat at a table, smoothing their papers and sharpening their quills. Then a soldier thumped his pikestaff on the ground and the whole company stood and bowed as a door behind the chair opened.

A squire bearing a silk banner preceded his master onto the podium and another set down a cushion of gold cloth on the seat as Francesco Foscari entered, shimmering in purple and scarlet, the horned headdress of his office sparkling with jewels. A shiver passed down my spine when I realised the Doge of Venice was to preside at the hearing for I had never imagined such a possibility and Foscari's reputation was daunting. Although, as Doge, he was meant to be simply first among his peers, he had held the position for more than twenty years and his supremacy was unchallenged. I soon found he was not a man for unnecessary preliminaries. He sat down, indicated that his counsellors should resume their places, turned to Signor Giustiniari and spoke one word: 'Proceed.'

The man who had taunted me in Verona rose and required me to state my name and profession, which I did. He smiled thinly as I confirmed that the University of Padua had conferred a doctorate of medicine upon me and proceeded to read out the charge.

'You are accused of conspiring against the interests of the Venetian Republic and acting to the serious detriment of those interests. Do you admit the accusation?'

I mustered my strength to give the answers I had prepared. 'It was never my intention to cause harm to the Most Serene Republic, my lord.'

'That does not suffice. Do you admit your guilt?'

'I can say no more.'

There was a rustling of paper at the clerks' table and some members of the Council murmured. A cadaverous fellow leaned forward and pointed at my face. 'Do you realise we have means to compel you to expand your shifty reply? We will start with a branding iron to make your right cheek as disfigured as the other.' One of his colleagues tittered but I said nothing.

Signor Giustiniari twitched with annoyance and resumed his questioning. 'It is true we can put you to the instruments but I invite you to cooperate with our enquiries. Let me refresh your memory on more specific issues. In what position did Signora Orsola Guarienti-Schioppa engage your services in Verona?'

'Physician to her household, my lord.'

He licked his thin lips. 'Did you discharge your physician's duties effectively?'

'I believe so. I treated many ailments and injuries among her servitors, both in Verona and on her estates. Among her senior attendants, her principal woman attested to my remedies which relieved pain in her back and I administered an enema successfully to the notary, Bernardino Biagio.'

This time the titter acknowledged perceived humour in what I had said but Francesco Foscari coughed and the company suppressed their whispers of amusement or fellow-feeling for the constipated sufferer.

'You knew the dwarf, Iacopo?'

I registered the naming of one person in the household and concluded that this was linked with Iacopo's betrayal of his former master to the Venetian authorities. 'I did.'

'You sought to bring about his downfall?'

'No, my lord, I tolerated a good deal of mockery from him, as one must, but felt no antipathy towards him until he attempted to kill Messer Biagio.'

'Why would he do that?'

'He believed Messer Biagio was concealing papers he wished to find.'

'Ah! So you admit there were secret papers of interest to the Most Serene Republic?'

'I hardly think the papers Iacopo wanted were of wider interest. They merely concerned a proposal by his former master to sell the dwarf to the Marquis of Mantua.'

321

'We note what you say.' Signor Giustiniari hoisted his gown up on his shoulders and his tone became more aggressive. 'Signora Orsola gave permission for you to visit Mantua?'

'She did, my lord.' I felt less comfortable at this change in the focus of his interrogation.

'You were attached temporarily to the household of Madonna Beatrice Gonzaga, were you not?'

'I was, my lord.'

The cadaverous councillor let out a squeak of excitement. 'The Commendatore's notorious whore? Did she reward you as she rewards any man? Did you have her, physician? By God, her standards are slipping if she lets an English quack into her bed.'

I gnawed the inside of my lip, praying to keep my equanimity, but the Doge banged his fist on the arm of his chair. 'Proceed,' he barked again at Signor Giustiniari.

'Why did you go to Mantua, Doctor Somers, if not to enjoy the favours of the incomparable Madonna Beatrice?'

'I went on an act of charity, my lord, to visit the mother of a dead priest who had lived in Verona.' I paused a moment and drew breath. 'He had been murdered.' I fixed my gaze on Giustiniari's face, hoping he read in my insolence an accusation that Father Mario had been killed on instructions from Venice.

'It is alleged that you sought secret papers in Mantua: papers which should have been handed to the Venetian Republic. It is alleged that you found these papers and destroyed them.'

I could not stop myself giving the hint of a smile. 'I have destroyed no papers, my lord.' It was a relief to reply honestly and without evasion.

'When your hands are crushed to pulp, physician, and your nails extracted with pliers, you may tell another story.' The intervention came from an austere looking

322

councillor sitting next to Giustiniari. He glanced down at his own manicured nails.

I began to feel faint and breathed deeply, desperate not to show weakness, but once again the Doge rescued me. He drew himself upright in his chair of state. 'You are English, I believe?'

'Yes, your grace,' I said, uncertain how he should be addressed. The honorific provoked another snigger.

Signor Giustiniari took up the questioning again, following the Doge's lead. 'Why did you leave England?'

There was no point in prevaricating as they clearly knew the reason already. 'I fled from certain execution, my lord. I was accused of connivance with witchcraft and treachery.'

A mutter ran along the ranks of councillors but the signor ignored it. 'Doubtless you protest your innocence?'

'I do.'

'You have an unfortunate knack for attracting erroneous accusations, it seems. Do you expect us to believe you are an incompetent nincompoop, Doctor Somers?'

'I have sometimes been too trusting, my lord.'

'The mere tool of others? A physician and scholar?'

I bowed my head in acquiescence. There seemed no more I could say.

The Doge rose to his feet and the whole company stood as he shook out the voluminous sleeves of his cassock and threw back his cloak. He raised his hand and his gold signet ring flashed in a beam of sunlight. 'We are ready to confer,' he said. 'Remove the prisoner but have him wait nearby.'

I staggered as the guards dragged me backwards to the door but I summoned enough control to make my obeisance at the portal. Then we were once more in the sweltering vestibule and my mind was spinning. The heat in the confined space swept over me and I gasped for air but a considerate soldier opened a window overlooking the courtyard so I could breathe more easily. Below me I saw a crowd of young people skipping about and laughing, holding up fantastic costumes and grotesque masks and I stared at them without comprehension, fearing I had lost my senses in some dreamlike vision. The soldier saw my confusion and tapped me on the shoulder.

'It's our Carnival in a few weeks,' he said. 'They're trying out their costumes. Look, see the choirboys trooping into the yard with their wings. They'll be dolled up as angels. Little perishers!'

I nodded dumbly, remembering that I had heard of the boisterous Venetian festival held just before the Lentan fast began. It seemed entirely appropriate that mischievous small boys should masquerade as angels, for everything I thought angelic had proved deceptive.

After a short delay the nobleman and the fair-haired youth I had noticed earlier left the Council Chamber and hurried past me with averted eyes. Then I was summoned back into the court and I was sorry to see the Doge was no longer present. He had seemed to me a benign figure, rigorous but just, who had not approved of his less scrupulous colleagues and their vulgar antics in ridiculing a prisoner. In his place Signor Giustiniari stood in the central position, in front of the empty chair, ready to pronounce my sentence.

'Doctor Somers, we find you have acted against the interests of our beloved Republic and to the comfort of our enemies. We therefore banish you henceforth from all the Most Serene Republic's lands, in the city and the *Terrafirma*.'

My mouth dropped open. Was he telling me I was free so long as I abandoned Venetian territory? Was it possible that, despite the verdict, they believed I intended no harm and were letting me go?

'In other circumstances,' the Signor continued, with an unpleasant smirk, 'we would have put you to the instruments to exact full details of your perfidy. Thereafter, I don't doubt, your battered body would have found its way into the lagoon. We have no doubt that is the treatment your actions merit. However, Venice is not the only state wishing to ensure you pay the penalty for your crimes. In recent weeks we have been entertaining an august embassy from the King of England who has personally requested us to return you to his realm. As you know, you are wanted there to stand trial on grievous charges and are likely to face the most severe punishment. Accordingly, we are content to accede to King Henry's courteous entreaty and you will be passed directly into the custody of his representative in order that you may be conveyed to England for judgement. May justice prevail!'

He clapped his hands and signalled to the guards as I rocked on my feet. 'Remove the prisoner and let the sentence be imposed.'

My wrists were bound together, as befitted a condemned criminal, and I was pushed roughly into the boat which conveyed me away from the filigree magnificence of the Doge's palace and along the great canal. I was not conscious of my surroundings and must have passed the mansion where I had been housed awaiting my trial, without noticing it or the subsidiary canal beside which the wretched gull had died. I glanced vaguely at the wooden bridge which spanned the waterway at the Rialto, my attention drawn to it by the cacophony of voices at the place where the merchants from a dozen lands congregated to do their business. Then my thoughts reverted to my misfortunes and my dejection increased. I supposed I had succeeded in putting Beatrice's treachery behind me, although my resolution was fragile and the love I had for her still lingered, but to hear the Council of Ten sniggering about her harlotry was unbearable. How had I been so blinded by her beauty? How could I have believed in her sincerity? My self-esteem was shattered by the revelation of her reputation and my own naiveté.

In the hidden pocket of my tattered physician's gown I still had the small box Beatrice sent me with its frivolous, derisive contents. I longed to hurl it into the water, to see it sink as my fortunes had sunk because of her false promise, but I could not move my hands to reach it. I felt its inconsequential weight dragging at my heart and silently I cursed her. It brought no comfort to think of Leone, whom she entrusted with the gift, and who might be ignorant of what was now to happen to me. How would he fare without a patron? Even more I was desolate at the thought of Rendell and feared he might already have paid the price of his boyish bravado in killing Carlo.

We moored at a jetty alongside a fine mansion, arcaded and with a latticed gallery like so many others. I paid it little attention as I was bundled up the steps but I noticed the pennant with the Plantagenet lions and lilies fluttering from a pole above the entrance. New attendants emerged from the doorway to escort me and the Venetian boatman pulled away with my erstwhile guards. I was now in the hands of King Henry's representative and all that I had gained by escaping from London had been rendered void. For more than two years I had lived in a foolish dream of freedom but this had been wiped away and nothing of value remained from my exile. I trudged up the steps and through a corridor to my new prison cell.

It was not what I expected. The room was plainly appointed with painted hessian on the walls but its furniture was serviceable and there was bread and a flask of wine on a side table. I remembered the poisoned sweetmeats from Signor Guarienti but did not care if this food and drink was similarly doctored. Indeed there was much to be said for ending my ordeal then and there, rather than facing the long journey as a captive and inevitable execution outside the Tower of London. I ate and drank with abandon and then I think I dozed, for I was wakened by a servant bringing a candelabrum of lit tapers when the light from the window grew dim. The man did not speak and quickly withdrew as we both heard footsteps along the passage outside. I did not relish the prospect of meeting my English masters and when the hinges of the door creaked I lowered my head to the table in pretence that I was still asleep.

'Well, well, Harry Somers, you do engage in the most tangled affairs, do you not?'

My head shot up at the familiar honeyed tones and I staggered to my feet. 'Lord Fitzvaughan!'

'The very same. Do sit. I'm sure you need to. I instructed that some opiate be added to your wine so that you might enjoy good rest. I'm sure you needed it after encountering a hostile Council of Ten. You did well by the accounts I've received.'

I was wary of his bonhomie because, although I knew him and he had facilitated my flight from England, he now stood in the place of King Henry and he was a man of integrity in matters affecting his duty. Besides, there was unspoken history between us, relating to the spirited Lady Maud, his wife. Moreover his opening words made clear his opinion of how I had squandered the opportunities given me in Italy. I could not marshal a response before he spoke again.

'By God, Harry, you are scarcely presentable. I'll send the barber to you and a new set of clothes. You are a doctor of the University of Padua, I hear. That is praiseworthy. My sweet Bartholomew was much impressed by your demeanour in front of the Doge. I am almost jealous.'

'Bartholomew?' My head was fuzzy and the name meant nothing.

'You may have noticed the handsome young fellow with locks the colour of straw. He observed your trial on my behalf.' I nodded and he laughed, reading my mind which remembered his previous companion. 'Oh, Gaston de la Tour is well but he has been compelled to travel to Normandy where his father lies on his deathbed. Bartholomew offers me consolation while he is absent.' He sat down on a chest and curled his lip. 'Mind you, I could be tempted by your well set-up apprentice. A comely youth.'

'Leone? You have met him?'

'He sought me out and was instrumental in the plan to save you. A lad of rare intelligence, I'd say. Will you take him with us to England?'

'He'd like to go there but I wouldn't want him associated with my ignominious fate.'

Lord Fitzvaughan flung himself back in his chair with a guffaw. 'Oh, I shouldn't tease you further, Harry. You are not facing execution on return to England. You are exonerated, given a royal pardon. I have the document in my possession, signed by King Henry, sealed with the Signet.

But it wouldn't do, you understand, to make the Venetian authorities aware of it. They must believe they have passed you over to obtain your just deserts. We must keep you close confined here for a week or two and then we will drag you in chains to the boat which will convey us to the mainland. You can play the part of a hapless captive, can't you? When we are away from the *Terrafirma* you can take your place in my train in your proper station. We are going first to Urbino and then to Rome. In the spring when the winds are favourable we will sail for England and on arrival you are to join the household of the Earl of Suffolk.'

'The Earl of Suffolk?'

'Do stop repeating what I've just told you. You should remember the Earl promised to support you. He couldn't do so openly at first, after the debacle involving witchcraft and treachery, but he's quietly built up his influence with the King and when the time was right he secured your pardon.'

'I'm sorry; this turnaround in my prospects is so sudden. I'd become used to miserable thoughts.'

'For all your talents you're rather pathetic, Doctor Somers. I never could understand what the beauteous Maud saw in you.'

I swallowed hard. 'Lady Maud is not with you in Venice?'

His expression was difficult to read. 'I haven't seen her for nearly a year. No doubt she will have been at King Henry's court for the Feast of the Nativity but I imagine she will return to my Norfolk estates shortly. I received her letter of felicitations when I arrived here. Oh, I recall: she sent a message for you. She knew I intended to run you to earth, though she'd no idea you would make it easy by getting yourself arrested and brought to Venice.'

Although it seemed like an echo from another life, the notion of Maud sending me a message filled me with misgiving but I resisted the urge to ask what she said.

'What was it now?' Lord Fitzvaughan stood and flicked a fair hair from the fur edging of his short gown. 'Ah, yes. It concerns that little serving maid of hers, who assisted your escape with great ingenuity.'

It seemed sacrilege for me to breathe her name. 'Bess?'

'That's right. Maud says the girl is to be wed on Easter Day. To my bailiff in Norfolk, a sturdy fellow. Maud seemed to think you'd be glad. Or was that her perverted sense of humour?' He put his hand on the latch of the door. 'There are others wanting to see you. I'll send them to you.'

I pulled myself together quickly despite the churning in my stomach. 'My lord, I'm deeply grateful to you and the Earl of Suffolk and I wish Bess well.'

After he had left me I sank back on my seat with my head in my hands. I had no right whatsoever to mourn for Bess's marriage. She had waited more than two years since her promise to me, while I had betrayed her affection and surrendered to a foolish, destructive passion. I thought that losing Bess after this long absence was a pinprick compared with the tearing of my entrails Beatrice's behaviour occasioned. And yet, and yet: there was new pain for me to bear.

*****

The barber duly arrived and removed my unkempt beard before I bathed and dressed myself in the unfamiliar garments Lord Fitzvaughan supplied. My old gown and hose were left crumpled on the floor when I was distracted by a delivery of fresh wine to my room. I took this to be unadulterated so I sipped it gladly but I had scarcely poured the glass when Leone came bounding through the unlocked door. He looked unusually stylish but I was disconcerted to see he was wearing the Fitzvaughan livery. He realised at once why my face fell and span round as if to exhibit his finery the better.

'It's safer,' he said. 'I can go in and out of the palazzo and all the world thinks I serve the King of England's ambassador.'

'How did you know to approach Lord Fitzvaughan? Surely his name meant nothing to you.'

He rubbed his nose and winked. 'A little bird told me about him. I'd no idea he wanted to find you and brought good news about your pardon. He's quite impressive, isn't he? He quickly worked out how to make representations to the Council of Ten and get you committed to King Henry's charge. You'll take me to England with you, won't you?'

'It's the least I can do, if that's what you want. I owe you my life.' Leone shrugged and shook his trimmed and perfumed hair. 'You need to watch yourself with Lord Fitzvaughan, you know,' I said.

He hooted with laughter. 'You don't need to tell me! But Bartholomew keeps a watchful eye on him. He's a good lad, Bartholomew. When he was satisfied I didn't see myself as a rival he become quite friendly. He's teaching me to play chess and I'm practising my English.'

'Very good.' Then I plucked up courage to ask the question which troubled me. 'Is there news of Rendell?'

'Holy mother! Hasn't Lord Fitzvaughan told you? Hold on a moment. I think I hear them coming.'

'Who? What about Rendell?' I could hear a child's voice getting nearer and was vexed that I might need to make polite conversation with other members of the household while ignorant of the boy's fate.

The door was held open and three people I took for strangers entered. They did not look like servants of the English embassy and when the elegant Venetian nobleman came forward I realised I had seen him before.

'Signor, I saw you at the Council of Ten.'

'Where you acquitted yourself bravely, Doctor Somers. Let me present myself. I am Enrico Capello. You once encountered my wife, Carlotta, in Padua, and you are well acquainted with her mother, Signora Orsola. When I learned what had befallen you I could hardly leave you friendless after all you have done for my family. Fortunately I had made the acquaintance of Lord Fitzvaughan so we were able to put our heads together.'

'Signor Capello, I am most grateful. I had no idea so many people were working on my behalf.'

'It was best you should not know in case things went awry. My wife sends her congratulations on your freedom.'

'Signora Carlotta is well I hope.'

'The Holy Mother be praised: Carlotta is in good health and she did me the honour not three weeks ago of presenting me with a robust son. I have an heir, Doctor Somers, after many years. Our beloved Signorina Capello may have her nose out of joint but I think she will come to appreciate her brother.'

He beckoned forward a neatly dressed maiden who had hung back behind her father and I realised with astonishment that this was the child who had caused so much trouble with the kitten on the tower in Padua. She was taller and less chubby, the lines of her face beginning to show a hint of the delightful young woman she would become. I bowed low to her while dreading that she might remember Rendell and ask after him. 'Signorina, I would not have recognised you.'

'I should think not, Doctor Somers, but I remember you. You were surly with your chivalrous servant who rescued my pet.'

I shut my eyes, blocking out the pain. 'I am rightly reprimanded.'

'Do you not think he makes a creditable page?'

I stared at her, at a loss as to her meaning, until I followed her glance towards the attendant in Capello livery standing by the door. It could not be, surely it could not be?

'Rendell!'

'Pretty smart, ain't I? It's just temporary, to give me protection. Like master, like man, you know. I'm exiled from Venice as well.' He sounded very pleased with himself.

'But you escaped worse punishment?'

'Yeah. Old Carlo, what I killed, turns out to have been wanted himself for murder, in Venice. He'd killed one of the Doge's men last year. The senators were glad to be rid of him and the crafty lawyer Signor Capello got to defend me argued I were rightfully defending my employer when I cut the rogue's throat. The lawyer said I'd been in honourable anger at the affront to my master's safety. That's his words. So they decided to kick me out of the city and leave it at that.'

'How did Signor Capello find out about your predicament?'

'Why, I got Leone to find him of course. I remembered Signorina Carlotta's father were a nobleman in the city and hoped she'd get him to help me. So she did, may Heaven bless the young lady.' With this florid outpouring, Rendell executed a deep bow and little Carlotta simpered as he kissed her hand. Despite my relief at his safety I found this display of gallantry rather sickening.

I poured wine for Signor Capello and we sat while he told me more about the scheme he and Lord Fitzvaughan had contrived, with Leone's help, in order to save my life. I was aware young Carlotta had discovered the heap of my discarded clothes and from the corner of my eye I saw her insist that Rendell try on the soiled gown. He did so amidst squeals of girlish laughter but when I heard something fall to the floor I swivelled in my chair, realising with embarrassment what it must be. Rendell stooped to pick up the small box which had fallen open.

'What's this then?'

'It's nothing, rubbish. It can be thrown away.'

Leone, who knew its origin, made to take the box but Carlotta was too quick for him and seized it from Rendell's hand. She examined it closely and strode to my side. 'It's not rubbish. I'd say it was a love token.'

'What makes you say that?' her father asked indulgently.

'Well, look, there's swansdown inside it, wrapped in silk. That's a pretty message.'

'It's just an old feather,' I said weakly.

'Nonsense! Don't you recognise it? It could have come from the costumes the boys in the choir wear at Carnival time. It's a feather from an angel's wing. It's a blessing. Like a lady gives her knight in the stories. Did your mistress give you it, Doctor Somers?'

I felt the flush rising from my throat as Signor Capello chided his daughter for unbecoming impertinence but she was determined to have the last word.

'I'm right, Doctor, aren't I? It's a lover's blessing. What else could it be?'

What indeed? I dared not speak but, with a feeble smile, I reached out and took back the ambiguous gift I had perhaps too rashly spurned.

HISTORICAL NOTE

In 1442 the wife of Humphrey, Duke of Gloucester, Duchess Eleanor, was imprisoned for life and her principal accomplices executed for complicity in a treasonable plot, involving witchcraft, which was designed to bring about the death of King Henry VI of England. The King was at that time unmarried and Duke Humphrey, his one surviving uncle and the youngest brother of King Henry V, was heir to the throne.

Those events form a background to the first book in this series which introduces the fictional character Harry Somers, *The Devil's Stain*.

The Angel's Wing follows on from that time when Harry Somers has taken refuge in the cities of the Venetian Republic. Padua and Verona were then part of the Venetian *Terrafirma,* governed by a mixture of devolved arrangements to the individual cities and overall control by Venice. There had been unsuccessful uprisings against Venetian authority in these cities in 1439. Milan, led by the Visconti Duke, and Mantua, led by the Gonzaga Marquis, were at this period frequently at war with Venice.

Most characters in the *Angel's Wing* are fictional but Gianfrancesco, Marquis of Mantua, Ludovico his heir, and Francesco Foscari, Doge of Venice, are significant historical leaders. The interpretations of their personalities given in the story are my own. A Veronese citizen named Guglielmo Guarienti was confined to Venice, from 1443 until 1454, by the Venetian authorities but the circumstances of his family and background described in the book are inventions.

The author

Pamela Gordon Hoad read history at Oxford University, which she enjoyed, but, despite the more austere approaches of her learned tutors, she continued also to love the drama and romance of characters and plot in historical fiction. She tried her hand at such creative writing over the years but, due to the exigencies of her career, she mainly wrote committee reports, policy papers and occasional articles for publication. After working for the Greater London Council, she held the positions of Chief Executive of the London Borough of Hackney and then Chief Executive of the City of Sheffield. Later she held public appointments, including that of Electoral Commissioner when the Electoral Commission was established.

Since 'retiring', Pamela has been active in the voluntary sector and for three years chaired the national board of Relationships Scotland. Importantly, during the last few years, she has also been able to pursue her aim of writing historical fiction and she published her first novel, *The Devil's Stain* in 2016. This introduced the young physician, Harry Somers, whose story is continued in *The Angel's Wing* and will be developed further in *The Cherub's Smile* which is due for publication in 2017.

Pamela has also published short stories with historical backgrounds in anthologies published by the Borders Writers Forum (which she chaired for three years). She is currently President of the Melrose Literary Society and is also a member of the Melrose Historical and Archaeological Association.

terrifying things in the universe than they ever learned at school, as a terrifying monster is awakened from a long hot sleep.'

For young adults:
Golden Jaguar of the Sun by prize-winning author, Oliver Eade: first book of a trilogy, spanning the USA and Mexico: a story of teenage love and its pitfalls and also a tale of adventure, fantasy and the merging of beliefs